William Allingham

The Ballad Book

A Selection of the Choicest British Ballads

William Allingham

The Ballad Book
A Selection of the Choicest British Ballads

ISBN/EAN: 9783744766227

Printed in Europe, USA, Canada, Australia, Japan

Cover: Foto ©Andreas Hilbeck / pixelio.de

More available books at **www.hansebooks.com**

THE

BALLAD BOOK

THE

BALLAD BOOK

A SELECTION OF THE CHOICEST BRITISH BALLADS

EDITED BY

WILLIAM ALLINGHAM

AUTHOR OF 'DAY AND NIGHT SONGS' ETC.

J. N. Paton.   C. H. Jeens.

London
MACMILLAN AND CO.
AND NEW YORK
1887

PRINTED BY
SPOTTISWOODE AND CO., NEW-STREET SQUARE
LONDON

PREFACE.

I. THIS little Book is intended to present, for the delight of lovers of poetry, some fourscore of the best Old Ballads in at once the best and the most authentic attainable form. But let it be understood, at the beginning, that in most cases the authority, if it deserve the name at all, for the text of an old ballad is of an obscure and evasive kind ; and the more scrutiny, the less assurance. To not many of the poems in this book could even an approximate date be affixed, and to not one the author's name. Ballad, *ballata*, is originally a song sung in dancing (*ballando*), or perhaps intermixed with dances.

II. 'The Old Ballads' suggests as distinct a set of impressions as the name of Shakspeare, Spenser, or Chaucer ; but on looking close we find ourselves puzzled ; the sharp bounding lines disappear ; the mountain chain so definite on the horizon is found to be a disunited and intricate region. Perhaps most people's notion of the Old Ballads is formed out of recollections of Percy's *Reliques*, Ritson's *Robin Hood* set, Scott's *Border Minstrelsy*, as repositories ; of ' Sir Patrick Spens,' ' Clerk Saunders,' ' The Twa Corbies,' ' Chevy Chace,' ' Thomas the Rhymer,' and a few more ballads individually ; and withal of the presence of certain joyless introductions, dissertations, notes, appendices, commentaries, controversies, of an antiquarian, historical, or pseudo-historical nature, wherein the poetry is packed, like pots of dainties and wine-flasks in straw and sawdust. In most of the collections, lyrics and metrical tales are associated with the Ballads proper, and it has been usual, besides, to load on a heap of Modern Imitations. All honour and gratitude to the collectors and editors, greater and lesser ; yet one must venture to say that the really fine and favourite Old Ballads have hitherto formed the vital portions of a set of volumes which are, on the whole, rather lumpish and unreadable. The feast they offer is somewhat like an ' olla podrida' of Spenser's *Fairy Queen*, Dodsley's *Miscellany*, the driest columns of *Notes and Queries*, and a selection from the Poet's Corner of the provincial newspapers.

The Ballads which we give have, one and all, no connection of the slightest importance with history. Things that did really happen are no doubt shadowed forth in many of them, but with such a careless confusion of names, places, and times, now thrice and thirty times confounded by alterations in course of oral transmission, various versions, personal and local adaptations, not to speak of editorial emendations, that it is mere waste of time and patience to read (if any one ever does read) those grave disquisitions, historical and antiquarian, wherewith it has been the fashion to encumber many of these rudely picturesque and pathetic poems. All the aforesaid wrap-pages, or nearly all, the present editor has taken the liberty to put aside, leaving the reader of this volume of Ballads to enjoy them simply as poems, unvexed with dull and trivial questions, to which, after all, no precise answers are forthcoming.

III. Those Ballads which give colour and value to this department of English literature are the best of the 'Robin Hood' set, and the Scottish and North-English Ballads of a romantic and supernatural kind. The truly historical Ballads are one and all inferior, and, considered as poetry, rather like chips in the porridge. The printers' ballads, by Deloney, Johnson, Elderton (who, as old Camden reports, 'did arm himself with ale when he ballated') and other professional writers, made in a prosaic pedestrian style, though some of them meritorious in their own way, and preserving here and there a tinge of the better sort of ballad-writing, are of little or no account in the estimate. Some of the best 'Robin Hood' Ballads were early printed; the 'Lytell Geste,' by Wynken de Worde, probably in 1489: but of the romantic Minstrel Ballads by far the greater number have been preserved by oral transmission, and gathered together by collectors during the last hundred years, chiefly in the remoter parts of the kingdom, and from the mouths of persons of humble rank. Of the comparatively few old MS. copies extant, most, if not all, were doubtless also taken down, directly or otherwise, from the oral delivery of professional minstrels, who themselves, whether as inventors or repeaters, were not accustomed to commit their verses to paper; and such MS. copies, made by anonymous and often, as in the case of Percy's Folio, illiterate hands, have really no more authority than oral versions obtained in our own day, except in so far as they may be held to represent the popular forms at such or such a date.

The Ballads owe no little of their merit to the countless riddlings, siftings, shiftings, omissions, and additions of innumerable reciters. The lucky changes hold, the stupid ones fall aside. Thus, with some effective fable, story, or incident for its soul, and taking form from the hands of a ' maker' who knew his business, the ballad (like the nursery rhyme) glides from generation to generation, and fits itself more and more to the brain and ear of its proper audience. At last the editors take it up, and then the alterations are huge and sudden—here with great and obvious improvement, there injurious and destructive. It is the quick work (good and evil) of a despotism compared with the gradual results of an old constitutional government.

IV. How to date most of our popular romantic ballads is to this day a much debated question. It has been usual to take for granted in a vague way that they are old—very old ; and to connect them with a certain marketable neatness, but with no true strength of link, with the bards, trouveres, court minstrels, and so on. On the other hand, a gentleman of much study in the matter has recently given it as his opinion [*The Romantic Scottish Ballads, their Epoch and Authorship*, by Robert Chambers, 1859] of most, if not all, the best of the romantic ballads, that some were written, and the others entirely recast, no further back than in the last century, by Elizabeth, Lady Wardlaw. To us, however, it appears that ' Hardyknute' (granting the

lady's authorship of that) has little or no poetical
merit, and owes its reputation to the novelty, in that
day, of its style; the true and pure examples (whereof
' Hardyknute' was a poorish imitation) lying hidden
as yet from the reading public. From ' Hardyknute '
alone Mr. Chambers argues Lady Wardlaw's capa-
bility of writing or putting into their present forms
' Sir Patrick Spens,' ' Edward, Edward,' ' The Jew's
Daughter,' ' Young Waters,' ' Edom o' Gordon,'
' The Gay Goshawk,' ' Gil Morice,' ' Annie o' Lochroyan,' and many other of our best ballads. ' Childe
Maurice' (printed by Jamieson *literatim* from Percy's
folio MS.) is ' a poor bald imperfect composition,'
says Mr. Chambers, ' in comparison with " Gil
Morice."' This old MS. copy is indeed imperfect,
in the sense of fragmentary; that is, it does not
give the whole ballad as then existing; yet even in
what it does give are to be seen the characteristics of
our finest ballad poetry, and we have gone back to
it for the use of the present work. That, like
every other ballad orally transmitted, this ballad
became modified and altered in the course of
successive generations, cannot be doubted; that,
once the epoch of editors set in, the ballads were in
a short time more touched, and by more, skilful
hands, than during their whole previous existence,
seems indubitable; but that Lady Wardlaw, or any
individual writer, recast ' Gil Morice,' or any other,
much less most, of our best ballads, we find no
evidence whatever. If not proved old, they have
certainly not been proved modern.

V. We look upon our romantic ballads as a class
of poems traceable backwards to perhaps the fif-

teenth century,—impressive stories in a simple style of verse, sung (and often filled in with prose narration) by professional strollers of a humbler sort than the courtly minstrels, who themselves by this time were beginning to decline from their high place. These narrative songs (some derived from ancient times and foreign countries, some abridged from the long metrical romances, some of new invention) were composed, not without genius in the best, by unlearned men for popular audiences ; and passing from mouth to mouth and generation to generation of singers and reciters, dull and clever, undergoing numerous alterations by the way by reason of slips of memory, personal tastes, local adaptations and prejudices, additions, omissions, patches, and lucky thoughts, and on the whole gaining in strength in the process, came in a later day into the baskets of literary collectors, were transferred into the editorial laboratories, there sifted, mixed, shaken, clarified, improved (or the contrary), no one can ever tell how much, and sent at last into the World of Books in a properly solemn shape, their triviality duly weighted with a load of antiquarianism, and garnished with fit apologies for the presentation of such ' barbarous productions' to 'a polished age like the present,' and assurances that those high literary personages, the 'ingenious' Mr. This and the 'elegant ' Mr. That, whose own poems are so justly, &c. (read now, forgotten), have given some countenance to the venture.

VI. Popular poems, similar in style and often in subject, are found in Denmark, Sweden, Germany, and other countries, all doubtless deriving no

little from the splendidly obscure Oriental nursery of
our race. In 1586, Sophia, Queen of Denmark,
visiting Tycho Brahe, prince of stars, in his island-
observatory, was there storm-sted three days; when
to amuse Her Majesty a store of old Danish Ballads,
collected by Pastor Sæffrensen, a friend of Tycho's,
was produced; and, with the Queen's encouragement,
a select hundred of them were published in 1591,
under the title of *Kæmpe Viser*, Heroic Ballads.
Just a century after this, Peter Say, another priest,
published a second hundred ballads of his own
collecting. A complete edition of the *Danske Viser*,
in 5 vols., appeared at Copenhagen in 1812–14.
Of the Swedish Ballads, collections have been
published at Stockholm in 3 vols. 1814–16, and in
3 vols. 1834–42.

Among these Scandinavian Ballads are found
parallel stories to our 'Fair Annie,' 'Kempion,'
'Douglas Tragedy,' 'Katharine Janfarie,' 'Etin the
Forester,' 'Binnorie,' 'Willy's Lady,' 'May Colvin,'
'The Cruel Brother,' 'Sweet William's Ghost;'
while 'Lord Ronald,' and 'Edward, Edward,' appear in the old German popular minstrelsy. This
strong family likeness to old foreign ballads (where-
soever we may look for the origin) is in itself no bad
evidence for the antiquity of ours. The existence
of many versions in various parts of the country
goes strongly to prove the same point. But this is
not all. 'The Lytell Geste,' as we have said, was
printed about 1485. The 'Hunting of the Cheviot'
must be at least as old as Henry the VIII.'s reign
(some think half a century earlier). 'Childe Maurice'
in Percy's MS. is apparently in 16th century spelling.

A verse from 'Little Musgrave' is quoted in 1611 by Beaumont and Fletcher, and another from 'Fair Margaret's Misfortunes' (see our notes). 'Hynd Horn,' 'Tamlane,' 'Thomas the Rhymer,' 'Fair Annie,' 'Kempion,' and others, are ballad versions of early metrical romances. Several are by subject and treatment clearly referable to the mediæval times, such as 'Hugh of Lincoln,' and 'Young Beichan.' 'Lord Thomas and Fair Ellinor' and 'The Bailiff's Daughter of Islington,' are among the black-letter broadsheets in Pepys's collection. In *Wit Restor'd* (1658) appear 'Johnie Armstrong,' 'The Miller and the King's Daughter' (a burlesque version of 'Binnorie'), and 'The Old Ballad of Little Musgrave and the Lady Barnard.' In short, we believe that many of our best Old Ballads were old ballads in Shakspeare's time, and, considering the conservatism of the commonalty in such matters, that, for all the verbal variations, they are *substantially* not much altered since then.

VII. From the ancient Skalds and Bards, who were historians and genealogists as well as poets, the high harpers and gleemen, trouveres, jongleurs, romancists, and minstrels of every nobler kind, we come, in those books which treat thereof, by obscure transition to the later ballad-singers of humble rank, strolling from house to hamlet, from tavern to cottage, with their songs old and new. Most of the ballads went to a fitting tune, but one tune did duty for many ballads. Some, perhaps, were rather chantingly recited than sung; and the song or the chant, when given by a professed performer, was usually accompanied by a harp, cithern (guitar), fiddle, or other suitable instrument. Here and there a skilled private person would be sure to emulate in his own little circle the completeness of the professor; while much more often the ballad would be given in the huge chimney-nook of a farmhouse or on the bench of a village-green, to some casual knot of listeners, in such irregular and imperfect fashion as the memory and voice of some old woman or peasant youth could attain. But the printer encroached more and more on the power and privileges of the minstrel, whose profession grew ever poorer and lower, till at last he is denounced in 39th Eliz. cap. iv. among 'rogues, vagabonds, and sturdy beggars.' This marks the decline of the once highly honourable class, some fragrance of whose ancient repute, however, still lingered round a few sad survivors in Scotland and Ireland within living memory.

VIII. As to the extent of ballad literature in the middle of the 16th century, take this fact (quoted from Collier by Mr. Chappell, *Music of the Olden Time*, i. 106), that, at the end of the year 1560, '796 ballads, left for entry at Stationers' Hall, remained in the cupboard of the council-chamber of the company, to be transferred to the new wardens; and only 44 books.' Most of these, however, were doubtless of that inferior London ballad literature written for the press, those broadsheets whereof the Roxburghe collection almost entirely consists, those 'Garlands' and 'Penny Merriments' so numerous in their day, a literature interesting in other ways, but not as poetry, saving some rare exceptions. Why comparatively so few

of our finest ballads are found early in print may
be accounted for thus, that the printing-press itself
gave rise to this new school of ballad makers, whose
really very inferior compositions had a novelty, and,
in a low sense, completeness of form and style
which brought them into favour, especially in the
cities and the more polished and 'progressive' parts
of the country. Ballad-making, through the dingiest
kind of printing-offices, has been continued from
that day to this, when it finds its issues in a
Seven Dials court, a Dublin lane near Thomas
Street, or some similar alley of Cork or Glasgow.
Meanwhile the nobler or wild-flower sort of popular
ballad still sprang up here and there till about the
time, we should guess, of Pope and Swift; chiefly,
if not exclusively, in the ruder Northern parts of
the kingdom, which all along have been the most
prolific in this kind, owing, perhaps, to the wild,
moory, and mountainous scenery, the adventurous
and martial habits, the old-world customs, and the
closer connection with ballad-loving Scandinavia.
The actual events to which the following ballads
refer (very inaccurately as a rule) occurred, as far as
we can trace, in or about the years affixed :—' Hughie
Graham,' 1560 ; 'Edom o' Gordon' (old version,
Captain Carre), 1571 ; 'Kinmont Willie,' 1596 ;
' Laird o' Drum,' 1643 ; 'Baron of Brackley, 1666 ;
'Bessie Bell and Mary Gray,' 1666.   With the
eighteenth century set in the epoch of ballad-
editing.

IX. After a good deal of reading and consideration
on this matter, our opinion is that our Old Ballads,
as a class of popular poems, took their rise in pre-

Shakspearian times (not to be more particular than we have warrant for), and were most of them transmitted orally for many generations, and, consequently, in countless varied versions; that in the century and a half after Shakspeare, ballads continued to be composed in Scotland and the North of England for popular audiences in the good old style; and that, half a century or so later than this, these, as well as similar remains in MS. and in rare books, began to excite the curiosity of 'the literary world,' and certain of the countless oral versions, picked up by chance or sought out in the likeliest quarters, took printed forms—manipulated more or less, or 'given exactly as recited' by this or that peasant or gentlewoman of the old school, according to the nature of the collector.

X. Now to say something of the chief collections. *Wit Restor'd* (London, 1658) contains a version of 'Johnnie Armstrong' and one of 'Little Musgrave;' and *Miscellany Poems*, edited by Dryden, 6 vols. (London, 1684-1708), a version of the latter. *A Collection of Old Ballads* (Br. Mus. set, vol. i. London 1723; vol. ii. 2nd ed. 1726; vol. iii. 2nd ed. 1738) has 'Johnie Armstrong,' several of 'Robin Hood,' 'Lord Thomas and Fair Ellinor,' 'Chevy Chase,' 'Gilderoy,' and 'The Baffled Knight.' Allan Ramsay's *Ever Green, Scots Poems wrote by the Ingenious before* 1600 (Edinburgh, 1724), has 'The Battle of Harlaw' and 'The Reid Squair Raid' (both of the dull local-historical kind), 'Johnie Armstrong' again, and the apocryphal 'Hardyknute;' his *Tea-table Miscellany* (Edinburgh, 1724) gives some better ballad-things, without saying where they come from—namely, 'Barbara Allan,' 'Sweet William's Ghost' (imperfect and with spurious additions), 'The Bonny Earl of Murray,' 'Waly, Waly,' and also 'Johny Faa, the Gypsie Laddie.' In 1765 came Bishop Percy's *Reliques of Ancient English Poetry*, gathered chiefly from 'an ancient folio MS. in the editor's possession, which contains near two hundred poems, songs, and metrical romances. This manuscript was written about the middle of the last century, but contains compositions of all times and dates, from the ages prior to Chaucer to the conclusion of the reign of Charles I.' This folio was given to Percy by Humphrey Pitt, Esq., of Prior's-Lee, Shropshire, who said it was purchased with a library of old books. The bishop's nephew, editing the fourth edition in 1794, adds some particulars of this MS. ' The first and last leaves are wanting ; and of fifty-four pages near the beginning half of every leaf hath been torn away, and several others are injured towards the end. Besides that, through a great part of the volume the top or bottom, and sometimes both, have been cut off in the binding. . . . Even where the leaves have suffered no injury, the transcripts, which seem to have been all made by one person (they are at least all in the same kind of hand) are sometimes extremely incorrect and faulty. Hence the public may judge *how much they are indebted* [equivocal !] to the *composer* of this collection.' The famous MS., seen but by a select few, is after all of no very great importance for our particular business. Of the ballads we deal in, but two—'Glasgerion' and 'Childe Waters '—are given by Percy as from the Folio only, though others have received insertions and corrections from that source. Four—'Lord Thomas and Fair Annet, 'The Jew's Daughter,' 'Edward, Edward,' 'Sir Patrick Spens'—are from MSS. 'sent from Scotland.' 'Young Waters,' 'Gil Morice,' and 'Edom o' Gordon,' are from copies recently printed at Glasgow; and 'Little Musgrave,' 'King John and the Abbot,' 'Lord Thomas and Fair Ellinor,' 'Barbara Allen,' 'The Bailiff's Daughter of Islington,' 'The Frolicksome Duke,' from old printed copies (emendated). For the rest, the *Reliques* consist of old poems, lyrics, and inferior ballads, some rare, some not. Speaking of his mode of dealing with his materials in the Folio and elsewhere, Percy says in his Preface: 'These old popular rhymes being many of them copied from illiterate transcripts, or the imperfect recitation of itinerant ballad-singers, have, as might be expected, been handed down to us with less care than any other writings in the world. And the old copies, whether MS. or printed, were often so defective and corrupted, that a scrupulous adherence to their wretched readings would only have exhibited unintelligible nonsense, or such poor meagre stuff as neither came from the bard nor was worthy the press; when, by a few slight corrections or additions, a most beautiful or interesting sense hath started forth, and so naturally and easily, that the editor could seldom prevail on himself to indulge the vanity of making a formal claim to the improvement; but must plead guilty to the charge of concealing his own share in the amendments, under some such general title as a " Modern Copy " or the like.' He adds that, ' where any considerable liberties were taken with the old copies,' three aste-risks are subjoined to the poem.

In 1769 (2nd ed. 1776) appeared Herd's *Ancient and Modern Scottish Songs, Heroic Ballads, &c.*, an indiscriminate gathering—no authorities given—including, among other ballads, versions of ' Lam-mikin,' 'The Bonny Lass of Lochryan ;' 'Fine Flowers in the Valley' [otherwise 'The Cruel Bro-ther '] ; ' Earl Richard ' [otherwise ' Young Redin '] ; 'The Lowlands of Holland;' ' May Colvin;' a fragment of ' Fair Annie,' of ' Kertonha',' [otherwise ' Tamlane,'] of ' The Cruel Mother,' and of ' Helen of Kirconnell.'

Now we come to Scott's *Minstrelsy of the Scottish Border*, the first two volumes published in 1802, the third in 1803, containing no fewer than forty ballads not published before, and among these, 'Thomas the Rhymer ;' 'The Twa Corbies ;' 'The Dowie Dens o' Yarrow' [' The Banks o' Yarrow']; ' Brown Adam ;' ' The Wife of Usher's Well ;' 'Annan Water;' ' The Douglas Tragedy;' ' Kempion;' 'Johnnie of Braidislee;' ' Katharine Janferie ;' ' Clerk Saunders;' ' The Song of the Outlaw Murray;' ' Kin-mont Willie ;' ' The Fray o' Suport ; ' ' The Dæmon Lover [' The Ship o' the Fiend ']; ' Lament of the Border Widow;' ' Willie's Lady; ' a version of ' Lord Randal [' Lord Ronald ']; of ' Helen of Kirconnell;' and of ' Tamlane.' With these, which seem to us the best, and with some more of the same class, the *Minstrelsy* includes a number of local-historical ballads (heavily loaded with antiquarian commen-tary), and a camp-following crowd of ' Imitations.'

As to where and how Scott got those ballads and versions which were not before in print, and still more in regard to his manipulations, we are generally left in fog. Of the local-historical ballads he says he 'has been obliged to draw his materials chiefly from oral tradition' (ed. 1851, i. 223). After pipers and other itinerants of the Border districts, he speaks of 'shepherds and aged persons,' and says, 'it is chiefly from this latter source that the editor has drawn his materials, most of which were collected many years ago,' adding and correcting from a manuscript collection of Border songs made by Mr. Riddell, 'a sedulous border antiquary.' Where copies disagreed, the editor preserved what seemed to him the best reading. The romantic ballads, Scott says, are 'much more extensively known among the peasantry of Scotland than the border-raid ballads, the fame of which is generally confined to the mountains where they were originally composed. Hence, it has been easy to collect these tales of romance, to a number much greater than the editor has chosen to insert.' Besides his own gatherings, Scott had the use of Mr. Herd's MSS., containing ballads published and unpublished. He also had two MS. books of ballads from Mr. A. F. Tytler (afterwards Lord Woodhouselee). Mr. Tytler's father got these from Professor Gordon, of Aberdeen. Professor Gordon's daughter, Mrs. Brown, remembered most of them from the singing of her aunt, Mrs. Farquhar of Braemar, who was full of the old songs and ballads which she had heard from nurses and country women; and these, with others of Mrs. Brown's own picking up, were at last written down. Much other assistance and information Scott received 'from various quarters.'. To some of Scott's many

arrangements and 'conjectural emendations' reference is made here and there in our notes. We
have no doubt that the ballads have gained very
much on the whole from his treatment, and lost
nothing of the least substantial importance. A sub-
sequent editor, who held it to be the strict and
stern duty of his tribe to give every ballad precisely
as found, speaks of 'the alembic established at
Abbotsford for the purification of Ancient Song'
(Motherwell's _Minstrelsy_, 131). Of versions printed
verbatim from the lips of the people, Motherwell's
book, Buchan's, and others, contain many specimens, not without interest; but is it, for example,
necessary to print a horse, in quarto, as 'that bonnie
apple-gray' (Motherwell, p. 237), because the line
was so recited by 'an old woman in Renfrewshire'?

Jamieson, in his _Popular Ballads and Songs_
(2 vol. Edin. 1806), gave about fifteen ballads not
before published (among them 'Burd Helen,' 'Willie
and May Margaret,' 'Young Beichan,' 'Alison
Gross,') and versions of many others; also 'Childe
Maurice,' from the Percy folio. He collected many
of his ballads himself, was furnished with others
by friends, and took down about a dozen from the
copious Mrs. Brown, whom he visited, and who
afterwards sent him several more. Jamieson (who
by-the-bye had a vein of poetic genius) put in many
stanzas; see, for instance, his note to 'Sweet Willie
and Fair Annie' (i. 35), and to 'The Twa Sisters'
(i. 49).

In 1808, came out Finlay's Ballads, containing different versions of several, nothing new of
importance. By Laing, Sharpe, Maidment, some

small contributions were made to this branch of literature. Kinloch (1827) gives some useful versions, with a half a dozen minor ballads. Motherwell's *Minstrelsy* (1827), gives interesting oral versions of several, and a few, not of high class, hitherto unpublished, mixed up incongruously with modern pieces of no great merit. Next comes Peter Buchan's *Ancient Ballads and Songs of the North of Scotland, hitherto unpublished* (2 vols. 1828). Here is much that is not to be found elsewhere ; and Peter's ballads are, we believe, more truly than any one else's (except Motherwell's few), real popular versions ; at the same time they are, as a rule, rude, vulgar and often silly. His volumes we have found very useful for collation with others, and have also gleaned from them the ballads of ' Earl Mar's Daughter,' ' Young John,' and ' Brown Robyn's Confession.' Of more recent ballad-books (none of which we believe profess to add anything to our old store), we may mention Mr. Robert Chambers' volume, *The Scottish Ballads* (1829), who 'associated what seemed [to him] the best stanzas and the best lines, nay, even the best words of the various copies extant ;' and, moreover, added many stanzas of his own composition; Mr. Whitelaw's *Book of Scottish Ballads* (1845), a close-printed volume of nearly 600 pages, crowded with modern compositions, and also with spurious verses in the older ballads ; Mr. Bell's *Ancient Poems, Ballads, and Songs, of the Peasantry of England* (1857), which has no ballads of our kind ; Professor Aytoun's *Ballads of Scotland* (2 vols. 1858, 3rd ed. 1861), a large miscellaneous collection, chiefly from the books which we have already named,

b

mixed with some Scottish poems not of the ballad
class, edited on the principle of selecting the best
versions and fragments, and where necessary, 'restoring' and 'consolidating' the ballads in a complete form.   This, which includes the insertion here
and there of new lines and stanzas, is skilfully done.

The largest collection of British ballads ever published has lately appeared in America, edited by
Professor Child (8 vols. Philadelphia, 1857-59), who
has done his work of amassment in an unpretend-
ing and gentlemanlike manner, copying down from
the collections a variety of versions, adopting a
quasi arrangement in 'books' and appendices, and
packing a large miscellaneous heap of ballad things,
good, bad, and indifferent, into eight trim volumes.

XI. *The Robin Hood Ballads* must be considered
by themselves. Though doubtless there was some
kind of foundation for the stories, Robin Hood is an
inhabitant of the world of fiction, not of history. The
general tradition runs thus : Robin Hood (in the
reigns of King Henry II. and Richard I., say some ;
others put him later), being a man of noble family,
for some reason outlawed, took to the woods of
Yorkshire and Nottinghamshire, and was there
joined by other 'merry men,' or bold fellows, the
chief of them named Little John (he being very
tall), Will Scathlock or Scarlett, George à Green,
pinner (poundkeeper) of Wakefield, Much, a miller's
son, and a jolly friar, Tuck. Also with him lived
in the green forest his sweetheart and wife, Maid
Marian. Robin and his men shot the king's deer,
robbed rich wayfarers in a gallant and jovial
fashion, with especial gusto if they were holy

churchmen ; rescued many from prison and gallows, and were always courteous to women, and ready with help for the poor and weak.

The Sheriff of Nottingham is *ex officio* the chief enemy of Robin and his men, and the relations between them are always those of a state of war.

The Robin Hood Ballads form a separate group on the above general theme. . They are some fifty in number, but include much repetition both of phrase and of incident. A dozen or so describe Robin's falling in with some unknown wayfarer, fighting him, getting worsted, and finally telling his own name, and offering to enrol his antagonist in the famous company of Lincoln-Green Archers.

Robin Hood has been a household word in England for five or six centuries ; and our literature, from *Piers Plowman* (circa 1362) downwards, has frequent allusions to ' Jolly Robin,' the ' gentle outlaw,' the ' honest thief.'· His adventures were the subject of several dramas ; Ben Jonson's unfinished pastoral play, *The Sad Shepherd,* is a tale of Robin Hood, and he was long a favourite hero in rustic revels and May games. ' I came once myselfe,' says Bishop Latimer (in his sixth sermon before King Edward VI.*), ' to a place riding on a journey homeward from London, and I sent word overnight into the town that I would preach there in the morning, because it was a holyday, and methought it was an holidayes worke ; the churche stode in my way, and I toke my horsse and my companye and went thither ; I thought I should have found a great

---

* Ritson, i. xciv. 1st edit.

companye in the churche, and when I came there
the churche dore was faste locked.   I tarried there
half an houre and more, and at last the keye was
founde ; and one of the parishe commes to me, and
sayes, Syr, thys ys a busye day with us, we cannot
heare you ; it is ROBYN HOODES DAYE. The
parishe are gone abroad to gather for Robyn Hoode,
I pray you let them not.   I was fayne there to geve
place to Robyn Hoode.   I thought my rochet
should have been regarded, though I were not ; but
it woulde not serve, it was fayne to geve place to
Robyn Hoodes Men.

  ' It is no laughyng matter, my friendes, it is a
wepynge matter, a heavy matter, under the pretence
for gatherynge for Robyn Hoode, a traytoure and a
thefe, to put out a preacher, to have his office lesse
estemed, to prefer Robyn Hoode before the myny-
stration of God's word,' &c.

  ' The bishop grows scurrilous,' says Ritson in a
note, taking up the cudgels for his favourite.

  Mock biographies of Robin were composed ;
various dates, birthplaces, and 'true names' assigned to him ; he was made Earl of Huntingdon,
his pedigree set forth in full, and opportunity given
to the antiquaries for their favourite amusement of
' winnowing three wechts o' naething.'   The people
gave his name to a bay on the Yorkshire coast, a
hill near Gloucester, a well near Doncaster, and
so on.

  The ballads were flying about the country, generation after generation, in the form of broad sheets
and of little collections called ' Garlands,' till Ritson
gathered them into his two volumes, published 1795.

Industrious and irritable Joe (who described Mr. *Ritson*
Gough of the *Gentleman's Magazine* as 'the scur- *Percy*
rilous and malignant editor of that degraded publication ') * is long and angry in defence of Robin
Hood's character, and particularly admires him for
robbing 'clerical drones or pious locusts.'

Among the oldest of the ballads, if not the oldest,
are those eight connected ones, entitled, 'A Lytell
Geste of Robyn Hode,' given in this volume in its
old form, with some slight correction of the lawless
spelling (what good in spelling 'high' four different
ways in nine lines ?), and an abatement of the very
strong swearing that was formerly in fashion.
'Robin Hood and the Monk' is another of the oldest,
and also of the best ; but it is a long ballad, and
we had not room for it.

The Robin Hood Ballads, taken in the lump, being
full of repetition, and often vulgar, or perhaps vulgarised in style, form a disappointing book, one of
those which people buy for its name and neglect for
its own sake.   Each ballad had a popularity, in its
own time and circle ; but taken together they have
no vital coherency or continuity, and form a chance
bundle, ticketed 'Robin Hood,' not, as one might
hope from the usual way of talking, a series with
some poetic movement and unity, a kind of rude
ballad-history.

* Speaking of Bishop Percy's version of ' Robin Hood and Guy of
Gisborne,' Ritson exclaims, 'How an editor . . . . can justify
such wanton, arbitrary, and even injudicious alterations in the publication of an ancient poem is beyond the conception of a person not
habituated to "liberties" of this nature, nor destitute of all manner
of regard for truth and probity' (*Robin Hood*, vol. ii. at end). Furious
Joe, by-the-bye, 'hisself,' if he took no liberties, made many a blunder.

The set of eight connected ballads, ' The Lytell
Geste' is the most important section of Robin
Hood song, and with those few others here presented will give our guests a good dish of lawless
venison.*   But if the ballads as a whole be tedious,
the central figure (whithersoever or howsoever come)
is a clear and delightful one, of that small class of
ideal personages to which Don Quixote and Robinson Crusoe also belong—a bold, generous, and
courteous Outlaw, famous in archery, living under
greenwood tree with his merry-men, taking from
the rich and giving to the poor—a figure that, once
lodged in the popular imagination, became an
easy and favourite subject for one rhymester after
another.

So let us into the forest-land of romance, and for
awhile 'live like the old Robin Hood of England'
—'fleet the time carelessly, as they did in the
golden world.'

XII. The set of ballads in our own volume is,
we believe, on the whole, much nearer to what
the sung and recited ballads really were, at their
best, than those which we have all accepted as *The
Old Ballads* in the collections of Percy, Jamieson,
Scott, and other editors.   Many modern interpolations, confessed or obvious, are now left out, greatly,
if we mistake not, to the improvement of the ballads.   Where rearrangement, or selection from different copies (freely practised by preceding editors),

---

* ' The Lytell Geste ' is probably of the early part of the sixteenth
century, and the older songs so often alluded to by early writers were
doubtless remodelled in that age for the popular amusement, and
have come to us in the form which they then got into ; the originals,
except fragments, being now lost.

appeared desirable, it has been done with diligent
examination of a large mass of materials, and with
the most punctilious caution ; and where the present
editor found occasion, which was rarely, to supply
some link, repair some dropt stitch, he has dealt
merely with things neutral, carefully avoiding to
foist in any touches of pseudo-antique, whether
in incident, language, or costume. A very few
words are altered for manners' sake. *Substantially,
he has added nothing to the ballads.* On the
general effect of his labours he would be content
to leave the verdict either to half a dozen true
knowers of English poetry (if so many could be
found at one time), or else to any group of ordinary
listeners, men, women, and children, who care to
listen to the like,—such a group as ballads were
made to please. Let, for example, ' Earl Mar's
Daughter ' be read as here given, or ' Young Redin,'
or ' The Jolly Goshawk,' or ' Etin,' or ' Binnorie,' or
' Little Musgrave,' or ' Willy's Lady,' and also those
versions of the same which are printed in any other
collection. No doubt, however, those who have
been bred up, as it were, in a particular form of a
ballad will be apt, at least at first, to mislike any
other form. One who has had impressed upon his
youthful mind—

> It was in or about the Martinmas time
> When the green leaves were a-fallin',
> That Sir John Graeme in the west countrie
> Fell in love with Barbara Allen—

may very likely be ill-content to find name of person
and season of year altered, as they are in the following equally authentic version—

> All in the merry month of May,
>   When green buds they were swellin',
> Young Jemmy Grove on his death-bed lay
>   For love of Barbara Allen.

But let him not, therefore, fall foul of the editor, who was bound to choose without prejudice between autumn and spring, Jemmy Grove and Sir John.

Most of the old ballads, as taken down from the mouths of nurses, peasants, itinerant musicians, or from broadsheets and ha'penny songbooks, would be found corrupt, incoherent, incomplete; and with here and there a striking bit, on the whole vexatious and tiresome to read. The various oral versions of a popular ballad obtainable throughout England, Scotland, and Ireland, are perhaps, even at this late day, practically innumerable—one as 'authentic' as another. What then to do? Various versions of half a dozen ballads would make a volume the size of this—and a very worthless volume. The right course has appeared to be this, to make one-self acquainted with all attainable versions of a ballad. Then (granting a 'turn' for such things, to begin; without which all were labour in vain), the editor may be supposed to get as much insight as may be had into the origin and character of the ballad in question; he sees or surmises more or less as to the earliest version or versions, as to blunders, corruptions, alterations of every sort (national, local, personal), on the part of reciters; he then comes to investigate the doings of former editors, adopting thankfully what he finds good, correcting at points whereupon he has attained better information, rejecting (when for the worse) acknowledged or obvious interpolations or changes. He is to give it in *one* form—the best according to his judgment and feeling—in firm black and white, for critics, and for readers cultivated and simple ; the ballad itself is multiform, and even shifting, vapourlike, as one examines it; the conditions of his task are therefore by no means easy; and when the work is done with his utmost care and skill, nothing can be easier than to pull it to pieces and prove it ' a thing of nought.' So much, not in deprecation of criticism, but to suggest to any one inclined to be critical the difficulties attending a task which, the more you look into the nature of it, the more is it found to be without solid basis or definite boundaries. To make the narrative clear, and bring out forcibly the dramatic points, is what every balladist aimed at ; the comparative success with which this is done tests the value of this version, or that, of a story.

Take the present version of ' Lamkin,' wherein, as usual in our book, no addition is made to the traditionary matter. Collating the existing versions, each more or less altered and corrupted, and viewing them by the light of imaginative truth, we have set forth the story (essentially unchanged) in a complete and consistent form. The incidents and the style remain unaltered. This is just what a good reciter or minstrel would do, and used to do. All the essentials remain ; but a better ballad is the result. Our Irish nurse's version (like several others) calls the murderer ' Lamkin,' and suggests that it was an epithet given to the cruel man, by rule of contrary. This much enhances the horror, although the hint for it may first have come by accident.

In short, the present editor has dealt, as poet
and critic, with a heap of confused materials, much
as he would have dealt orally with the same materials, had fortune placed him in the world some three
centuries ago in the condition of a ballad-minstrel
(many worse conditions for a poet), singing in hall
or cottage to groups of old and young.

XIV. Without entering upon a discussion of the re-
spective claims of England and Scotland in ballad
making, we merely say that there is in the present
volume at least as much of English as of Scottish
produce. For old ballads, as a class, belong to both
countries ; and though one here and there may be
assigned to each, attempts to divide them are on
the whole vain and useless. Many a ballad is found
in an old Scottish form and in an old English form,
as for instance, ' The Twa Corbies ' and ' The Three
Ravens ;' ' Young Beichan ' (several versions);
' Hugh of Lincoln ' (several); ' Little Musgrave ;'
' The Fair Flower of Northumberland ;' ' Edom o'
Gordon ' and ' Captain Car.' Percy gave ' Edom o'
Gordon,' printed in Glasgow, 1755, but 'with several
fine stanzas,' 'from a fragment of the same ballad
in folio MS.' ' Uniformity required that the additional stanzas supplied from that copy should be
clothed in the Scottish orthography and idiom ;
this has, therefore, been attempted, though perhaps
imperfectly' (i. 123) [an instructive little confession !]: Ritson in his *Ancient Songs and Ballads*
(ii. 38) gives ' an entire ancient copy, the undoubted
original of the Scottish ballad, and one of the few
specimens now extant of the genuine proper old
English ballad' [though founded on a fact which

happened in Scotland]. It is in a ' collection in the
Cotton Library, marked Vespasian A xxv. At the
top of the original stands the word *Ihus* (Jesus), and
at the end is *Finis*, Pme Willm̄ Asheton clericū ; the
name and quality, we may presume, of the original
author. The MS. having received numerous alterations or corrections, all or most of which are evidently for the better, they are here adopted as part of
the text.' Car or Ker, sent by Sir Adam Gordon,
burned Alex. Forbes's Castle of Towey in 1571.

This English ballad begins :—

> It befell at Martynmas,
>   When wether waxed colde,
> Captaine Care saide to his men,
>   We must go take a holde.

Some of the best stanzas of ' Edom o' Gordon '
are here :—

> Then bespake the yongest sonn,
>   That sat on the nurse's knee ;
> Sayth, mother gay, geve over your house,
>   [The smoke] it smoldereth me.
>
> I would geve my gold, she saith,
>   And so I wolde my fee,
> For a blaste of the ' western ' wind,
>   To dryve the smoke from thee.

But we do not find the pathetic death of the young
daughter in the older ballad.

The English version of ' The Fair Flower of
Northumberland,' is by ' the great ballade-maker
T. D. or Thomas Deloney ;' and though vulgarly
handled, has in its form recognisably the smack of
old ballad literature :

> It was a knight, in Scotland born
> 　(*Follow, my love, come over the strand*),
> Was taken prisoner and left forlorn,
> 　Even by the good Earl of Northumberland.
>
> And as in sorrow thus he lay,
> 　(*Follow, my love, come over the strand*),
> The Earl's sweet daughter walks that way,
> 　And she's the fair flower of Northumberland.

Kinloch gives a Scottish version of the same story, 'The Provost's Dochter,' with this burden :—

> The Provost's dochter went out a walking,
> 　*A may's love whiles is easy won;*
> She heard a fair prisoner making her meane [moan],
> 　And she was the fair flow'r o' Northumberland.

Deloney's ballad ends :—

> All you fair maidens, be warned by me,
> 　(Follow, my love, come over the strand),
> Scots never were true, and never will be,
> 　To lord, nor lady, nor fair England.'

But the Scottish version has it :—

> She's na the first that the Scots hae beguil'd,
> 　And she's still the flow'r o' Northumberland.

XV. The editor of this book, moved by a natural affection for ballads, has not only made himself acquainted with all ballads and ballad literature that came within his reach, but might perhaps, if he chose, set up some claim to be considered as an original collector in a small way—Ireland being his principal field.　Ireland would certainly have contributed her full share to our general store of ballads, but for one sufficient reason—her tongue was Keltic; her native popular songs and ballads lie hid in that little-known and expiring language. Many of the English and Scottish ballads, however,

were carried over to the neighbouring island, and
are still borne in the memory of humble people.
Unable here to discuss this matter of Anglo-
Hibernian versions, we may mention as specimens
those of 'Binnorie' and 'Lamkin,' sung (among other
ballads) by a nurse in the family of a relative of
ours in Ireland. They are chiefly remarkable for
corruption of language and neglect of rhyme.
' Lamkin' begins thus :

> As my lord and my lady were out walking one day,
> Says my lord to my lady, ' Beware of Lamkin ! '
> ' O why should I fear him, or any such man,
> When my doors are well barr'd and my windows well pinn'd ?
>   When my doors,' &c.

But there are some good points :

> O keep your gold and silver, it will do you some good,
> It will buy you a coffin when you are dead.
> There's blood in the kitchen, and blood in the hall,
> And the young Mayor of England lies dead by the wall.

The version of 'Binnorie,' called ' Sister, dear Sister,'
and sung to a peculiar and beautiful air, begins

> Sister, dear sister, where shall we go play ?
>   *Cold blows the wind, and the wind blows low,*
>   We shall go to the salt sea's brim,
>   *And the wind blows cheerily around us, High ho!*

The editor has also a large collection of the ballads
and songs, printed on slips of whitey-brown paper,
sold by hawkers and professional ballad-singers
throughout Ireland at the present day. Among these,
oddly enough, he does not recollect one version of any
of the good British ballads. An account of the collection may be found in a paper published some
years ago in *Household Words*, entitled ' Irish Ballad-
singers and Irish Ballads.' Moreover, he has visited

several of the chief ballad printing-offices—in Dublin, in Belfast, and lately in Seven Dials. In the latter place he found two of the old ballads, and only two, still in the market—the usual version of 'Lord Thomas and Fair Eleanor,' and a very corrupt version of 'Barbara Allen,' beginning

> In Reading town where I was born,
> A fair maid there was dwelling,
> I picked her out to be my wife,
> Her name was Barbara Allen.

XVI. To sum up, in regard to the ballads here presented,—they are narrative poems of an old simple kind, modified in form in transmission to our own day. They have no historical value, except in so far as they convey a general impression of a state of society very different from ours in externals, being hot, rude, violent, and picturesque. Below the surface, perhaps, the difference is not so great. The same passions and motives show themselves in human history, with their outward fashion changed, in all places and at all times.

The old ballads abound in 'strong situations;' they are full of crime, of 'battle, murder, and sudden death.' Such is the very substance of which the best of them are wrought; and those who are unwilling to look on the tragic side of human life must turn their eyes elsewhere. Two or three fine ballads have been omitted as too painful or horrible for our audience. Many gloomy stories remain, but all told with simple seriousness and right feeling. When sin and crime are spoken of, it is with due gravity. The dignity of human nature is upheld. In the varieties of character and fortune, some facts present themselves which are by general consent deemed unsuitable for literary treatment, and they who deal with such, however well, narrow their audience from millions to units; but there are many incidents and combinations of a tragical kind of which it is wholesome to speak, and whereof no one has so good a right to speak as the poet—provided he speaks rightly. We do well for our humanity by looking at the darker incidents of life, in their turn, in the mirror of art, when there presented with a true sense of their solemn and fathomless import. There is nothing finer in literature in the same compass, than ' Childe Maurice,' ' Little Musgrave,' ' Clerk Saunders,' ' Fine Flowers in the Valley,' ' Young Redin,' ' Childe Vyet,' and ' Glasgerion.' But all is not darkness and tempest in this region of song; gay stories of true-love with a happy ending are many; and they who love enchantments, and to be borne off into fairy-land, may have their wish at the turning of a leaf.

And now the editor sends forth the little book, with the feeling that he has done what in him lay to make it generally acceptable.

CONTENTS.

C

Contents. xli

d

Thomas the Rhymer.

I

TRUE Thomas lay on Huntley bank ;
   A ferlie spied he wi' his ee ;
'There he saw a lady bright
   Come riding doun by the Eildon Tree.

2

Her skirt was o' the grass-green silk,
   Her mantle o' the velvet fine ;
At ilka tett o' her horse's mane,
   Hung fifty siller bells and nine.

3

True Thomas he pu'd aff his cap,
   And louted low doun on his knee :
' Hail to thee, Mary, Queen of Heaven !
   For thy peer on earth could never be.'

4

' O no, O no, Thomas,' she said,
   ' That name does not belong to me ;
I'm but the Queen o' fair Elfland,
   That hither have come to visit thee.

'ferlie,' marvel.   ' tett,' tassel.

5

' Harp and carp, Thomas,' she said ;
  ' Harp and carp along wi' me ;
And if ye dare to kiss my lips,
  Sure of your body I shall be.'

6

' Betide me weal, betide me woe,
  That weird shall never daunten me.'
Syne he has kiss'd her on the lips,
  All underneath the Eildon Tree.

7

' Now ye maun go wi' me,' she said,
  ' Now, Thomas, ye maun go wi' me ;
And ye maun serve me seven years,
  Through weal or woe as may chance to be.'

8

She's mounted on her milk-white steed,
  And she's ta'en Thomas up behind ;
And aye, whene'er her bridle rang,
  The steed gaed swifter than the wind.

9

O they rade on, and farther on,
  The steed gaed swifter than the wind ;
Until they reach'd a desert wide,
  And living land was left behind.

10

' Now, Thomas, light doun, light doun,' she said,
  ' And lean your head upon my knee ;
Abide ye there a little space,
  And I will show you ferlies three.

' Harp and carp,' talk merrily and familiarly ?
    ' weird,' doom.

11

'O see ye not yon narrow road,
  So thick beset wi' thorns and briars?
That is the Path of Righteousness,
  Though after it but few enquires.

12

'And see ye not yon braid, braid road,
  That lies across the lily leven?
That is the Path of Wickedness,
  Though some call it the road to Heaven.

13

'And see ye not yon bonny road
  That winds about the ferny brae?
That is the road to fair Elfland,
  Where thou and I this night maun gae.

14

'But, Thomas, ye sall haud your tongue,
  Whatever ye may hear or see;
For speak ye word in Elfin-land,
  Ye'll ne'er win back to your ain countrie.'

15

O they rade on, and further on,
  And they waded rivers abune the knee;
And they saw neither sun nor moon,
  But they heard the roaring of a sea.

16

It was mirk, mirk night, there was nae starlight,
  They waded through red blude to the knee;
For a' the blude that's shed on the earth
  Rins through the springs o' that countrie.

'leven,' lawn.

17

Syne they came to a garden green,
　　And she pu'd an apple frae a tree :
'Take this for thy wages, Thomas,' she said ;
　　'It will give thee the tongue that can never lee.'

18

'My tongue is my ain,' then Thomas he said ;
　　'A gudely gift ye wad gie to me !
I neither dought to buy or sell
　　At fair or tryst where I might be.

19

'I dought neither speak to prince or peer,
　　Nor ask of grace from fair ladye !'—
'Now haud thy peace, Thomas,' she said,
　　'For as I say, so must it be.'

20

He has gotten a coat of the even cloth,
　　And a pair o' shoon of the velvet green ;
And till seven years were come and gane,
　　True Thomas on earth was never seen.

II

The Twa Corbies.

1

As I was walking all alane,
I heard twa corbies making a mane :
The tane unto the tither did say,
'Whar sall we gang and dine the day ?'

'dought,' could.　　'corbies,' ravens.

2

' In behint yon auld fail dyke,
I wot there lies a new-slain knight ;
And naebody kens that he lies there
But his hawk, his hound, and his lady fair.

3

' His hound is to the hunting gane,
His hawk to fetch the wild-fowl hame,
His lady's ta'en anither mate,
Sae we may mak' our dinner sweet.

4

' Ye'll sit on his white hause-bane,
And I'll pike out his bonny blue e'en ;
Wi' ae lock o' his gowden hair
We'll theek our nest when it grows bare.

5

' Mony's the one for him makes mane,
But nane sall ken whar he is gane.
O'er his white banes, when they are bare,
The wind sall blaw for evermair.'

III

Hynd Horn.

I

NEAR the King's court was a young child born,
With a hey lillelu and a how lo lan;
And his name it was called Young Hynd Horn,
And the birk and the broom blooms bonnie.

' fail,' turf, sod.　　' hause,' neck.　　' theek,' thatch.

2

Seven lang years he served the King,
  With a hey lillelu and a how lo lan;
And it's a' for the sake o' his daughter Jean,
  And the birk and the broom blooms bonnic.

3

The King an angry man was he,
  With a hey lillelu and a how lo lan;
He sent Young Hynd Horn to the sea,
  And the birk and the broom blooms bonnic.

4

O his love gave him a gay gold ring,
  With a hey lillelu and a how lo lan;
With three shining diamonds set therein,
  And the birk and the broom blooms bonnic.

5

'As lang as these diamonds keep their hue,
  With a hey lillelu and a how lo lan,
Ye'll know I am a lover true,
  And the birk and the broom blooms bonnic.

6

' But when your ring turns pale and wan,
  With a hey lillelu and a how lo lan,
Then I'm in love with another man,
  And the birk and the broom blooms bonnic.'

7

He's gone to the sea and far away,
  With a hey lillelu and a how lo lan;
And he's stayed for seven lang years and a day,
  And the birk and the broom blooms bonnic :

8

Seven lang years by land and sea,
  With a hey lillelu and a how lo lan ;
And he's aften look'd how his ring may be,
  And the birk and the broom blooms bonnie.

9

One day when he look'd this ring upon,
  With a hey lillelu and a how lo lan,
The shining diamonds were pale and wan,
  And the birk and the broom blooms bonnie.

10

He hoisted sails, and hame cam' he,
  With a hey lillelu and a how lo lan ;
Hame unto his ain countrie,
  And the birk and the broom blooms bonnie.

11

He's left the sea and he's come to land,
  With a hey lillelu and a how lo lan ;
And the first he met was an auld beggar-man,
  And the birk and the broom blooms bonnie.

12

' What news, what news, my silly auld man ?
  With a hey lillelu and a how lo lan ;
For it's seven lang years since I saw this land,
  And the birk and the broom blooms bonnie.'

13

' No news, no news,' doth the beggar-man say,
  With a hey lillelu and a how lo lan ;
' But our King's ae Daughter she's wedded to-day,
  And the birk and the broom blooms bonnie.'

14

'Wilt thou give to me thy begging coat?
　With a hey lillelu and a how lo lan;
And I'll give to thee my scarlet cloak,
　And the birk and the broom blooms bonnie.

15

'Give me your auld pike-staff and hat,
　With a hey lillelu and a how lo lan;
And ye sall be right weel paid for that,
　And the birk and the broom blooms bonnie.

16

The auld beggar-man cast off his coat,
　With a hey lillelu and a how lo lan,
And he's ta'en up the scarlet cloak,
　And the birk and the broom blooms bonnie.

17

He's gi'en him his auld pike-staff and hat,
　With a hey lillelu and a how lo lan;
And he was right weel paid for that,
　And the birk and the broom blooms bonnie.

18

The auld beggar-man was bound for the mill,
　With a hey lillelu and a how lo lan;
But Young Hynd Horn for the King's ain hall,
　And the birk and the broom blooms bonnie.

19

When he came to the King's ain gate,
　With a hey lillelu and a how lo lan,
He asked a drink for Young Hynd Horn's sake,
　And the birk and the broom blooms bonnie.

20

These news unto the bonnie bride cam',
With a hey lilleln and a how lo lan,
That at the gate there stands an auld man,
And the birk and the broom blooms bonnie.

21

There stands an auld man at the King's gate.
With a hey lilleln and a how lo lan ;
He asketh a drink for Young Hynd Horn's sake,
And the birk and the broom blooms bonnie.

22

The Bride cam' tripping down the stair,
With a hey lilleln and a how lo lan ;
The combs o' fine goud in her hair,
And the birk and the broom blooms bonnie ;

23

A cup o' the red wine in her hand,
With a hey lilleln and a how lo lan ;
And that she gave to the beggar-man,
And the birk and the broom blooms bonnie.

24

Out o' the cup he drank the wine,
With a hey lilleln and a how lo lan ;
And into the cup he dropt the ring,
And the birk and the broom blooms bonnie.

25

' O gat thou this by sea or by land ?
With a hey lilleln and a how lo lan.
Or gat thou it aff a dead man's hand ?
And the birk and the broom blooms bonnie.'

26

' I gat it neither by sea nor land,
  With a hey lillelu and a how lo lan,
Nor gat I it from a dead man's hand,
  And the birk and the broom blooms bonnie.

27

' But I gat it at my wooing gay,
  With a hey lillelu and a how lo lan;
And I gie it to you on your wedding-day,
  And the birk and the broom blooms bonnie.

28

' I'll cast aside my satin goun,
  With a hey lillelu and a how lo lan,
And I'll follow you frae toun to toun,
  And the birk and the broom blooms bonnie.

29

' I'll tak' the fine goud frae my hair,
  With a hey lillelu and a how lo lan,
And follow you for evermair,
  And the birk and the broom blooms bonnie!

30

He let his cloutie cloak doun fa',
  With a hey lillelu and a how lo lan;
Young Hynd Horn shone above them a',
  And the birk and the broom blooms bonnie.

31

The Bridegroom thought he had her wed,
  With a hey lillelu and a how lo lan;
But she is Young Hynd Horn's instead,
  And the birk and the broom blooms bonnie.

IV

The Banks o' Yarrow.

1

LATE at e'en, drinking the wine,
    And ere they paid the lawing,
They set a combat them between,
    To fight it in the dawing.

2

' What though ye be my sister's lord,
    We'll cross our swords to-morrow.'
' What though my wife your sister be,
    I'll meet ye then on Yarrow.'

3

' O stay at hame, my ain gude lord!
    O stay, my ain dear marrow!
My cruel brither will you betray
    On the dowie banks o' Yarrow.'

4

' O fare ye weel, my lady dear!
    And put aside your sorrow;
For if I gae, I'll sune return
    Frae the bonny banks o' Yarrow.'

5

She kiss'd his cheek, she kaim'd his hair,
    As oft she'd done before, O ;
She belted him wi' his gude brand,
    And he's awa' to Yarrow.

'lawing,' reckoning.   'marrow' (married), husband or wife.
'dowie,' doleful.

6

When he gaed up the Tennies bank,
  As he gaed mony a morrow,
Nine armed men lay in a den,
  On the dowie braes o' Yarrow.

7

' O come ye here to hunt or hawk
  The bonny Forest thorough ?
Or come ye here to wield your brand
  Upon the banks o' Yarrow ?'

8

' I come not here to hunt or hawk,
  As oft I've dune before, O,
But I come here to wield my brand
  Upon the banks o' Yarrow.

9

' If ye attack me nine to ane,
  That God may send ye sorrow !—
Yet will I fight while stand I may,
  On the bonny banks o' Yarrow.'

10

Two has he hurt, and three has slain,
  On the bloody braes o' Yarrow ;
But the stubborn knight crept in behind,
  And pierced his body thorough.

11

' Gae hame, gae hame, you brither John,
  And tell your sister sorrow,—
To come and lift her leafu' lord
  On the dowie banks o' Yarrow.'

' leafu',' lawful.

12

Her brither John gaed ower yon hill,
　　As oft he'd dune before, O ;
There he met his sister dear,
　　Cam' rinnin' fast to Yarrow.

13

' I dreamt a dream last night,' she says,
　　' I wish it binna sorrow ;
I dreamt I pu'd the heather green
　　Wi' my true love on Yarrow.'

14

' I'll read your dream, sister,' he says,
　　' I'll read it into sorrow ;
Ye're bidden go take up your love,
　　He's sleeping sound on Yarrow.'

15

She's torn the ribbons frae her head
　　That were baith braid and narrow ;
She's kilted up her lang claithing,
　　And she's awa' to Yarrow.

16

She's ta'en him in her arms twa,
　　And gi'en him kisses thorough ;
She sought to bind his mony wounds,
　　But he lay dead on Yarrow.

17

' O haud your tongue,' her father says,
　　' And let be a' your sorrow ;
I'll wed you to a better lord
　　Than him ye lost on Yarrow.'

18

'O haud your tongue, father,' she says,
  'Far warse ye mak' my sorrow;
A better lord could never be
  Than him that lies on Yarrow.'

19

She kiss'd his lips, she kaim'd his hair,
  As aft she had dune before, O;
And there wi' grief her heart did break,
  Upon the banks o' Yarrow.

V

Earl Mar's Daughter.

1

IT was intill a pleasant time,
  Upon a simmer's day,
The noble Earl Mar's daughter
  Went forth to sport and play.

2

And as she play'd and sported
  Below a green aik tree,
There she saw a sprightly doo
  Set on a branch sae hie.

3

'O Coo-my-doo, my love sae true,
  If ye'll come doun to me,
Ye'se hae a cage o' gude red goud
  Instead o' simple tree.

‘ doo,’ dove.

4

'I'll tak' ye hame and pet ye weel,
　Within my bower and ha';
I'll gar ye shine as fair a bird
　As ony o' them a'.'

5

And she had nae these words weel spoke,
　Nor yet these words weel said,
Till Coo-my-doo flew frae the branch,
　And lighted on her head.

6

Then she has brought this pretty bird
　Hame to her bower and ha',
And made him shine as fair a bird
　As ony o' them a'.

7

When day was gane, and night was come,
　About the evening-tide,
This lady spied a bonny youth
　Stand straight up by her side.

8

'Now whence come ye, young man,' she said,
　'To put me into fear?
My door was bolted right secure,
　And what way cam' ye here?'

9

'O haud your tongue, my lady fair,
　Lat a' your folly be;
Mind ye not o' your turtle-doo
　Ye coax'd from aff the tree?'

10

' O wha are ye, young man ?' she said,
    ' What country come ye frae ? '
' I flew across the sea,' he said,
    ''Twas but this verra day.

11

' My mither is a queen,' he says,
    ' Likewise of magic skill ;
'Twas she that turn'd me in a doo,
    To fly where'er I will.

12

'And it was but this verra day
    That I cam' ower the sea :
I loved you at a single look ;
    With you I'll live and dee.'

13

' O Coo-my-doo, my love sae true,
    Nae mair frae me ye'se gae.'
' That's never my intent, my love ;
    As ye said, it shall be sae.'

14

There he has lived in bower wi' her,
    For sax lang years and ane ;
Till sax young sons to him she bare,
    And the seventh she's brought hame.

15

But aye, as soon 's a child was born,
    He carried them away,
And brought them to his mither's care,
    As fast as he could fly.

16

Thus he has stay'd in bower wi' her
　For seven lang years and mair ;
Till there cam' a lord o' hie renown
　To court that lady fair.

17

But still his proffer she refused,
　And a' his presents too ;
Says, ' I'm content to live alane
　Wi' my bird Coo-my-doo.'

18

Her father sware an angry oath,
　He sware it wi' ill-will :
' To-morrow, ere I eat or drink,
　That bird I'll surely kill.'

19

The bird was sitting in his cage,
　And heard what he did say ;
He jump'd upon the window-sill :
　' 'Tis time I was away.'

20

Then Coo-my-doo took flight and flew
　Beyond the raging sea,
And lighted at his mither's castle,
　Upon a tower sae hie.

21

The Queen his mither was walking out,
　To see what she could see,
And there she saw her darling son
　Set on the tower sae hie.

C

22

' Get dancers here to dance,' she said ,
  'And minstrels for to play ;
For here's my dear son Florentine
  Come back wi' me to stay.'

23

' Get nae dancers to dance, mither,
  Nor minstrels for to play ;
For the mither o' my seven sons,
  The morn's her wedding-day.'

24

' Now tell me, dear son Florentine,
  O tell, and tell me true ;
Tell me this day, without delay,
  What sall I do for you ?'

25

' Instead of dancers to dance, mither,
  Or minstrels for to play,
Turn four-and-twenty well-wight men,
  Like storks, in feathers gray ;

26

' My seven sons in seven swans,
  Aboon their heads to flee ;
And I mysell a gay goshawk,
  A bird o' high degree.'

27

Then, sighing, said the Queen to hersell,
  ' That thing's too high for me !'
But she applied to an auld woman,
  Who had mair skill than she.

' well-wight,' very strong.

28

Instead o' dancers to dance a dance,
    Or minstrels for to play,
Were four-and-twenty well-wight men
    Turn'd birds o' feathers gray;

29

Her seven sons in seven swans,
    Aboon their heads to flee;
And he himsell a gay goshawk,
    A bird o' high degree.

30

This flock o' birds took flight and flew
    Beyond the raging sea;
They landed near the Earl Mar's castle,
    Took shelter in every tree.

31

They were a flock o' pretty birds,
    Right wondrous to be seen;
The weddin'eers they look'd at them
    Whilst walking on the green.

32

These birds flew up frae bush and tree,
    And lighted on the ha';
And, when the wedding-train cam' forth,
    Flew down amang them a'.

33

The storks they seized the boldest men,
    That they could not fight or flee;
The swans they bound the bridegroom fast
    Unto a green aik tree.

34

They flew around the bride-maidens,
    Around the bride's own head;
And, wi' the twinkling o' an ee,
    The bride and they were fled.

35

There's ancient men at weddings been
    For eighty years or more;
But siccan a curious wedding-day
    They never saw before.

36

For naething could the company do,
    Nor naething could they say;
But they saw a flock o' pretty birds
    That took their bride away.

VI

Brown Adam.

1

O WHA wad wish the wind to blaw,
    Or the green leaves fa' therewith?
Or wha wad wish a lealer love
    Than Brown Adam the Smith?

2

But they hae banish'd him, Brown Adam,
    Frae father and frae mother;
And they hae banish'd him, Brown Adam,
    Frae sister and frae brother.

3

And they hae banish'd him, Brown Adam,
  The flower o' a' his kin;
And he's bigged a bower in gude greenwood
  Above his ladye and him.   ·

4

It fell upon a summer's day,
  Brown Adam he thought lang;
And, for to hunt some venison,
  To greenwood he wad gang.

5

He has ta'en his bow his arm o'er,
  His bolts and arrows lang;
And he is to the gude greenwood
  As fast as he could gang.

6

O he's shot up, and he's shot down,
  The bird upon the brier;
And he sent it hame to his ladye,
  Bade her be of gude cheer.

7

O he's shot up, and he's shot down,
  The bird upon the thorn;
And sent it hame to his ladye,
  Said he'd be hame the morn.

8

When he cam' to his lady's bower-door
  He stood a little forbye,
And there he heard a fu' fause knight
  Tempting his gay ladye.

9

For he's ta'en out a gay goud ring,
　Had cost him many a poun':
' O grant me love for love, ladye,
　And this sall be thy own.'

10

' I lo'e Brown Adam weel,' she said ;
　' I trow sae does he me ;
I wadna gie Brown Adam's love
　For nae fause knight I see.'

11

Out has he ta'en a purse o' gowd,
　Was a' fou to the string :
' O grant me love for love, ladye,
　And a' this sall be thine.'

12

' I lo'e Brown Adam weel,' she says ;
　' I wot sae does he me :
I wadna be your light leman,
　For mair than ye could gie.'

13

Forth he drew his sharp bright brand ;
　His arm was stout and strang :
' Now grant me love for love, ladye,
　Or thro' ye this sall gang !'
Then, sighing, says that lady fair,
　' Brown Adam tarries lang !'

14

Then in and starts him Brown Adam,
　Says, ' I'm just at your hand.'

He's gar'd him leave his bonny bow,
　He's gar'd him leave his brand,
He's gar'd him leave a dearer pledge—
　Four fingers o' his right hand.

VII

Edom o' Gordon.

1

IT fell about the Martinmas,
　When the wind blew shrill and cauld,
Said Edom o' Gordon to his men,
　'We maun draw to a hauld.

2

'And whatna hauld sall we draw to,
　My merry men and me?
We will gae to the house of the Rodes,
　To see that fair ladye.'

3

The lady stood on her castle wa',
　Beheld baith dale and down;
There she was aware of a host of men
　Came riding towards the town.

4

'O see ye not, my merry men a',
　O see ye not what I see?
Methinks I see a host of men;
　I marvel who they be.'

'hauld,' hold, stronghold.　'town,' enclosed place.

5

She ween'd it had been her lovely lord,
    As he cam' riding hame ;
It was the traitor, Edom o' Gordon,
    Wha reck'd nor sin nor shame.

6

She had nae sooner buskit hersell,
    And putten on her gown,
Till Edom o' Gordon an' his men
    Were round about the town.

7

They had nae sooner supper set,
    Nae sooner said the grace,
But Edom o' Gordon an' his men
    Were lighted about the place.

8

The lady ran up to her tower-head,
    As fast as she could hie,
To see if by her fair speeches
    She could wi' him agree.

9

' Come doun to me, ye lady gay,
    Come doun, come doun to me ;
This night sall ye lig within mine arms,
    To-morrow my bride sall be.'

10

' I winna come down, ye fause Gordon,
    I winna come down to thee ;
I winna forsake my ain dear lord,—
    And he is na far frae me.'

                    ' buskit,' readied.

11

'Gie owre your house, ye lady fair,
    Gie owre your house to me;
Or I sall burn yoursell therein,
    But and your babies three.'

12

'I winna gie owre, ye fause Gordon,
    To nae sic traitor as thee;
And if ye burn my ain dear babes,
    My lord sall mak' ye dree.

13

'Now reach my pistol, Glaud, my man,
    And charge ye weel my gun;
For, but an I pierce that bluidy butcher,
    My babes, we been undone!'

14

She stood upon her castle wa',
    And let twa bullets flee:
She miss'd that bluidy butcher's heart,
    And only razed his knee.

15

'Set fire to the house!' quo' fause Gordon,
    Wud wi' dule and ire:
'Fause ladye, ye sall rue that shot
    As ye burn in the fire!'

16

'Wae worth, wae worth ye, Jock, my man!
    I paid ye weel your fee;
Why pu' ye out the grund-wa' stane,
    Lets in the reek to me?

'dree,' suffer.   'wud,' mad.   'reek,' smoke.

17

'And e'en wae worth ye, Jock, my man !
   I paid ye weel your hire ;
Why pu' ye out the grund-wa' stane,
   To me lets in the fire ?'

18

' Ye paid me weel my hire, ladye,
   Ye paid me weel my fee :
But now I'm Edom o' Gordon's man, —
   Maun either do or dee.'

19

O then bespake her little son,
   Sat on the nurse's knee :
Says, 'O mither dear, gie owre this house,
   For the reek it smothers me.'

20

' I wad gie a' my goud, my bairn,
   Sae wad I a' my fee,
For ae blast o' the western wind,
   To blaw the reek frae thee.'

21

O then bespake her daughter dear,—
   She was baith jimp and sma' :
' O row' me in a pair o' sheets,
   And tow me owre the wa' !'

22

They row'd her in a pair o' sheets,
   And tow'd her owre the wa' ;
But on the point o' Gordon's spear
   She gat a deadly fa'.

23

O bonnie, bonnie was her mouth,
  And cherry were her cheeks,
And clear, clear was her yellow hair,
  Whereon the red blood dreeps.

24

Then wi' his spear he turn'd her owre ;
  O gin her face was wan !
He said, ' Ye are the first that e'er
  I wish'd alive again.'

25

He cam' and lookit again at her ;
  O gin her skin was white !
' I might hae spared that bonnie face
  To hae been some man's delight.'

26

' Busk and boun, my merry men a',
  For ill dooms I do guess ;—
I cannot look on that bonnie face
  As it lies on the grass.'

27

' Wha looks to freits, my master dear,
  Its freits will follow them ;
Let it ne'er be said that Edom o' Gordon
  Was daunted by a dame.'

28

But when the ladye saw the fire
  Come flaming o'er her head,
She wept, and kiss'd her children twain,
  Says, ' Bairns, we been but dead.'

' Busk and boun,' trim up and prepare to go.　　' freits,' ill omens.

29

The Gordon then his bugle blew,
  And said, ' Awa', awa'!
This house o' the Rodes is a' in a flame ;
  I hauld it time to ga'.'

30

And this way lookit her ain dear lord,
  As he came owre the lea ;
He saw his castle a' in a lowe,
  Sae far as he could see.

31

' Put on, put on, my wighty men,
  As fast as ye can dri'e !
For he that's hindmost o' the thrang
  Sall ne'er get good o' me.'   ·   ·

32

Then some they rade, and some they ran,
  Out-owre the grass and bent ;
But ere the foremost could win up,
  Baith lady and babes were brent.

33

And after the Gordon he is gane,
  Sae fast as he might dri'e ;
And soon i' the Gordon's foul heart's blude
  He's wroken his fair ladye.

'lowe,' blaze.   'wighty,' sturdy.   'wroken,' avenged.

VIII

𝔜oung 𝔚aters.

1

IT was about Yule, when the wind blew cool,
  And the round tables began,
O there is come to our King's court
  Many a well-favour'd man.

2

The Queen look'd over the castle wall,
  Beheld both dale and down,
And there she saw the brave young Waters
  Come riding to the town.

3

His footmen they ran on before,
  His horsemen rode behind ;
A mantle seam'd with burning gold
  Did keep him from the wind.

4

Then careless spake a wily lord,
  And to the Queen said he,
' Now which might seem the comeliest man
  That rides in that company ?'

5

' I've seen lord, and I've seen laird,
  And knights of high degree ;
But so fair a face as Young Waters'
  Mine eyes did never see.'

6

Out then spake the jealous King,
  And an angry man was he :
' Now if he had been twice as fair,
  You might have excepted me.'

7

' You're neither laird nor lord,' she says,
  ' But the King that wears the crown ;
There is not a knight in fair Scotland
  But to thee maun bow down.'

8

For all that she could do or say,
  Appeased he would not be ;
But for the words which she had said
  Young Waters he must dee.

9

' Young Waters is a traitor bold,
  I have proof enough,' says he ;
And vile fause-witness though it was,
  Young Waters he must dee.

10

Now they have ta'en Young Waters,
  Put fetters on his feet ;
Now they have ta'en Young Waters,
  And thrown him in dungeon deep.

11

' Oft I have ridden through Stirling town
  In wind, and snow, and sleet ;
But I never rode through Stirling town
  With fetters at my feet.

12

'Oft I have ridden through Stirling town
  In the sunshine and the rain ;
But now I ride through Stirling town,
  Ne'er to return again.'

13

They brought unto the heading-hill
  His hounds within a leash ;
They brought unto the heading-hill
  His goshawk in a jess.

14

They led unto the heading-hill
  His horse and golden saddle ;
The nurse came to the heading-hill
  With his young son from the cradle.

15

His wife came to the heading-hill :
  'Adieu, dear love, to thee !'
And for the words the Queen had spoke
  Did brave Young Waters dee.

IX

The Wife of Usher's Well.

I

THERE lived a wife at Usher's Well,
  And a wealthy wife was she ;
She had three stout and stalwart sons,
  And sent them o'er the sea.

2

They hadna been a week from her,
　　A week but barely ane,
When word cam' to the carline wife
　　That her three sons were gane.

3

They hadna been a week from her,
　　A week but barely three,
When word cam' to the carline wife
　　That her sons she'd never see.

4

' I wish the wind may never cease,
　　Nor fish be in the flood,
Till my three sons come hame to me,
　　In earthly flesh and blood !'

5

It fell about the Martinmas,
　　When nights are lang and mirk,
The carline wife's three sons cam' hame,
　　And their hats were o' the birk.

6

It neither grew in syke nor ditch,
　　Nor yet in any sheugh ;
But at the gates o' Paradise
　　That birk grew fair eneugh.

7

' Blow up the fire, my maidens !
　　Bring water from the well !
For a' my house shall feast this night,
　　Since my three sons are well.'

'carline-wife,' an old peasant-woman.　　'birk,' birch.
'syke,' marsh.　　'sheugh,' trench.

8

And she has made to them a bed,
　She's made it large and wide ;
And she's ta'en her mantle round about,
　Sat down at the bedside.

9

Up then crew the red, red cock,
　And up and crew the gray;
The eldest to the youngest said,
　' 'Tis time we were away.

10

' The cock doth craw, the day doth daw,
　The channerin' worm doth chide ;
Gin we be miss'd out o' our place,
　A sair pain we maun bide.'

11

' Lie still, lie still but a little wee while,
　Lie still but if we may ;
Gin my mother should miss us when she wakes
　She'll go mad ere it be day.

12

' Our mother has nae mair but us ;
　See where she leans asleep ;
The mantle that was on herself,
　She has happ'd it round our feet.'

13

O it's they have ta'en up their mother's mantle,
　And they've hung it on a pin :
' O lang may ye hing, my mother's mantle,
　Ere ye hap us again !

D

14

' Fare ye weel, my mother dear!
　Fareweel to barn and byre!
And fare ye weel, the bonny lass
　That kindles my mother's fire!'

X

The Death of Parcy Reed.

1

GOD send the land deliverance
　Frae every reaving, riding Scot!
We'll sune hae neither cow nor ewe,
　We'll sune hae neither staig nor stot.

2

The outlaws come frae Liddesdale,
　They herry Redesdale far and near;
The rich man's gelding it maun gang,
　They canna pass the puir man's mear.

3

Sure it were weel, had ilka thief
　Around his neck a halter strang;
And curses heavy may they light
　On traitors vile oursels amang!

4

Now Parcy Reed has Crosier ta'en,
　He has delivered him to the law;
But Crosier says he'll do waur than that,
　He'll make the tower o' Troughend fa'.

'reaving' (reave or rive; reft), taking by violence.
'staig nor stot,' young horse nor ox.　'herry,' plunder.

5

And Crosier says he will do waur—
 He will do waur if waur can be ;
He'll make Parcy's bairns a' fatherless ;
 And Parcy's land may then lie lee.

6

' To the hunting, ho ! ' cried Parcy Reed,
 ' The morning sun is on the dew ;
The cauler breeze frae off the fells
 Will lead the dogs to the quarry true.

7

' To the hunting, ho ! ' cried Parcy Reed,
 And to the hunting he has gane ;
And the three fause Ha's o' Girsonsfield
 Alang wi' him he has them ta'en.

8

They hunted high, they hunted low,
 By heathery hill and birken shaw ;
They raised a buck on Rooken Edge,
 And blew the mort at Ealylawe.

9

They hunted high, they hunted low,
 They made the echoes ring amain ;
With music sweet o' horn and hound,
 They merry made fair Redesdale glen.

10

They hunted high, they hunted low,
 They hunted up, they hunted down,
Until the day was past the prime,
 And it grew late in the afternoon.

11

They hunted high in Batinghope,
　When as the sun was sinking low,
Says Parcy then, 'Ca' off the dogs,
　We'll bait our steeds and homeward go.'

12

They lighted aff in Batinghope,
　Atween the brown and benty ground;
They had but rested a little while,
　Till Parcy Reed was sleeping sound.

13

There's nane may lean on a rotten staff,
　But him that risks to get a fa';
There's nane may in a traitor trust,
　And traitors black were every Ha'.

14

They've stown the bridle aff his steed,
　And they've put water in his lang gun;
They've fixed his sword within the sheath,
　That out again it winna come.

15

'Awaken ye, waken ye, Parcy Reed,
　Or by your enemies be ta'en;
For yonder are the five Crosiers
　A-coming owre the Hingin-stane.'

16

'If they be five, and we be four,
　Sae that ye stand alang wi' me,
Then every man ye will take one,
　And only leave but two to me:

We will them meet as brave men ought,
  And make them either fight or flee.'

17
' We mayna stand, we canna stand,
  We daurna stand alang wi' thee ;
The Crosiers haud thee at a feud,
  And they wad gar us a' to dee.'

18
' O, turn thee, turn thee, Johnnie Ha',
  O, turn thee, man, and fight wi' me ;
When ye come to Troughend again,
  My gude black naig I will gie thee ;
He cost full twenty pound o' goud,
  Atween my brother John and me.'

19
' I mayna turn, I canna turn,
  I daurna turn and fight wi' thee ;
The Crosiers haud thee at a feud,
  And they wad kill baith thee and me!'

20
' O, turn thee, turn thee, Willie Ha',
  O, turn thee, man, and fight wi' me ;
When ye come to Troughend again,
  A yoke o' owsen I'll gie thee.'

21
' I mayna turn, I canna turn,
  I daurna turn and fight wi' thee ;
The Crosiers haud thee at a feud,
  And they wad kill baith thee and me.

22

' O, turn thee, turn thee, Tommy Ha',
  O, turn now, man, and fight wi' me ;
If ever we come to Troughend again,
  My daughter Jean I'll gie to thee.'

23

' I mayna turn, I canna turn,
  I daurna turn and fight wi' thee ;
The Crosiers haud thee at a feud,
  And they wad kill baith thee and me.'

24

' O, shame upon ye, traitors a' !
  I wish your hames ye may never see ;
Ye've stown the bridle aff my naig,
  And I can neither fight nor flee.

25

' Ye've stown the bridle aff my naig,
  And ye've put water i' my lang gun ;
Ye've fixed my sword within the sheath,
  That out again it winna come.'

26

He had but time to cross himsel',
  A prayer he hadna time to say,
Till round him came the Crosiers keen,
  All riding graithed, and in array.

27

'Weel met, weel met, now, Parcy Reed,
  Thou art the very man we sought ;
Owre lang hae we been in your debt,
  Now will we pay you as we ought.

' graithed,' accoutred.

. 28

' We'll pay thee at the nearest tree,
    Where we shall hang thee like a hound ; '
Brave Parcy rais'd his fankit sword,
    And fell'd the foremost to the ground.

29

Alake, and wae for Parcy Reed,
    Alake, he was an unarmed man ;
Four weapons pierced him all at once,
    As they assailed him there and than.

30

They fell upon him all at once,
    They mangled him most cruellie ;
Their slightest wound might caused his deid,
    And they have gi'en him thirty-three.
They hacket off his hands and feet,
    And left him lying on the lee.

31

' Now, Parcy Reed, we've paid our debt,
    Ye canna weel dispute the tale,'
The Crosiers said, and off they rade—
    They rade the airt o' Liddesdale.

32

It was the hour o' gloamin' gray,
    When herds come in frae fauld and pen ;
A herd he saw a huntsman lie,
    Says he, ' Can this be Laird Troughen' ? '

33

' There's some will ca' me Parcy Reed,
    And some will ca' me Laird Troughen' ;

' fankit,' entangled.

It's little matter what they ca' me,
My faes hae made me ill to ken.

34

' There's some will ca' me Parcy Reed,
And speak my praise in tower and town;
It's little matter what they do now,
My life-blood rudds the heather brown.

35

' There's some will ca' me Parcy Reed,
And a' my virtues say and sing;
But now I would much rather hae
A draught o' water frae the spring!'

36

The herd flung aff his clouted shoon,
And to the nearest fountain ran;
He made his bonnet serve a cup,
And wan the blessing o' the dying man.

37

' Now, honest herd, ye maun do mair,—
Ye maun do mair as I ye tell;
Ye maun bear tidings to Troughend,
And bear likewise my last farewell.

38

'A farewell to my wedded wife,
A farewell to my brother John,
Wha sits into the Troughend tower,
Wi' heart as hard as any stone.

39

'A farewell to my daughter Jean,
A farewell to my young sons five;

Had they been at their father's hand,
 I had this night been man alive.

40

'A farewell to my followers a',
 And a' my neighbours gude at need;
Bid them think how the treacherous Ha's
 Betrayed the life o' Parcy Reed.

41

'The laird o' Clennel bears my bow,
 The laird o' Brandon bears my brand;
Whene'er they ride i' the border side,
 They'll mind the fate o' the laird Troughend.'

XI

Waly, Waly.

1

O WALY, waly, up the bank,
 O waly, waly, doun the brae,
And waly, waly, yon burn-side,
 Where I and my love were wont to gae!
I lean'd my back unto an aik,
 I thocht it was a trustie tree,
But first it bow'd and syne it brak',—-
 Sae my true love did lichtlie me.

2

O waly, waly, but love be bonnie
 A little time while it is new!
But when it's auld it waxeth cauld,
 And fadeth awa' like the morning dew.

O wherefore should I busk my heid,
  Or wherefore should I kame my hair?
For my true love has me forsook,
  And says he'll never lo'e me mair.

3
Noo Arthur's Seat sall be my bed,
  The sheets sall ne'er be press'd by me;
Saint Anton's well sall be my drink;
  Since my true love's forsaken me.
Martinmas wind, when wilt thou blaw,
  And shake the green leaves off the tree?
O gentle death, when wilt thou come?
  For of my life I am wearie.

4
'Tis not the frost that freezes fell,
  Nor blawing snaw's inclemencie,
'Tis not sic cauld that makes me cry;
  But my love's heart grown cauld to me.
When we cam' in by Glasgow toun,
  We were a comely sicht to see;
My love was clad in the black velvet,
  An' I mysel' in cramasie.

5
But had I wist before I kiss'd
  That love had been so ill to win,
I'd lock'd my heart in a case o' goud,
  And pinn'd it wi' a siller pin.
Oh, oh! if my young babe were born,
  And set upon the nurse's knee;
And I mysel' were dead and gane,
  And the green grass growing over me!

  'cramasie' (cramoisie), crimson.

XII

The Laird o' Drum.

1

THE Laird o' Drum is a-hunting gane,
  All in a morning early,
And he has spied a weel-faur'd May,
  A-shearing at her barley.

2

' My bonny May, my weel-faur'd May,
  O will ye fancy me, O ?
Wilt gae and be the Leddy o' Drum,
  And let your shearing a-be, O ?'

3

' It's I winna fancy you, kind sir,
  Nor let my shearing a-be, O ;
For I'm ower low to be Leddy Drum,
  And your light love I'll never be, O.'

4

' Gin ye'll cast aff that gown o' grey,
  Put on the silk for me, O,
I'll make a vow, and keep it true,
  A light love you'll never be, O.'

5

' My father he is a shepherd mean,
  Keeps sheep on yonder hill, O,
And ye may gae and speer at him,
  For I am at his will, O.'

6

Drum is to her father gane,
    Keeping his sheep on yon hill, O :
' I am come to marry your ae daughter,
    If ye'll gie me your good-will, O.'

7

' My dochter can naether read nor write,
    She ne'er was brocht up at scheel, O ;
But weel can she milk baith cow and ewe,
    And mak' a kebbuck weel, O.

8

' She'll shake your barn, and win your corn,
    And gang to kiln and mill, O ;
She'll saddle your steed in time o' need,
    And draw aff yer boots hersell, O.'

9

.' I'll learn your lassie to read and write,
    And I'll put her to the scheel, O ;
She shall neither need to saddle my steed,
    Nor draw aff my boots hersell, O.

10

' But wha will bake my bridal bread,
    Or brew my bridal ale, O ;
And wha will welcome my bonnie bride,
    Is mair than I can tell, O.'

11

Four-and-twenty gentlemen
    Gaed in at the yetts of Drum, O ;
But no a man has lifted his hat,
    When the Leddy o' Drum came in, O.

'kebbuck,' cheese.

12

' Peggy Coutts is a very bonnie bride,
   And Drum is big and gawsy;
But he might hae chosen a higher match
   Than ony shepherd's lassie!'

13

Then up bespak his brother John,
   Says, ' Ye've done us meikle wrang, O ;
Ye've married ane far below our degree,
   A mock to a' our kin, O.'

14

' Now haud your tongue, my brother John ;
   What needs it thee offend, O ?
I've married a wife to work and win,
   And ye've married ane to spend, O.

15

' The first time that I married a wife,
   She was far abune my degree, O ;
She wadna hae walk'd thro' the yetts o' Drum,
   But the pearlin' abune her bree, O,
And I durstna gang in the room where she was,
   But my hat below my knee, O !'

16

He has ta'en her by the milkwhite hand,
   And led her in himsell, O ;
And in through ha's, and in through bowers,—
   ' And ye're welcome, Leddy Drum, O.'

17

When they had eaten and well drunken,
   And a' men bound for bed, O,

'gawsy,' portly.   'pearlin',' lace.   'bree,' brow.

The Laird of Drum and his Leddy fair,
In ae bed they were laid, O.

18

' Gin ye had been o' high renown,
  As ye're o' low degree, O,
We might hae baith gane doun the street
  Amang gude companie, O.'

19

' I tauld ye weel ere we were wed,
  Ye were far abune my degree, O ;
But now I'm married, in your bed laid,
  And just as gude as ye, O.

20

' For an I were dead, and ye were dead,
  And baith in ae grave had lain, O ;
Ere seven years were come and gane,
  They'd no ken your dust frae mine, O.'

XIII

Annan Water.

I

' ANNAN Water's wading deep,
  And my love Annie's wondrous bonny ;
I will keep my tryst to-night,
  And win the heart o' lovely Annie.'

2

He's loupen on his bonny grey,
  He rade the right gate and the ready ;
For a' the storm he wadna stay,
  For seeking o' his bonny lady.

3

And he has ridden o'er field and fell,
  Through muir and moss, and stones and mire;
His spurs o' steel were sair to bide,
  And frae her four feet flew the fire.

4

' My bonny grey, noo play your part!
  Gin ye be the steed that wins my dearie,
Wi' corn and hay ye'se be fed for aye,
  And never spur sall mak' you wearie.'

5

The grey was a mare, and a right gude mare;
  But when she wan the Annan Water,
She couldna hae found the ford that night
  Had a thousand merks been wadded at her.

6

' O boatman, boatman, put off your boat,
  Put off your boat for gouden money!'
But for a' the goud in fair Scotland,
  He dared na tak' him through to Annie.

7

' O I was sworn sae late yestreen,
  Not by a single aith, but mony.
I'll cross the drumly stream to-night,
  Or never could I face my honey.'

8

The side was stey, and the bottom deep,
  Frae bank to brae the water pouring;
The bonny grey mare she swat for fear,
  For she heard the water-kelpy roaring.

'wadded,' wagered.   'stey,' steep.
' water-kelpy,' water-spirit or goblin.   'drumly,' troubled.

9

He spurred her forth into the flood,
  I wot she swam both strong and steady;
But the stream was broad, her strength did fail,
  And he never saw his bonny lady.

10

O wae betide the frush saugh wand!
  And wae betide the bush of brier!
That bent and brake into his hand,
  When strength of man and horse did tire.

11

And wae betide ye, Annan Water!
  This night ye are a drumly river;
But over thee we'll build a brig,
  That ye nae mair true love may sever.

XIV

The Hunting of the Cheviot.

1

THE Percy out of Northumberland,
  And a vow to God made he,
That he would hunt in the mountains
  Of Cheviot within days three,
In the maugre of doughty Douglas,
  And all that with him be.

2

The fattest harts in all Cheviot
  He said he would kill, and carry away;
' By my faith,' said the doughty Douglas again,
  ' I will let that hunting if I may.'

  'frush,' brittle.   'saugh,' sallow.

3

Then the Percy out of Bamborough came,
   And with him a mighty meyné,
Fifteen hundred archers, of blood and bone,
   They were chosen out of shires three.

4

This began on a Monday at morn,
   In Cheviot the hills so hie ;
The child may rue it that is unborn ;
   It was the more pitie.

5

The drivers thorough the woodès went,
   For to raise the deer;
Bowmen bicker'd upon the bent
   With their broad arrows clear.

6

Then the wild thorough the woodès went,
   On every side shear ;
Greyhounds thorough the greves glent
   For to kill their deer.

7

They began in Cheviot, the hills above,
   Early on Monanday ;
By that it drew to the hour of noon,
   A hundred fat hartès dead there lay.

8

They blew a mort upon the bent,
   They assembled on sides shear ;
To the quarry then the Percy went,
   To the brittling of the deer.

'meyné,' company.   'wild,' wild creatures.   'shear,' straight and swift.   'greves,' groves.   'glent,' glanced. 'quarry,' prey.   'brittling,' cutting up.

9

He said, ' It was the Douglas's promise
    This day to meet me here :
But I wist he would fail, verament,'—
    A great oath the Percy sware.

10

At last a squire of Northumberland
    Looked at his hand full nigh ;
He was ware of the doughty Douglas coming,
    With him a mighty meyné ;

11

Both with spear, bill, and brand ;
    It was a mighty sight to see ;
Hardier men, both of heart and hand,
    Were not in Christiantie.

12

They were twenty hundred spearmen good,
    Withouten any fail ;
They were born along by the Water of Tweed,
    In the bounds of Tivydale.

13

' Leave off brittling the deer,' he said,
    ' To your bows look ye take good heed ;
For since ye were of your mothers born
    Had ye never so mickle need.'

14

The doughty Douglas on a steed
    He rode all his men beforne ;
His armour glittered as a glede ;
    A bolder barne was never born.

'bill and brand,' pike and sword.   'glede,' fire.   'barne,' man-child.

15

'Tell me who ye are,' he says,
　'Or whose men that ye be ;
Who gave you leave to hunt in this chace
　In the spite of me ?'

16

The first man that ever him answer made,
　It was the good Lord Percy ;
'We will not tell thee who we are,
　Nor whose men that we be ;
But we will hunt here in this chace,
　In spite of thine and thee.

17

'The fattest harts in all Cheviot
　We have kill'd, and cast to carry away.'
'By my troth,' said the doughty Douglas again,
　'Therefor shall one of us die this day.'

18

Then said the doughty Douglas
　Unto the Lord Percy,
'To kill all these **guiltless men,**
　Alas, it were great pitie !

19

'But, Percy, thou art a lord of land,
　And I am earl called in my countrie ;
Let all our men apart from us stand,
　And do the battle off thee and me.'

20

'Now, curse on his crown,' said the Lord Percy,
　'Whosoever thereto says nay !—
By my troth, doughty Douglas,' he says,
　'Thou never shalt see that day.

'cast,' intend.

E 2

21

'Neither in England, Scotland, nor France,
  Of woman born there is none,
But, an fortune be my chance,
  I dare meet him, one man for one.'

22

Then spake a squire of Northumberland,
  Richard Witherington was his name :
' It shall never be told in South-England,' he says,
  ' To King Harry the Fourth, for shame !

23

' I wot ye bin great lordès two,
  I am a poor squire of land ;
I'll ne'er see my captain fight on a field,
  And a looker-on to stand :
But while I may my weapon wield
  I will fail not, heart and hand.'

24

That day, that day, that dreadful day !—
  The first fytte here I find.
An ye will hear more of the Hunting of Cheviot,
  Yet more there is behind.

THE SECOND FYTTE.

1

THE Englishmen had their bowès bent,
  Their hearts were good enow ;
The first [flight] of arrows that they shot off,
  Seven score spearmen they sloughe.

2

Yet bides Earl Douglas upon the bent,
    A captain good enow,
And that was soon seen, verament,
    For he wrought [the English wo].

3

The Douglas parted his host in three,
    Like a chieftain [full] of pride;
With sure spears of mighty tree
    They came in on every side

4

Thorough our English archery,
    And gave many a wound full wide;
Many a doughty they gar'd to die,
    Which gained them no [small] pride.

5

The Englishmen let their bowès be,
    And pull'd out brands that were bright:
It was a heavy sight to see
    Bright swords on basnets light.

6

Thorough rich mail and maniple
    Stern they struck down straight;
Many a freke that was full free,
    There under-foot did light.

7

At last the Douglas and Percy met,
    Like two captains of might and main;
They swapt together till they both swat,
    With swords of the fine Milán.

'basnets,' small helmets.   'maniple' (of many folds), a
coat worn under the armour.   'freke,' man.

8

These worthy frekes for to fight
  Thereto they were full fain,
Till the blood out of their basnets sprent
  As ever did hail or rain.

9

' Hold thee, Percy ! ' said the Douglas,
  ' And i' faith I shall thee bring
Where thou shalt have an earl's wages
  Of Jamie our Scottish king.

10

' Thou shalt have thy ransom free ;
  I hight thee here this thing ;
For the manfullest man yet art thou
  That ever I conquerèd in fighting.'

11

' Nay,' said the Lord Percy,
  ' I told it thee beforne,
That I would never yielded be
  To no man of a woman born.'

12

With that came an arrow hastily
  Forth of a mighty wane ;
And it hath stricken the Earl Douglas
  In at the breast bane.

13

Thorough liver and lungs both
  The sharp arrow is gone,
That never after in all his life-days
  He spake more words but one :
That was, ' Fight ye, my merry men, while ye may !
  For my life-days be done.'

        ' hight,' promise.   ' wane,' ?

14

The Percy leanèd on his brand,
  And saw the Douglas die;
He took the dead man by the hand,
  And said, 'Wo is me for thee!

15

'To have saved thy life, I would have given
  My landès for years three;
For a better man, of heart nor of hand,
  Was not in the north countrie.'

16

Of all that saw a Scottish knight,
  Sir Hugh the Montgomerie;
He saw the Douglas to death was dight;
  He spended a spear, a trusty tree;

17

He rode upon a courser
  Through a hundred archery;
He never stinted, nor never blan,
  Till he came to good Lord Percy.

18

He set upon the Lord Percy
  A dint that was full sore;
With a sure spear of a mighty tree
  Clean thorough his body he bore,

19

On the other side that a man might see
  A large cloth-yard and mair.
Two better captains in Christentie
  Were not, than the two slain there.

'spended,'?   'blan,' stopped.

20

An archer of Northumberland
　Saw slain was the Lord Percy:
He bare a bend-bow in his hand
　Was made of trusty tree.

21

An arrow, that was a cloth-yard long,
　To the hard steel haled he;
A dint he set, was both sad and sore,
　On Sir Hugh the Montgomerie.

22

The dint it was both sad and sore
　That he on Montgomerie set;
The swan-feathers the arrow bore
　With his heart's-blood they were wet.

23

There was never a freke one foot would flee,
　But still in stour did stand,
Hewing on each other, while they might dree,
　With many a baleful brand.

24

This battle began in Cheviot
　An hour before the noon,
And still when even-song bell was rung
　The battle was not half done.

25

They took [off] on either hand
　By the light of the moon;
Many had no strength for to stand,
　In Cheviot the hills aboon.

'stour,' turmoil of fight.　　'dree,' endure.

26

Of fifteen hundred archers of England,
  Went away but fifty and three;
Of twenty hundred spearmen of Scotland,
  But even five and fiftie,

27

That were not slain in Cheviot;
  They had no strength to stand on hie.
The child may rue that is unborn:
  It was the more pitie.

28

There was slain with Lord Percy,
  Sir John of Agerstone;
Sir Roger, the hyndè Hartley;
  Sir William, the bold Heron.

29

Sir George, the worthy Lovel,
  A knight of great renown;
Sir Ralph, the rich Rugby;
  With dints were beaten down.

30

For Witherington my heart was wo,
  That ever he slain should be;
For when both his legs were hewn in two,
  Yet he kneeled and fought on his knee.

31

There was slain with the doughty Douglas,
  Sir Hugh the Montgomerie;
Sir Davy Liddale, that worthy was,
  His sister's son was he;

'hyndè,' courteous.

32

Sir Charles à Murray in that place,
  That never a foot would flee ;
Sir Hugh Maxwell, a lord he was,
  With the Douglas did he dee.

33

So on the morrow they made them biers
  Of birch and hazel gray ;
Many widows with weeping tears
  Came to fetch their makès away.

34

Tivydale may carp of care,
  Northumberland make great moan ;
For two such captains as there were slain
  On the Marches shall never be none.

35

Word is come to Edinborough,
  To Jamie the Scottish King,
Doughty Douglas, lieutenant of the Marches,
  Lay slain Cheviot within.

36

His handès did he weal and wring :
  ' Alas, and wo is me !
Such another captain in Scotland wide
  There is not left,' said he.

37

Word is come to lovely London,
  To Harry the Fourth our King,
Lord Percy, lieutenant of the Marches,
  Lay slain Cheviot within.

' makes,' mates.   ' Marches,' Borders.   ' weal,' ?

38

'God have mercy on his soul,' said King Harry,
  'Good Lord, if Thy will it be!
I've a hundred captains in England,' he said,
  'As good as ever was he :
But, Percy, an I brook my life,
  Thy death well quit shall be.'

39

And now may Heaven amend us all,
  And into bliss us bring!
This was the Hunting of the Cheviot:
  God send us all good ending!

XV

Bessie Bell and Mary Gray.

I

O BESSIE BELL and Mary Gray,
  They were twa bonny lasses ;
They built a house on yon burn-brae,
  And theek't it o'er wi' rashes.

2

They theek't it o'er wi' birk and brume,
  They theek't it o'er wi' heather ;
Till the pest cam' frae the neib'rin town,
  And strack them baith thegither.

3

They werena buried in Meffin kirkyard,
  Amang the rest o' their kin ;
But they were buried on Dornoch Haugh,
  On the bent before the sun.

'theek't,' thatch'd.

4

Sing, Bessie Bell and Mary Gray,
    They were twa bonny lasses ;
They built a bower on yon burn-brae,
    And theek't it o'er wi' rashes.

XVI

Sir Patrick Spens.

1

THE king sits in Dunfermline town,
    Drinking the blude-red wine :
' O whare will I get a skeely skipper
    To sail this new ship o' mine ? '

2

O up and spake an eldern knight
    Sat at the king's right knee :
' Sir Patrick Spens is the best sailor
    That ever sailed the sea.'

3

Our king has written a braid letter
    And sealed it wi' his hand,
And sent it to Sir Patrick Spens,
    Was walking on the sand.

4

' To Noroway, to Noroway,
    To Noroway o'er the faem ;
The king's daughter to Noroway,
    'Tis thou maun bring her hame.'

'skeely,' skilful.

5

' Be it wind or weet, be it hail or sleet,
   Our ship must sail the faem ;
The king's daughter to Noroway,
   'Tis we must bring her hame.'

6

They hoisted their sails on Monenday morn
   Wi' a' the speed they may ;
They hae landed safe in Noroway
   Upon a Wodensday.

7

They hadna been a week, a week,
   In Noroway but twae,
When that the lords o' Noroway
   Began aloud to say:

8

' Ye Scottishmen spend a' our king's goud
   And a' our queenis fee.'
' Ye lie, ye lie, ye liars loud,
   Fu' loud I hear ye lie !

9

' For I brought as mickle white monie
   As gane my men and me,—
And I brought a half-fou o' gude red goud
   Out-o'er the sea wi' me.

10

' Mak' ready, mak' ready, my merry men a' !
   Our gude ship sails the morn.'
' Now ever alake ! my master dear,
   I fear a deadly storm.

      ' gane,' sufficed.   ' half-fou,' half-bushel.

11

' I saw the new moon late yestreen,
  Wi' the auld moon in her arm ;
And if we gang to sea, master,
  I fear we'll come to harm.'

12

They hadna sail'd upon the sea
  A day but barely three,
Till loud and boisterous grew the wind,
  And gurly grew the sea.

13

' O where will I get a gude sailor
  To tak' my helm in hand,
Till I gae up to the tall topmast
  To see if I can spy land ?'

14

' O here am I, a sailor gude,
  To tak' the helm in hand,
Till you gae up to the tall topmast,—
  But I fear you'll ne'er spy land.'.

15

He hadna gane a step, a step,
  A step but barely ane,
When a bolt flew out o' our goodly ship,
  And the salt sea it came in.

16

' Gae fetch a web o' the silken claith,
  Anither o' the twine,
And wap them into our ship's side,
  And letna the sea come in.'

17

They fetched a web o' the silken claith,
    Anither o' the twine,
And they wapped them into that gude ship's side,
    But still the sea cam' in.

18

O laith, laith were our gude Scots lords
    To weet their milk-white hands ;
But lang ere a' the play was ower
    They wat their gouden bands.

19

O laith, laith were our gude Scots lords
    To weet their cork-heel'd shoon ;
But lang ere a' the play was play'd
    They wat their hats aboon.

20

O lang, lang may the ladies sit
    Wi' their fans into their hand,
Before they see Sir Patrick Spens
    Come sailing to the land !

21

And lang, lang may the maidens sit
    Wi' their goud kaims in their hair
Awaiting for their ain dear loves,
    For them they'll see nae mair.

22

Half ower, half ower to Aberdour,
    It's fifty fathoms deep ;
And there lies gude Sir Patrick Spens,
    Wi' the Scots lords at his feet.

XVII
King John and the Abbot of Canterbury.

I

AN ancient story I'll tell you anon,
Of a notable prince, that was callèd King John;
He ruled over England with main and might,
But he did great wrong, and maintain'd little right.

2

And I'll tell you a story, a story so merry,
Concerning the Abbot of Canterbury;
How for his housekeeping and high renown,
They rode post to bring him to London town.

3

A hundred men, as the King heard say,
The Abbot kept in his house every day;
And fifty gold chains, without any doubt,
In velvet coats waited the Abbot about.

4

'How now, Father Abbot? I hear it of thee,
Thou keepest a far better house than me;
And for thy housekeeping and high renown,
I fear thou work'st treason against my crown.'

5

'My Liege,' quoth the Abbot, 'I would it were known,
I am spending nothing but what is my own;
And I trust your Grace will not put me in fear,
For spending my own true-gotten gear.'

6

' Yes, yes, Father Abbot, thy fault is high,
And now for the same thou needest must die;
And except thou canst answer me questions three,
Thy head struck off from thy body shall be.

7

' And first,' quo' the King, ' as I sit here,
With my crown of gold on my head so fair,
Among all my liegemen of noble birth,—
Thou must tell to one penny what I am worth.

8

' Secondly, tell me, beyond all doubt,
How soon I may ride the whole world about;
And at the third question thou must not shrink,
But tell me here truly, what do I think?'

9

' O, these are deep questions for my shallow wit,
And I cannot answer your Grace as yet:
But if you will give me a fortnight's space,
I'll do my endeavour to answer your Grace.'

10

' Now a fortnight's space to thee will I give,
And that is the longest thou hast to live;
For unless thou answer my questions three,
Thy life and thy lands are forfeit to me.'

11

Away rode the Abbot all sad at this word;
He rode to Cambridge and Oxenford;
But never a doctor there was so wise,
That could by his learning an answer devise.

F

12

Then home rode the Abbot, with comfort so cold,
And he met his Shepherd, a-going to fold :
' Now, good Lord Abbot, you are welcome home ;
What news do you bring us from great King John?'

13

' Sad news, sad news, Shepherd, I must give ;
That I have but three days more to live.
I must answer the King his questions three,
Or my head struck off from my body shall be.

14

' The first is to tell him, as he sits there,
With his crown of gold on his head so fair
Among all his liegemen of noble birth,
To within one penny, what he is worth.

15

' The second to tell him, beyond all doubt,
How soon he may ride this whole world about ;
And at question the third I must not shrink,
But tell him there truly, what does he think?'

16

' O cheer up, my Lord ; did you never hear yet
That a fool may teach a wise man wit ?
Lend me your serving-men, horse, and apparel,
And I'll ride to London to answer your quarrel.

17

' With your pardon, it oft has been told to me
That I'm like your Lordship as ever can be :
And if you will but lend me your gown,
There is none shall know us at London town.'

18

' Now horses and serving-men thou shalt have,
With sumptuous raiment gallant and brave;
With crozier, and mitre, and rochet, and cope,
Fit to draw near to our Father the Pope.'

19

' Now welcome, Sir Abbot,' the King he did say,
"'Tis well thou'rt come back to keep thy day;
For and if thou canst answer my questions three,
Thy life and thy living both saved shall be.

20

' And first, as thou seest me sitting here,
With my crown of gold on my head so fair,
Among my liegemen of noble birth,—
Tell to one penny what I am worth.'

21

' For thirty pence our Saviour was sold
Among the false Jews, as I have been told;
And twenty-nine is the worth of thee;
For, I think, thou art one penny worse than he.'

22

The King he laugh'd, and swore by St. Bittle,
' I did not think I was worth so little!
Now secondly tell me, beyond all doubt,
How soon I may ride this world about.'

23

' You must rise with the sun, and ride with the same.
Until the next morning he riseth again;
And then your Grace need never doubt
But in twenty-four hours you'll ride it about.

24

The King he laugh'd, and swore by St. Jone,
"I did not think I could do it so soon!
Now from question the third thou must not shrink,
But tell me truly, what do I think?'

25

'Yea, that I shall do, and make your Grace merry :
You think I'm the Abbot of Canterbury;
But I'm his poor shepherd, as plain you may see,
That am come to beg pardon for him and for me.'

26

The King he laugh'd, and swore by the mass,
'I'll make thee Lord Abbot this day in his place!'
'Now nay, my Liege, be not in such speed;
For, alas! I can neither write nor read.'

27

'Four nobles a week, then, I'll give to thee,
For this merry jest thou hast shown to me;
And tell the old Abbot, when thou gettest home,
Thou hast brought him free pardon from King John.'

XVIII

The Douglas Tragedy.

I

'RISE up, rise up, Lord Douglas!' she says,
'And put on your armour so bright;
Let it ne'er be said that a daughter of ours
Was married to a lord under night.

2

' Rise up, rise up, my two bold sons,
    And put on your armour so bright ;
And take better care o' your youngest sister,
    For your eldest's awa' this night ! '

3

Lady Margaret was on a milkwhite steed,
    Lord William was on a grey,
A buglet-horn hung down by his side,
    And swiftly they rode away.

4

Lord William look'd over his left shoulder
    To see what he could see,
And there he spied her two bold brothers
    Come riding o'er the lea.

5

' Light down, light down, Lady Margaret,' he said,
    ' And hold my steed in your hand,
Until that against your two bold brothers,
    And your father, I make a stand.'

6

She held his steed in her milkwhite hand,
    And never shed one tear,
Until she saw her two brothers fa',
    And hard-fighting her father dear.

7

' O haud your hand, Lord William ! ' she said,
    ' Your strokes they are wondrous sair ;
Though lovers I might get mony a ane,
    A father I canna get mair.'

8

Then she's ta'en aff her neckerchief,
  It was o' the cambrick fine,
And aye she dighted her father's wounds;
  His blood ran down like wine.

9

' Now choose, now choose, Lady Margaret :
  Will ye gang wi' me, or bide?'
' I'll gang, I'll gang, Lord William,' she said;
  ' Ye've left me no other guide.'

10

He lifted her up on her milkwhite steed,
  And mounted his dapple-grey,
With his buglet-horn hung down by his side,
  And slowly they rade away.

11

O they rade on, and on they rade,
  And a' by the light o' the moon,
Until they came to a wan water,
  And there they lighted down.

12

They lighted down to tak' a drink
  O' the spring that ran so clear,
But down the stream ran his gude heart's blood,
  And sair she 'gan to fear.

13

' Hold up, hold up, Lord William,' she said,
  ' I fear me you are slain!'
' 'Tis but the shadow o' my scarlet cloak
  That shines in the water sae plain.'

14

O they rade on, and on they rade,
  And a' by the light o' the moon,
Until they came to his mother's ha',
  And there they lighted down.

15

' Get up, get up, lady mother,' he says,
  ' Get up, and let in your son !
Open the door, lady mother,' he says,
  ' For this night my fair lady I've won !

16

' Now, mak' my bed, lady mother,' he says,
  ' O mak' it baith wide and deep,
And lay Lady Margaret close at my back,
  And the sounder I will sleep !'

17

Lord William was dead lang ere midnight,
  Lady Margaret lang ere day.
May all true lovers that go thegither
  Have mair gude luck than they !

18

Lord William was buried in Mary's Kirk,
  Lady Margaret in Mary's Quire;
And out o' her grave grew a bonny red rose,
  And out o' the knight's a briar.

19

And they twa met, and they twa plat,
  And fain they wad be near;
And a' the warld right weel might ken
  These were twa lovers dear.

20

Till bye and rade the Black Douglas,
    And O but he was rough!
For he pu'd up the bonny briar,
    And flang't in St. Mary's Lough.

XIX

Kempion.

1

HER mither died when she was young,
    Which gave her cause to make great moan;
Her father married the warse woman
    That ever lived in Christendom.

2

She servèd well wi' foot and hand,
    In everything that she could dee;
But her stepmither hated her warse and warse,
    And a powerful wicked witch was she.

3

'Come hither, come hither, ye cannot choose;
    And lay your head low on my knee;
The heaviest weird I will you read
    That ever was redd to gay ladye.

4

'Mickle dolour sall ye dree
    When o'er the saut seas maun ye swim;
And far mair dolour sall ye dree
    When up to Estmere Crags ye climb.

'weird,' doom.   'dree,' suffer.

5

'I weird ye to be a fiery snake ;
  And borrowed sall ye never be,
Unless that Kempion, the king's own son,
  Come to the crag and thrice kiss thee.
Until the warld comes to an end,
  Borrowed sall ye never be !'

6

O mickle dolour did she dree,
  And aye the saut seas o'er she swam ;
And far mair dolour did she dree
  On Estmere Crags, when up she clamb.

7

And aye she cried on Kempion,
  Gin he would but come to her hand :—
Now word has gane to Kempion,
  That siccan a beast was in the land.

8

'Now, by my sooth,' said Kempion,
  'This fiery beast I'll gang and see.'
'And by my sooth,' said Segramour,
  'My ac brother, I'll gang wi' thee.'

9

They twa hae biggit a bonny boat,
  And they hae set her to the sea ;
But a mile before they reach'd the land,
  Around them 'gan the red fire flee.

10

The worm leapt out, the worm leapt down,
  She plaited nine times round stock and stane ;
And aye as the boat came to the beach
  She struck and banged it off again.

'borrowed,' rescued.

11

'Mind how you steer, my brother dear :
    Keep further off!' said Segramour;
'This beast will drown us in the sea,
    Or burn us up, if we come on shore.'

12

Syne Kempion has bent an arblast bow,
    And aimed an arrow at her head ;
And swore, if she didna quit the shore,
    Wi' that same shaft to shoot her dead.

13

'Out o' my stythe I winna rise,
    Nor quit my den for awe o' thee,
Till Kempion, the king's own son,
    Come to the crag and thrice kiss me.'

14

He's louted him o'er the Estmere Crags,
    And he has gi'en that beast a kiss :
In she swang, and again she cam',
    And aye her speech was a wicked hiss.

15

'Out o' my stythe I winna rise,
    Nor quit my den for the fear o' thee,
Till Kempion, that courteous knight,
    Come to the crag and thrice kiss me.'

16

He's louted him o'er the Estmere Crag,
    And he has gi'en her kisses twa :
In she swang, and again she cam',
    The fiercest beast that ever you saw.

'stythe,' staying-place.   'louted,' bended.

17

'Out o' my stythe I winna rise,
   Nor quit my den for the dread o' thee,
Till Kempion, that noble prince,
   Come to the crag and thrice kiss me.'

18

He's louted him o'er the lofty crag,
   And he has gi'en her kisses three :
In she swang, a loathly worm ;
   And out she stepped, a fair ladye.

19

Nae cleeding had this lady fair,
   To keep her body frae the cold ;
But Kempion took his mantle off,
   And around his ain true love did fold.

20

'And by my sooth,' says Kempion,
   'My ain true love !—for this is she—
They surely had a heart o' stane,
   Could put thee to this misery.

21

'O was it wer-wolf in the wood,
   Or was it mermaid in the sea,
Or a wicked man, or a vile woman,
   My ain true love, that mis-shaped thee ?'

22

'It wasna wer-wolf in the wood,
   Nor was it mermaid in the sea ;
But it was my wicked stepmother,
   And wae and weary may she be !'

23

'O a heavy weird sall her light on ;
   Her hair sall grow rough, and her teeth grow lang;
   And aye upon four feet maun she gang ;
And aye in Wormeswood sall she wonn ! '

XX

Johnnie of Braidislee.

I

JOHNNIE róse up in a May morning,
   Call'd for water to wash his hands :
'Gar loose to me the twa gray dogs,
   That are bound wi' iron bands.'

2

When Johnnie's mother gat word o' that,
   Her hands for dule she wrang :
'O Johnnie ! for my blessing,
   To the greenwood dinna gang !

3

'Eneugh ye hae o' gude wheat bread,
   And eneugh o' the blude-red wine ;
And therefore for nae venison, Johnnie,
   I pray thee, stir frae hame.'

4

But Johnnie 's buskit his gude bend-bow,
   His arrows, ane by ane,
And he has gane to Durrisdeer
   To hunt the dun deer down.

'wonn,' dwell.   'dule,' grief.   'buskit,' prepared.

5

He lookit east, and he lookit west,
    And a little below the sun ;
And there he spied a dun deer lying
    Aneath a bush o' broom.

6

Johnnie he shot and the dun deer lap,
    And he wounded her on the side,
But atween the water and the brae
    His hounds they laid her pride.

7

And Johnnie has brittled the deer sae weel,
    Ta'en out her liver and lungs ;
And wi' these he has feasted his bluidy hounds,
    As if they had been earl's sons.

8

They ate their fill o' the venison,
    And drank their fill o' the blude ;
And Johnnie and his twa gude hounds
    Fell asleep as they had been dead.

9

By there came a silly auld carle,
    A silly auld carle was he ;
And he is aff to the proud foresters,
    To tell what he did see.

10

' Now why sae fast, thou greyheaded carle ?
    What news, what news, bring ye ?'
' I bring nae news,' said the greyheaded carle,
    ' Save what these·eyes did see.

11

'As I came over by Merriemass,
　And doun amang the scroggs,
The bonniest chiel that ever I saw
　Lay sleeping atween twa dogs.

12

'The shirt he wore upon his back,
　It was o' the Holland fine;
The doublet that he wore over that,
　It was o' the Lincoln twine.

13

'The buttons that were upon his sleeve,
　Were made o' the goud sae gude;
The great gray dogs that he lay atween,
　Their mouths were dyed wi' blude.'

14

Then out and spak' the First Forester,
　The head man ower them a':
'Gin this be Johnnie o' Braidislee,
　Nae nearer will we draw.'

15

But out spak' the Seventh Forester,
　(His sister's son was he):
'If this be Johnnie o' Braidislee,
　We sune sall gar him die!'

16

The first flight of arrows the Foresters shot,
　They wounded him on the knee;
And ane to anither the Foresters said,
　'The next will gar him dee.'

'scroggs,' low bushes.

17

Johnnie has set his back to an aik,
   His foot against a stane ;
He has shot against the Foresters,
   Though they be seven to ane.

18

' Stand stout, stand stout, my noble hounds,
   Stand stout, and dinna flee !
Stand fast, stand fast, my gude gray dogs,
   And we will mak' them dee ! '

19

Johnnie he shot twa Foresters,
   His hounds they pu'd doun three ;
Out shot the Master Forester,
   Strak' Johnnie aboon the bree.

20

' O is there nae bird in a' this forest
   Will do as mickle for me
As dip its wing in the wan water
   And straik it on my ee-bree ?

21

' O is there nae bird in a' the forest
   To sing as I can say,—
To flee fu' fast to my mither's window,
   And bid fetch Johnnie away ? '

22

They made a rod o' the hazel bush,
   Anither o' slae-thorn tree,
And mony were the men, I trow,
   At fetching hame Johnnie.

' bree,' brow.

23

Out and spak' his auld mither,
　And fast her tears did fa' :
' Ye wadna be warned, my son Johnnie,
　Frae the hunting to bide awa' ! '

24

Now Johnnie's gude bend-bow is broke,
　And his gude gray dogs are slain ;
And his body lies dead in Durrisdeer ;
　And his hunting it is done.

XXI

𝕿𝖍𝖊 𝕭𝖎𝖗𝖙𝖍 𝖔𝖋 𝕽𝖔𝖇𝖎𝖓 𝕳𝖔𝖔𝖉.

I

O WILLIE 's large o' limb and lith,
　And come o' high degree ;
And he is gone to Earl Richard
　To serve for meat and fee.

2

Earl Richard had but ae daughter,
　Fair as a lily flower ;
And they made up their love-contract
　Like proper paramour.

3

It fell upon a simmer's nicht,
　Whan the leaves were fair and green,
That Willie met his gay ladie
　Intil the wood alane.

'lith,' joint.

4

' O narrow is my gown, Willie,
   That wont to be sae wide,
And gane is a' my fair colour,
   That wont to be my pride.

5

' But gin my father should get word
   What's past between us twa,
Before that he should eat or drink,
   He'd hang you o'er that wa'.

6

' But ye'll come to my bower, Willie,
   At the setting o' the sun ;
And kep me in your arms twa,
   And latna me fa' down.'

7

O whan the sun was near gane down,
   He's doen him till her bower ;
And there, by the lee licht o' the moon,
   Her window she lookit o'er.

8

Intill a robe o' red scarlet
   She lap, and caught nae harm ;
Willie was large o' lith and limb,
   And keepit her in his arm.

9

And they've gane to the gude greenwood,
   And ere the night was dune,
She's borne to him a bonny young son,
   Amang the leaves sae green.

'lee,' calm.   'kep,' catch.

G

10

Whan night was gane and day was come,
     And the sun began to peep,
Up and raise the Earl Richard
     Out o' his drowsy sleep.

11

He's ca'd upon his merry young men,
     By ane, by twa, and by three,
'O what's come o' my daughter dear,
     That she's na come to me ?

12

'I dreamt a dreary dream last night—
     God grant it come to gude !
I dreamt I saw my daughter dear
     Drown in the saut sea flood.

13

'My daughter, maybe, is dead or sick ;
     Or gin she be stown awa',
I mak' a vow, and I'll keep it true,
     I'll hang ye ane and a' !'

14

They sought her back, they sought her fore,
     They sought her up and down ;
They got her in the gude greenwood
     Nursing her bonny young son.

15

He took the bonny boy in his arms,
     And kist him tenderlie ;
Says, 'Though I would your father hang,
     Your mother's dear to me.'

16

He kist him o'er and o'er again;
  ' My grandson I thee claim;
And Robin Hood in gude greenwood,
  'Tis that shall be your name.'

17

There's mony ane sings o' grass, o' grass,
  And mony ane sings o' corn;
And mony ane sings o' Robin Hood,
  Kens little whar' he was born.

18

It was na in the ha', the ha',
  Nor in the painted bower;
But it was in the gude greenwood,
  Amang the lily flower.

XXII

ffair Annie.

1

THE reivers they stole Fair Annie,
  As she walked by the sea;
But a noble knight was her ransom soon,
  Wi' goud and white monie.

2

She bided in strangers' land wi' him,
  And none knew whence she came;
She lived in the castle wi' her love,
  But never told her name.

' reivers,' takers by violence, robbers, pirates.

G 2

3

' It's narrow, narrow, mak' your bed,
    And learn to lie your lane ;
For I'm gaun o'er the sea, Fair Annie,
    A braw Bride to bring hame.
Wi' her I will get goud and gear,
    Wi' you I ne'er gat nane.

4

' And wha will bake my bridal bread,
    Or brew my bridal ale ?
And wha will welcome my bright Bride,
    That I bring o'er the dale ? '

5

' It's I will bake your bridal bread,
    And brew your bridal ale ;
And I will welcome your bright Bride,
    That you bring o'er the dale.'

6

' But she that welcomes my bright Bride
    Maun gang like maiden fair ;
She maun lace up her robe sae jimp,
    And comely braid her hair.

7

' Bind up, bind up your yellow hair,
    And tie it on your neck ;
And see you look as maiden-like
    As the day that first we met.'

8

' O how can I gang maiden-like,
    When maiden I am nane ?
Have I not borne six sons to thee,
    And am wi' child again ? '

' jimp,' trim.

9

' I'll put cooks into my kitchen,
  And stewards in my hall,
And I'll have bakers for my bread,
  And brewers for my ale;
But you're to welcome my bright Bride,
  That I bring owre the dale.'

10

Three months and a day were gane and past,
  Fair Annie she gat word,
That her love's ship was come at last,
  Wi' his bright young Bride aboard.

11

She's ta'en her young son in her arms,
  Anither in her hand;
And she's gane up to the highest tower,
  Looks over sea and land.

12

'Come doun, come doun, my mother dear,
  Come aff the castle wa'!
I fear if langer ye stand there,
  Ye'll let yoursell doun fa'.'

13

She's ta'en a cake o' the best bread,
  A stoup o' the best wine;
And a' the keys upon her arm,
  And to the yett is gane.

14

' O ye're welcome hame, my ain gude lord,
  To your castles and your towers;
Ye're welcome hame, my ain gude lord,
  To your ha's, but and your bowers.

' yett,' gate.

And welcome to your hame, fair lady !
　For a' that's here is yours.'

15

' Owhatna lady's that, my lord,
　That welcomes you and me ?
Gin I be lang about this place,
　Her friend I mean to be.'

16

Fair Annie served the lang tables
　Wi' the white bread and the wine ;
But aye she drank the wan water
　To keep her colour fine.

17

And she gaed by the first table,
　And smiled upon them a' ;
But ere she reach'd the second table,
　The tears began to fa'.

18

She took a napkin lang and white,
　And hung it on a pin ;
It was to wipe away the tears,
　As she gaed out and in.

19

When bells were rung and mass was sung,
　And a' men bound for bed,
The bridegroom and the bonny bride
　In ae chamber were laid.

20

Fair Annie 's ta'en a harp in her hand,
    To harp thir twa asleep ;
But aye, as she harpit and she sang,
    Fu' sairly did she weep.

21

' O gin my sons were seven rats,
    Rinnin' on the castle wa',
And I mysell a great grey cat,
    I soon wad worry them a' !

22

'O gin my sons were seven hares,
    Rinnin' o'er yon lily lee,
And I mysell a good greyhound,
    Soon worried they a' should be ! '

23

Then out and spak' the bonny young Bride,
    In bride-bed where she lay :
' That's like my sister Annie,' she says ;
    ' Wha is it doth sing and play ?

24

' I'll put on my gown,' said the new-come Bride,
    ' And my shoes upon my feet ;
I will see wha doth sae sadly sing,
    And what is it gars her greet.

25

' What ails you, what ails you, my housekeeper,
    That ye mak' sic a mane ?
Has ony wine-barrel cast its girds,
    Or is a' your white bread gane ? '

26

' It is na because my wine is spilt,
　Or that my white bread's gane ;
But because I've lost my true love's love,
　And he's wed to anither ane.'　　　　.

27

' Noo tell me wha was your father ?' she says,
　' Noo tell me wha was your mother ?
And had ye ony sister ?' she says,
　' And had ye ever a brother ?'

28

' The Earl of Wemyss was my father,
　The Countess of Wemyss my mother,
Young Elinor she was my sister dear,
　And Lord John he was my brother.'

29

' If the Earl of Wemyss was your father,
　I wot sae was he mine ;
And it's O my sister Annie !
　Your love ye sall na tyne.

30

' Tak' your husband, my sister dear ;
　You ne'er were wrang'd for me,
Beyond a kiss o' his merry mouth
　As we came o'er the sea.

31

' Seven ships, loaded weel,
　Came o'er the sea wi' me ;
Ane o' them will tak' me hame,
　And six I'll gie to thee.'

　　　　　　' tyne,' lose.

XXIII

Childe Maurice.

1

CHILDE MAURICE was a handsome young man,
　His locks waved wi' the wind;
He rode about in the merry greenwood,
　And hunted the hart and hind.

2

He called to his little footpage,
　'You don't see what I see;
For yonder I see the very first woman
　That ever loved me.

3

' Here is a glove, a glove,' he says,
　' Edged wi' the silver gris;
Bid that lady come to Silver-wood,
　To speak to Childe Maurice.

4

' Here is a ring, a ring,' he says,
　' It's set wi' an emerald stane;
Tell her to come to Silver-wood,
　And ask the leave o' nane.'

5

' Well do I love you, my master dear,
　But better I love my life.
Would ye have me go to John Steward's castle,
　To tryst away his wife?'

'gris,' a costly fur.

6

'O don't I give you meat?' he says,
　'And don't I pay you fee?
I'll gar your body bleed,' he says,
　'Gin my word you won't obey.'

7

When the boy he came to John Steward's castle,
　He ran right through the gate,
Until he came to the high, high hall
　Where great folk sat at meat.

8

'Here is a glove, my lady,' he says,
　'Edged wi' the silver gris;
You're bidden to come to Silver-wood,
　And speak to Childe Maurice.

9

'Here is a ring, my lady,' he says,
　'It is set wi' an emerald stane;
You're bidden to come to Silver-wood,
　And ask the leave o' nane.'

10

The lady she stampèd wi' her foot,
　And winkèd wi' her e'e;
But for a' that she could say or do,
　Forbidden he wadna be.

11

Out then spak' her bower-woman;
　A wily woman was she:
'If this be come frae Childe Maurice,
　It's dearly welcome to me!'

12

' Thou liest, thou liest,' says the little boy,
  ' Sae loud as I hear thee lie!
I brought it to John Steward's lady;
  I trow thou binna she.'

13

John Steward he quickly rose from the table;
  An angry man was he:
' I little thought there was man in the world
  My lady loved but me!'

14

O he dressed himself in his lady's gown,
  And a wimple over his face;
And he is away to Silver-wood,
  Sae well as he knew that place.

15

Merry it was in Silver-wood,
  Amang the leaves sae fair;
Childe Maurice he sat upon a stane,
  Kaiming his yellow hair.

16

Gil Morice he climbed on yonder tree,
  He whistled and he sang:
' Wae is me!' says Childe Maurice;
  ' My mother tarries lang!'

17

Childe Maurice came quickly out of the tree,
  His mother to lift from her horse:
' O what is here?' says Childe Maurice;
  ' My mother was ne'er so gross!'

' wimple,' veil.

18

' Nae wonder, nae wonder,' John Steward thinks,
　' My lady should lo'e thee weel;
The fairest part o' my bodie
　Is blacker than thy heel!'

19

John Steward he had a sharp, sharp sword,
　That hung low down by his knee;
He slew Childe Maurice, cut off his head,
　And his body put in a tree.

20

And when he came to his castle,
　And into his lady's hall,
He threw the head into her lap,
　Says, ' Lady, there is a ball!'

21

Says, ' Canst thou know Childe Maurice's head,
　When that thou dost it see?
Now lap it soft, and kiss it oft,
　For thou loved'st him better than me.'

22

But when she look'd on Childe Maurice,
　Her answer thus made she:
' I never bare a child but one,
　And you have slain him, trulye.'

23

And she hath ta'en the bloody head,
　And kissed it, cheek and chin:
' I was once as fu' o' Childe Maurice
　As the haw is o' the stane!'

24

' I bare thee in my father's house,
  Wi' mickle sin and shame;
I brought thee up in good greenwood
  Under the dew and rain.'

25

And syne she kissed him on the mouth,
  She kissed him on the chin:
' O better I lo'ed my Childe Maurice
  Than a' my kith and kin!'

26

' O an evil chance!' John Steward he said,
  And a waefu' man was he;
' If you had told me he was your son,
  He had never been slain by me.'

XXIV
Brown Robyn's Confession.

1

IT fell upon a Wodensday
  Brown Robyn's men went to sea;
But they saw neither moon nor sun
  Nor starlight wi' their e'e.

2

' We'll cast kevels us amang,
  See wha the man may be:'
The kevel fell on Brown Robyn,
  The master-man was hee.

'kevels,' lots.

3

'It is nae wonder,' said Brown Robýn,
  'Altho' I dinna thrive;
[For I murther'd my ain auld father,' says he;
  'I would he were yet alive!]

4

'But tie me to a plank o' wood,
  And throw me in the sea;
And if I sink, ye may bid me sink,
  If I [swim] just lat me be.'

5

They've tied him to a plank o' wood
  And thrown him in the sea;
He didna sink, tho' they bade him sink,
  He swim'd, and they bade lat him be.

6

He hadna been into the sea
  An hour but barely three,
Till by and came Our Blessed Ladie,
  Her dear young son her wi'.

7

'Will ye gang to your men again?
  Or will ye gang wi' me?
Will ye gang to the high heavens
  Wi' my dear son and me?'

8

'I winna gang to my men again,
  For they wou'd be fear'd at me;
But I wou'd gang to the high heavens
  Wi' thy dear son and thee.'

9

'It's for nae honour ye did, Brown Robyn,
    It's for nae gude ye did to me;
But it's a' for your fair confession
    You've made upon the sea.'

XXV.

𝕿𝖍𝖊 𝕵𝖔𝖑𝖑𝖞 𝕲𝖔𝖘𝖍𝖆𝖜𝖐.

I

'O WELL is me, my jolly goshawk,
    That you can speak and flee ;
For you can carry a love-letter
    To my true love frae me.'

2

'O how can I carry a letter to her,
    Or how should I her know ?
I bear a tongue ne'er wi' her spak',
    And eyes that ne'er her saw.'

3

'The white o' my love's skin is white
    As down o' dove or maw ;
The red o' my love's cheek is red
    As blood that's spilt on snaw.

4

'When ye come to the castle,
    Light on the tree of ash,
And sit you there and sing our loves
    As she comes frae the mass.

        ' maw,' mew. sea-gull.

5

'Four and twenty fair ladies
   Will to the mass repair;
And weel may ye my lady ken,
   The fairest lady there.'

6

When the goshawk flew to that castle,
   He lighted on the ash;
And there he sat and sang their loves
   As she came frae the mass.

7

'Stay where ye be, my maidens a',
   And sip red wine anon,
Till I go to my west window
   And hear a birdie's moan.'

8

She's gane unto her west window,
   The bolt she fainly drew;
And into that lady's white, white neck
   The bird a letter threw.

9

'Ye're bidden to send your love a send,
   For he has sent you twa;
And tell him where he may see you soon,
   Or he cannot live ava.'

10

'I send him the ring from my finger,
   The garland off my hair,
I send him the heart that's in my breast;
   What would my love have mair?
And at the fourth kirk in fair Scotland,
   Ye'll bid him wait for me there.'

11

She hied her to her father dear
  As fast as gang could she:
' I'm sick at the heart, my father dear;
  An asking grant you me !'
' Ask me na for that Scottish lord,
  For him ye'll never see ! '

12

' An asking, an asking, dear father !' she says,
  ' An asking grant you me ;
That if I die in fair England,
  In Scotland ye'll bury me.

13

' At the first kirk o' fair Scotland,
  You cause the bells be rung ;
At the second kirk o' fair Scotland,
  You cause the mass be sung ;

14

' At the third kirk o' fair Scotland,
  You deal gold for my sake ;
At the fourth kirk o' fair Scotland,
  O there you'll bury me at !

15

' This is all my asking, father,
  I pray you grant it me ! '
' Your asking is but small,' he said ;
  ' Weel granted it shall be.
But why do ye talk o' suchlike things ?
  For ye arena going to dee.'

H

16

The lady's gane to her chamber,
  And a moanfu' woman was she,
As gin she had ta'en a sudden brash,
  And were about to dee.

17

The lady's gane to her chamber
  As fast as she could fare;
And she has drunk a sleepy draught,
  She mix'd it wi' mickle care.

18

She's fallen into a heavy trance,
  And pale and cold was she;
She seemed to be as surely dead
  As ony corpse could be.

19

Out and spak' an auld witch-wife,
  At the fireside sat she:
Gin she has killed hersell for love,
  I wot it weel may be:

20

' But drap the het lead on her cheek,
  And drap it on her chin,
And drap it on her bosom white,
  And she'll maybe speak again.
'Tis much that a young lady will do
  To her true love to win.'

21

They drapped the het lead on her cheek,
  They drapped it on her chin,
They drapped it on her bosom white,
  But she spake none again.

' brash,' attack of illness.

22

Her brothers they went to a room,
    To make to her a bier;
The boards were a' o' the cedar wood,
    The edges o' silver clear.

23

Her sisters they went to a room,
    To make to her a sark;
The cloth was a' o' the satin fine,
    And the stitching silken-wark.

24

'Now well is me, my jolly goshawk,
    That ye can speak and flee !
Come show me any love-tokens
    That you have brought to me.'

25

'She sends you the ring frae her white finger,
    The garland frae her hair;
She sends you the heart within her breast ;
    And what would you have mair ?
And at the fourth kirk o' fair Scotland,
    She bids you wait for her there.'

26

'Come hither, all my merry young men !
    And drink the good red wine ;
For we must on towards fair England
    To free my love frae pine.'

27

The funeral came into fair Scotland,
    And they gart the bells be rung ;
And when it came to the second kirk,
    They gart the mass be sung.

28

And when it came to the third kirk,
    They dealt gold for her sake ;
And when it came to the fourth kirk,
    Her love was waiting thereat.

29

At the fourth kirk in fair Scotland
    Stood spearmen in a row ;
And up and started her ain true love,
    The chieftain over them a'.

30

'Set down, set down the bier,' he says,
    'Till I look upon the dead ;
The last time that I saw her face,
    Its colour was warm and red.'

31

He stripped the sheet from aff her face
    A little below the chin ;
The lady then she open'd her eyes,
    And lookèd full on him.

32

'O give me a shive o' your bread, love,
    O give me a cup o' your wine !
Long have I fasted for your sake,
    And now I fain would dine.

33

'Gae hame, gae hame, my seven brothers,
    Gae hame and blaw the horn !
And ye may say that ye sought my skaith,
    And that I hae gi'en you the scorn.

'shive,' slice.   'skaith,' injury.

34

' I cam' na here to bonny Scotland
    To lie down in the clay ;
But I cam' here to bonny Scotland
    To wear the silks sae gay !

35

' I cam' na here to bonny Scotland
    Amang the dead to rest ;
But I cam' here to bonny Scotland
    To the man that I lo'e best ! '

XXVI

Alison Gross.

I

O ALISON GROSS, that lives in yon tower,
    The ugliest witch in the north countrie,
She trysted me ae day up till her bower,
    And mony fair speeches she made to me.

2

She straiked my head and she kaimed my hair,
    And she set me doun saftly on her knee ;
Says, ' Gin ye will be my lemman sae true,
    Sae mony braw things as I would you gie ! '

3

She shaw'd me a mantle o' red scarlett,
    Wi' gouden flowers and fringes fine ;
Says, ' Gin ye will be my lemman sae true,
    This gudely gift it sall be thine.'

'lemman,' sweetheart.

4

'Awa', awa', ye ugly witch,
 Haud far awa', and lat me be !
I never will be your lemman sae true,
 And I wish I were out o' your company.'

5

She neist brought a sark o' the saftest silk,
 Well wrought wi' pearls about the band ;
Says, ' Gin ye will be my ain true love,
 This gudely gift ye sall command.'

6

She shaw'd me a cup o' the gude red goud,
 Weel set in jewels sae fair to see ;
Says, ' Gin ye will be my lemman sae true,
 This gudely gift I will ye gie.'

7

'Awa', awa', ye ugly witch,
 Haud far awa', and lat me be !
For I wadna ance kiss your ugly mouth
 For a' the gifts that you could gie.'

8

She's turned her richt and round about,
 And thrice she blew on a grass-green horn ;
And she sware by the moon and the stars aboon
 That she'd gar me rue the day I was born.

9

Then out has she ta'en a silver wand,
 And she's turned her three times round and round ;
She's mutter'd sic words that my strength it fail'd,
 And I fell doun senseless on the ground.

'sark,' shirt.

10

She turned me into an ugly worm,
  And gar'd me twine about the tree ;
And aye on ilka Saturday's night
  Alison Gross she cam' to me ;

11

Wi' silver basin and silver kaim,
  To kaim my headie upon her knee ;
But ere that I'd kiss her ugly mouth,
  I'd sooner gae twining around the tree.

12

But as it fell out, on last Hallowe'en,
  When the Seely Court cam' ridin' by,
The Queen lighted doun on a gowan bank,
  Close by the tree where I wont to lie.

13

She took me up in her milkwhite hand,
  She straiked me three times o'er her knee ;
She changed me back to my proper shape,
  And nae mair do I twine about the tree.

XXVII

Johnnie Armstrong.

1

Is there ever a man in all Scotland,
  From the highest estate to the lowest degree,
That can show himself now before our King,
  Scotland's so full of treacherie ?

'gowan,' daisy.
'The Seely Court,' the Happy Court, i.e. of the Fairies.

2

There dwelt a man in fair Westmorland,
  Johnnie Armstrong they did him call;
He had neither lands nor rents coming in,
  Yet eightscore men he kept in his hall.

3

He had horses and harness for them all,
  Goodly steeds that were all milkwhite,
Goodly bands about their necks,
  Wi' hats and feathers all alike.

4

But news was brought unto the King
  That there was sic a one as he,
That livèd like a bold outlaw,
  And robbèd all the north countrie.

5

The King he sent a broad letter
  Sign'd wi' his own hand so lovinglie,
And hath bidden Johnnie Armstrong therein
  To come and speak wi' him speedilie.

6

When Johnnie looked this letter upon,
  His heart was blithe as bird on tree:
' I was never before a King in my life,
  My father, my grandfather, none of us three.

7

' And now, since we're going before the King,
  Lord, we will go most gallantlie!
Ye shall every one have a velvet coat,
  Laid down wi' golden laces three.

8

' Ye shall every one have a scarlet cloak,
    Laid down wi' silver laces white ;
Wi' your golden bands about your necks,
    Black hats, white feathers, all alike.'

9

But when Johnnie went from Giltnock Hall,
    The wind blew hard, and fast did it rain :
' Now fare thee well, thou Giltnock Hall !
    I fear I shall never see thee again.'

10

Now Johnnie he is to Edinborough gone,
    Wi' his eightscore men so gallantlie ;
Every one on a milkwhite steed,
    Wi' sword and buckler at his knee.

11

When Johnnie came before the King,
    He fell down low upon his knee :
' O pardon, my sovereign liege ! ' he said,
    ' O pardon my eightscore men and me ! '

12

' Thou shalt have no pardon, thou traitor strong,
    For those thy eightscore men nor thee ;
To-morrow morning, by ten o' the clock,
    Ye all shall hang on the gallows-tree.'

13

Then Johnnie look'd over his left shoulder,
    And to his merry men thus said he :
' I have askèd grace of a graceless face ;
    No pardon there is for you and me.'

14

At Johnnie's belt was a bright broadsword,
    That swiftly out of his sheath pull'd he ;
And had not the King moved his foot aside,
    He had smitten the head from his fair bodie.

15

Saying, ' Fight on, my merry men all,
    And see that none of you be ta'en ;
Rather than men shall say we were hang'd,
    Let them report how we were slain.'

16

Then, I wot, fair Edinborough rose,
    And so beset poor Johnnie around,
That fourscore and ten of John's best men
    Lay gasping there on bloody ground.

17

Like a bold fellow John laid about,
    And like a madman there fought he ;
Till a false Scot drew in behind,
    And ran him through the fair bodie.

18

Says Johnnie, ' Fight on, my merry men all !
    I'm a little wounded, but I'm not slain ;
I will lay me down to bleed awhile,
    And then rise and fight with you again.'

19

So they fought on courageously,
    Till every man of them was slain ;
But little Musgrave, that was Johnnie's foot-page,
    On his master's horse rode off unta'en.

20

But when he came to Giltnock Hall,
  The lady spièd him presentlie :
' What news, what news, thou little foot-page ?
  What news from thy master, and his companie ?'

21

' My news is bad news, lady,' he said, ·
  'And very bad, as you may see ;
My master, Johnnie Armstrong, is slain,
  And all his gallant companie.'

22

Out then spake his little son,
  As he stood by his nurse's knee :
' If ever I live to be a man,
  I'll revenge my father's death,' said he.

XXVIII

Katharine Janfarie.

1

THERE was a may, and a weel-far'd may,
  Lived high up in yon glen :
Her name was Katharine Janfarie,
  She was courted by mony men.

2

Doun cam' the Laird o' Lamington,
  Doun frae the South Countrie ;
And he is for this bonny lass,
  Her bridegroom for to be.

3

He ask'd no her father and mither,
　Nor the chief o' a' her kin ;
But he whisper'd the bonny lass hersel',
　And did her favour win.

4

Doun cam' an English gentleman,
　Doun frae the English border ;
He is for this bonny lass,
　To keep his house in order.

5

He ask'd her father and mither,
　And a' the lave o' her kin ;
But he never ask'd the lassie hersel'
　Till on her wedding-e'en.

6

But she has wrote a long letter,
　And sealed it with her hand ;
And sent it away to Lamington,
　To let him understand.

7

The first line o' the letter he read,
　He was baith fain and glad ;
But or he has read the letter o'er,
　He's turn'd baith wan and sad.

8

Then he has sent a messenger,
　To run through all his land ;
And four and twenty armèd men
　Were all at his command.

9

But he has left his merry men all,
    Left them on the lee ;
And he's awa' to the wedding-house,
    To see what he could see.

10

They all rose up to honour him,
    For he was of high renown ;
They all rose up to welcome him,
    And bade him to sit down.

11

O mickle was the gude red wine
    In silver cups did flow ;
But aye she drank to Lamington,
    And fain with him would go.

12

' O come ye here to fight, young lord ?
    Or come ye here to play ?
Or come ye here to drink gude wine
    Upon the wedding-day ?'

13

' I come na here to fight,' he said,
    ' I come na here to play ;
I'll but lead a dance wi' the bonny bride,
    And mount and go my way.'   .

14

He's caught her by the milkwhite hand,
    And by the grass-green sleeve ;
He's mounted her hie behind himsel',
    At her kinsfolk spier'd na leave.

' spier'd,' asked.

15

It's up, it's up the Couden bank,
  It's doun the Couden brae ;
And aye they made the trumpet sound,
  ' It's a' fair play ! '

16

Now, a' ye lords and gentlemen
  That be of England born,
Come ye na doun to Scotland thus,
  For fear ye get the scorn !

17

They'll feed ye up wi' flattering words,
  And play ye foul play ;
They'll dress you frogs instead of fish
  Upon your wedding-day !

XXIX

Robin Hood rescuing the Widow's Three Sons.

1

THERE are twelve months in all the year,
  As I hear many say,
But the merriest month in all the year
  Is the merry month of May.

2

Now Robin Hood is to Nottingham gone,
  With a link a down, and a day,
And there he met a silly old woman,
  Was weeping on the way.

3

'What news? what news? thou silly old woman,
  What news hast thou for me?'
Said she, 'There's my three sons in Nottingham town
  To-day condemned to die.'

4

'O, have they parishes burnt?' he said,
  'Or have they ministers slain?
Or have they robbed any virgin?
  Or other men's wives have ta'en?'

5

'They have no parishes burnt, good sir,
  Nor yet have ministers slain,
Nor have they robbed any virgin,
  Nor other men's wives have ta'en.'

6

'O, what have they done?' said Robin Hood,
  'I pray thee tell to me.'
'It's for slaying of the king's fallow deer,
  Bearing their long bows with thee.'

7

'Dost thou not mind, old woman,' he said,
  'How thou madest me sup and dine?
By the truth of my body,' quoth bold Robin Hood,
  'You could not tell it in better time.'

8

Now Robin Hood is to Nottingham gone,
  With a link a down, and a day,
And there he met with a silly old palmer,
  Was walking along the highway.

'palmer,' pilgrim.

9

'What news? what news? thou silly old man,
  What news, I do thee pray?'
Said he, 'Three squires in Nottingham town
  Are condemn'd to die this day.'

10

'Come change thy apparel with me, old man,
  Come change thy apparel for mine;
Here is ten shillings in good silvèr,
  Go drink it in beer or wine.'

11

'O, thine apparel is good,' he said,
  'And mine is ragged and torn;
Wherever you go, wherever you ride,
  Laugh not an old man to scorn.'

12

'Come change thy apparel with me, old churl,
  Come change thy apparel with mine;
Here is a piece of good broad gold,
  Go feast thy brethren with wine.'

13

Then he put on the old man's hat,
  It stood full high on the crown:
'The first bold bargain that I come at,
  It shall make thee come down.'

14

Then he put on the old man's cloak,
  Was patch'd black, blue, and red;
He thought it no shame, all the day long,
  To wear the bags of bread.

15

Then he put on the old man's breeks,
 Was patch'd from leg to side :
' By the truth of my body,' bold Robin can say,
 ' This man loved little pride.'

16

Then he put on the old man's hose,
 Were patch'd from knee to wrist :
' By the truth of my body,' said bold Robin Hood,
 ' I'd laugh if I had any list.'

17

Then he put on the old man's shoes,
 Were patch'd both beneath and aboon ;
Then Robin Hood swore a solemn oath,
 ' It's good habit that makes a man.'

18

Now Robin Hood is to Nottingham gone,
 With a link a down and a down,
And there he met with the proud sheriff,
 Was walking along the town.

19

' Save you, save you, sheriff!' he said ;
 ' Now heaven you save and see !
And what will you give to a silly old man
 To-day will your hangman be?'

20

' Some suits, some suits,' the sheriff he said,
 ' Some suits I'll give to thee ;
Some suits, some suits, and pence thirteen,
 To-day 's a hangman's fee.'

I

21

Then Robin he turns him round about,
  And jumps from stock to stone :
' By the truth of my body,' the sheriff he said,
  ' That's well jumpt, thou nimble old man.'

22

' I was ne'er a hangman in all my life,
  Nor yet intends to trade ;
But curst be he,' said bold Robin,
  ' That first a hangman was made !

23

· I've a bag for meal, and a bag for malt,
  And a bag for barley and corn ;
A bag for bread, and a bag for beef,
  And a bag for my little small horn.

24

' I have a horn in my pockèt,
  I got it from Robin Hood,
And still when I set it to my mouth,
  For thee it blows little good.'

25

' O, winð thy horn, thou proud fellòw !
  Of thee I have no doubt.
I wish that thou give such a blast,
  Till both thy eyes fall out.'

26

The first loud blast that he did blow,
  He blew both loud and shrill ;
A hundred and fifty of Robin Hood's men
  Came riding over the hill.

27

The next loud blast that he did give,
  He blew both loud and amain,
And quickly sixty of Robin Hood's men
  Came shining over the plain.

28

' O, who are those,' the sheriff he said,
  ' Come tripping over the lee ? '
' They're my attendants,' brave Robin did say ;
  ' They'll pay a visit to thee.'

29

· They took the gallows from the slack,
  They set it in the glen,
They hanged the proud sheriff on that,
  Released their own three men.

XXX

ffair Annie of Locħroyan.

1

' O WHA will shoe my bonny foot,
  And wha will glove my hand ?
And wha will lace my middle jimp
  Wi' a new-made London band ?

2

' Or wha will kaim my yellow hair
  Wi' a new-made silver kaim ?
O wha will father my young son
  Till Lord Gregory comes hame ? '

' slack,' lower ground.   ' jimp,' neat.   ' kaim,' comb.
I 2

3

'Thy father will shoe thy bonny foot,
   Thy mother will glove thy hand,
Thy sister will lace thy middle jimp,
   Till Lord Gregory comes to land.

4

'Thy brethren will kaim thy yellow hair
   Wi' a new-made silver kaim ;
And God will be thy bairn's father,
   Till Lord Gregory comes hame.'

5

'O gin I had a bonny boat,
   And men to sail wi' me,
It's I wad gang to my true love,
   Sin' he winna come to me !'

6

Her father's gi'en her a bonny boat,
   And sent her to the strand ;
She's ta'en her young son in her arms,
   And turn'd her back to the land.

7

Her mast was cover'd wi' beaten gold,
   And it shone across the sea ;
The sails were o' the grass-green silk,
   And the ropes o' taffetie.

8

And now she has been on the sea sailing
   For seven lang days or more,
She's landed one night frae her bonny boat
   Near to her true love's door.

9

The night was dark, and the wind blew cauld,
　And her love was fast asleep,
And the bairn that was in her twa arms
　Fu' sair began to greet.

10

' O open the door, Lord Gregory !
　O open, and let me in !
For the wind blaws through my yellow hair,
　And the rain draps o'er my chin.'

11

Lang stood she at Lord Gregory's door,
　And lang she tirled the pin ;
At length up gat his fause mother,
　Says, ' Wha's that wad be in ?'

12

' O it's Annie of Lochroyan,
　Your love, come o'er the sea,
But and your young son in her arms ;
　So open the door to me.' ‧

13

' Awa', awa', ye ill woman !
　You're no come here for gude ;
You're but a witch, or a vile warlock,
　Or a mermaid o' the flood.'

14

' I'm no a witch, nor vile warlock,
　Nor mermaiden,' said she ;
' I'm but your Annie of Lochroyan,—
　O open the door to me ! '

15

' O gin ye be Annie of Lochroyan
   (As I trow ye binna she),
Tell me some o' the love-tokens
   That passed 'tween me and thee.'

16

' O dinna ye mind, Lord Gregory,
   When we sat at the dine,
How we changed the napkins frae our necks?
   It's no sae lang sinsyne.

17

' And yours was good, and good enough,
   But no sae good as mine ;
For yours was o' the cambrick dear
   But mine o' the silk sae fine.

18

' And dinna ye mind, Lord Gregory,
   As we twa sat at wine,
How we changed the rings frae our fingers ?
   And I can show thee thine.

19

' And yours was good, and good enough,
   But aye the best was mine ;
For yours was o' the good red gold,
   But mine o' the diamonds fine.

20

' Sae open the door, love Gregory,
   And open it wi' speed ;
Or your young son that's in my arms,
   For cauld will soon be dead.'

        ' sinsyne,' since then.

21

‘ Awa’, awa’, ye ill woman !
   Gae frae my door for shame ;
For I hae gotten anither love,
   Sae you may hie you hame.’

22

‘ O hae ye gotten anither love,
   For a’ the oaths ye sware ?
Then fare ye weel, fause Gregory,
   For me ye’ll never see mair ! ’

23

Slowly, slowly, gaed she back,
   As the day began to peep ;
She set her foot intill her boat,
   And sair, sair did she weep.

24

‘ Tak’ down, tak’ down the mast o’ gold,
   Set up the mast o’ tree ;
It ill becomes a forsaken lady
   To sail sae gallantlie.’

25

Lord Gregory started out o’ his sleep,
   And to his mother did say,
‘ O I hae dreamt a dream, mother,
   That mak’s my heart right wae.

26

‘ I dreamt that Annie of Lochroyan,
   ˊThe flower o’ a’ her kin,
E’en now was standing at my door,
   But nane wad let her in.

27

'O I hae dreamt a dream, mother—
    The thought o't gars me greet—
That the bonnie Lass of Lochroyan
    Lay cauld dead at my feet.'

28

'O there was a woman stood at the door
    Wi' a bairn intill her arm;
But I couldna let her come within,
    For fear she had done you harm.'

29

O quickly, quickly raise he up,
    And fast ran to the strand;
And there he saw her, fair Annie,
    A-sailing frae the land. .

30

And 'hey, Annie!' and 'how, Annie!'
    'O Annie, winna ye bide?'
But aye the mair that he cried 'Annie,'
    The rougher grew the tide.

31

And 'hey, Annie!' and 'how, Annie!'
    'O Annie, speak to me!'
But aye the louder that he cried 'Annie,'
    The louder rair'd the sea.

32

High blew the blast, the waves ran fast,
    The boat was overthrown, ·
And soon he saw his fair Annie
    Come floating in the foam.

33

He caught her by the yellow hair,
  And drew her up on the sand ;
Fair Annie's corpse lay at his feet,
  And his young son came never to land.

34

And syne he kissed her on the cheek,
  And kissed her on the chin ;
And syne he kissed her on the mouth,
  But there was nae breath within.

35

' O wae betide my mother !
  An ill death may she dee !
She turned my true love frae my door,
  Wha cam' sae far to me !

36

' O wae to my cruel mother !
  An ill death may she dee !
She turned fair Annie frae my door,
  Wha died for love o' me ! '

XXXI

A Lyke-wake Dirge.

THIS ae nighte, this ae nighte,
  Everie nighte and alle,
Fire, and sleete, and candle-lighte,
  And Christe receive thy saule.

When thou from hence away art past,
    Everie nighte and alle,
To Whinny-muir thou comest at last,
    And Christe receive thy saule.

If ever thou gavest hosen and shoon,
    Everie nighte and alle,
Sit thee down and put them on,
    And Christe receive thy saule.

If hosen and shoon thou gavest nane,
    Everie nighte and alle,
The whinnes shall pricke thee to the bare bane,
    And Christe receive thy saule.

From Whinny-muir when thou mayst passe,
    Everie nighte and alle,
'To Brigg o' Dread thou comest at last,
    And Christe receive thy saule.
    *   *   *   *

From Brigg o' Dread when thou mayst passe,
    Everie nighte and alle,
To Purgatory Fire thou comest at last,
    And Christe receive thy saule.

If ever thou gavest meate or drinke,
    Everie nighte and alle,
The fire shall never make thee shrinke
    And Christe receive thy saule,

If meate or drinke thou gavest nane,
　Everie nighte and alle,
The fire will burne thee to the bare bane,
　And Christe receive thy saule.

This ae nighte, this ae nighte,
　Everie nighte and alle,
Fire, and sleete, and candle-lighte,
　And Christe receive thy saule.

XXXII

𝔈tin t𝔥e 𝔉orester.

1

YOUNG Lady Margaret sits in her bower,
　Sewing her silken seam ;
She took a thought o' Elmond-wood,
　And wish'd she there had been.

2

She loot the seam fa' frae her side,
　The needle to her tae,
And she is aff to Elmond-wood
　As fast as she could gae.

3

She hadna pu'd a nut, a nut,
　Nor broken a branch but ane,
Till by there came the bold Etin,
　Says, ' Lady, lat alane.

　　　　' loot,' let.　　　　　　　' tae,' toe.

4

'O why pu' ye the nut?' he says;
   'O why break ye the tree?
For I am forester o' this wood:
   Ye should spier leave at me.'

5

'I'll ask nae leave o' living man,
   Nor yet will I o' thee;
My father's lord o' a' this land,
   This wood belongs to me.'

6

'O rest thee, Lady Margaret!
   O stay in the wood wi' me!
It's there I'll build a secret bower,
   And dearly I'll lo'e thee.'

7

He's kept her in the deep forest
   For six lang years and ane;
Six pretty sons to him she bore,
   And the seventh she's brought hame.

8

And ance it fell upon a day,
   When the hunting was begun,
The forester he went through the wood,
   Took wi' him his eldest son.

9

'O I wad ask ye something, father,
   Gin ye wadna angry be.'
'Say on, say on, my bonny boy;
   Ye'se na be quarrell'd by me.'

'spier,' ask.

10

' My mither's cheeks are afttimes weet,
   I never see them dry ;
I wonder what is it aileth her
   To mourn sae constantly.'

11

' Your mither was an earl's daughter,
   Sprung frae a high degree ;
She might hae wed wi' the first in the land,
   Had she na been stolen by me.

12

' I lo'e her true, I lo'e her weel ;
   She lo'es me weel and true ;
But still she thinks on former times,
   Which aften gars her rue.'

13

' I'll shoot the deer amang the fern,
   The bird upon the tree,
And bring them to my mither hame,
   See if she'll merrier be.'

14

It fell upon anither day,
   This forester thought lang ;
And he is to the hunting gane
   The forest leaves amang.

15

Wi' bow and arrow by his side,
   He took his path alane ;
And left his seven young children
   To stay wi' their mither at hame.

'gars,' makes.

16

' I'd ask ye something, mither,
    An ye wadna angry be.'
' Ask on, ask on, my eldest son ;
    Ask ony thing at me.'

17

' Your cheeks are afttimes weet, mither ;
    You're weeping, as I can see.'
' Nae wonder, nae wonder, my little son,
    Nae wonder though I should dee !

18

' For I was ance an earl's daughter,
    Of noble birth and fame ;
And now I'm the mither o' seven sons
    Wha ne'er gat christendame.'

19

He's ta'en his mither by the hand,
    His six brithers also,
And they are on through Elmond-wood
    As fast as they could go.

20

They wistna weel whar' they were gaen,
    And weary were their feet ;
They wistna weel whar' they were gaen,
    Till they stopp'd at her father's gate.

21

' I hae nae money in my pocket,
    But jewel-rings I hae three ;
I'll gie them to you, my little son,
    And ye'll enter there for me.

22

' Ye'll gie the first to the proud porter,
  And he will lat you in ;
Ye'll gie the next to the butler-boy,
  And he will show you ben.

23

' Ye'll gie the third to the minstrel
  That's harping in the ha',
To play good luck to the bonny boy
  That comes frae the greenwood shaw.'

24

He ga'e the first ring to the proud porter,
  And he open'd and lat him in ;
He ga'e the next to the butler-boy,
  And he has shown him ben ;

25

He ga'e the third to the minstrel
  That was harping in the ha',
And he play'd success to the bonny boy
  That cam' frae the greenwood shaw.

26

Now when he cam' before the Earl,
  He fell down low on his knee ;
The Earl he turned round about,
  And the saut tear blint his e'e.

27

' Win up, win up, my bonny boy,
  Gang frae my companie ;
Ye look sae like my dear daughter,
  My heart will burst in three ! '

                ' ben,' to the inner.

28

'If I look like your dear daughter,
    A wonder it is nane ;
If I look like your dear daughter,
    I am her eldest son.'

29

'O tell me soon, ye little wee boy,
    Where may my Margaret be?'
'She's just now standing at your gates,
    And my six brithers her wi'.'

30

'Now where are a' my porter-boys
    That I pay meat and fee,
To open my gates baith braid and wide,
    And let her come in to me?'

31

When she cam' in before the Earl,
    She fell down low on her knee :
'Win up, win up, my daughter dear ;
    This day ye'll dine wi' me.'

32

'Ae bit I canna eat, father,
    Ae drop I canna drink,
Till I see Etin, my dear husband ;
    Sae long for him I think !'

33

'Now where are a' my rangers bold
    That I pay meat and fee,
To search the forest far and wide,
    And bring Etin to me?'

34

Out then speaks the little wee boy :
   ' Na, na, this mauna be ;
Without ye grant a free pardon,
   I hope ye'll na him see ! '

35

' O here I grant a free pardon
   Well seal'd wi' my own han' ;
And mak' ye search for Etin,
   As soon as ever ye can.'

36

They search'd the country braid and wide,
   The forest far and near,
And they found him into Elmond-wood,
   Tearing his yellow hair.

37

' Win up, win up now, Etin,
   Win up and boun' wi' me ;
For we are come frae the castle,
   And the Earl wad fain you see.'

38

' O lat him tak' my head,' he says,
   ' Or hang me on a tree ;
For since I've lost my dear lady,
   Life's no pleasure to me ! '

39

' Your head will no be touch'd, Etin,
   Nor sall you hang on tree ;
Your lady's in her father's house,
   And all he wants is thee.'

'boun',' go.

40

When he came in before the Earl,
  He fell down low on his knee :
' Win up, win up now, Etin ;
  This day ye'se dine wi' me.'

41

As they were set at their dinner,
  The boy he asked a boon :
' I wish we were in haly kirk,
  To get our christendoun.

42

' For we hae lived in guid greenwood
  These seven years and ane ;
But a' this time since e'er I mind
  Was never a kirk within.'

43

' Your asking's na sae great, my boy,
  But granted it sall be :
This day to haly kirk sall ye gang,
  And your mither sall gang you wi'.'

44

When she cam' to the haly kirk,
  . She at the door did stan' ;
She was sae sunken down wi' shame,
  She couldna come farther ben.

45

Till out and spak' the haly priest,
  Wi' a kindly word spak' he :
' Come ben, come ben, my lily-flower,
  And bring your babes to me.'

XXXIII
The Lawlands o' Holland.

I

' The love that I hae chosen,
  I'll therewith be content ;
The saut sea sall be frozen
  Before that I repent.
Repent it sall I never
  Until the day I dee ;
But the Lawlands o' Holland
  Hae twinn'd my love and me.

2

' My love he built a bonny ship,
  And set her to the main,
Wi' twenty-four brave mariners
  To sail her out and hame.
But the weary wind began to rise,
  The sea began to rout,
And my love and his bonny ship
  Turned withershins about.

3

' There sall nae mantle cross my back,
  No kaim gae in my hair,
Neither sall coal nor candle-light
  Shine in my bower mair ;
Nor sall I choose anither love
  Until the day I dee,
Sin' the Lawlands o' Holland
  Hae twinn'd my love and me.'

' Lawlands,' Lowlands.   ' twinn'd,' separated.
      ' withershins,' the wrong way.
            K 2

4

'Noo haud your tongue, my daughter dear,
    Be still, and bide content ;
There's ither lads in Galloway ;
    Ye needna sair lament.'
'O there is nane in Galloway,
    There's nane at a' for me.
I never lo'ed a lad but ane,
    And he's drown'd in the sea.'

XXXIV

The Twa Sisters o' Binnorie.

I

THERE were twa sisters sat in a bow'r ;
    (Binnorie, O Binnorie !)
A knight cam' there, a noble wooer,
    By the bonny mill-dams o' Binnorie.

2

He courted the eldest wi' glove and ring,
    (Binnorie, O Binnorie !)
But he lo'ed the youngest aboon a' thing,
    By the bonny mill-dams o' Binnorie.

3

The eldest she was vexed sair,
    (Binnorie, O Binnorie !)
And sair envìed her sister fair,
    By the bonny mill-dams o' Binnorie.

4

Upon a morning fair and clear,
  (Binnorie, O Binnorie !)
She cried upon her sister dear,
    By the bonny mill-dams o' Binnorie.

5

' O sister, sister, tak' my hand,'
  (Binnorie, O Binnorie !)
' And let's go down to the river-strand,
    By the bonny mill-dams o' Binnorie.'

6

She's ta'en her by the lily hand,
  (Binnorie, O Binnorie !)
And down they went to the river-strand,
    By the bonny mill-dams o' Binnorie.

7

The youngest stood upon a stane,
  (Binnorie, O Binnorie !)
The eldest cam' and pushed her in,
    By the bonny mill-dams o' Binnorie.

8

' O sister, sister, reach your hand !
  (Binnorie, O Binnorie !)
' And ye sall be heir o' half my land' —
    By the bonny mill-dams o' Binnorie.

9

' O sister, reach me but your glove !'
  (Binnorie, O Binnorie !)
' And sweet William sall be your love '—
    By the bonny mill-dams o' Binnorie.

10

Sometimes she sank, sometimes she swam,
  (Binnorie, O Binnorie !)
Till she cam' to the mouth o' yon mill-dam,
  By the bonny mill-dams o' Binnoric.

11

Out then cam' the miller's son
  (Binnorie, O Binnorie !)
And saw the fair maid soummin' in,
  By the bonny mill-dams o' Binnoric.

12

' O father, father, draw your dam ! '
  (Binnorie, O Binnorie !)
' There's either a mermaid or a swan,'
  By the bonny mill-dams o' Binnoric.

13

The miller quickly drew the dam,
  (Binnorie, O Binnorie !)
And there he found a drown'd womàn,
  By the bonny mill-dams o' Binnoric.

14

Round about her middle sma'
  (Binnorie, O Binnoric !)
There went a gouden girdle bra',
  By the bonny mill-dams o' Binnoric.

15

All amang her yellow hair
  (Binnoric, O Binnorie !)
A string o' pearls was twisted rare,
  By the bonny mill-dams o' Binnoric.

' bra',' brave, rich.

16

On her fingers lily-white,
  (Binnorie, O Binnorie!)
The jewel-rings were shining bright,
  By the bonny mill-dams o' Binnorie.

17

And by there cam' a harper fine,
  (Binnorie, O Binnorie!)
Harpèd to nobles when they dine,
  . By the bonny mill-dams o' Binnorie.

18

And when he looked that lady on,
  (Binnorie, O Binnorie!)
He sigh'd and made a heavy moan,
  By the bonny mill-dams o' Binnorie.

19

He's ta'en three locks o' her yellow hair,
  (Binnorie, O Binnorie!)
And wi' them strung his harp sae rare,
  By the bonny mill-dams o' Binnorie.

20

He went into her father's hall,
  (Binnorie, O Binnorie!)
And played his harp before them all,
  By the bonny mill-dams o' Binnorie.

21

And sune the harp sang loud and clear
  (Binnorie, O Binnorie!)
' Fareweel, my father and mither dear!'
  By the bonny mill-dams o' Binnorie.

22

And neist when the harp began to sing,
  (Binnorie, O Binnorie !)
'Twas 'Farewcel, sweetheart !' said the string,
  By the bonny mill-dams o' Binnorie.

23

And then as plain as plain could be,
  (Binnorie, O Binnorie !)
' There sits my sister wha drownèd me !'
  By the bonny mill-dams o' Binnorie.

XXXV

Glenlogie.

I

THREESCORE o' nobles rade to the king's ha',
But bonnie Glenlogie's the flower o' them a' ;
Wi' his milkwhite steed and his bonnie black e'e,
' Glenlogie, dear mither, Glenlogie for me !'

2

' O haud your tongue, dochter, ye'll get better than he.'
' O say na sae, mither, for that canna be ;
Though Drumlie is richer, and greater than he,
Yet if I maun lo'e him, I'll certainly dee.

3

' Where will I get a bonnie boy, to win hose and shoon,
Will gae to Glenlogie, and come again soon ?'
' O here am I, a bonnie boy, to win hose and shoon,
Will gae to Glenlogie, and come again soon.'

4

When he gaed to Glenlogie,'twas 'Wash and go dine;'
'Twas ' Wash ye, my pretty boy, wash and go dine.'
' O 'twas ne'er my father's fashion, and it ne'er shall
  be mine,
To gar a lady's errand wait till I dine.

5

' But there is, Glenlogie, a letter for thee.'
The first line he read, a low smile ga'e he ;
The next line he read, the tear blindit his e'e ;
But the last line he read, he gart the table flee.

6

' Gar saddle the black horse, gar saddle the brown ;
Gar saddle the swiftest steed e'er rade frae town ; '
But lang ere the horse was brought round to the green,
O bonnie Glenlogie was twa mile his lane.

7

When he cam' to Glenfeldy's door, sma' mirth was
  there ;
Bonnie Jean's mother was tearing her hair ;
' Ye're welcome, Glenlogie, ye're welcome,' said she,
' Ye're welcome, Glenlogie, your Jeanie to see.'

8

Pale and wan was she, when Glenlogie gaed ben,
But red rosy grew she whene'er he sat down ;
She turned awa' her head, but the smile was in her e'e :
' O binna feared, mither, I'll maybe no dee.'

'his lane,' alone.

XXXVI
The Children in the Wood.

1

Now ponder well, you parents dear,
  These words which I shall write ;
A doleful story you shall hear,
  In time brought forth to light.
A gentleman of good account
  In Norfolk dwelt of late,
Who did in honour far surmount
  Most men of his estate.

2

Sore sick he was and like to die,
  No help his life could save ;
His wife by him as sick did lie,
  ·And both possest one grave.
No love between these two was lost,
  Each was to other kind ;
In love they lived, in love they died,
  And left two babes behind :

3

The one a fine and pretty boy
  Not passing three years old,
The other a girl more young than he,
  And framed in beauty's mould.
The father left his little son,
  As plainly did appear,
When he to perfect age should come,
  Three hundred pounds a year ;

4

And to his little daughter Jane
  Five hundred pounds in gold,
To be paid down on marriage-day,
  Which might not be controll'd.
But if the children chance to die
  Ere they to age should come,
Their uncle should possess their wealth ;
  For so the will did run.

5

' Now, brother,' said the dying man,
  ' Look to my children dear ;
Be good unto my boy and girl,
  No friends else have they here :
To God and you I recommend
  My children dear this day ;
But little while be sure we have
  Within this world to stay.

6

' You must be father and mother both,
  And uncle, all in one ;
God knows what will become of them
  When I am dead and gone.'
With that bespake their mother dear :
  ' O brother kind,' quoth she,
' You are the man must bring our babes
  ·To wealth or misery.

7

' And if you keep them carefully,
  Then God will you reward ;
But if you otherwise should deal,
  God will your deeds regard.'

With lips as cold as any stone,
    They kiss'd their children small :
' God bless you both, my children dear !'
    With that the tears did fall.

8

These speeches then their brother spake
    To this sick couple there :
' The keeping of your little ones,
    Sweet sister, do not fear ;
God never prosper me nor mine,
    Nor aught else that I have,
If I do wrong your children dear
    When you are laid in grave !'

9

The parents being dead and gone,
    The children home he takes,
And brings them straight unto his house,
    Where much of them he makes.
He had not kept these pretty babes
    A twelvemonth and a day,
But, for their wealth, he did devise
    To make them both away.

10

He bargain'd with two ruffians strong,
    Which were of furious mood,
That they should take these children young,
    And slay them in a wood.
He told his wife an artful tale :
    He would the children send
To be brought up in London town
    With one that was his friend.

11

Away then went those pretty babes,
    Rejoicing at that tide,
Rejoicing with a merry mind
    They should on cock-horse ride.
They prate and prattle pleasantly,
    As they ride on the way,
To those that should their butchers be
    And work their lives' decay :

12

So that the pretty speech they had
    Made Murder's heart relent ;
And they that undertook the deed
    Full sore did now repent.
Yet one of them, more hard of heart,
    Did vow to do his charge,
Because the wretch that hirèd him
    Had paid him very large.

13

The other won't agree thereto,
    So here they fall to strife ;
With one another they did fight
    About the children's life :
And he that was of mildest mood
    Did slay the other there,
Within an unfrequented wood ;
    The babes did quake for fear !

14

He took the children by the hand,
    Tears standing in their eye,
And bade them straightway follow him,
    And look they did not cry ;

And two long miles he led them on,
    While they for food complain :
' Stay here,' quoth he ; ' I'll bring you bread
    When I come back again.'

15

These pretty babes, with hand in hand,
    Went wandering up and down ;
But never more could see the man
    Approaching from the town.
Their pretty lips with blackberries
    Were all besmear'd and dyed ;
And when they saw the darksome night,
    They sat them down and cried.

16

Thus wander'd these poor innocents,
    Till death did end their grief ;
In one another's arms they died,
    As wanting due relief :
No burial this pretty pair
    From any man receives,
Till Robin Redbreast piously
    Did cover them with leaves.

17

And now the heavy wrath of God
    Upon their uncle fell ;
Yea, fearful fiends did haunt his house,
    His conscience felt an hell :
His barns were fired, his goods consumed,
    His lands were barren made,
His cattle died within the field,
    And nothing with him stay'd.

18

And in a voyage to Portugal
  Two of his sons did die ;
And, to conclude, himself was brought
  To want and misery :
He pawn'd and mortgaged all his land
  Ere seven years came about.
And now at last this wicked act
  Did by this means come out.

19

The fellow that did take in hand
  These children for to kill,
Was for a robbery judged to die,
  Such was God's blessed will :
Who did confess the very truth,
  As here hath been display'd :
The uncle having died in jail,
  Where he for debt was laid.

20

You that executors be made,
  And overseers eke,
Of children that be fatherless,
  And infants mild and meek,
Take you example by this thing,
  And yield to each his right,
Lest God with suchlike misery
  Your wicked minds requite.

'eke,' also.

XXXVII

Young Beichan.

1

In London was Lord Beichan born,
   He longed strange countries for to see ;
But he was ta'en by a savage Moor,
   Who handled him right cruellie.

2

For he viewed the fashions of that land ;
   Their way of worship viewèd he ;
But to Mahound, or Termagant,
   Would Beichan never bend a knee.

3

So on every shoulder they've putten a rope,
   To every rope they've putten a tree ;
And they have made him trail the wine
   And spices on his fair bodie.

4

They've casten him in a dungeon deep,
   Where he could neither hear nor see ;
And fed him on nought but bread and water
   Till he for hunger's like to dee.

5

This Moor he had but ae daughter,
   Her name was called Susie Pye ;
And every day as she took the air,
   Near Beichan's prison she passed by.

6

Now so it fell upon a day,
  About the middle time of Spring,
As she was passing by that way,
  She heard young Beichan sadly sing :

7

' My hounds they all go masterless,
  My hawks they fly from tree to tree,
My younger brother will heir my land ;
  Fair England again I'll never see ! '

8

All the night long no rest she got,
  Young Beichan's sang for thinking on ;
She's stown the keys from her father's head,
  And to the prison strang is gone.

9

And she has open'd the prison-doors :
  I wot she open'd two or three
Ere she could come young Beichan at,
  He was locked up so curiouslie.

10

But when she cam' young Beichan till,
  Sore wondered he that May to see ;
He took her for some fair captive :
  ' Fair lady, I pray, of what countrie ? '

11

' O have ye ony lands,' she said,
  ' Or castles in your own countrie ?
Or what could ye give to a lady fair,
  From prison strong would set ye free ? '

' stown,' stolen.

L

12

'Near London town I have a hall,
　And other castles two or three ;
I'll give them all to the lady fair
　That out of prison will set me free.'

13

'Give me the truth of your right hand,
　The truth of that now give to me,
For seven years ye'll no lady wed,
　Unless that ye be wed with me.'

14

'I give thee the truth of my right hand,
　The truth of that I freely gie,
That for seven years I'll stay unwed,
　For the kindness thou dost show to me.'

15

She's gi'en him to eat the good spice-cake,
　She's gi'en him to drink the blood-red wine ;
She's bidden him sometimes think on her
　That's kindly freed him out o' pine.

16

And she has broken her finger-ring ;
　To Beichan half of it gave she :
'Keep it to mind you in foreign land
　Of the lady's love that set you free.

17

'And set your foot on good ship-board,
　And haste ye back to your ain countrie ;
And before that seven years have an end,
　Come back again, love, and marry me.'

18

But long ere seven years had an end,
  She longed full sore her love to see ;
So she's set her foot on good ship-board,
  And turned her back on her own countrie.

19

She sailed east, she sailed west,
  Till to fair England's shore she came,
Where a bonny shepherd she espied,
  Feeding his sheep upon the plain.

20

' What news, what news, thou bonny shepherd ?
  What news hast thou to tell to me ? '
' Such news I hear, ladie,' he says,
  ' The like was never in this countrie.

21

' There is a wedding in yonder hall,
  And ever the bells ring merrilie ;
It is Lord Beichan's wedding-day
  Wi' a lady fair o' high degree.'

22

She's putten her hand into her pocket,
  Gi'en him the gold and white monie :
' Hey, take ye that, my bonny boy,
  All for the news thou tellest to me.'

23

When she came to young Beichan's gate,
  She tirled softly at the pin ;
So ready was the proud porter
  To open and let this lady in.

24

'Is this young Beichan's house?' she said,
  'Or is that noble lord within?'
'Yea, he sits in hall among them all,
  And this is the day o' his weddin'.'

25

'O has he wed anither love?
  O has he clean forgotten me?'
And sighing said that fair ladie,
  'I wish I were in my own countrie!'

26

And she has ta'en her gay gold ring,
  That with her love she brake so free;
Says, 'Gie him that, ye proud porter,
  And bid the bridegroom speak with me.'

27

The porter came his lord before,
  And kneeled low down on his knee:
'What aileth thee, my proud porter,
  And wherefore is thy courtesie?'

28

'I have been porter at your gates,
  It's now for thirty years and three;
But there stands a lady now thereat,
  And so fair a lady I never did see.'

29

Then out and spak' the bride's mother;
  An angry woman, I wot, was she:
'Ye might have excepted our bonny bride,
  And twa or three of our companie.'

30

' My dame, your daughter's fair enough,
 And aye the fairer mote she be,
But the fairest time that ever she was,
 She'll no compare wi' this ladie.

31

' On every finger she has a ring,
 On her mid-finger she has three ;
And as mickle gold aboon her head
 As would buy an earldom unto me.

32

' And this golden ring that's broken in twa,
 This half o' a golden ring sends she :
" Ye'll carry that to Lord Beichan," she says,
 " And bid him to come and speak wi' me." '

33

Then up and started Lord Beichan ;
 I wot he made the table flee :
' I would gie a' my yearly rent
 'Twere Susie Pye come over the sea ! '

34

And quickly hied he down the stair,
 Of fifteen steps he made but three ;
He's ta'en his bonny love in his arms,
 And kiss'd, and kiss'd her tenderlie.

35

' O have ye ta'en anither bride ?
 And have ye clean forgotten me
And have ye clean forgotten her
 That gave you life and libertie ? '

' mote,' may.

36

She looked over her left shoulder,
　To hide the tears stood in her e'e :
' Now, fare thee well, young Beichan,' she says;
　' I'll try to think no more on thee.'

37

' O never, never, Susie Pye,
　O never, never can it be,
That I shall wed in all the world
　Another woman but only thee !'

38

Then up and spak' the bride's mother ;
　She never was heard to speak so free :
' Ye cannot forsake my ae daughter,
　Though Susie Pye has crossed the sea !'

39

' Take home, take home your daughter, madam,
　For she is never the worse for me ;
I'll send her back in a coach and four,
　And a double sum shall her dowry be.'

40

He's ta'en Susie Pye by the milkwhite hand,
　And led her through his halls so hie ;
He's kiss'd her on the red-rose lips :
　' Ye're dearly welcome, jewel, to me.'

41

He's ta'en her by the milkwhite hand,
　And led her to yon fountain-stane ;
He's changed her name from Susie Pye,
　And call'd her his bonny wife, Lady Jane.

XXXVIII

Clerk Saunders.

1

CLERK SAUNDERS and may Margaret
    Walk'd ower yon garden green ;
And deep and heavy was the love
    That fell thir twa between.

2

' A bed, a bed,' Clerk Saunders said,
    ' A bed for you and me ! '
' Fye na, fye na,' said may Margaret,
    ' Till anes we married be ! '

3

' Then I'll take the sword frae my scabbard
    And slowly lift the pin ;
And you may swear, and save your aith,
    Ye ne'er let Clerk Saunders in.

4

' Take you a napkin in your hand,
    Tie up your bonnie een,
And you may swear, and save your aith,
    Ye saw me na since yestreen.'

5

It was about the midnight hour,
    When they asleep were laid,
When in and came her seven brothers,
    Wi' torches burning red :

Called ' Clerk,' as being a learned young nobleman.

6

When in and came her seven brothers,
　Wi' torches burning bright :
They said, ' We hae but one sister,
　And behold her lying with a knight ! '

7

Then out and spake the first o' them,
　' We will awa' and let them be.'
And out and spake the second o' them,
　' His father has nae mair but he.'

8

And out and spake the third o' them,
　' I wot that they are lovers dear.'
And out and spake the fourth o' them,
　' They hae been in love this mony a year.'

9

Then out and spake the fifth o' them,
　' It were great sin true love to twain.'
And out and spake the sixth o' them,
　' It were shame to slay a sleeping man.'

10

Then up and gat the seventh o' them,
　And never a word spake he ;
But he has striped his bright brown brand
　Out through Clerk Saunders' fair bodye.

11

Clerk Saunders he started, and Margaret she turn'd
　Into his arms as asleep she lay ;
And sad and silent was the night
　That was atween thir twae.

'striped,' thrust.

12

And they lay still and sleepit sound
  Until the day began to daw ;
And kindly she to him did say,
  ' It is time, true love, you were awa'.'

13

But he lay still, and sleepit sound,
  Albeit the sun began to sheen ;
She look'd atween her and the wa',
  And dull and drowsie were his een.

14

Then in and came her father dear ;
  Said, ' Let a' your mourning be ;
I'll carry the dead corpse to the clay,
  And I'll come back and comfort thee.'

15

' Comfort weel your seven sons,
  For comforted I will never be :
I trow 'twas neither knave nor loon
  Was in the bower last night wi' me.'

16

The clinking bell gaed through the town,
  And carried the dead corpse to the clay.
Young Saunders stood at may Margaret's window,
  I wot, an hour before the day.

17

' Are ye sleeping, Margaret ?' he says,
  ' Or are ye waking presentlie ?
Give me my faith and troth again,
  True love, as I gied them to thee.'

18

' Your faith and troth ye sall never get,
　Nor our true love sall never twin,
Until ye come within my bower,
　And kiss me cheek and chin.'

19

' My mouth it is full cold, Margaret ;
　It has the smell, now, of the ground ;
And if I kiss thy comely mouth,
　Thy days will soon be at an end.

20

' O, cocks are crowing a merry midnight ;
　I wot the wild fowls are boding day.
Give me my faith and troth again,
　And let me fare me on my way.'

21

' Thy faith and troth thou sall na get,
　And our true love sall never twin,
Until ye tell what comes o' women,
　Wot ye, who die in strong traivelling ? '

22

' Their beds are made in the heavens high,
　Down at the foot of our good Lord's knee,
Weel set about wi' gillyflowers ;
　I wot, sweet company for to see.

23

' O, cocks are crowing a merry midnight ;
　I wot the wild fowls are boding day ;
The psalms of heaven will soon be sung,
　And I, ere now, will be miss'd away.'

'twin,' break in two.

24

Then she has taken a crissom wand,
  And she has stroken her troth thereon ;
She has given it him out at the shot-window,
  Wi' mony a sad sigh and heavy groan.

25

' I thank ye, Marg'ret ; I thank ye, Marg'ret ;
  Ever I thank ye heartilie ;
But gin I were living, as I am dead,
  I'd keep my faith and troth with thee.'

26

It's hosen and shoon, and gown alone,
  She climb'd the wall, and follow'd him,
Until she came to the green forest,
  And there she lost the sight o' him.

27

' Is there ony room at your head, Saunders ?
  Is there ony room at your feet ?
·Is there ony room at your side, Saunders,
  Where fain, fain, I wad sleep ?'

28

' There's nae room at my head, Marg'ret.
  There's nae room at my feet ;
My bed it is fu' lowly now,
  Amang the hungry worms I sleep.

29

' Cauld mould is my covering now,
  But and my winding-sheet ;
The dew it falls nae sooner down
  Than my resting-place is weet.'

'crissom' (?)

30

Then up and crew the red, red cock,
  And up and crew the gray :
' 'Tis time, 'tis time, my dear Marg'ret,
  That you were going away.

31

' And fair Marg'ret, and rare Marg'ret,
  And Marg'ret, o' veritie,
Gin e'er ye love another man,
  Ne'er love him as ye did me.'

XXXIX

𝕿𝖍𝖊 𝕭𝖆𝖎𝖑𝖎𝖋𝖋'𝖘 𝕯𝖆𝖚𝖌𝖍𝖙𝖊𝖗 𝖔𝖋 𝕴𝖘𝖑𝖎𝖓𝖌𝖙𝖔𝖓.

I

THERE was a youth, and a well-beloved youth,
  And he was a squire's son ;
He loved a bailiff's daughter dear,
  That lived in Islington.

2

Yet she, being coy, would not believe
  That he did love her so,
Nor would she any countenance
  Unto this young man show.

3

But when his friends did understand
  His fond and foolish mind,
They sent him up to fair London,
  An apprentice him to bind.

Perhaps ' Islington,' in Norfolk.   ' bailiff,' a magistrate.

4
And now he's gone 'tis seven long years,
    And never his love could see :
' O many a tear have I shed for her sake,
    When she little thought of me ! '

5
One day the maids of Islington
    Went forth to sport and play ;
And then the bailiff's daughter dear,
    She secretly stole away.

6
She pull'd off her pretty gown of pink,
    And put on ragged attire,
And to fair London she would go,
    ·For her true love to enquire.

7
And as she went along the road,
    The weather being hot and dry,
She sat her down on a grassy bank,
    And her true love came riding by.

8
She started up, with a colour so red,
    Catching hold of his bridle-rein :
' One penny, one penny, kind sir,' she said,
    ' Would ease me of much pain.'

9
' Before I give you one penny, sweetheart,
    Pray tell me where you were born.'
' At Islington, kind sir,' said she,
    ' Where I have had many a scorn.'

10

' I prithee, sweetheart, then tell to me,
    O tell me whether you know
The bailiff's daughter of Islington ?'
    ' She is dead, sir, long ago.'

11

' If she be dead, then take my horse,
    My saddle and bridle also ;
For I'll sail away for some far country,
    Where no man shall me know.'

12

' O stay, good youth ! O look, dear love !
    She standeth by thy side ;
She's here alive, she is not dead,
    She's ready to be thy bride.'

13

' O farewell grief, and welcome joy,
    Ten thousand times, therefore !
For now I have found mine own true love,
    Whom I thought I should never see more.'

XL

A Lytell Geste of Robyn Hode.

THE FIRSTE FYTTE.

[How Robin lent a poor Knight four hundred pounds.]

I

LITHE and lysten, gentylmen,
    That be of frebore blode ;
I shall you tell of a good yemàn,
    His name was Robyn Hode.

2

Robyn was a proude outlawe,
    Whyles he walked on grounde,
So curteyse an outlawe as he was one
    Was never none yfounde.

3

Robyn stode in Barnysdale, ·
    And lened hym to a tree,
And by hym stode Lytell Johan,
    A good yeman was he ;

4

And also dyd good Scathelock,
    And Much the miller's sone ;
There was no ynche of his body,
    But it was worthe a grome.

'Geste' (gero), act, thing done; also, account of the like, history, tale.   'lithe,' attend.   'frebore,' freeborn. 'yeman,' yeoman.   'Barnysdale,' in Yorkshire.   'grome' (?)

5

Then bespake him Lytell Johan
　All unto Robyn Hode,
‘ Mayster, yf ye wolde dyne betyme,
　It wolde do you moch good.’

6

Then bespake good Robyn,
　‘ To dyne I have no lust,
Tyll I have some bolde baròn,
　Or some unketh guest,

7

‘ [Or els some byshop or abbot]
　That may paye for the best ;
Or some knyght or some squyere
　That dwelleth here by west.’

8

A good maner than had Robyn,
　In londe where that he were :
Every daye or he wolde dyne
　Thre messes wolde he here.

9

Robyn loved Our Dere Lady ;
　For doute of dedely synne
Wolde he never do company harme
　That ony woman was ynne.

10

‘ Mayster,’ than sayd Lytell Johan,
　‘ And we our borde shall sprede,
Tell us whither we shall gone,
　And what lyfe we shall lede ;

‘lust,’ desire.　‘unketh,’ uncouth, strange.　‘messes,’ masses.
‘Our Dere Lady,’ the Virgin.　‘doute,’ dread.　‘ynne,’ in.

11

' Where we shall take, where we shall leve,
    Where we shall abide behynde,
Where we shall robbe, where we shall reve,
    Where we shall bete and bynde.'

12

' Thereof no fors,' sayd Robyn,
    ' We shall do well enow ;
But loke ye do no housbonde harme
    That tylleth with his plough ;

13

' No more ye shall no good yemàn,
    That walketh by grene wode shawe,
Ne no knyght, ne no squyèr,
    That wolde be a good felawe.

14

' These bysshoppes, and thyse archebysshoppes,
    Ye shall them bete and bynde ;
The hye sheryfe of Notynghame,
    Hym holde in your mynde.'

15

' This worde shall be holde,' sayd Lytyll Johan,
    ' And this lesson shall we lere ;
It is ferre dayes, god sende us a guest,
    That we were at our dynere.'

16

' Take thy good bowe in thy hande,' said Robyn,
    ' Let Moche wende with the,
And so shall Wyllyam Scathelocke,
    And no man abyde with me :

'reve,' take by force.   'Thereof no fors,' no matter, never
mind. 'housbonde,' husbandman. 'ferre dayes,' far in the day.

M

17

'And walke up to the Sayles,
  And so to Watlynge-strete,
And wayte after some unketh guest,
  Up-chaunce ye mowe them mete.

18

' Be he erle or ony baròn,
  Abbot or ony knyght,
Brynge hym to lodge to me,
  Hys dyner shall be dyght.'

19

They wente unto the Sayles,
  These yemen all thre,
They loked est, they loked west,
  They myght no man see.

20

But as they loked in Barnysdale,
  By a derne strete
Then came there a knyght rydynge,
  Full sone they gan hym mete.

21

All dreri then was his semblaunte,
  And lytell was hys pryde,
Hys one fote in the sterope stode,
  That other waved besyde.

'Watlynge-strete,' one of the Roman roads: 'This seems to
have been, and in many parts is still, the name used by the vulgar for Erming-street. The course of the real Watling-street was
from Dover to Chester.'—*Ritson.*
  'unketh guest,' stranger.   'dyght,' dressed.
  'derne strete,' secret or private way.

22

Hys hode hangynge over hys cyen two,
  He rode in symple aray ;
A soryer man than he was one
  Rode never in somers-day.

23

Lytell Johan was curteyse,
  And set hym on his kne :
' Welcome be ye, gentyll knyght,
  Welcome are you to me ;

24

' Welcome be thou to grene wood,
  Hende knyght and fre ;
My mayster hath abyden you fastynge,
  Syr, all these oures thre.'

25

' Who is your mayster ? ' sayd the knyght.
  Johan sayde, ' Robyn Hode.'
' He is a good yeman,' sayd the knyght,
  ' Of hym I have herde moch good.

26

' I graunte,' he sayd, ' with you to wende,
  My brethren all in-fere ;
My purpose was to have deyned to day
  At Blythe or Dankastere.'

27

Forthe than went this gentyll knyght,
  With a carefull chere,
The teres out of his eyen ran,
  And fell downe by his lere.

' hode,' hood.   ' soryer,' shabbier (?)   ' hende,' gentle.
' in-fere,' together.   ' Dankastere,' Doncaster.   ' lere,' cheek.
M 2

28

They brought hym unto the lodge dore ;
  When Robyn gan hym se,
Full curteysly dyd of his hode,
  And set hym on his kne.

29

' Welcome, syr knyght,' then said Robyn,
  ' Welcome thou art to me ;
I haue abyde you fastynge, syr,
  All these houres thre.'

30

Then answered the gentyll knyght,
  With wordes fayre and fre,
' God the save, good Robyn,
  And all thy fayre meynè !'

31

They washed togyder and wyped bothe,
  And set tyll theyr dynere ;
Brede and wyne they had ynough,
  And nombles of the dere ;

32

Swannes and fesauntes they had full good,
  And foules of the rivere ;
There fayled never so lytell a byrde,
  That ever was bred on brere.

33

' Do gladly, syr knyght,' sayd Robyn.
  ' Gramercy, syr,' sayd he,
' Suche a dyner had I not
  Of all these wekes thre :

' meyne,' company.   ' nombles,' umbles, eatable parts of the
entrails.   ' brere,' briar.   ' gramercy,' grand merci, much thanks.

34

' If I come agayne, Robyn,
Here by this countrè,
As good a dyner I shall thee make,
As thou hast made to me.'

35

' Gramercy, knyght,' sayd Robyn,
' My dyner whan I have,
I was never so gredy [I swear to thee],
My dyner for to crave.

36

' But pay or ye wende,' sayd Robyn,
' Me thynketh it is good ryght ;
It was never the maner, by my troth,
A yeman to pay for a knyght.'

37 ·

' I have nought in my cofers,' sayd the knyght,
' That I may profer for shame.'
' Lytell Johan, go loke,' sayd Robyn,
' Ne let not for no blame.

38

' Tell me trouth,' sayd Robyn,
' So god have parte of thee.'
' I have no more but ten shillings,' sayd the knyght,
' So god have parte of me.

39

' Yf thou have no more,' sayd Robyn,
' I wyll not one peny ;
And yf thou have nede of ony more,
More shall I len thee.

' or ye wende,' ere you go.
' Ne let not for no blame,' stop not for any chiding.

40

'Go now forth, Lytell Johan,
    The trouthe tell thou me :
Yf there be no more but ten shillings,
    Not one peny that I se.'

41

Lytell Johan spred downe his mantèll
    Full fayre upon the grounde,
And there he founde in the knyghtes cofer
    But even halfe a pounde.

42

Lytyll Johan let it lye full styll,
    And went to his mayster full lowe.
'What tydynge, Johan?' sayd Robyn.
    'Syr, the knyght is trewe inough.'

· 43

'Fyll of the best wyne,' sayd Robyn,
    'The knyght shall begynne ;
Moch wonder thynketh me
    Thy clothynge is so thynne.

44

'Tell me one worde,' sayd Robyn,
    'And counsell shall it be ;
I trowe thou were made a knyght of forse,
    Or elles of yemanry ;

45

'Or elles thou hast ben a sory housband,
    And leved in stroke and stryfe ;
An okerer, or elles a lechoure,' sayd Robyn,
    'With wronge hast thou lede thy lyfe.'

'counsell,' in confidence. 'of forse' (?). 'trowe,' hold for truth,
am sure. 'sory housband,' ill-manager. 'okerer,' usurer.

46

' I am none of them,' sayd the knyght,
 ' By [him] that made me :
An hondreth wynter here before,
 Myne aunsetters knyghtes have be.

47

' But ofte it hath befal, Robyn,
 A man hath be dysgrate ;
But [he] that syteth in heven above
 May amend his state.

48

' Within two or thre yere, Robyn,' he sayd,
 ' My neyghbores well it kende,
Foure hondreth pounde of good money
 Full wel than myght I spende.

49

' Now have I no good,' sayd the knyght,
 ' But my chyldren and my wyfe ;
God hath shapen such an ende,
 Tyll it may amende my lyfe.'

50

' In what maner,' sayd Robyn,
 ' Hast thou lore thy richès ?'
' For my grete foly,' he sayd,
 ' And for my kindenesse.

51

' I had a sone, for soth, Robyn,
 That sholde have ben my eyre,
When he was twenty wynter olde,
 In felde wolde juste full feyre ;

' aunsetters,' ancestors.   ' dysgrate,' disgraced.   ' than,'
then.   ' lore,' lost.   ' for soth,' forsooth, truly.   ' eyre,' heir.
' In felde wolde juste full feyre,' in field would tilt full fair.

52

'He slewe a knyght of Lancastshyre,
 And a squyre bold ;
For to save hym in his ryght
 My goodes beth sette and solde ;*

53

'My londes beth set to wedde, Robyn,
 Untyll a certayne daye,
To a ryche abbot here besyde,
 Of Saynt Mary abbay.'

54

'What is the somme?' sayd Robyn,
 'Trouthe than tell thou me.'
'Syr,' he sayd, 'foure hondred pounde,
 The abbot tolde it to me.'

55

'Now, and thou lese thy londe,' sayd Robyn,
 'What shall fall of thee?'
'Hastely I wyll me buske,' sayd the knyght,
 'Over the salte see,

56

'And se where Cryst was quycke and deed,
 On the mounte of Calvarè.
Fare well, frende, and have good daye,
 It may noo better be—'

57

Teeres fell out of his eyen two,
 He wolde haue gone his waye—
'Farewell, frendes, and have good day ;
 I ne have more to say.'

'to wedde,' in pawn. 'buske,' betake.
'quycke and deed,' alive and dead.
* His son had to pay a heavy fine, or else go to prison.

58

'Where be thy frendes?' sayd Robyn.
 'Syr, never one wyll me know;
Whyle I was ryche inow at home,
 Grete bost then wolde they blowe,

59

'And now they renne awaye fro me,
 As bestes on a rawe;
They take no more heed of me
 Then they me never sawe.'

60

For ruthe then wepte Lytell Johan,
 Scathelocke and Much in fere.
'Fyll of the best wyne,' sayd Robyn,
 'For here is a symple chere.

61

'Hast thou ony frendes,' sayd Robyn,
 'Thy borowes that wyll be?'
'[None other] but Our Dere Lady:
 She [never hath] fayled me.'

62

'Now by my hand,' sayd Robyn,
 'To serche all Englond thorowe,
Yet founde I never to my pay,
 A moch better borowe.

63

'Come now forthe, Lytell Johan,
 And goo to my tresourè,
And brynge me foure hondred pounde,
 And loke that it well tolde be.'

'inow,' enough. 'bost,' boast. 'As bestes on a rawe,' like
beasts in a row. 'ruthe,' pity. 'in fere,' together. 'here
is a symple chere,' here is but poor cheer. 'borowes,' sureties,

64

Forthe then wente Lytell Johan,
  And Scathclocke went before,
He tolde out foure houndred pounde,
  By two and twenty score.

65

' Is this well tolde ?' sayd lytell Much.
  Johan sayd, ' What greveth thee ?
It is almes to helpe a gentyll knyght
  That is fall in povertè.'

66

' Mayster,' than sayd Lytell Johan,
  ' His clothynge is full thynne ;
Ye must gyve the knyght a lyveray,
  To lappe his body ther in.

67

' For ye have scarlet and grene, mayster,
  And many a ryche aray ;
There is no marchaunt in mery Englònde
  So ryche, I dare well saye.'

68

' Take hym thre yerdes of every coloure,
  And loke that well mete it be.'
Lytell Johan toke none other mesure
  But his bowe tre,

69

And of every handfull that he met
  He lept over fotes thre.
' What devilkyns draper,' sayd litell Much,
  ' Thynkyst thou to be ?'

'lyveray,' dress.   ' mete,' measured.   ' his bowe tre,' the
        wood of his bow.   ' fotes,' feet.

70

Scathelocke stoode full styll and lough,
   [And swore it was but right] ;
Johan may give hym the better mesure,
   It costeth him but lyght.

71

' Mayster,' sayd Lytell Johan,
   All unto Robyn Hode,
' Ye must gyve that knight an hors,
   To lede home al this good.'

72

' Take hym a gray courser,' sayd Robyn,
   ' And a sadell newe ;
He is our ladyes messengere,
   [I hope] that he be true.'

73

' And a good palfraye,' sayd lytell Moch,
   ' To mayntayne hym in his ryght.
' And a payre of botes,' sayd Scathelocke,
   ' For he is a gentyll knyght.'

74   [Robyn.

'What shalt thou gyve hym, Lytel Johan ?' sayd
   ' Syr, a payre of gylte spurres clene,
To pray for all this company—
   God brynge hym out of tene ! '

75

' Whan shall my daye be,' sayd the knyght,
   ' Syr, and your wyll be ? '
' This daye twelve moneth,' sayd Robyn,
   ' Under this grene wode tre.

'tene,' affliction.

76

'It were grete shame,' sayd Robyn,
  'A knyght alone to ryde,
Without squyer, yeman, or page,
  To walke by hys sydc.

77

'I shall thee lene Lytyll Johan my man,
  For he shall be thy knave ;
In a yeman's steed he may thee stonde,
  Yf thou grete nede have.'

THE SECONDE FYTTE.

*[The Knight releases his pawned lands; and
afterwards, going to repay Robin Hood, suc-
cours a yeoman for Robin's sake.]*

1

NOWE is the knyght went on his way ;
  This game hc thought full good ;
Whan he loked on Barnysdale,
  He blyssed Robyn Hode ;

2

And whan he thought on Barnysdale,
  On Scathelock, Much, and Johan,
He blyssed them for the best company
  That ever he in come.

'lene,' lend.   'knave,' servant.   'in a yeman's steed,' in
                    yeoman's stead,

3

Then spake that gentyll knyght,
    To Lytel Johan gan he saye,
' To morowe I must to Yorke toune,
    To Saynt Mary abbay ;

4

' And to the abbot of that place
    Foure hondred pounde I must pay :
And but I be there upon this nyght
    My londe is lost for ay.'

5

The abbot sayd to his covent,
    There he stode on grounde,
' This day twelfe moneth came there a knyght
    And borowed foure hondred pounde.

6

' [He borowed foure hondred pounde]
    Upon all his londe fre,
But he come this ylke day
    Disheryted shall he be.'

7

' It is full erely,' sayd the pryoure,*
    ' The day is not yet ferre gone ;
I had lever to pay an hondred pounde,
    And lay it downe a none.

'covent,' convent.   'a none,' anon, at once.   'lever,' rather.
    * The prior, in an abbey, was the officer immediately under the
abbot ; in priories and conventual cathedrals he was the superior.
                                                        Ritson.

8

'The knyght is ferre beyonde the see,
    In Englonde is his ryght,
And suffreth honger and colde
    And many a sory nyght :

9

' It were grete pytè,' sayd the pryoure,
    ' So to have his londe ;
And ye be so lyght of your conseyence,
    Ye do to him moch wronge.'

10

' Thou arte ever in my berde,' sayd the abbot,
    ' By our saynt Rycharde.'
With that cam in a fat-heded monke,
    The high cellarer :

11

' He is dede or hanged,' sayd the monke
    ' By him that bought me dere ;
And we shall have to spende in this place
    Foure hondred pounde by yere.'

12

The abbot and the high cellarer,
    Sterte forthe full bolde ;
The High Justyce of Englonde
    [With] the abbot there dyd holde.

13

The High Justyce and many mo
    Had take into their honde
Wholly all the knyghtes det,
    To put that knyght to wronge.

14

They demed the knyght wonder sore,
    The abbot and hys meynè :
' But he come this ylke day
    Disheryted shall he be.'

15

' He wyll not come yet,' sayd the justyce,
    ' I dare well undertake.'
But in sorry tyme for them all,
    The knyght came to the gate.

16

Than bespake that gentyll knyght
    Untyll his meynè,
' Now put on your simple wedes
    That ye brought fro the see.'

17

[They put on their simple wedes,]
    And came to the gates anone,
The porter was redy hymselfe,
    And welcomed them everychone.

18

' Welcome, syr knyght,' sayd the portèr,
    ' My lord to mete is he,
And so is many a gentyll man,
    For the love of thee.'

19

The porter swore a full grete othe,
    [When he his horse did see] :
' Here be the best coresed horse
    That ever yet sawe I me.

'demed,' doomed, judged.   'meyne,' company.   'ylke,'
same.   'wedes,' clothes.   'mete,' meat.   'so,' should be
'wo' (?)   'coresed,' harnessed (*Halliwell*).

20

‘ Lede them into the stable,’ he sayd,
 ‘ That eased myght they be.’
‘ They shall not come therin,’ sayd the knyght,
 [‘ Thy stable liketh not me.’]

21

Lordes were to mete isette
 In that abbotes hall,
The knyght went forth and kneled downe,
 And salved them grete and small.

22

‘ Do gladly, syr abbot,’ sayd the knyght,
 ‘ I am come to holde my day.’
The fyrst word the abbot spake,
 ‘ Hast thou brought my pay?’

23

‘ Not one peny,’ sayd the knyght,
 [‘ Alas ! it might not be.’]
‘ Thou art a shrewed dettour,’ sayd the abbot ;
 ‘ Syr justyce, drynke to me.

24

‘ What doost thou here,’ sayd the abbot,
 ‘ But thou haddest brought thy pay ?’
‘ Fore heaven,’ than sayd the knyght,
 ‘ To pray of a lenger daye.’

25

‘ Thy daye is broke,’ sayd the justyce,
 ‘ Londe getest thou none.’
‘ Now, good syr justice, be my frende,
 And fende me of my fone.’

 ‘salved,’ said ‘ save you ! ’   ‘fone,’ foes.

26

'I am holde with the abbot,' sayd the justyce.
  'Bothe with cloth and fee.'
'Now, good syr sheryf, be my frende!'
  'Nay, fore heaven,' sayd he.

27

'Now, good syr abbot, be my frende,
  For thy curteysè,
And holde my londes in thy honde
  Tyll I have made thee gree ;

28

'And I wyll be thy true servaunte,
  And trewely serve the,
Tyl ye have foure hondred pounde
  Of money good and free.'

29

The abbot sware a full grete othe,
  [A solemn othe sware he :]
'Get the londe where thou may,
  For thou getest none of me.'

30

['Now by our Lady,'] sayd the knyght,
  ['Whose aidance have I besought,]
But I have my londe agayne,
  Full dere it shall be bought.'

31

The abbot lothely on hym gan loke,
  And vylaynesly hym gan call :
'Out,' he sayd, 'thou false knyght,
  Spede thee out of my hall!'

'gree,' satisfaction.   'but,' unless.

N

32

'Thou lyest,' then sayd the gentyll knyght,
  'Abbot in thy hal ;
False knyght was I never,
  By him that made us all.'

33

Up then stode that gentyll knyght,
  To the abbot sayd he,
'To suffre a knyght to knele so longe,
  Thou canst no curteysye ;

34

'In joustes and in tournement
  Full ferre than have I be,
And put myselfe as ferre in prees
  As ony that ever I se.'

35

'What wyll ye gyve more?' said the justyce,
  'And the knyght shall make a releyse ;
And elles dare I safely swere
  Ye holde never your londe in pecs.'

36

'An hondred pounde,' sayd the abbot.
  The justyce sayd, 'Gyve him two.'
'Nay, be heaven,' sayd the knyght,
  'Yet gete ye it not soo :

37

'Though ye wolde gyve a thousande more,
  Yet were ye never the nere ;
Shall there never be myn eyre,
  Abbot, justyse, ne frere.'

'in prees,' in press, i. e. of combat.   'soo,' so.   'eyre,' heir.
'frere,' friar.

38

He sterte hym to a borde anone;
  Tyll a table rounde,
And there he shoke out of a bagge
  Even foure hondred pounde.

39

' Have here thy golde, syr abbot,' sayd the knyght,
  ' Which that thou lentest me ;
Haddest thou ben curteys at my comynge,
  Rewarde sholdest thou have be.'

40

The abbot sat styll, and ete no more,
  For all his ryall chere,
He cast his hede on his sholdèr,
  And fast began to stare.

41

' [Bring] me my golde agayne,' sayd the abbot,
  ' Syr justyce, that I toke thee.'
' Not a peny,' sayd the justyce,
  [' Thou diddest but pay my fee.']

42

' Sýr abbot, and ye men of lawe,
  Now have I holde my daye,
Now shall I have my londe agayne,
  For aught that you can saye.'

43

The knyght stert out of the dore,
  Awaye was all his care,
And on he put his good clothynge,
  The other he lefte there.

'ryall chere,' royal cheer.   'holde my daye,' kept my day.

44

He wente hym forthe full mery syngynge,
   As men have tolde in tale,
His lady met hym at the gate,
   At home in ' Wierysdale.'

45

' Welcome, my lorde,' sayd his lady ;
   ' Syr, lost is all your good ? '
' Be mery, dame,' sayd the knyght,
   ' And praye for Robyn Hode,

46

' That ever his soule be in blysse,
   He holpe me out of my tene ;
Ne had not be his kyndenesse,
   Beggars had we bene.

47

' The abbot and I acordyd bene ;
   He is served of his pay ;
The good yeman lent it me,
   As I came by the way.'

48

This knyght than dwelled fayre at home,
   The soth for to say,
Tyll he had got foure hondreth pounde,
   All redy for to paye.

49

He purveyed hym an hondred bowes,
   The strenges [were] welle dyght,
An hondred shefe of arowes good,
   The hedes burnyshed full bryght,

   'tene,' grief.   'dyght,' prepared, finished.

50

And every arowe an elle longe,
  With pecocke well ydyght,
Inocked all with whyte sylvèr,
  It was a semly syght.

51

He purveyed hym an hondreth men,
  Well harneysed in that stede,
And hymsclfc in that same sete,
  And clothed in whyte and rede.

52

He bare a launsgay in his honde,
  And a man ledde his male,
And reden with a lyght songe,
  Unto Barnysdale.

53

As he went at a brydge ther was a wrastelyng,
  And there taryed was he,
And there was all the best yemèn
  Of all the west countree.

54

A full fayre game there was upset,
  A whyte bull up ipyght ;
A grete courser with sadle and brydil,
  With golde burneyshed full bryght ;

55

A payre of gloves, a rede golde rynge,
  A pype of wyne, in good fay :
What man bereth him best, I wys,
  The pryce shall bere away.

'inocked,' notched.   'stede,' place (?)   'sete' (?)
'launsgay,' lance (?)   'male,' baggage.   'upset,' set up.
'ipyght,' fixed, fastened.   'fay,' faith.   'pryce,' prize.

56

There was a yeman in that place,
  And best worthy was he ;
And for he was ferre, [without] frend bestad,
  Islayne he sholde have be.

57

The knyght had ruth of this yemàn,
  In place where that he stode,
He said that yoman sholde have no harme,
  For love of Robyn Hode.

58

The knyght presed into the place,
  An hondred folowed hym fre,
With bowes bent, and arowes sharpe,
  For to shende that company.

59

They sholdred all, and made hym rome,
  To wete what he wolde say,
He toke the yeman by the honde,
  And gave hym all the playe ;

60

He gave hym fyve marke for his wyne,
  There it laye on the molde,
And bad it sholde be sette a-broche,
  Drynke who so wolde.

61

Thus longe taryed this gentyll knyght,
  Tyll that playe was done,—
So longe abode Robyn fastynge,
  Thre houres after the none.

'ferre,' from afar.   'bestad,' beset (?)   'shende,' hurt, punish.
  'there,' where.   'molde,' ground.

THE THYRDE FYTTE.

[Little John goes into the service of the Sheriff, robs his house, and entices him into the hands of Robin Hood.]

1

LYTH and lysten, gentyll men,
    All that now be here,
Of Lytell Johan, that was the knyghtes man,
    Good myrthe shall ye here.

.

2

It was upon a mery day,
    That yonge men wolde go shete,
Lytell Johan fet his bowe anone,
    And sayd he wolde them mete.

3

Thre tymes Lytell Johan shot about,
    And alway cleft the wande,
The proude sheryf of Notyngham
    By the markes gan stande.

4

The sheryf saw how Johan shot,
    And a great oath sware he :
' This man is the best archere ·
    That yet sawe I me.

'shete,' shoot.   'fet,' fetched

5

'Say me now, wyght yonge man,
　　Thy name now tell to me, ·
In what countre were thou born,
　　And where may thy wonnynge be?'

6

'In Holdernesse I was bore,
　　I wys, all of my dame;
Men call me Reynolde Grenclefe,
　　Whan I am at hame.'

7

'Say me, Reynaud Grenelefe,
　　Wolte thou dwell with me?
And every yere I wyll the gyve
　　Twenty marke to thy fee.'

8

'I have a mayster,' sayd Lytell Johan,
　　'A curteys knyght is he;
May ye gete leve of hym,
　　The better may it bee.'

9

The sheryfe gate Lytell Johan
　　Twelve monethes of the knyght,
Therfore he gave him ryght anone
　　A good hors and a wyght.

10

Now is Lytel Johan the sheryffes man,
　　Heaven gyve us well to spede;
But alway thought Lytell Johan
　　To quyte hym well his mede.

'wyght,' strong, active.　　'I wys,' I know, i. e. truly.
'To quyte' &c., to pay him well his due.

11

' Now so heaven me helpe,' sayd Lytel Johan,
  ' And by my trewe lewtè,
I shall be the worste servaunte to hym
    That ever yet had he.'

12

It befell upon a wednesday,
    The sheryfe on hontynge was gone,
And Lytel Johan lay in his bed,
    And was foryete at home.

13

Therfore he was fastynge
    Tyl it was past the none.
' Good syr stuard, I pray thee,
    Geve me to dyne,' sayd Lytel Johan.

14

' It is too long for Grenelefe,
    Fastynge so long to be ;
Therfore I pray the, stuarde,
    My dyner gyve thou me.'

15

' Shalt thou never ete ne drynke,' sayd the stuarde,
    ' Tyll my lord be come to towne.'
' I make myn avowe,' sayd Lytell Johan,
    ' I had lever to cracke thy crowne.'

16

The butler was ful uncurteys,
    There he stode on flore,
He sterte to the buttery,
    And shet fast the dore.

'lewte,' loyalty, faith.   'foryete,' forgotten.   'none,' noon.

17

Lytell Johan gave the buteler such a rap,
  His backe yede nygh on two ;
Tho he lyved an hundreth wynter,
  The wors he sholde go.

18

He sporned the dore with his fote,
  It went up wel and fyne,
And there he made a large lyveray
  Both of ale and wyne.

19

' Syth ye wyl not dyne,' sayd Lytel Johan,
  ' I shall gyve you to drynke,
And though ye lyve an hondred wynter,
  On Lytell Johan ye shall thynk.'

20

Lytell Johan ete, and Lytell [Johan] dronke,
  The whyle that he wolde.
The sheryfe had in his kechyn a coke,
  A stoute man and a bolde.

21

' I make myn avowe,' sayd the coke,
  ' Thou arte a shrewde hynde,
In an housholde to dwel,
  For to ask thus to dyne.'

22

And there he lent Lytel Johan
  Good strokes thre.
' I make myn avowe,' sayd Lytell Johan,
  ' These strokes lyketh well me.

' yede,' went.   ' lyveray :' the quantity of provisions delivered
at one time by the butler was called a livery (*Ritson*).   ' hynde,'
servant.

23

' Thou arte a bolde man and an hardy,
　And so thynketh me ;
And or I passe fro this place,
　Asayed better shalt thou be.'

24

Lytell Johan drewe a good swerde,
　The coke toke another in honde ;
They thought nothynge for to fle,
　But styfly for to stonde.

25

' I make myn avowe,' sayd Lytell Johan,
　' And be my trewe lewtè,
Thou art one of the best swerdemen
　That ever yet sawe I me.

26

' Coowdest thou shote as well in a bowe,
　To grene wood thou sholdest with me,
And two tymes in the yere thy clothynge
　Ichaunged sholde be ;

27

' And every yere of Robyn Hode
　Twenty marke to thy fee.'
' Put up thy swerde,' sayd the coke,
　' And felowes wyll we be.'

28

Then he fette to Lytell Johan
　The numbles of a doe,
Good brede and full good wyne,
　They ete and dranke therto.

'asayed,' tried.

29

And whan they had dronken well,
  Ther trouthes togyder they plyght,
That they wolde be with Robyn
  That ylke same day at nyght.

30

The dyde them to the tresure-hous,
  As fast as they myght gone,
The lockes that were of good stele
  They brake them everychone ;

31

They toke away the sylver vessell,
  And all that they myght get,
Peces, masars, and spones,
  Wolde they non forgete ;

32

Also they toke the good pence,
  Thre hondred pounde and three ;
And dyd them strayt to Robyn Hode,
  Under the grene wode tre.

33

‘ God the save, my dere mayster,’
  [Little Johan said he,]
And than say'd Robyn to Lytell Johan,
  ‘ Welcome myght thou be ;

34

‘ And also be that fayre yemàn
  Thou bryngest there with thee.
What tydynges fro Notyngham ?
  Lytell Johan, tell thou me.’

‘ trouthes,’ troths.   ‘ plyght,’ pledged.
‘ Peces, masars, and spones,’ drinking cups, bowls, and spoons.

35

'Well thee greteth the proude sheryfe,
  And sende thee here by me
His coke and his sylver vessell,
  And thre hondred pounde and thre.'

36

'I make myn avow,' sayd Robyn,
  'However the thing may be,
It was never by his good wyll,
  This good is come to me!'

37

Lytell Johan hym there bethought
  On a shrewed wyle.
Fyve myle in the forest he ran,
  Hym happed at his wyll ;

38

Than he met the proud sheryf,
  Huntynge with hounde and horne,
Lytell Johan coud his curteysye,
  And kneled hym beforne :

39

God thee save, my dere maystèr,
  Keep thee well,' sayd he.
'Raynolde Grenelefe,' sayd the sheryfe,
  'Where hast thou nowe be ?'

40

'I have be in this forest,
  A fayre syght can I se,
It was one of the fayrest syghtes
  That ever yet sawe I me ;

'Hym happed at his wyll,' i. e. it chanced to him as he wished '?'

41

' Yonder I se a ryght fayre hart,
  His couloure is [full shene],
Seven score of dere upon an herde
  Be all with hym bedene ;

42

' His tynde are so sharp, maystèr,
  Of sexty and well mo,
That I durst not shote for drede
  Lest they wolde me sloo.'

43

' I make myn avowe ! ' sayd the sheryf,
  ' That syght wolde I fayn se.'
' Buske you thyderwarde, my dere maystèr,
  Anone, and wende with me.'

44

The sheryfe rode, and Lytell Johan
  Of fote he was full smarte,
And whan they came afore Robyn :
  ' Lo, here is the mayster harte ! '

45

Styll stode the proude sheryf,
  A sory man was he :
' Wo worth the, Raynolde Grenelefe !
  Thou hast now betrayed me ! '

46

' I make myn avowe,' sayd Lytell Johan,
  ' Mayster, ye be to blame ;
I was mysserved of my dynere,
  When I was with you at hame.'

'shene,' bright.   'bedene,' besides (?)   'tynde,' antlers.
'buske,' betake.

47

Soone he was to supper sette,
   And served with sylver whyte ;
And whan the sheryf se his vessell,
   For sorowe he myght not ete.

48

' Make good chere,' sayd Robyn Hode,
   ' Sheryfe, for charytè,
And for the love of Lytell Johan,
   Thy lyfe is graunted to the.'

49

When they had supped well,
   The day was all agone,
Robyn commaunded Lytell Johan
   To drawe off his hosen and his shone,

50

His kyrtell and his cote a pye,
   That was furred well fyne,
And take him a grene mantèll,
   To lappe his body therin.

51

Robyn commaunded his wyght yong men,
   Under the grene wood tre,
They shall lay in that same sorte
   That the sheryf myght them se.

52

All nyght laye that proud sheryf,
   In his breche and in his sherte,
No wonder it was, in grene wode,
   Tho his sydes do smerte.

' kyrtell and cote a pye,' jacket and cloak.

53

'Make glad chere,' sayd Robyn Hode,
  'Sheryfe, for charytè,
For this is our order I wys,
  Under the grene wood tre.'

54

'This is harder order,' sayd the sheryfe,
  'Than ony anker or frere;
For al the golde in mery Englonde
  I wolde not longe dwell here.'

55

'All these twelve monethes,' sayd Robyn,
  'Thou shalte dwell with me;
I shall thee teche, proud sheryfe,
  An outlawe for to be.'

56

'Or I here another nyght lye,' sayd the sheryfe,
  'Robyn, nowe I praye thee,
Smyte of my hede rather to-morne,
  And I forgyve it thee.

57

'Lete me go,' then sayd the sheryf,
  'For saynt Charytè,
And I wyll be thy best frende
  That ever yet had thee.'

58

'Thou shalte swere me an othe,' sayd Robyn,
  'On my bryght bronde,
Thou shalt never awayte me scathe,
  By water ne by londe;

'anker,' anchorite.   'scathe,' injury.

59

'And if thou fynde ony of my men,
　By nyght or by day,
Upon thyne othe thou shalt swere,
　To helpe them that thou may.'

60

Now have the sheryf iswore his othe,
　And home he began to gone,
He was as full of grene wode
　As ever was [haw] of stone.' *

THE FOURTH FYTTE.

*[Robin reimburses himself of his loan by means of
a Monk of St. Mary's Abbey, and the Knight
is free.]*

1

THE sheryf dwelled in Notynghame,
　He was fayne that he was gone,
And Robyn and his mery men
　Went to wode anone.

2

'Go we to dyner?' sayd Lytell Johan.
　Robyn Hode sayd, 'Nay;
For I drede our lady be wroth with me,
　For she sent me not my pay.'

---

* i.e. he had enough of it.　This seems to have been a popular
saying (see *Childe Maurice*); but 'hip,' the word used in each
place, means, now at least, the dog-rose berry, which has woolly
seeds, not a stone; while 'haw' makes the image perfect.

3

'Have no dout, mayster,' sayd Lytell Johan,
   ' Yet is not the sonne at rest ;
For I dare saye, and saufly swere,
   The knyght is trewe and trust.'

4

'Take thy bowe in thy hande,' sayd Robyn,
   ' Let Moch wende with thee,
And so shall Wyllyam Scathelock,
   And no man abyde with me,

5

' And walke up into the Sayles,
   And to Watlynge-strete,
And wayte after some unketh gest,
   Up-chaunce ye may them mete.

6

' Whether he be messengere,
   Or a man that myrthes can,
Or yf he be a pore man,
   Of my good he shall have some.'

7

Forth then stert Lytel Johan,
   Half in tray and tene,
And gyrde hym with a full good swerde,
   Under a mantel of grene.

8

They went up to the Sayles,
   These yemen all thre ;
They loked est, they loked west,
   They myght no man se.

'tray and tene,' anger and vexation.

9

But as they loked in Barnysdale,
    By the hye waye,
Than were they ware of two blacke monkes,
    Eche on a good palferay.

10

Then bespake Lytell Johan,
    To Much he gan say,
' I dare lay my lyfe to wedde,
    That these monkes have brought our pay.

11

' Make glad chere,' sayd Lytell Johan,
    ' And frese our bowes of ewe,
And loke your hertes be seker and sad,
    Your strynges trusty and trewe.

12

' The monke hath fifty two men,
    And seven somers full stronge ;
There rydeth no bysshop in this londe
    So ryally, I understond.

13

' Brethern,' sayd Lytell Johan,
    ' Here are no more but we thre ;
But we brynge them to dyner,
    Our mayster dare we not se.

14

' Bende your bowes,' sayd Lytell Johan,
    ' Make all yon prese to stonde ;
The formost monke, his lyfe and his deth
    Is closed in my honde.

'wedde,' pawn. 'frese,' try (?) 'ewe,' yew. 'seker and sad,' sure and settled. 'somers,' sumpter-beasts, carrying baggage. 'prese.' press, crowd.

15

'Abyde, chorle monke,' sayd Lytell Johan,
  ' No ferther that thou gone ;
Yf thou doost, by dere worthy god,
  Thy deth is in my honde.

16

'And evyll thryfte on thy hede,' sayd Lytell Johan,
  ' Ryght under thy hattes bonde,
For thou hast made our mayster wroth,
  He is fastynge so longe.'

17

'Who is your mayster?' sayd the monke.
  Lytell Johan sayd, ' Robyn Hode.'
' He is a stronge thefe,' sayd the monke,
  ' Of hym herd I never good.'

18

' Thou lyest,' than sayd Lytell Johan,
  ' And that shall rewe thee ;
He is a yeman of the forèst,
  To dyne he hath bode thee.

19

Much was redy with a bolte,
  Reddily and a-none,
He set the monke to fore the brest,
  To the grounde that he can gone.

20

Of fyfty two wyght yonge men,
  There abode not one,
Saf a lytell page, and a grome
  To lede the somers with Johan.

' rewe,' repent.　' bode,' bidden.　' grome,' groom.

21

They brought the monke to the lodge dore,
  Whether he were loth or lefe,
For to speke with Robyn Hode,
  Maugre in theyr tethe.

22

Robyn dyd adowne his hode,
  The monke whan that he see ;
The monke was not so curtcyse,
  His hode then let he be.

23

' He is a chorle, mayster, I swere,'
  Than sayd Lytell Johan.
' Thereof no force,' sayd Robyn,
  ' For curteysy can he none.

24

' How many men,' sayd Robyn,
  ' Had this monke, Johan ? '
' Fyfty and two whan that we met,
  But many of them be gone.'

25

' Let blowe a horne,' sayd Robyn,
  ' That felaushyp may us knowe.'
Seven score of wyght yemen
  Came pryckynge on a rowe,

26

And everych of them a good mantèll,
  Of scarlet and of raye,
All they came to good Robyn,
  To wyte what he wolde say.

'lefe,' willing.   ' thereof no force,' no matter.
'pryckynge,' spurring—seems here used for hastening
  ' raye,' striped cloth (*Halliwell*).   ' wyte,' know.

27

They made the monke to wasshe and wype,
  And syt at his denere.
Robyn Hode and Lytel Johan
  They served him bothe in fere.

28

' Do gladly, monke,' sayd Robyn.
  ' Gramercy, syr,' sayd he.
' Where is your abbay, whan ye are at home,
  And who is your avowè ?'

29

' Saynt Mary abbay,' sayd the monke,
  ' Though I be symple here.'
' In what offyce ?' sayd Robyn.
  ' Syr, the hye selerer.'

30

' Ye be the more welcome, sayd Robyn,
  ' So ever mote I the.
Fyll of the best wyne,' sayd Robyn,
  ' This monke shall drynke to me.

31

' But I have grete mervayle,' sayd Robyn,
  ' Of all this longe day,
I drede our lady be wroth with me,
  She sent me not my pay.'

32

' Have no doute, mayster,' sayd Lytell Johan,
  ' Ye have no nede I saye,
This monke it hath brought, I dare well swere,
  For he is of her abbay.'

' in fere,' together.   ' gramercy,' much thanks.   ' avowe,'
patron.   ' hye selerer,' high-cellarer.   ' mote I the,' may I
thrive.

33

' She was a borowe,' sayd Robyn
   ' Betwene a knyght and me,
Of a lytell money that I hym lent,
   Under the grene wode tree ;

34

' And yf thou hast that sylver ibroughte,
   I praye the let me se,
And I shall helpe thee eftsones,
   Yf thou have nede of me.'

35

The monke swore a full grete othe,
   With a sory chere :
' Of the borowehode thou spekest to me,
   Herde I never ere.'

36

' I make myn avowe,' sayd Robyn,
   ' Monke, thou arte to blame,
For god is holde a ryghtwys man,
   And so is his dame.

37

' Thou toldest with thyn owne tonge,
   Thou may not say nay,
How thou arte her servaunt,
   And servest her every day :

38

' And thou art made her messengere,
   My money for to pay,
Therfore I con thee more thanke,
   Thou arte come at thy day.

' borowe,' surety.   ' eftsones,' hereafter (*Ritson*) ; immediately
(*Halliwell*).   ' sory chere,' sad countenance.   ' ere,' before.

39

'What is in your cofers?' sayd Robyn,
  ' Trewe then tell thou me.'
' Syr,' he sayd, 'twenty marke,
  Al so mote I the.'

40

' Yf there be no more,' sayd Robyn,
  ' I wyll not one peny ;
Yf thou hast myster of ony more,
  · Syr, more I shall lende to the ;

41

' And yf I fynde more,' sayd Robyn,
  ' I wys thou shalte it forgone ;
For of thy spendynge sylver, monk,
  Therof wyll I ryght none.

42

' Go nowe forthe, Lytell Johan,
  And the trouth tell thou me ;
If there be no more but twenty marke,
  No peny that I se.'

43

Lytell Johan spred his mantell downe,
  As he had done before,
And he tolde out of the monkes male,
  Eyght hundreth pounde and more.

44

Lytell Johan let it lye full styll,
  And went to his mayster in hast :
' Syr,' he sayd, 'the monke is trewe ynowe,
  Our lady hath doubled your cost.'

'myster,' need.   'male,' budget.   ·

45

' I make myn avowe,' sayd Robyn,
  ' (Monke, what tolde I thee?)
Our lady is the trewest womàn
  That ever yet founde I me.

46

' By all that's good,' sayd Robyn,
  ' To seche all Englond thorowe,
Yet founde I never to my pay
  A moche better borowe.

47

'Fyll of the best wyne, do hym drynke,' sayd Robyn;
  ' And grete well thy lady hende,
And yf she have nede of Robyn Hode,
  She shall hym fynde a frende ;

48

' And yf she nedeth ony more sylvèr,
  Come thou agayne to me,
And, by this token she hath me sent,
  She shall have such thre.'

49

The monke was going to London ward,
  There to holde grete mote,
The knyght that rode so hye on hors,
  To brynge hym under fote.

50

' Whither be ye away ?' sayd Robyn.
  ' Syr, to manors in this londe,
To reken with our reves,
  That have done moch wronge.'

    ' hende,' gentle. * ' mote,' meeting.   ' reves,' bailiffs.

51

The monke toke the hors with spurre,
  No lenger wolde he abyde.
' Aske to drynke,' than sayd Robyn,
  ' Or that ye forther ryde.'

52

' Nay, fore heaven,' than sayd the monke,
  ' Me reweth I cam so nere ;
For better chepe I myght have dyned
  In Blythe or in Dankestere.'

53

' Grete well your abbot,' sayd Robyn,
  ' And your pryour, I you pray,
And byd hym sende me such a monke
  To dyner every day.'

54

Now lete we that monke be styll,
  And speke we of that knyght,
Yet he came to holde his day
  Whyle that it was lyght.

55

He dyde him streyt to Barnysdale,
  Under the grene wode tre,
And he founde there Robyn Hode,
  And all his mery meynè.

56

The knyght lyght downe of his good palfrày,
  Robyn whan he gan see,
So curteysly he dyde adoune his hode,
  And set hym on his knee.

'Dankestere,' Doncaster.   'meynè,' company.

57

'God the save, good Robyn Hode,
    And al this company.'
'Welcome be thou, gentyll knyght,
    And ryght welcome to me.'

58

Than bespake hym Robyn Hode
    To that knyght so fre :
'What nede dryveth the to grene wode ?
    I pray the, syr knyght, tell me.

59

'And welcome be thou, gentyl knyght,
    Why hast thou be so longe ?'
'For the abbot and the hye justyce
    Wolde have had my londe.'

60

'Hast thou thy londe agayne ?' sayd Robyn,
    'Treuth than tell thou me.'
'Ye, truly,' sayd the knyght,
    'And that thanke I god and the.

61

'But take not a grefe, I have be so longe ;
    I came by a wrastelynge,
And there I dyd holpe a pore yemàn,
    With wronge was put behynde.'

62

'Nay, that is well,' sayd Robyn,
    'Syr knyght, that thanke I the ;
What man that helpeth a good yemàn,
    His frende than wyll I be.'

'for,' because.

63

'Have here foure hondred pounde,' sayd the knyght,
  'The whiche ye lent to me;
And here is also an hondred more
  For your curteysy.'

64

'Nay, syr knyght,' than sayd Robyn,
  'Thou broke it well for ay;
For our lady, by her selerer,
  Hath sent to me my pay;

65

'And yf I toke it twyse,
  A shame it were to me:
But trewely, gentyll knyght,
  Welcom arte thou to me.'

66

Whan Robyn had tolde his tale,
  He leugh and had good chere.
'By my trouthe,' then sayd the knyght,
  'Your money is redy here.'

67

'Broke it well,' sayd Robyn,
  'Thou gentyll knyght so fre;
And welcome be thou, gentill knyght,
  Under my trystell tree.

68

'But what shall these bowes do?' sayd Robyn,
  'And these arowes ifedered fre?'
'By my troth,' than sayd the knyght,
  'A pore present to thee.'

'broke,' enjoy.   'trystell,' where he kept tryst or
appointment of meeting with his men (?)

69

'Come now forth, Lytell Johan,
 And go to my treasurè,
And brynge me there foure hondred pounde,
 The monke over-tolde it to me.

70

'Have here foure hondred pounde,
 Thou gentyll knyght and trewe,
And bye hors and harnes good,
 And gylte thy spurres all newe :

71

'And yf thou fayle ony spendynge,
 Come to Robyn Hode,
And by my trouth thou shalt none fayle
 The whyles I have any good.

72

'And broke well thy four hundred pound,
 Whiche I lent to the,
And make thy selfe no more so bare,
 By the counsell of me.'

THE FYFTH FYTTE.

[*How Robin Hood went to a public shooting at Nottingham, was attacked by the Sheriff, and received into Sir Richard's castle.*]

1

Now hath the knyght his leve itake,
 And wente hym on his way ;
Robyn Hode and his mery men
 Dwelled styll full many a day.

'bye,' buy.

2

Lyth and lysten, gentil men,
　And herken what I shall say,
How the proud sheryfe of Notyngham
　Dyde crye a full fayre play :

3

That all the best archers of the north
　Sholde come upon a day,
And he that shoteth alderbest
　The game shall bere away.

4

' He that shoteth alderbest,
　Furthest fayre and lowe,
At a payre of fynly buttes,
　Under the grene wode shawe.

5

' A ryght good arowe he shall have,
　The shaft of sylver whyte,
The heade and the feders of ryche rede golde,
　In Englonde is none lyke.'

6

This then herde good Robyn,
　Under his trystell tre :
' Make you redy, ye wyght yonge men,
　That shotynge wyll I se.

7

' Buske you, my mery yonge men,
　Ye shall go with me ;
And I wyll wete the shryves fayth,
　Trewe and yf he be.'

'lyth,' attend.　　'alderbest,' best of all.　　'fynly,' goodly.
'buske,' make ready.　　'wyght,' strong, active.　　'wete
the shryves fayth,' know the sheriff's faith.

8

Whan they had theyr bowes ibent,
  Theyr takles fedred fre,
Seven score of wyght yonge men
  Stode by Robyns kne.

9

Whan they cam to Notyngham,
  The buttes were fayre and longe,
Many was the bold archere
  That shoted with bowes stronge.

10

' There shall but syx shote with me,
  The others shal kepe my hede,
And stande with good bowes bent,
  That I be not desceyvèd.'

11

The fourth outlawe his bowe gan bende,
  And that was Robyn Hode,
And that behelde the proude sheryfe,
  All by the butt he stode.

12

Thryes Robyn shot about,
  And alway he slist the wand,
And so dyde good Gylberte,
  With the whyte hande.

13

Lytell Johan and good Scatheloke
  Were archers good and fre;
Lytell Much and good Reynolde,
  The worste wolde they not be.

'takles,' tackles, i. e. arrows.   'slist,' sliced.

14

Whan they had shot aboute,
　These archours fayre and good,
Evermore was the best,
　Forsoth, Robyn Hode.

15

Hym was delyvered the goode aròw,
　For best worthy was he ;
He toke the yeſt so curteysly ;
　To grene wode wolde he.

16

They cryed out on Robyn Hode,
　And great hornes gan they blowe.
' Wo worth thee, treason !' sayd Robyn,
　' Full evyl thou art to knowe.

17

' And wo be thou, thou proud sheryf,
　Thus gladdynge thy gest,
Other wyse thou behote me
　In yonder wvlde forèst ;

18

' But had I thee in grene wode,
　Under my trystell tre,
Thou sholdest leve me a better wedde
　Than thy trewe lewtè.'

19

Full many a bowe there was bent,
　And arowes let they glyde,
Many a kyrtell there was rent,
　And hurt many a syde.

' yeſt,' gift.　　' gest,' guest.　　' behote,' promised.　　' wedde,'
pledge.　　' lewte,' loyalty, good faith.　　' kyrtell,' short coat.

20

The outlawes' shot was so stronge,
That no man myght them dryve,
And the proud sheryfes men
They fled away full blyve.

21

Robyn sawe the busshement to-broke;
In grene wode he wolde have be;
Many an arowe there was shot
Amonge that company.

22

Lytell Johan was hurte full sore,
With an arowe in his kne,
That he myght neyther go nor ryde;
It was full grete pytè.

23

' Mayster,' then sayd Lytell Johan,
' If ever thou lovest me,
And for that ylke lordes love,
That dyed upon a tre,

24

' And for the medes of my servyce,
That I have served the,
Lete never the proude sheryf
Alyve now fynde me;

25

' But take out thy browne swerde,
And smyte all of my hede,
Or gyve me woundes deep and wyde,
So to leve me dede.'

'blyve,' briskly.   'busshement to-broke,' ambush broken up.
'ylke,' same.   'medes,' reward.

P

26

'I wolde not that,' sayd Robyn,
   'Johan, that thou were slawe,
For all the golde in mery Englond,
   Though it lay now on a rawe.'

27

'God forbede,' sayd lytell Much,
   'That dyed on a tre,
That thou sholdest, Lytell Johan,
   Parte our company.'

28

Up he toke hym on his backe,
   And bare hym well a myle,
Many a tyme he layd hym downe,
   And shot another whyle.

29

Then was there a fayre castèll,
   A lytell within the wode,
Double-dyched it was about,
   And walled, by the rode ;

30

And there dwelled that gentyll knyght,
   Syr Rychard at the Lee,
That Robyn had lent his good,
   Under the grene wode tre.

31

In he toke good Robyn,
   And all his company :
'Welcome be thou, Robyn Hode,
   Welcome arte thou [to] me ;

'rawe,' row.   'rode,' rood.

32

' And moche [I] thanke the of thy comfort,
  And of thy curteysye,
And of thy grete kyndenesse,
  Under the grene wode tre.

33

' I love no man in all this worlde
  So moch as I do the ;
For all the proud sheryf of Notyngham,
  Ryght here shalt thou be.

34

' Shet the gates, and drawe the bridge,
  And let no man com in ;
And arme you well, and make you redy,
  And to the walle ye wynne.

35

' For one thyng, Robyn, I thee behote :
  I swere by saynt Quyntyn,
These twelve dayes thou wonest with me,
  To suppe, ete, and dyne.'

36

Bordes were layed, and clothes spred,
  Reddely and anone ;
Robyn Hode and his mery men
  To mete gan they gone.

'behote,' promise.

THE SYXTE FYTTE.

*[The Sheriff casts the Knight into prison, and
Robin rescues him.]*

1

Lythe and lysten, gentylmen,
And herken unto your songe ;
How the proude sheryfe of Notyngham,
And men of armes stronge,

2

Full faste came to the hye sheryfe,
The countre up to rout,
And they beset the knyghts castèll,
The walles all about.

3

The proude sheryf loude gan crye,
And sayd, 'Thou traytour knyght,
Thou kepeste here the kynges enemye,
Agayne the lawes and ryght.'

4

'Syr, I wyll avowe that I have done
The dedes that here be dyght,
Upon all the londes that I have,
As I am a trewe knyght.

5

'Wende forthe, syrs, on your waye,
And doth no more to me,
Tyll ye wytte our kynges wyll
What he woll say to the.'

'dyght,' done.

6

The sheref thus had his answere,
   With out ony leasynge,
Forthe he yode to London toune,
   All for to tel our kynge.

7

There he tolde him of that knyght,
   And eke of Robyn Hode,
And also of the bolde archeres,
   That [wonned in the grene wode].

8

' He wolde avowe that he had done,
   To mayntayne the outlawes stronge,
He wolde be lorde, and set you at nought,
   In all the north londe.'

9

' I woll be at Notyngham,' sayd the kynge,
   ' Within this fourtynyght,
And take I wyll Robyn Hode,
   And so I wyll that knyght.

10

' Go home, thou proud sheryf,
   And do as I bydde the,
And ordayne good archeres inowe,
   Of all the wyde countree.'

11

The sheryf had his leve itake,
   And went hym on his way ;
And Robyn Hode to grene wode [went]
   Upon a certayn day ;

' leasynge,' lying.

12

And Lytell Johan was hole of the arowe,
   That shote was in his kne,
And dyd hym strayte to Robyn Hode,
   Under the grene wode tre.

13

Robyn Hode walked in the foreste,
   Under the leves grene,
The proud sheryfe of Notyngham,
   Therefore he had grete tene.

14

The sheryf there fayled of Robyn Hode,
   He myght not have his pray ;
Then he awayted that gentyll knyght,
   Bothe by nyght and by daye.

15

Ever he awayted that gentyll knyght,
   Syr Rychard at the Lee ;
As he went on haukynge by the ryver syde,
   And let his haukes flee,

16

Toke he there this gentyll knyght,
   With men of armes stronge,
And lad hym home to Notyngham warde,
   Ibonde both fote and honde.

17

The sheryf swore a full grete othe,
   By all that sacred be,
He had lever than an hondrede pounde,
   That Robyn Hode had he.

'tene,' vexation.   'warde,' prison.

18

Then the lady, the knygbtes wyfe,
  A fayre lady and fre,
She set her on a gode palfrày,
  To grene wode anon rode she.

19

When she came to the forèst,
  Under the grene wode tre,
Founde she there Robyn Hode,
  And all his fayre meynè.

20

'God the save, good Robyn Hode,
  And all thy company ;
For Our Dere Ladyes love,
  A bone graunte thou me.

21

' Let thou never my wedded lorde
  Shamfully slayne to be ;
He is fast ibounde to Notyngham warde,
  For the love of the.'

22

Anone then sayd good Robyn
  To that lady fre,
'What man hath your lorde itake?'
  ' The proude shirife,' than sayd she.

23

'[The proude sheryfe hath hym itake,]
  Forsoth as I the say ;
He is not yet thre myles
  Passed on his waye.'

'bone,' boon.

24

Up then sterte good Robyn,
　As a man that had be wode :
' Buske you all, my mery younge men,
　[To Nottingham lieth our road.']

25

Sone there were good bowes ibent,
　Mo than seven score,
Hedge ne dyche spared they none,
　That was them before.

26

' I make myn avowe,' sayd Robyn,
　' The knyght wolde I fayn se,
And yf I may hym take,
　Iquyt than shall he bee.'

27

And whan they came to Notyngham,
　They walked in the strete,
And with the proud sheryf, I wys,
　Sone gan they mete.

28

' Abyde, thou proud sheryf,' he sayd,
　' Abyde and speake with me ;
Of some tydynges of our kynge
　I wolde fayne here of the.

29

' This seven yere, by my troth,
　Ne yede I so fast on fote :
I make myn avowe, thou proud sheryfe,
　It is not for thy good.'

' wode,' mad.　　' iquyt,' quit.　　' yede,' went.

30

Robyn bent a good bowe,
　An arrowe he drewe at his wyll,
He hyt so the proud sheryf,
　Upon the grounde he lay full styll ;

31

And or he myght up arysc,
　On his fcte to stonde,
He smote of the sheryves hede
　With his bryght bronde.

32

' Lye thou there, thou proud sheryf,
　. Evyll mote thou thryve ;
There myght no man to the trust,
　The whyles thou were alyve.'

33

His men drewe out theyr bryght swerdes,
　That were so sharpe and kene,
And layde on the sheryves men,
　And dryved them downe bydene.

34

Robyn stert to that knyght,
　And cut a two his bonde,
And toke hym in his hand a bowe,　　　`
　And bade hym by hym stonde.

35

' Leve thy hors the behynde,
　And lerne for to renne ;
Thou shalt with me to grene wode,
　Through myre, mosse, and fenne ;

　　　　' bydene,' together, or forthwith.

36

'Thou shalt with me to grene wode,
    Without ony leasynge,
Tyll that I have gete us grace
    Of Edwarde our comly kynge.'

THE SEVENTH FYTTE.

[The King visits Robin Hood.]

1

THE kynge came to Notynghame,
    With knyghtes in grete araye,
For to take that gentyll knyght,
    And Robyn Hode, yf he may.

2

He asked men of that countrè,
    After Robyn Hode,
And after that gentyll knyght,
    That was so bolde and stout.

3

Whan they had tolde hym the case,
    Our kynge understonde ther tale,
And seased in his honde
    The knyghtes londes all.

4

All the passe of Lancasshyre,
    He went both ferre and nere,
Tyll he came to Plomton parke,
    He faylyd many of his dere.

'faylyd,' missed.

5

There our kynge was wont to se
  Herdes many one,
He coud unneth fynde one dere,
  That bare ony good horne.

6

The kynge was wonder wroth withall,
  And swore by the trynytè,
' I wolde I had Robyn Hode,
  With eyen I myght hym se ;

7

' And he that wolde smyte of the knyghtes hede,
  And brynge it to me,
He shall have the knyghtes londes,
  Syr Rycharde at the Le ;

8

' I gyve it hym with my chartèr,
  And sele it with my honde,
To have and holde for evermore,
  In all mery Englonde.'

9

Than bespake a fayre olde knyght,
  That was treue in his fay :
' A, my lege lorde the kynge,
  One worde I shall you say ;

10

' There is no man in this countrè
  May have the knyghtes londes,
While Robyn Hode may ryde or gone,
  And bere a bowe in his hondes,

' unneth,' hardly.　　' fay,' faith.

11

' That he ne shall lese his hede,
    That is the best ball in his hode :
Give it no man, my lorde the kynge,
    That ye wyll any good.'

12

Half a yere dwelled our comly kynge
    In Notyngham, and well more ;
[Yet] coude he not here of Robyn Hode,
    In what countre that he were ;

13

But alway went good Robyn
    By halke and eke by hyll,
And alway slewe the kynges dere,
    And welt them at his wyll.

14

Than bespake a proude fostere,
    That stode by our kynges kne :
' If ye wyll se good Robyn,
    Ye must do after me.

15

' Take fyve of the best knyghtes
    That be in your lede,
And walke downe by yon abbay,
    And gete you monkes wede.

16

' And I wyll be your ledesman,
    And lede you the way,
And or ye come to Notyngham,
    Myn hede then dare I lay,

' lese his hede,' lose his head.   ' hode,' hood.   ' here,' hear.
' halke,' corner (?)   ' welt,' overthrew.   ' fostere,' forester.
' after me,' as I say.   ' lede,' train (?) or land (?)   ' wede,' dress.
' ledesman,' guide.

17

'That ye shall mete with good Robyn,
  On lyve yf that he be,
Or ye come to Notyngham,
  With eyen ye shall hym se.'

18

Full hastly our kynge was dyght,
  So were his knyghtes fyve,
Everych of them in monkes wedc,
  And hasted them thyder blyth.

19

Our kynge was grete above his cole,
  A brode hat on his crowne,
Ryght as he were abbot-lyke,
  They rode up in-to the towne.

20

Styf botes our kynge had on,
  Forsoth as I you say,
He rode syngynge to grene wode,
  The covent was clothed in graye,

21

His male hors, and his grete somèrs,
  Folowed our kynge behynde,
Tyll they came to grene wode,
  A myle under the lynde,

22

There they met with good Robyn,
  Stondynge on the waye,
And so dyde many a boldc archerc,
  For soth as I you say.

'cole,' neck (?) or cowl (?)   'male hors,' baggage-horse.
  'somers,' sumpters.   'lynde,' trees (lindens).

23

Robyn toke the kynges hors
    Hastely in that stede,
And sayd, ' Syr abbot, by your leve,
    A whyle ye must abyde ;

24

' We be yemen of this foreste,
    Under the grene wode tre,
We lyve by our kynges dere,
    Other shyft have not we ;

25

' And ye have chyrches and rentes both,
    And gold full grete plentè ;
Gyve us some of your spendynge,
    For saynt Charytè.'

26

Than bespake our cumly kynge,
    Anone than sayd he,
' I brought no more to grene wode
    But forty pounde with me.

27

' I have layne at Notyngham
    This fourtynyght with our kynge,
And spent I have full moche good,
    On many a grete lordynge ;

28

' And I have but forty pounde,
    No more than have I me,
But yf I had an hondred pounde,
    I would geve it to the.'

29

Robyn toke the forty pounde,
  And departed it in two partye,
Halfendell he gave his mery men,
  And bad them mery to be.

30

Full curteysly Robyn gan say,
  ' Syr, have this for your spendyng,
We shall mete a nother day.'
  ' Gramercy,' than sayd our kynge ;

31

' But well the greteth Edwarde our kynge,
  And sent to the his seale,
And byddeth the com to Notyngham,
  Both to mete and mele.'

32

He toke out the brode tarpe,
  And sone he lete hym se ;
Robyn coud his courteysy,
  And set hym on his kne :

33

' I love no man in all the worlde
  So well as I do my kynge.
Welcome is my lordes seale ;
  And, monke, for thy tydynge.

34

' Syr abbot, for thy tydynges,
  To day thou shalt dyne with me
For the love of my kynge
  Under my trystell tre.'

' tarpe,' (?).

35

Forth he lad our comly kynge,
  Full fayre by the honde,
Many a dere there was slayne,
  And full fast dyghtande.

36

Robyn toke a full grete horne,
  And loude he gan blowe :
Seven score of wyght yonge men
  Came redy on a rowe,

37

All they kneeled on theyr kne,
  Full fayre before Robyn.
The kynge sayd hymselfe untyll,
  And swore by saynt Austyn,

38

' Here is a wonder semely syght ;
  Me thynketh by this sign,
His men are more at his byddynge,
  Then my men be at myn.'

39

Full hastly was theyr dyner idyght,
  And therto gan they gone,
They served our kynge with al theyr myght,
  Both Robyn and Lytell Johan.

40

Anone before our kynge was set
  The fatte venyson,
The good whyte brede, the good red wyne,
  And therto the fyne ale browne.

' dyghtande,' readied.   ' wyght,' active.

41

'Make good chere,' sayd Robyn,
  'Abbot, for charytè ;
And for this ylke tydynge,
  Blyssed mote thou be.

42

'Now shalte thou se what lyfe we lede,
  Or thou hens wende,
Than thou may enfourme our kynge,
  Whan ye togyder lende.'

43

Up they sterte all in hast,
  Theyr bowes were smartly bent,
Our kynge was never so sore agast,
  He wende to have be shente.

44

Two yerdes there were up set,
  Thereto gan they gange ;
By fifty pase, our kynge sayd,
  The merkes were too longe.

45

On every syde a rose garlonde,
  They shot under the lyne.
'Who so fayleth of the rose garlonde,' sayd Robyn,
  'His takyll he shall tyne,

46

'And yelde it to his mayster,
  Be it never so fyne ;
For no man wyll I spare,
  So drynke I ale or wyne ;

'lende,' tarry.   'shente,' destroyed.   'yerdes,' rods.
'gan they gauge,' began they to go.   'merkes,' marks.
'takyll,' tackle.   'tyne,' lose.

Q

47

'And bere a buffet on his hede,
  I wys ryght all bare.'
And all that fell in Robyn's lote,
  He smote them wonder sare.

48

Twyse Robyn shot aboute,
  And ever he cleved the wande,
And so dyde good Gylberte,
  With the whyte hand ;

49

Lytell Johan and good Scathelocke,
  For nothyng wolde they spare, ·
When they fayled of the garlonde,
  Robyn smote them full sair.

50

At the last shot that Robyn shot,
  For all his frendes fare,
Yet he fayled of the garlonde,
  Thre fyngers and mair.

51

Than bespake good Gylberte,
  And thus he gan say :
'Mayster,' he sayd, 'your takyll is lost,
  Stand forth and take your pay.'

52

'If it be so,' sayd Robyn,
  'That may no better be ;
Syr abbot, I delyver the myn arowe,
  I pray the, syr, serve thou me.'

'fare,' boast (?)

53

' It falleth not for myn order,' sayd our kynge,
    ' Robyn, by thy leve,
For to smyte no good yemàn,
    For doute I sholde hym greve.'

54

' Smyte on boldely,' sayd Robyn,
    ' I give the large leve.'
Anone our kynge, with that worde,
    He folde up his sleve,

55

And sych a buffet he gave Robyn,
    To grounde he yede full nere.
' I make myn avowe,' sayd Robyn,
    ' Thou arte a stalworthe frere ;

56

' There is pith in thyn arme,' sayd Robyn,
    ' I trowe thou canst well shote.'
Thus our kynge and Robyn Hode
    Togeder than they met.

57

Robyn behelde our comly kynge
    Wystly in the face,
So dyde syr Richarde at the Le,
    And kneled downe in that place ;

58

And so dyde all the wylde outlawes,
    Whan they se them knele.
' My lorde the kynge of Englonde,
    Now I knowe you well.'

59

' Mercy,' then Robyn sayd to our kynge,
  ' Under your trystyll tre,
Of thy goodnesse and thy grace,
  For my men and me !

60

' Yes, for by my troth,' sayd Robyn,
  ' And also god me save ;
I aske mercy, my lorde the kynge,
  And for my men I crave.'

61

' Be it so,' than sayd our kynge ;
  ' Thy peticion I graunt the,
With that thou leve the grene wode,
  And all thy company ;

62

' And come home, syr, to my courte,
  And there dwell with me.'
' I make myn avowe,' sayd Robyn,
  ' And ryght so shall it be ;

63

' I wyll come to your courte,
  Your servyse for to se,
And brynge with me of my men
  Seven score and thre.

64

' But me lyke well your servyse,
  I come agayne full soone,
And shote at the donne dere,
  As I am wonte to done.'

'donne,' dun.

THE EIGHTH FYTTE.

[Robin enters the King's service, but after a time returns to the greenwood, where he abides till his death.]

1

'HASTE thou ony grene cloth?' sayd
    our kynge,
  'That thou wylte sell nowe to me?'
'Ye, in troth,' sayd Robyn,
  'Thyrty yerdes and thre.

2

'Robyn,' sayd our kynge,
  'Now pray I the
To sell me some of that cloth,
  To me and my meynè.'

3

'Yes, in troth,' then sayd Robyn,
  'Or elles I were a fole;
A nother day ye wyll me clothe,
  I trowe, ayenst the Yole.'

4

The kynge kest of his cote then,
  A grene garment he dyde on,
And every knyght had so, I wys,
  They clothed them full soone.

'fole,' fool.   'Yole,' Christmas.

5

Whan they were clothed in Lyncolne grene,
    They kest away theyr graye.
‘ Now we shall to Notyngham,’
    All thus our kynge gan say.

6

Theyr bowes bente and forth they went,
    Shotynge all in-fere,
Towarde the towne of Notyngham,
    Outlawes as they were.

7

Our kynge and Robyn rode togyder,
    For soth as I you say,
And they shote plucke-buffet,
    As they went by the way ;

8

And many a buffet our kynge wan
    Of Robyn Hode that day :
And nothynge spared good Robyn
    Our kynge in his pay.

9

‘ So heaven me helpe,’ sayd our kynge,
    ‘ Thy game is nought to lere ;
I sholde not get a shote of the,
    Though I shote all this yere.’

10

All the people of Notyngham
    They stode and behelde ;
They sawe nothynge but mantels of grene,
    They covered all the felde ;

‘ as,’ as if.   ‘ wan,’ received.   ‘ nought to lere,’ nowise to learn.

11

Than every man to other gan say,
  ' I drede our kynge be slone ;
Come Robyn Hode to the towne, I wys,
  On lyve he leveth not one.'

12

Full hastly they began to fle,
  Both yemen and knaves,
And olde wyves that myght evyll goo,
  They hypped on theyr staves.

13

The kynge loughe full fast,
  And commanded theym agayne ;
When they se our comly kynge,
  I wys they were full fayne.

14

They ete and dranke, and made them glad,
  And sange with notes hye.
Than bespake our comly kynge
  To syr Rycharde at the Lee :

15

He gave hym there his londe agayne,
  A good man he bad hym be.
Robyn thanked our comly kynge,
  And set hym on his kne.

16

Had Robyn dwelled in the kynges courte
  But twelve monethes and thre,
That he had spent an hondred pounde,
  And all his mennes fee.

' on lyve,' alive. ' yemen and knaves,' yeomen and lads.
  ' hypped,' limped. ' fayne,' glad.

17

In every place where Robyn came,
　Ever more he layde downe,
Both for knyghtes and for squyres,
　To gete hym grete renowne.

18

By than the yere was all agone,
　He had no man but twayne,
Lytell Johan and good Scathelocke,
　Wyth hym all for to gone.

19

Robyn sawe yonge men shote,
　Full fayre upon a day:
'Alas!' than sayd good Robyn,
　'My welthe is went away.

20

'Somtyme I was an archere good,
　A styffe and eke a stronge;
I was commytted the best archere
　That was in mery Englonde.

21

'Alas!' then sayd good Robyn,
　'Alas and well a woo!
Yf I dwele lenger with the kynge,
　Sorowe wyll me sloo.'

22

Forth than went Robyn Hode,
　Tyll he came to our kynge:
'My lorde the kynge of Englonde,
　Graunte me myn askynge.

'commytted,' settled to be.

23

' I made a chapell in Barnysdale,
   That semely is to se,
It is of Mary Magdalene,
   And thereto wolde I be ;

24

' I myght never in this seven nyght,
   No tyme to slepe ne wynke,
Nother all these seven dayes,
   Nother ete ne drynke.

25

' Me longeth sore to Barnysdale,
   I may not be therfro,
Barefote and wolwarde I have hyght
   Thyder for to go.'

26

' Yf it be so,' than sayd our kynge,
   ' It may no better be ;
Seven nyght I gyve the leve,
   No lengre, to dwell fro me.'

27

' Gramercy, lorde,' then sayd Robyn,
   And set hym on his kne ;
He toke his leve full courteysly,
   To grene wode then went he.

28

Whan he came to grene wode,
   In a May mornynge,
There he herde the notes small
   Of byrdes mery syngynge.

' wolwarde,' in a woollen shirt.   ' hyght,' declared, promised.

29

' It is ferre gone,' sayd Robyn,
  ' That I was last here,
Me lyste a lytell for to shote
  At the donne dere.'

30

Robyn slewe a full grete harte ;
  His horne than gan he blow,
That all the outlawes of that forèst
  That horne coud they knowe,

31

And gadred them togyder,
  In a lytell throwe,
Seven score of wyght yonge men,
  Came redy on a rowe ;

32

And fayre dyde off theyr hodes,
  And set them on theyr kne :
' Welcome,' they sayd, ' our maystèr,
  Under this grene wode tre.'

33

Robyn dwelled in grene wode
  Twenty yere and two ;
For all drede of Edwarde our kynge,
  Agayne wolde he not goo.

34

Yet he was begyled, I wys,
  Through a wycked womàn,
The pryoresse of Kyrkesly,
  That nye was of his kynne,

'ferre gone,' a long time past.　'donne,' dun.　'lytell throwe,
  a short time, soon.　'for all drede of,' notwithstanding.

35

For the love of a knyght,
  Syr Roger of Donkestèr,
That was her owne speciall,—
  Full evyll mote they fare !

36

They toke togyder theyr counsell
  Robyn Hode for to sle,
And how they myght best do that dede,
  His banis for to be.

37

Than bespake good Robyn,
  In place where as he stode,
' To morow I muste to Kyrkesley,
  Craftely to be leten blode.'

38

Syr Roger of Donkestere
  With the pryoresse was there,
And there betrayed was good Robyn Hode,
  Through this false payre.

39

Cryst have mercy on his soule,
  That dyed on the rode !
For he was a good outlawe,
  And dyde pore men moch god.

'banis,' bane.   'rode,' rood, cross.

XLI

Bonnie George Campbell.

I

Hie upon Hielands,
  And low upon Tay,
Bonnie George Campbell
  Rode out on a day;
Saddled and bridled,
  And gallant to see:
Hame cam' his gude horse,
  But hame cam' na he.

2

Out ran his auld mither,
  Greeting fu' sair;
Out ran his bonnie bride,
  Reaving her hair.
He rade saddled and bridled,
  Wi' boots to the knee:
Hame cam' his gude horse,
  But never cam' he.

3

'My meadow lies green,
  And my corn is unshorn,
My barn is to bigg,
  And my babie's unborn.'
He rade saddled and bridled,
  Careless and free:
Toom hame cam' the saddle,
  And never cam' he.

'bigg,' build.   'toom,' empty.

XLII

Lord Thomas and Fair Ellinor.

1

LORD THOMAS he was a bold forester,
  And a chaser of the king's deer ;
Fair Ellinor was a fine woman,
  Lord Thomas he loved her dear.

2

' Come riddle my riddle, dear mother,' he said,
  ' And riddle for both in one ;
Whether I shall marry with fair Ellinor,
  And let the brown girl alone ?'

3

' The brown girl she has houses and land,
  Fair Ellinor she has none,
And I charge you, on my blessing,
  Bring me the brown girl home.'

4

As it befell on a high holiday,
  As many there are beside,
Lord Thomas he went to fair Ellinor,
  That should have been his bride.

5

But when he came to fair Ellinor's bower
  He knocked there at the ring,
And who was so ready as fair Ellinor
  For to let Lord Thomas in.

6

'What news? what news? Lord Thomas,' she said,
'What news hast thou brought unto me?'
'I am come to bid thee to my wedding,
And that is bad news for thee.'

7

'O God forbid, Lord Thomas,' she said,
'That such a thing should be done!
I thought to have been thy bride my own self,
And you to have been bridegroom.'

8

'Come riddle my riddle, dear mother,' she said,
'And riddle it all in one;
Whether I shall go to Lord Thomas's wedding,
Or whether I shall tarry at home?'

9

'There's many that are your friend, daughter,
But there's many that are your foe;
And I charge you, on my blessing,
To Lord Thomas's wedding don't go.'

10

'There's many that are my friend, mother,
If a thousand more were my foe:
Betide me life, betide me death,
To Lord Thomas's wedding I'll go.'

11

She clothed herself in gallant attire,
And her merry men all in green,
And as they rid through every town,
They took her to be some queen.

12

But when she came to Lord Thomas's gate,
  She knocked there at the ring,
And who was so ready as Lord Thomas
  To let fair Ellinor in.

13

' Is this your bride ?' fair Ellinor said ;
  ' Methinks she looks wonderful brown.
Thou mightest have had as fair a woman
  As ever trod on the ground.'

14

' Despise her not, fair Ellin,' he said,
  ' Despise her not unto me,
For better I love thy little finger
  Than all her whole bodie.'

15

The brown bride had a little penknife—
  The blade was slender and sharp—
And, between the short ribs and the long,
  Prick'd fair Ellinor to the heart.

16

' O, Christ now save thee !' Lord Thomas he said ;
  ' Methinks thou look'st wondrous wan ;
Thou used to look with as fresh a colour
  As ever the sun shined on.'

17

' O art thou blind, Lord Thomas ?' she said,
  ' O canst thou not very well see—
O dost thou not see my own heart's blood
  Run trickling down by my knee ?'

18

Lord Thomas had a sword by his side,
 As he walked about the hall;
He cut off his bride's head from her shoulders,
 And threw it against the wall.

19

He set the hilt against the ground,
 The point against his heart :
There never were three lovers met,
 That sooner did depart.

XLIII

Hugh of Lincoln.

[*Showing the cruelty of a Jew's daughter.*]

I

A' the boys of merry Lincoln
 Were playing at the ba',
And up it stands him sweet Sir Hugh,
 The flower among them a'.

2

He kicked the ba' there wi' his foot,
 And keppit it wi' his knee,
Till even in at the Jew's window
 He gart the bonny ba' flee.

3

' Cast out the ba' to me, fair maid,
 Cast out the ba' to me.'
' Never a bit,' says the Jew's daughter,
 ' Till ye come up to me.'

     ' keppit,' caught.

4

'Come up, sweet Hugh, come up, dear Hugh,
　Come up and get the ba'.'
'I winna come, I mayna come,
　Without my bonny boys a'.'

5

She's ta'en her to the Jew's garden,
　Where the grass grew lang and green,
She's pu'd an apple red and white,
　To wyle the bonny boy in.

6

She's wyled him in through ae chamber,
　She's wyled him in through twa,
She's wyled him into the third chamber,
　And that was the warst o' a'.

7

She's tied the little boy, hands and feet,
　She's pierced him wi' a knife,
She's caught his heart's blood in a golden cup,
　And twinn'd him o' his life.

8

She row'd him in a cake o' lead,
　Bade him lie still and sleep,
She cast him in a deep draw-well
　Was fifty fathom deep.

9

When bells were rung, and mass was sung,
　And every bairn went hame,
Then ilka lady had her young son,
　But Lady Helen had nane.

'twinn'd,' deprived.　　'ilka,' each.

R

10

She row'd her mantle her about,
    And sair, sair 'gan she weep ;
And she ran unto the Jew's house,
    When they were all asleep.

11

' My bonny Sir Hugh, my pretty Sir Hugh,
    I pray thee to me speak ! '
' Lady Helen, come to the deep draw-well
    'Gin ye your son wad seek.'

12

Lady Helen ran to the deep draw-well,
    And knelt upon her knee :
' My bonny Sir Hugh, an ye be here,
    I pray thee speak to me ! '

13

' The lead is wondrous heavy, mither,
    The well is wondrous deep ;
A keen penknife sticks in my heart,
    It is hard for me to speak.

14

' Gae hame, gae hame, my mither dear,
    Fetch me my winding-sheet ;
And at the back o' merry Lincoln,
    It's there we twa sall meet.'

15

Now Lady Helen she's gane hame,
    Made him a winding-sheet ;
And at the back o' merry Lincoln,
    The dead corpse did her meet.

16

And a' the bells o' merry Lincoln
  Without men's hands were rung ;
And a' the books o' merry Lincoln
  Were read without men's tongue :
Never was such a burial
  Sin' Adam's days begun.

XLIV

Barbara Allen's Cruelty.

1

ALL in the merry month of May,
  When green buds they were swelling,
Young Jemmy Grove on his death-bed lay
  For love o' Barbara Allen.

2

He sent his man unto her then,
  To the town where she was dwelling :
' O haste and come to my master dear,
  If your name be Barbara Allen.'

3

Slowly, slowly rase she up,
  And she cam' where he was lying ;
And when she drew the curtain by,
  Says, ' Young man, I think you're dying.'

4

' O it's I am sick, and very, very sick,
  And it's a' for Barbara Allen.'
' O the better for me ye'se never be,
  Tho' your heart's blude were a-spilling !

R 2

5

'O dinna ye min', young man,' she says,
    ' When the red wine ye were filling,
That ye made the healths gae round and round,
    And ye slighted Barbara Allen?'

6

He turn'd his face unto the wa',
    And death was wi' him dealing :
' Adieu, adieu, my dear friends a' ;
    Be kind to Barbara Allen.'

7

As she was walking o'er the fields,
    She heard the dead-bell knelling ;
And every jow the dead-bell gave,
    It cried, 'Woe to Barbara Allen !'

8

' O mother, mother, mak' my bed,
    To lay me down in sorrow.
My love has died for me to-day,
    I'll die for him to-morrow.'

XLV

May Colvin.

I

FALSE Sir John a-wooing came
    Unto a maiden fair ;
May Colvin was the lady's name,
    Her father's only heir.

'jow,' toll.

2

He's courted her but, he's courted her ben,
    He's courted her in the ha';
Till at last he got this lady's consent
    To mount and ride awa'.

3

She's gane to her father's coffers,
    Where all his money lay;
She's ta'en the red, and she's left the white,
    And lightly tripped away.

4

She's gane down to her father's stable,
    Where a' his steeds did stand;
She's ta'en the best, and she's left the warst,
    And they rode from her father's land.

5

He rode on, and she rode on,
    They rode a lang simmer's day,
Till they came through the woods to a hie, hie rock,
    Above the deep, deep sea.

6

' Loup off the steed!' says false Sir John;
    ' Your bridal bed you see :
Seven women I've drowned here,
    And eight I'll make out wi' thee.

7

' Cast off, cast off your silks so fine,
    And lay them on a stone ;
For they are too good and too costly
    To rot in the salt sea-foam,

8

'Cast off, cast off your Holland smock,
  And lay it from your hand;
It is too fine and too costly
  To toss in the wet sea-sand.'

9

'O turn thee about, thou false Sir John,
  And look to the leaf o' the tree,
For it never became a gentleman
  A woman thus to see.'

10

He turned himself right round about,
  To look to the leaf o' the tree;
She's twined her arms about his waist,
  And thrown him into the sea.

11

'O lie thou there, thou false Sir John,
  O lie thou there,' said she,
'For you lie not in a caulder bed
  Than you intended for me.'

12

So she rade back on her father's steed,
  As swift as she could flee,
And she won hame to her father's gates
  At the breaking of the day.

13

Up then spake the pretty parrot,
  In the bonny cage where it lay:
'O what hae ye done wi' your Sir John,
  That ye went wi' yesterday?'

14

‘ Now hold your tongue, my pretty parrot,
  And talk nae mair o’ me ;
Your cage shall be made o’ the beaten gold,
  And the spakes o’ ivorie.’

15

Up then spake her father dear,
  In the chamber where he lay :
‘ What ails the pretty parrot,
  To prattle ere break of day ?’

16

‘ A cat that came to my cage-door,
  I thought ’twould have worried me,
And I was calling on fair May Colvin
  To take the cat from me.’

XLVI

Edward, Edward.

1

‘ WHY does your brand sae drop wi’ blude,
      Edward, Edward ?
Why does your brand sae drop wi’ blude,
      And why sae sad gang ye, O ?’
‘ O I hae killed my hawk sae gude,
      Mither, mither ;
O I hae killed my hawk sae gude,
      And I hae nae mair but he, O.’

‘ spakes,’ bars.

2

' Your hawk's blude was never sae red,
  Edward, Edward ;
Your hawk's blude was never sae red,
  My dear son, I tell thee, O.'
' O I hae killed my red-roan steed,
  Mither, mither ;
O I hae killed my red-roan steed,
  That was sae fair and free, O.'

3

' Your steed was auld, and ye've plenty mair,
  Edward, Edward ;
Your steed was auld, and ye've plenty mair ;
  Some ither dule ye dree, O.'
' O I hae killed my father dear,
  Mither, mither ;
O I hae killed my father dear,
  Alas, and wae is me, O ! '

4

' And whatten penance will ye dree for that,
  Edward, Edward ?
Whatten penance will ye dree for that ?
  My dear son, now tell me, O.'
' I'll set my feet in yonder boat,
  Mither, mither ;
I'll set my feet in yonder boat,
  And I'll fare over the sea, O.'

5

' And what will ye do wi' your tow'rs and your ha',
  Edward, Edward ?
And what will ye do wi' your tow'rs and your ha',
  That were sae fair to see, O ? '

' dule ye dree,' grief you suffer.

‘ I’ll let them stand till they doun fa’,
　　Mither, mither ;
I’ll let them stand till they doun fa’,
　　For here never mair maun I be, O.’ ·

6

‘ And what will ye leave to your bairns and your wife,
　　Edward, Edward ?
And what will ye leave to your bairns and your wife,
　　When ye gang ower the sea, O ?’
‘ The warld’s room : let them beg through life,
　　Mither, mither ;
The warld’s room : let them beg through life ;
　　For them never mair will I see, O.’

7

‘ And what will ye leave to your ain mither dear,
　　Edward, Edward ?
And what will ye leave to your ain mither dear,
　　My dear son, now tell me, O ?’
‘ The curse of hell frae me sall ye bear,
　　Mither, mither ;
The curse of hell frae me sall ye bear :
　　Sic counsels ye gave to me, O ! ’

XLVII

𝕿𝖍𝖊 𝕺𝖚𝖙𝖑𝖆𝖜 𝕸𝖚𝖗𝖗𝖆𝖞.

I

ETTRICK FOREST is a fair forest,
　　In it grows many a seemly tree ;
There’s hart and hind, and dae and rae,
　　And of a’ wild beasts great plentie.

2

There's a fair castle, bigged wi' lime and stane ;
　O gin it stands not pleasantlie !
In the fore front o' that castle fair,
　Twa unicorns are bra' to see ;
There's the picture of a knight, and a lady bright,
　And the green hollin abune their bree.

3

There an Outlaw keeps five hundred men,
　He keeps a royal company ;
His merry men are a' in ae livery clad,
　O' the Lincoln green sae gay to see ;
He and his lady in purple clad,
　O gin they live not royallie !

4

Word is gane to our noble King,
　In Edinburgh where that he lay,
That there was an Outlaw in Ettrick Forest,
　Counted him nought, nor a' his courtrie gay.

5

' I make a vow,' then the gude King said,
　' Unto the man that dear bought me,
I'se either be King of Ettrick Forest,
　Or King of Scotland that Outlaw sall be !'

6

Then spake the lord hight Hamilton,
　And to the noble King said he,
' My sovereign prince, some counsel take,
　First at your nobles, syne at me.

<hr>

'hollin,' holly.　　'bree,' brow.

7

' I rede ye, send yon braw Outlaw till,
  And see gif your man come will he :
Desire him come and be your man,
  And hold of you yon forest free.

8

' Gif he refuses to do that,
  We'll conquer baith his lands and he !
Or else we'll throw his castle down,
  And mak' a widow o' his gay ladye.'

9

The King then call'd a gentleman,
  James Boyd (the Earl of Arran's brother was he);
When James he came before the King,
  He kneeled before him on his knee.

10

' Welcome, James Boyd ! ' said our noble King,
  ' A message ye maun gang for me ;
Ye maun hie to Ettrick Forest,
  To yon Outlaw, where bideth he.

11

' Ask him of whom he holds his lands,
  Or man wha may his master be,
And desire him come and be my man,
  And hold of me yon forest free.

12 .

' To Edinburgh to come and gang,
  His safe warrant I sall gie ;
And gif he refuses to do that,
  We'll conquer baith his lands and he.

' rede,' advise.

13

'Thou mayst vow I'll cast his castle down,
    And mak' a widow o' his gay ladye ;
I'll hang his merry men, pair by pair,
    In ony frith where I may them see.'

14

James Boyd took his leave o' the noble King,
    To Ettrick Forest fair cam' he ;
Down Birkendale Brae when that he cam',
    He saw the fair forest wi' his ee.

15

Baith dae and rae, and hart and hind,
    And of a' wild beasts great plentie ;
He heard the bows that boldly ring,
    And arrows whidderan' him near by.

16

Of that great castle he got a sight ;
    The like he ne'er saw wi' his ee !
On the fore front o' that castle fair,
    Twa unicorns were bra' to see ;
The picture of a knight, and lady bright,
    And the green hollin abune their bree.

17

Thereat he spyed five hundred men,
    Shooting with bows on Newark Lee ;
They were a' in ae livery clad,
    O' the Lincoln green sae gay to see.

18

His men were a' clad in the green,
    The knight was armed capapie,
With a bended bow, on a milkwhite steed ;
    And I wot they rank'd right bonnilie.

'frith,' field ; or, perhaps, place of shelter. See Dr. Jamieson's Scottish Dictionary.

19

Thereby Boyd kend he was master man,
  And served him in his ain degree.
' God mote thee save, brave Outlaw Murray !
  Thy ladye, and all thy chivalrie ! '
' Marry, thou's welcome, gentleman,
  Some king's messenger thou seems to be.'

20

' The King of Scotland sent me here,
  And, gude Outlaw, I am sent to thee ;
I wad wot of whom ye hold your lands,
  Or man wha may thy master be ?'

21

' Thir lands are mine,' the Outlaw said ;
  ' I ken nae king in Christentie ;
Frae Soudron I this forest wan,
  When the King nor his knights were not to see.'

22

' He desires you'll come to Edinburgh,
  And hauld of him this forest free ;
And, gif ye refuse to do this thing,
  He'll conquer baith thy lands and thee.
He hath vow'd to cast thy castle down,
  And mak' a widow o' thy gay ladye ;

23

' He'll hang thy merry men, pair by pair,
  In ony frith where he may them find.'
' Ay, by my troth ! ' the Outlaw said,
  ' Than wauld I think me far behind.

' Soudron,' Southern (?)

24

'Ere the King my fair country get,
　This land that's nativest to me,
Mony o' his nobles sall be cauld,
　Their ladies sall be right wearie.'

25

Then spak' his lady, fair of face :
　She said, ' 'Twere without consent of me,
That an outlaw suld come before a King ;
　I am right rad of treasonrie.
Bid him be gude to his lords at hame,
　For Edinburgh my lord sall never see.'

26

James Boyd took his leave o' the Outlaw keen,
　To Edinburgh boun' is he ;
When James he cam' before the King,
　He kneeled lowly on his knee.

27

' Welcome, James Boyd !' said our noble King,
　' What forest is Ettrick Forest free ?'
' Ettrick Forest is the fairest forest
　That ever man saw wi' his ee.

28

' There's the dae, the rae, the hart, the hind,
　And of a' wild beasts great plentie ;
There's a pretty castle of lime and stane,
　O gif it stands not pleasantlie !

29

' There's in the fore front o' that castle
　Twa unicorns, sae bra' to see ;
There's the picture of a knight, and a lady bright,
　Wi' the green hollin abune their bree.

'rad,' afraid.

30

' There the Outlaw keeps five hundred men,
    He keeps a royal companie ;
His merry men in ae livery clad,
    O' the Lincoln green sae gay to see :
He and his lady in purple clad ;
    O gin they live not royallie !

31

' He says, yon forest is his awn ;
    He wan it frae the Southronie ;
Sae as he wan it, sae will he keep it,
    Contrair all kings in Christentie.'

32

' Gar warn me Perthshire, and Angus baith,
    Fife, up and down, and Lothians three,
And graith my horse !' said our noble King,
    ' For to Ettrick Forest hie will I me.

33

Then word is gane the Outlaw till,
    In Ettrick Forest, where dwelleth he,
That the King was coming to his countrie,
    To conquer baith his lands and he.

34

' I mak' a vow,' the Outlaw said,
    ' I mak' a vow, and that trulie :
Were there but three men to tak' my part,
    Yon King's coming full dear suld be !'

35

Then messengers he called forth,
    And bade them hie them speedilye :
' Ane of ye gae to Halliday,
    The Laird of the Corehead is he.

' graith,' armour.

36

'He certain is my sister's son ;
  Bid him come quick and succour me ;
The King comes on for Ettrick Forest,
  And landless men we a' will be.'

37

'What news ? what news ?' said Halliday,
  'Man, frae thy master unto me ?'
'Not as ye would ; seeking your aid ;
  The King's his mortal enemie.'

38

'Ay, by my troth !' said Halliday,
  'Even for that it repenteth me ;
For gif he lose fair Ettrick Forest,
  He'll tak' fair Moffatdale frae me.

39

'I'll meet him wi' five hundred men,
  And surely mair, if mae may be ;
And before he gets the forest fair,
  We a' will die on Newark Lee !'

40

The Outlaw call'd a messenger,
  And bid him hie him speedilye
To Andrew Murray of Cockpool :
  'That man's a dear cousin to me ;
Desire him come and mak' me aid
  With a' the power that he may be.'

41

'It stands me hard,' Andrew Murray said,
  'Judge gif it stand na hard wi' me ;

To enter against a king wi' crown,
  And set my lands in jeopardie !
Yet, if I come not on the day,
  Surely at night he sall me see.'

42

To Sir James Murray of Traquair,
  A message came right speedilye :
' What news? what news?' James Murray said,
  ' Man, frae thy master unto me ? '

43

' What needs I tell ? for weel ye ken
  The King's his mortal enemie ;
And now he is coming to Ettrick Forest,
  And landless men ye a' will be.'

44

' And, by my troth,' James Murray said,
  ' Wi' that Outlaw will I live and dee ;
The King has gifted my lands lang syne—
  It cannot be nae warse wi' me.'

45

The King was coming thro' Caddon Ford,
  And full five thousand men was he ;
They saw the dark forest them before,
  They thought it awsome for to see.

46

Then spak' the lord hight Hamilton,
  And to the noble King said he,
' My sovereign liege, some counsel tak',
  First at your nobles, syne at me.

S

47

' Desire him meet thee at Permanscore,
  And bring four in his companie ;
Five earls sall gang yoursell before,
  Gude cause that you suld honour'd be.

48

' And, gif he refuses to do that,
  We'll conquer baith his lands and he ;
There sall never a Murray, after him,
  Hold land in Ettrick Forest free.'

49

The King then call'd a gentleman,
  Royal banner-bearer there was he,
James Hoppringle of Torsonse by name ;
  He cam' and kneeled upon his knee.

50

' Welcome, James Pringle of Torsonse !
  A message ye maun gang for me :
Ye maun gae to yon Outlaw Murray,
  Surely where boldly bideth he.

51

' Bid him meet me at Permanscore,
  And bring four in his companie ;
Five earls sall come wi' mysell,
  Gude reason I suld honour'd be.

52

' And gif he refuses to do that,
  Bid him look for nae good o' me ;
There sall never a Murray, after him,
  Have land in Ettrick Forest free.'

53

James cam' before the Outlaw keen,
   And served him in his ain degree :
'Welcome, James Pringle of Torsonse !
   What message frae the King to me ?'

54

' He bids ye meet him at Permanscore,
   And bring four in your company ;
Five earls sall gang himsell before,
   Nae mair in number will he be.

55

'And gif you refuse to do that,
   (I freely here upgive wi' thee,)
He'll cast yon bonny castle down,
   And mak' a widow o' that gay ladye.

56

' He'll loose yon bloodhound Borderers,
   Wi' fire and sword to follow thee ;
There will never a Murray, after thysell,
   Have land in Ettrick Forest free.'

57

' It stands me hard,' the Outlaw said,
   ' Judge gif it stands na hard wi' me :
What reck o' the losing of mysell,
   But a' my offspring after me !

58

'Auld Halliday, young Halliday,
   Ye sall be twa to gang wi' me ;
Andrew Murray, and Sir James Murray,
   We'll be nae mae in companie.'

s 2

59

When that they cam' before the King,
    They fell before him on their knee :
' Grant mercy, mercy, noble King !
    E'en for his sake that dyed on tree.'

60

' Sicken like mercy sall ye have,
    On gallows ye sall hangit be !'
' Over God's forbode,' quoth the Outlaw then,
    ' I hope your grace will better be !
Else, ere you come to Edinburgh port,
    I trow thin guarded sall ye be.

61

' Thir lands of Ettrick Forest fair,
    I wan them from the enemie ;
Like as I wan them, sae will I keep them,
    Contrair a' kings in Christentie.'

62

All the nobles the King about,
    Said pity it were to see him dee.
' Yet grant me mercy, sovereign prince,
    Extend your favour unto me !

63

' I'll give thee the keys of my castle,
    Wi' the blessing o' my gay ladye,
Gin thou'lt make me sheriff of this forest,
    And a' my offspring after me.'

64

' Wilt thou give me the keys of thy castle,
    Wi' the blessing of thy gay ladye ?

' sicken,' such.

I'se make thee sheriff of Ettrick Forest,
  Surely while upward grows the tree ;
If you be not traitor to the King,
  Forfaulted sall thou never be.'

65

' But, Prince, what sall come o' my men ?
  When I gae back, traitor they'll ca' me.
I had rather lose my life and land,
  Ere my merry men rebuked me.'

66

' Will your merry men amend their lives,
  And a' their pardons I grant thee ?
Now, name thy lands where'er they lie,
  And here I render them to thee.'

67

' Fair Philiphaugh is mine by right,
  And Lewinshope still mine shall be ;
Newark, Foulshiells, and Tinnies baith,
  My bow and arrow purchased me.

68

' And I have native steads to me,
  The Newark Lee and Hanginshaw ;
I have mony steads in Ettrick Forest,
  But them by name I dinna knaw.'

69

The keys of the castle he gave the King,
  Wi' the blessing o' his fair ladye ;
He was made sheriff of Ettrick Forest,
  Surely while upward grows the tree ;
And if he was na traitor to the King,
  Forfaulted he suld never be.

70

Wha ever heard, in ony times,
　Sicken an outlaw in his degree
Sic favour get before a King,
　As did Outlaw Murray of the forest free?

XLVIII

The Cruel Brother.

1

' O FAIREST lady ever seen,
　With a heigh-ho! and a lily gay,
Give consent to be my queen,'
　As the primrose spreads so sweetly.

2

' O you must ask my father dear,
　With a heigh-ho! and a lily gay,
And the mother, too, that did me bear,'
　As the primrose spreads so sweetly.

3

' And you must ask my sister Anne,
　With a heigh-ho! and a lily gay,
And not forget my brother John,'
　As the primrose spreads so sweetly.

4

' To anger him it were not good,
　With a heigh-ho! and a lily gay,
For he is of a heavy mood,'
　As the primrose spreads so sweetly.

5

Now he has asked her father dear,
With a heigh-ho! and a lily gay,
And the mother, too, that did her bear,
As the primrose spreads so sweetly.

6

And he has asked her sister Anne,
With a heigh-ho! and a lily gay;
But he left out her brother John,
As the primrose spreads so sweetly.

7

Her father handed her down the stair,
With a heigh-ho! and a lily gay;
Her mother kindly kiss'd her there,
As the primrose spreads so sweetly.

8

Her sister Anne through the close her led,
With a heigh-ho! and a lily gay;
Her brother John put her up on her steed,
As the primrose spreads so sweetly.

9

'You are high and I am low,
With a heigh-ho! and a lily gay;
Let me have a kiss before you go,'
As the primrose spreads so sweetly.

10

She was louting down to kiss him sweet,
With a heigh-ho! and a lily gay;
Wi' his penknife he wounded her deep,
As the primrose spreads so sweetly.

11

'Ride saftly on,' said the best young man,
　With a heigh-ho! and a lily gay;
'I think our bride looks pale and wan,'
　As the primrose spreads so sweetly.

12

'O take me from my horse, I pray,
　With a heigh-ho! and a lily gay,
And let me breathe, if so I may,'
　As the primrose spreads so sweetly.

13

'O lean me on my true love's breast,
　With a heigh-ho! and a lily gay;
I want a little time to rest,'
　As the primrose spreads so sweetly.

14

'I wish I had an hour,' she said,
　With a heigh-ho! and a lily gay,
'To make my will ere I am dead,'
　As the primrose spreads so sweetly.

15

'O what would ye leave to your father dear?'
　With a heigh-ho! and a lily gay.
'The milkwhite steed that brought me here,'
　As the primrose spreads so sweetly.

16

'What would ye give to your mother dear?'
　With a heigh-ho! and a lily gay.
'My wedding-shift which I do wear,'
　As the primrose spreads so sweetly.

17

' But she must wash it very clean,
  With a heigh-ho! and a lily gay,
For my heart's blood sticks in every seam,'
  As the primrose spreads so sweetly.

18

' What would ye give to your sister Anne?'
  With a heigh-ho! and a lily gay.
' My gay gold ring and my feathered fan,'
  As the primrose spreads so sweetly.

19

' What would ye give to your brother John?'
  With a heigh-ho! and a lily gay.
' A rope and a gallows to hang him on!'
  As the primrose spreads so sweetly.

20

' What would ye give to your brother John's wife?'
  With a heigh-ho! and a lily gay.
' Grief and sorrow to end her life!'
  As the primrose spreads so sweetly.

21

' What would ye give to your own true lover?'
  With a heigh-ho! and a lily gay.
' My dying kiss, and my love for ever!'
  As the primrose spreads so sweetly.

XLIX

Little Musgrave and the Lady Barnard.

1

IT fell upon a holy-day,
　As many there be in the year,
When young men and maids together did go
　Their matins and mass to hear,

2

Little Musgrave came to the church-door,
　When the priest was at private mass ;
But he had more mind of the fair women
　Than he had of Our Lady's grace.

3

This one of them was clad in green,
　That other was clad in pall ;
And then came in my Lord Barnard's wife,
　The fairest amongst them all.

4

She cast an eye on little Musgrave,
　As bright as the summer sun ;
And then bethought this little Musgrave,
　'This lady's heart have I won.'

5

'A good day unto thee, my handsome youth !'
　In passing forth said she ;
'Will you come to my bower in Dalisbury,
　And lodge for a while with me ?'

6

'O fain would I go with you, lady,
  But I dare not for my life ;
For I ken by the rings on your fingers
  That you are Lord Barnard's wife.'

7

'Lord Barnard's wife although I be,
  Yet what is that to thee ?
For we'll beguile him for this one night ;
  And far away is he.'

8

Quoth he, 'I thank thee, fair lady,
  For the kindness thou showest to me ;
And whether it be to my weal or woe,
  This night I will lodge with thee.'

9

All that heard a little tiny page,
  By his lady's coach he ran.
Quoth he, 'Though my lady's footpage I be,
  Yet I am Lord Barnard's man.

10

'My good Lord Barnard shall know of this,
  Whether I sink or swim.'
And footsore he came to Lord Barnard's lodging,
  When the stars shone pale and dim.

11

'Awaken ! awaken ! my Lord Barnard,
  As thou art a man of life ;
For little Musgrave is at Dalisbury
  Along with thy wedded wife.'

12

'If this be true, thou little tiny page,
  This thing thou tellest to me,
The broadest field in Dalisbury
  I freely will give to thee.

13

'If this be a lie, thou little tiny page,
  This thing thou tellest to me,
On the highest tree in Dalisbury
  Hanged shalt thou be.'

14

He called up his merry men all :
  'Come saddle to me my steed ;
For this night I must to Dalisbury,
  I never had greater need.'

15

There was a man of Lord Barnard's train,
  And he was of Musgrave's kin ;
And aye as fast as the horsemen rode
  More nimbly he did run.

16

He set a horn unto his mouth,
  Which loudly seem'd to say,
When he blew his blast so clear and shrill,
  'Away, Musgrave, away !'

17

Then up he raised him, little Musgrave,
  And drew to him his shoon :
'Lie still, lie still !' the lady she cried ;
  'Why get ye up so soon ?'

18

'O, methought I heard a wee horn blow,
　And it blew wondrous clear ;
And the turning of the bugle-note
　Was aye " Lord Barnard's here ! "

19

' Methought I heard a horn blow shrill,
　And ever it seem'd to say,
" Lord Barnard's here ! Lord Barnard's here !
　Away, Musgrave, away ! " '

20

' Lie still, lie still, thou little Musgrave,
　And huggle me from the cold ;
'Tis nothing at all but the wintry wind
　That bloweth across the wold.'

21

Up they looked, and down they lay,
　And so fell sound asleep ;
And there of a sudden Lord Barnard stood
　Close at their bed feet.

22

He lifted up the coverlet,
　He lifted up the sheet :
' Dost thou like my bed, thou little Musgrave ?
　Dost thou find my lady sweet ? '

23

' I find her sweet,' quoth little Musgrave,
　' The more it is to my pain ;
I would gladly give three hundred pounds
　That I were on yonder plain.'

24

'Arise, thou little Musgrave,' quoth he,
　' And put thy clothing on ;
It shall ne'er be said in my country
　I've killed a naked man.

25

' Here are two swords,' said Lord Barnard,
　' They are both sharp and shear ;
Take you the best and I the worst,
　And we'll end the matter here.'

26

The first stroke little Musgrave struck,
　He hurt Lord Barnard sore ;
The next stroke that Lord Barnard struck,
　Little Musgrave never struck more.

27

With that bespake this fair lady,
　In bed whereas she lay :
'Although thou'rt dead, thou little Musgrave,
　Yet I for thee will pray ;

28

' And wish well to thy soul will I,
　So long as I have life ;
So will I not for thee, Barnard,
　Although I'm thy wedded wife.'

29

Then he has ta'en his bright dagger,
　It was both keen and sharp,
And he has stricken that fair lady
　A deep wound to the heart.

30

'Now dig ye a grave,' Lord Barnard said,
'And hastily put them in ;
Yet lay ye her o' the upper hand,
Because o' her noble kin.'

L

Kinmont Willie.

1

O HAVE ye na heard o' the fause Sakelde ?
O have ye na heard o' the keen Lord Scroope ?
How they hae ta'en bauld Kinmont Willie,
On Haribee to hang him up ?

2

Had Willie had but twenty men,
But twenty men as stout as he,
Fause Sakelde had never the Kinmont ta'en,
Wi' eight score in his companie.

3

They band his legs beneath the steed,
They tied his hands behind his back ;
They guarded him, fivesome on each side,
And they brought him ower the Liddel-rack.

4

They led him thro' the Liddel-rack,
And also thro' the Carlisle sands ;
They brought him on to Carlisle castle,
To be at my Lord Scroope's commands.

'Haribee,' the gallows.

5

' My hands are tied, but my tongue is free,
   And wha will dare this deed avow ?
Or answer by the Border law ?
   Or answer to the bauld Buccleuch ?'

6

' Now haud thy tongue, thou rank reiver !
   There's never a Scot shall set thee free :
Before ye cross my castle yate,
   I trow ye shall take farewell o' me.'

7

' Fear na ye that, my lord,' quo' Willie :
   ' By the faith o' my body, Lord Scroope,' he said,
' I never yet lodged in a hostelrie,
   But I paid my lawing before I gaed.'

8

Now word is gane to the bauld Keeper,
   In Branksome Ha' where that he lay,
That Lord Scroope has ta'en the Kinmont Willie,
   Between the hours of night and day.

9

He has ta'en the table wi' his hand,
   He garr'd the red wine spring on hie :
' Now a curse upon my head,' he said,
   ' But avengèd of Lord Scroope I'll be !

10

' O is my basnet a widow's curch ?
   Or my lance a wand of the willow-tree ?
Or my arm a lady's lily hand,
   That an English lord should lightly me !

'basnet,' small helmet.   'curch,' cap.

11

'And have they ta'en him, Kinmont Willie,
Against the truce of Border tide,
And forgotten that the bauld Buccleuch
Is keeper here on the Scottish side?

12

'And have they e'en ta'en him, Kinmont Willie,
Withouten either dread or fear,
And forgotten that the bauld Buccleuch
Can back a steed, or shake a spear?

13

'O were there war between the lands,
As well I wot that there is none,
I would slight Carlisle castle high,
Though it were builded of marble stone.

14

'I would set that castle in a low,
And sloken it with English blood!
There's never a man in Cumberland
Should ken where Carlisle castle stood.

15

'But since nae war's between the lands,
And there is peace, and peace should be,
I'll neither harm English lad or lass,
And yet the Kinmont freed shall be!'

16

He has call'd him forty Marchmen bauld,
I trow they were of his ain name,
Except Sir Gilbert Elliot, call'd
The Laird of Stobs, I mean the same.

T

17

He has call'd him forty Marchmen bauld,
　Were kinsmen to the bauld Buccleuch ;
With spur on heel, and splent on spauld,
　And gluves of green, and feathers blue.

18

There were five and five before them a',
　Wi' hunting-horns and bugles bright :
And five and five cam' wi' Buccleuch,
　Like warden's men, array'd for fight.

19

And five and five, like masons gang,
　That carried the ladders lang and hie ;
And five and five, like broken men ;
　And so they reach'd the Woodhouselee.

20

And as we cross'd the 'Bateable Land,
　When to the English side we held,
The first o' men that we met wi',
　Whae sould it be but fause Sakelde ?

21

' Where be ye gaun, ye hunters keen ?'
　Quo' fause Sakelde ; 'come tell to me !'
' We go to hunt an English stag,
　Has trespass'd on the Scots countrie.'

22

' Where be ye gaun, ye marshal men ?'
　Quo' fause Sakelde ; 'come tell me true !'
' We go to catch a rank reiver,
　Has broken faith wi' the bauld Buccleuch.'

'splent on spauld,' armour on shoulder.

23

'Where are ye gaun, ye mason lads,
Wi' a' your ladders lang and hie?'
'We gang to herry a corbie's nest,
That wons not far frae Woodhouselee.'

24

'Where be ye gaun, ye broken men?'
Quo' fause Sakelde; 'come tell to me!'
Now Dickie of Dryhope led that band,
And the nevir a word of lear had he.

25

'Why trespass ye on the English side?
Row-footed outlaws, stand!' quo' he;
The nevir a word had Dickie to say,
Sae he thrust the lance through his fause bodie.

26

Then on we held for Carlisle toun,
And at Staneshaw-bank the Eden we cross'd
The water was great and meikle of spait,
But the never a horse nor man we lost.

27

And when we reach'd the Staneshaw-bank,
The wind was rising loud and hie;
And there the Laird garr'd leave our steeds,
For fear that they should stamp and neigh.

28

And when we left the Staneshaw-bank,
The wind began full loud to blaw;
But 'twas wind and weet, and fire and sleet,
When we came beneath the castle wa'.

'herry,' rob.   'corbie,' raven.   'lear,' learning.
'row-footed,' rough-footed (?)   'spait,' flood.

29

We crept on knees, and held our breath,
    Till we placed the ladders against the wa';
And sae ready was Buccleuch himsell
    To mount the first before us a'.

30

He has ta'en the watchman by the throat,
    He flung him down upon the lead :
' Had there not been peace between our lands,
    Upon the other side thou hadst gaed !

31

. ' Now sound out, trumpets !' quo' Buccleuch ;
    ' Let's waken Lord Scroope right merrilie !'
Then loud the warden's trumpet blew—
    O wha dare meddle wi' me?

32

Then speedilie to wark we gaed,
    And raised the slogan ane and a',
And cut a hole through a sheet of lead,
    And so we wan to the castle ha'.

33

They thought King James and a' his men
    Had won the house wi' bow and spear ;
It was but twenty Scots and ten,
    That put a thousand in sic a stear !

34

Wi' coulters, and wi' forehammers,
    We garr'd the bars bang merrilie,
Until we came to the inner prison,
    Where Willie o' Kinmont he did lie.

' slogan,' war-cry.   ' stear,' stir.   ' coulters,' ploughshares.

35

And when we cam' to the lower prison,
　Where Willie o' Kinmont he did lie—
'O sleep ye, wake ye, Kinmont Willie,
　Upon the morn that thou's to die?'

36

'O I sleep saft, and I wake aft ;
　It's lang since sleeping was fley'd frae me ;
Gie my service back to my wife and bairns,
　And a' gude fellows that spier for me.'

37

Then Red Rowan has hente him up,
　The starkest man in Teviotdale—
'Abide, abide now, Red Rowan,
　Till of my Lord Scroope I take farewell.

38

' Farewell, farewell, my gude Lord Scroope !
　My gude Lord Scroope, farewell !' he cried ;
' I'll pay you for my lodging maill,
　When first we meet on the Border side.'

39

Then shoulder high, with shout and cry,
　We bore him down the ladder lang ;
At every stride Red Rowan made,
　I wot the Kinmont's airns play'd clang.

40

'O mony a time,' quo' Kinmont Willie,
　' I have ridden horse baith wild and wood ;
But a rougher beast than Red Rowan
　I ween my legs have ne'er bestrode.

'maill,' rent.　　'airns,' irons.

41

'And mony a time,' quo' Kinmont Willie,
  ' I've prick'd a horse out oure the furs ;
But since the day I back'd a steed,
  I never wore siccan heavy spurs.'

42

We scarce had won the Staneshaw-bank,
  When a' the Carlisle bells were rung,
And a thousand men on horse and foot
  Cam' wi' the keen Lord Scroope along.

43

Buccleuch has turn'd to Eden Water,
  Even where it flow'd frae bank to brim,
And he has plunged in wi' a' his band,
  And safely swam them through the stream.

44

He turn'd him on the other side,
  And at Lord Scroope his glove flung he :
' If ye like na my visit in merry England,
  In fair Scotland come visit me !'

45

All sore astonish'd stood Lord Scroope,
  He stood as still as rock of stane ;
He scarcely dared to trew his eyes,
  When through the water they had gane.

46

' He is either himsell a devil frae hell,
  Or else his mother a witch maun be ;
I wadna have ridden that wan water
  For a' the gowd in Christentie.'

'furs,' furrows?   'trew,' trust.

LI

𝔉ine 𝔉lowers in the 𝔙alley.

1

SHE sat down below a thorn,
 Fine flowers in the valley;
And there she has her sweet babe born,
 And the green leaves they grow rarely.

2

' Smile na sae sweet, my bonny babe,
 Fine flowers in the valley;
An ye smile sae sweet, ye'll smile me dead,'
 And the green leaves they grow rarely.

3

She's ta'en out her little penknife,
 Fine flowers in the valley;
And twinn'd the sweet babe o' its life,
 And the green leaves they grow rarely.

4

She's howket a grave by the light o' the moon,
 Fine flowers in the valley;
And there she's buried her sweet babe in,
 And the green leaves they grow rarely.

5

As she was going to the church,
 Fine flowers in the valley,
She saw a sweet babe in the porch,
 And the green leaves they grow rarely.

6

'O sweet babe, if thou wert mine,
  Fine flowers in the valley,
I wad cleed thee in silk and sabelline,'
  And the green leaves they grow rarely.

7

'O mother mine, when I was thine,
  Fine flowers in the valley,
You did na prove to me sae kind,'
  And the green leaves they grow rarely.

8

'But now I'm in the heavens hie,
  Fine flowers in the valley;
And ye have the pains o' hell to dree'—
  And the green leaves they grow rarely.

LII

Robin Hood's Death and Burial.

1

WHEN Robin Hood and Little John,
  Down a down, a down, a down,
Went o'er yon bank of broom,
Said Robin Hood to Little John,
  'We have shot for many a pound :
  Hey down, a down, a down.

2

'But I am not able to shoot one shot more,
  My arrows will not flee ;
But I have a cousin lives down below,
  Please God. she will bleed me.'

3

Now Robin is to fair Kirkley gone,
　As fast as he can win ;
But before he came there, as we do hear,
　He was taken very ill.

4

And when that he came to fair Kirkley-hall,
　He knock'd all at the ring,
But none was so ready as his cousin herself
　For to let bold Robin in.

5

'Will you please to sit down, cousin Robin,' she said,
　'And drink some beer with me?'
'No, I will neither eat nor drink
　Till I am blooded by thee.'

6

'Well, I have a room, cousin Robin,' she said,
　'Which you did never see,
And if you please to walk therein,
　You blooded by me shall be.'

7

She took him by the lily-white hand,
　And led him to a private room,
And there she blooded bold Robin Hood,
　Whilst one drop of blood would run.

8

She blooded him in the vein of the arm,
　And locked him up in the room ;
There did he bleed all the live-long day,
　Until the next day at noon.

9

He then bethought him of a casement door,
　Thinking for to be gone;
He was so weak he could not leap,
　Nor he could not get down.

10

He then bethought him of his bugle-horn,
　Which hung low down to his knee;
He set his horn unto his mouth,
　And blew out weak blasts three.

11

Then Little John, when hearing him,
　As he sat under the tree,
'I fear my master is near dead,
　He blows so wearily.'

12

Then Little John to fair Kirkley is gone,
　As fast as he can dri'e;
But when he came to Kirkley-hall,
　He broke locks two or three:

13

Until he came bold Robin to,
　Then he fell on his knee:
'A boon, a boon,' cries Little John,
　'Master, I beg of thee.'

14

'What is that boon,' quoth Robin Hood,
　'Little John, thou begs of me?'
'It is to burn fair Kirkley-hall,
　And all their nunnery.'

'dri'e,' drive.

15

'Now nay, now nay,' quoth Robin Hood,
  'That boon I'll not grant thee ;
I never hurt woman in all my life,
  Nor man in woman's company.

16

'I never hurt fair maid in all my time,
  Nor at my end shall it be ;
But give me my bent bow in my hand,
  And a broad arrow I'll let flee ;
And where this arrow is taken up,
  There shall my grave digg'd be.

17

'Lay me a green sod under my head,
  And another at my feet ;
And lay my bent bow by my side,
  Which was my music sweet ;
And make my grave of gravel and green,
  Which is most right and meet.

18

'Let me have length and breadth enough,
  With a green sod under my head ;
That they may say, when I am dead,
  Here lies bold Robin Hood.'

19

These words they readily promis'd him,
  Which did bold Robin please ;
And there they buried bold Robin Hood,
  Near to the fair Kirklèys.

LIII

Young Redin.

1

FAIR CATHERINE from her bower-window
  Look'd over heath and wood ;
She heard a smit o' bridle-reins,
  And the sound did her heart good.

2

' Welcome, young Redin, welcome !
  And welcome again, my dear !
Light down, light down from your horse,' she says,
  ' It's long since you were here.'

3

' O good morrow, lady, good morrow, lady ;
  God make you safe and free !
I'm come to take my last farewell,
  And pay my last visit to thee.

4

' I mustna light, and I canna light,
  I winna stay at a' ;
For a fairer lady than ten of thee
  Is waiting at Castleswa'.'

5

' O if your love be changed, my dear,
  Since better may not be,
Yet, ne'ertheless, for auld lang syne,
  Ye'll stay this night wi' me.'

6

She birl'd him wi' the ale and wine,
  As they sat down to sup ;
A living man he laid him down,
  But I wot he ne'er rose up.

7

'Now lie ye there, young Redin,' she says,
  'O lie ye there till morn—-
Though a fairer lady than ten of me
  Is waiting till you come home!

8

'O lang, lang is the winter night,
  Till day begins to daw ;
There is a dead man in my bower,
  And I would he were awa'.'

9

She cried upon her bower-maiden,
  Aye ready at her ca' :
'There is a knight into my bower,
  'Tis time he were awa'.'

10

They've booted him and spurred him,
  As he was wont to ride,
A hunting-horn tied round his waist,
  A sharp sword by his side ;
And they've flung him into the wan water,
  The deepest pool in Clyde.

11

Then up bespake a little bird
  That sat upon a tree,
'Gae hame, gae hame, ye fause lady,
  And pay your maid her fee.'

12

'Come down, come down, my pretty bird,
    That sits upon the tree ;
I have a cage of beaten gold,
    I'll gie it unto thee.'

13

'Gae hame, gae hame, ye fause lady ;
    I winna come down to thee ;
For as ye have done to young Redin,
    Ye'd do the like to me.'

14

O there came seeking young Redin
    Mony a lord and knight,
And there came seeking young Redin
    Mony a lady bright.

15

They've call'd on Lady Catherine,
    But she sware by oak and thorn
That she saw him not, young Redin,
    Since yesterday at morn.

16

The lady turn'd her round about,
    Wi' mickle mournfu' din :
'It fears me sair o' Clyde water
    That he is drown'd therein.'

17

Then up spake young Redin's mother,
    The while she made her mane :
'My son kenn'd a' the fords o' Clyde,
    He'd ride them ane by ane.'

18

'Gar dive, gar dive!' his father he cried,
  'Gar dive for gold and fee!
O wha will dive for young Redin's sake
  And wha will dive for me?'

19

They dived in at ae pool-side,
  And out again at the other:
'We'll dive nae mair for young Redin,
  Although he were our brother.'

20

Then out it spake a little bird
  That flew above their head:
'Dive on, dive on, ye divers all,
  For there he lies indeed.

21

'But leave off your day diving,
  And dive at dark of night;
In the pool where young Redin lies in
  The candles they'll burn bright.'

22

They left off their day diving,
  And dived at dark of night;
In the pool where young Redin lay
  The candles they burn'd bright

23

The deepest pool in a' the stream
  They found young Redin in;
Wi' a great stone tied across the breast
  To keep his body down.

24

Then up and spake the little bird,
  Says, 'What needs a' this din?
It was his light leman took his life,
  And hided him in the linn.'

25

She sware her by the sun and moon,
  She sware by grass and corn,
She hadna seen him, young Redin,
  Since Monanday at morn.

26

'It's surely been my bower-woman—
  O ill may her betide!
I ne'er wad hae slain my young Redin,
  And thrown him in the Clyde.'

27

Now they hae cut baith fern and thorn,
  The bower-woman to brin ;
And they hae made a big balefire,
  And put this maiden in ;
But the fire it took na on her cheek,
  It took na on her chin.

28

Out they hae ta'en the bower-woman,
  And put her mistress in ;
The flame took fast upon her cheek,
  Took fast upon her chin,
Took fast upon her fair body,
  Because of her deadly sin.

'brin,' burn.

LIV

The Fray o' Suport.

1

SLEEP'RY Sim of the Lamb-hill,
And snoring Jock of Suport-mill,
Ye are baith right het and fou';
But my wae wakens na you.
Last night I saw a sorry sight—
Nought left me o' four-and-twenty gude ousen
    and ky,
My weel-ridden gelding, and a white quey,
But a toom byre and a wide,
And the twelve nogs on ilka side.
> Fy, lads! shout a' a' a' a' a',
> My gear's a' gane.

2

Weel may ye ken,
Last night I was right scarce o' men:
But Toppet Hob o' the Mains had guesten'd in
    my house by chance;
I set him to wear the fore-door wi' the speir, while
    I kept the back-door wi' the lance;
But they hae run him thro' the thick o' the thie,
    and broke his knee-pan,
And the mergh o' his shin-bane has run down on
    his spur-leather whang:
He's lame while he lives, and wherc'er he may
    gang.
> Fy, lads! shout a' a' a' a' a',
> My gear's a' gane.

'het and fou',' hot and full.   'ousen and ky,' oxen and cows.
'quey,' young cow.   'toom,' empty.   'nogs,' stakes.
'wear,' guard (?) 'mergh,' marrow.

U

3

But Peenye, my gude son, is out at the Hagbut-
    head,
His een glittering for anger like a fiery gleed;
Crying—' Mak' sure the nooks
Of Maky's-muir crooks;
For the wily Scot takes by nooks, crooks, and
    hooks.
Gin we meet a' together in a head the morn,
We'll be merry men.'
        Fy, lads! shout a' a' a' a' a',
        My gear's a' gane.

4

There's doughty Cuddy in the Heugh-head,
Thou was aye gude at a need;
With thy brock-skin bag at thy belt,
Aye ready to mak' a puir man help.
Thou maun awa' out to the Cauf-craigs
(Where anes ye lost your ain twa naigs),
And there toom thy brock-skin bag.
        Fy, lads! shout a' a' a' a' a',
        My gear's a' ta'en.

5

Doughty Dan o' the Houlet Hirst,
Thou was aye gude at a birst;
Gude wi' a bow, and better wi' a speir,
The bauldest March-man that e'er follow'd gear:
Come thou here.
        Fy, lads! shout a' a' a' a' a',
        My gear's a' gane.

' gleed,' glowing coal.   ' birst,' burst, battle, fight.

6

Rise, ye carle coopers, frae making o' kirns and
    tubs,
In the Nicol forest woods.
Your craft hasna left the value of an oak rod.
But if you had ony fear o' God,
Last night ye hadna slept sae sound,
And let my gear be a' ta'en.
        Fy, lads ! shout a' a' a' a' a',
        My gear's a' ta'en.

7

Ah ! lads, we'll fang them a' in a net,
For I hae a' the fords o' Liddel set ;
The Dunkin and the Door-loup,
The Willie-ford and the Water-slack,
The Black-rack and the Trout-dub of Liddel.
There stands John Forster, wi' five men at his
    back,
Wi' bufft coat and cap of steil.
Boo ! ca' at them e'en, Jock ;
That ford's sicker, I wat weil.
        Fy, lads ! shout a' a' a' a' a',
        My gear's a' ta'en.

8

Hoo ! hoo ! gar raise the Reid Souter, and
    Ringan's Wat.
Wi' a broad elshin and a wicker
I wat weil they'll mak' a ford sicker.
Sae, whether they be Elliots or Armstrangs,
Or rough-riding Scots, or rude Johnstones,

'kirn,' churn. 'fang,' catch. 'sicker,' sure. 'Souter,'
shoemaker. 'elshin,' awl. 'wicker,' switch. [They'll
make a ford sure, if they have but a broad awl and a switch for
weapons.]

Or whether they be frae the Tarras or Ewsdale,
They maun turn and fight, or try the deeps o'
    Liddel.
             Fy, lads! shout a' a' a' a' a',
             My gear's a' ta'en.

9

'Ah! but they will play ye anither jigg,
For they will out at the big rig,
And thro' at Fargy Grame's gap.'
But I hae anither wile for that:
For I hae little Will, and Stalwart Wat,
And lang Aicky, in the Souter Moor,
Wi' his sleuth-dog sits in his watch right sure.
Gin the dog gie a bark,
He'll be out in his sark,
And die or win.
             Fy, lads! shout a' a' a' a' a',
             My gear's a' ta'en.

10

Ha! boys!—I see a party appearing—wha's yon?
Methinks it's the Captain of Bewcastle, and
    Jephtha's John,
Coming down by the foul steps of Catlowdie's
    loan:
They'll make a' sicker, come which way they will.
             Ha, lads! shout a' a' a' a' a',
             My gear's a' ta'en.

11

Captain Musgrave, and a' his band,
Are coming down by the Siller-strand,

'rig,' ridge.

And the Muckle toun-bell o' Carlisle is rung :
My gear was a' weel won,
And before it's carried o'er the Border, mony a
    man's gae down.
        Fy, lads ! shout a' a' a' a' a',
        My gear's a' gane.

LV

𝔗𝔥𝔢 𝔖𝔥𝔦𝔭 o' 𝔱𝔥𝔢 𝔉𝔦𝔢𝔫𝔡.

1

'O WHERE hae ye been, my lang-lost lover,
    This lang seven years and mair ?'
'O I'm come again to seek your love
    And the vows that ye did swear.'

2

'Now haud your tongue o' my love and vows,
    For they can breed but strife ;
Now haud your tongue o' my former vows,
    For I am anither man's wife.'

3

He turn'd him right and round about,
    And the tear blinded his e'e :
'I wad never hae trodden on Irish ground,
    If it had not been for thee.

4

'I might hae had a noble lady,
    Far beyond the sea ;
I might hae had a noble lady,
    Were it no for the love o' thee.'

5 .

'If ye might hae had a noble lady,
　Yoursel' ye hae to blame;
Ye might hae taken the noble lady,
　For ye kenn'd that I was nane.'

6

'O fause are the vows o' womankind,
　But fair is their fause bodie;
I wad never hae trodden on Irish ground,
　Were it no for the love o' thee!

7

'For I despised the pearls and rings,
　And the fair ladye also;
And I am come back to my ain true love,
　But with me she'll not go.'

8

'My husband he is a carpenter,
　And earns gude bread wi' his hand;
And I hae borne him a little son;
　Wi' you I winna gang.'

9

'Ye may leave your husband to himsel',
　And your little son also;
And sail wi' me across the sea:
　Sae fair the wind doth blow.'

10

'O what hae you to keep me wi',
　If I wi' you should go—
If I should forsake my good husband,
　My little young son also?'

11

'See ye not yon seven pretty ships—
  The eighth brought me to land—
With merchandise and mariners,
  And music on every hand?

12

'There's mantles warm to wrap my love,
  O' the silk and soft velvet,
And rich attires to deck her head,
  And costly shoon for her feet.'

13

She turn'd her round upon the shore,
  Her love's ships to behold ;
Their mainyards and their topmasts high
  Were cover'd o'er wi' gold.

14

And she has gone to her little young son,
  Kiss'd him baith cheek and chin :
'O fare ye weel, my little son !
  For I'll never see you again.'

15

She has drawn the slippers on her feet,
  Weel wrought wi' threads o' gold,
And he's wrapt her round wi' the soft velvet
  To haud her frae the cold.

16

'O how do you like the ship?' he said,
  'Or how do you like the sea?
And how do you like the bold mariners,
  That wait upon thee and me?'

17

'O weel I like the ship,' she said,
  'And weel I like the sea;
But where are a' your mariners?
  I see nane but thee and me.'

18

She hadna sailed a league frae land,
  A league but barely three,
Till she minded on her dear husband,
  And her little young son tee.

19

'O gin I were on shore again,
  On shore where I wad be,
Nae living man should flatter me
  To sail upon the sea!'

20

'O haud your tongue o' weeping,' says he,
  'Let a' your mourning be;
I'll show ye how the lilies grow
  On the banks o' Italie.'

21

'O what hills are yon, yon pleasant hills,
  That the sun shines sweetly on?'
'O yon are the hills o' Heaven,' he said,
  'Where you will never win.'

22

'O whatna mountain is yon,' she said,
  'Sae dreary wi' frost and snow?'
'O yon is the mountain o' Hell,' he cried,
  'Where you and I maun go!'

'tee,' too.   'maun,' must.

23

And aye when she turn'd her round about,
 Aye taller he seem'd for to be ;
Until that the tops o' that gallant ship
 Nae taller were than he.

24

He strack the mainmast wi' his hand,
 The foremast wi' his knee ;
The gallant ship was broken in twain
 And sank into the sea.

LVI

Lamkin.

1

LAMKIN was as good a mason
 As ever hewed a stane ;
He biggit Lord Weare's great castle,
 But payment gat he nane.

2

'O pay me now, Lord Weare,
 Come pay me out o' hand.'
'I canna pay you, Lamkin,
 Unless I sell my land.'

3

'O gin ye winna pay me,
 I here sall make a vow,
Before that ye come hame again,
 Ye sall hae cause to rue.'

4

The lord said to his lady,
  As he mounted his horse,
' Beware, beware of Lamkin,
  That lieth in the moss.'

5

The lord said to his lady,
  As he rode away,
' Beware, beware of Lamkin,
  That lieth in the clay.'

6

' What care I for Lamkin,
  Or any of his gang?
I'll keep my doors weel guarded,
  My windows all penn'd in.'

7

When all the doors were guarded,
  And all the windows shut,
There was still one little window,
  And that one was forgot.

8

And the nourice was a fause limmer
  As e'er hung on a tree ;
And she laid a plot wi' Lamkin
  When her lord went over the sea.

9

She laid a plot wi' Lamkin,
  When the servants were awa',
Loot him in at the little window
  And brought him to the ha'.

' nourice,' nurse.

10

'O where's a' the men o' this house,
   That ca' me Lamkin?'
'They're at the barn thrashing;
   'Twill be lang ere they come in.'

11

'O where's the women o' this house,
   That ca' me Lamkin?'
'They're at the well washing;
   'Twill be lang ere they come in.'

12

'O where's the lady o' this house,
   That ca's me Lamkin?'
'She's up in her bower sewing,
   But we soon can bring her down.'

13

'And how are we to bring her down?'
   Says the Lamkin.
'Pinch the babe in the cradle here,'
   Says the fause nourice to him.

14

'O still my bairn, nourice,
   Still him if you can.'
'He will not still, madam,
   For a' his father's land.'

15

'O still my bairn, good nourice,
   O still him wi' the keys.'
'He will not still, my lady,
   Let me do what I please.'

16

'O still my bairn, kind nourice,
　O still him wi' the ring.'
'He will not still, dear mistress,
　Let me do anything.'

17

'O still my bairn, sweet nourice,
　O still him wi' the bell.'
'He will not still, my lady dear,
　Till ye come down yoursel'.'

18

The first step the lady stepped,
　She stepped on a stane ;
The last step the lady stepped,
　There she met Lamkin.

19

'O mercy, mercy, Lamkin !
　Have mercy upon me !
O harm ye not my little son,
　I pray you let him be !'

20

'Now sall I kill her, nourice?
　Or sall I let her be ?'
'O kill her, kill her, Lamkin,
　For she ne'er was good to me.'

21

'Then scour the basin, nourice,
　And mak' it fair and clean,
For to keep this lady's heart's blood,
　For she comes o' noble kin.'

22

'There needs nae basin, Lamkin;
　Let it run upon the floor;
What better is the heart's blood
　O' the rich than o' the poor?'

23

Lord Weare he sat in England
　A-drinking o' the wine;
He felt his heart fu' heavy
　At this very same time.

24

'I wish a' may be weel,' he says,
　'Wi' my dear lady at hame;
For the rings upon my fingers
　They've bursten into twain.'

25

He sailed in his bonny ship
　Upon the saut sea-faem;
He leap'd upon his horse,
　And swiftly he rade hame.

26

'O wha's blude is this,' he says,
　'That lieth in my ha'?'
'It is your little son's heart's blude,
　The clearest ava'.'

27

'O wha's blude is this,' he says,
　'That lies in the bower?'
'It is your lady's heart's blude,
　Where Lamkin he slew her.'

28

O sweetly sang the blackbird,
　That sat upon the tree ;
But sair moaned Lamkin,
　When he was judged to dee.

29

O bonny sang the mavis
　Out o' the thorny brake ;
But sair grat the nourice,
　When she was tied to the stake.

LVII

𝕿𝖍𝖊 𝕱𝖗𝖔𝖑𝖎𝖈𝖐𝖘𝖔𝖒𝖊 𝕯𝖚𝖐𝖊 ; 𝖔𝖗, 𝕿𝖍𝖊 𝕿𝖎𝖓𝖐𝖊𝖗'𝖘 ﹒𝕲𝖔𝖔𝖉 𝕱𝖔𝖗𝖙𝖚𝖓𝖊.

I

Now, as fame does report, a young Duke keeps a
　court,
One that pleases his fancy with frolicksome sport :
But amongst all the rest, here is one, I protest,
Which will make you to smile when you hear the
　true jest :
A poor tinker he found, lying drunk on the ground,
As secure in sleep as if laid in a swound.

2

The Duke said to his men, 'William, Richard,
　and Ben,
Take him home to my palace ; we'll sport with
　him then.'
O'er a horse he was laid, and with care soon
　convey'd
To the palace, altho' he was poorly arrai'd :

'grat,' wept.

Then they stript off his cloaths, both his shirt,
    shoes, and hose,
And they put him to bed for to take his repose.

3

Having pull'd off his shirt, which was all over dirt,
They did give him clean holland, this was no
    great hurt :
On a bed of soft down, like a lord of renown,
They did lay him to sleep the drink out of his
    crown.
In the morning, when day, then admiring he lay,
For to see the rich chamber, both gaudy and gay.

4

Now he lay something late, in his rich bed of
    state,
Till at last knights and squires they on him did
    wait ;
And the chamberlain bare then did likewise
    declare,
He desired to know what apparel he'd wear :
The poor tinker, amaz'd, on the gentleman gaz'd,
And admired how he to this honour was rais'd.

5

Tho' he seem'd something mute, yet he chose a
    rich suit,
Which he straitways put on without longer
    dispute,
With a star on his side, which the tinker oft ey'd,
And it seem'd for to swell him no little with
    pride ;
For he said to himself, ' Where is Joan my sweet
    wife ?
Sure she never did see me so fine in her life.'

6

From a convenient place, the right Duke, his good
    grace,
Did observe his behaviour in every case.
To a garden of state, on the tinker they wait,
Trumpets sounding before him : thought he, this
    is great :
Where an hour or two, pleasant walks he did
    view,
With commanders and squires in scarlet and
    blue.

7

A fine dinner was drest, both for him and his
    guests :
He was plac'd at the table above all the rest,
In a rich chair [or bed,] lin'd with fine crimson
    red,
With a rich golden canopy over his head :
As he sat at his meat, the musick play'd sweet,
With the choicest of singing his joys to compleat.

8

While the tinker did dine, he had plenty of wine,
Rich canary, with sherry and tent superfine.
Like a right honest soul, faith, he took off his bowl,
Till at last he began for to tumble and roul
From his chair to the floor, where he sleeping did
    snore,
Being seven times drunker than ever before.

9

Then the Duke did ordain, they should strip him
    amain,
And restore him his old leather garments again :

'Twas a point next the worst, yet perform it they
    must,
And they carry'd him strait where they found
    him at first.
Then he slept all the night, as indeed well he
    might ;
But when he did waken, his joys took their flight.

10

For his glory [to him] so pleasant did seem,
That he thought it to be but a meer golden dream ;
Till at length he was brought to the Duke, where
    he sought
For a pardon, as fearing he had set him at nought.
But his highness he said, ' Thou'rt a jolly bold
    blade :
Such a frolick before, I think, never was plaid.'

11

Then his highness bespoke him a new suit and
    cloak,
Which he gave for the sake of this frolicksome
    joke,
Nay, and five hundred pound, with ten acres of
    ground :
' Thou shalt never,' said he, ' range the counteries
    round,
Crying old brass to mend, for I'll be thy good
    friend,
Nay, and Joan thy sweet wife shall my duchess
    attend.'

12

Then the tinker reply'd : ' What ! must Joan my
    sweet bride
Be a lady in chariots of pleasure to ride ?

X

Must we have gold and land ev'ry day at com-
    mand?
Then I shall be a squire, I well understand.
Well I thank your good grace, and your love I
    embrace ;
I was never before in so happy a case! '

LVIII

Childe Vyet ; or, The Brothers.

I

LORD INGRAM and Childe Vyet
    Were both born in one hall ;
And both laid their loves on one lady,—
    The worse did them befall.

2

Lord Ingram woo'd Lady Maisry
    From father and from mother ;
Lord Ingram woo'd Lady Maisry
    From sister and from brother.

3

Lord Ingram woo'd Lady Maisry
    With leave of all her kin :
But Childe Vyet woo'd herself alone,
    And she loved none but him.

4

Now Lady Maisry she sat in her bower
    Dressing her hair one day ;
And in there came her proud father,
    In robes and rich array.

5

'Get up now, Lady Maisry,
  Put on your wedding-gown;
For this is the day, and Lord Ingram's here,
  And your wedding must be done!'

6

'O where shall I get a bonny boy
  Will win gold to his fee—
Will run unto Childe Vyet's ha'
  With this letter from me?

7

'I'd rather be Childe Vyet's wife,
  The white fish for to sell,
Before I'd be Lord Ingram's wife,
  To wear the silks so well.

8

'I'd rather be Childe Vyet's wife,
  With him to beg my bread,
Before I'd be Lord Ingram's wife,
  To wear the gold so red.'

9

'O here I am, the boy,' says one,
  'Will win gold to his fee,
And carry any letter away
  To Childe Vyet from thee.'

10

The first line that Childe Vyet read,
  The tear blinded his e'e;
The next line that he looked on,
  An angry man was he.

X 2

11

'What ails my own brother,' he says,
  'That he'll not let my Love be ?
But I'll come in haste to my brother's wedding;
  My lady she shall be free !'

12

But when he came to his brother's wedding,
  Childe Vyet could ne'er get in ;
For every gate was guarded weel,
  And his way he might not win.

13

'Tween Mary Kirk and the Castle
  'Twas all spread o'ar with garl,
To keep the lady and her maidens
  From treading upon the marl.

14

From Mary Kirk to the Castle
  Was spread a cloth of gold,
To keep that lady and her maidens
  From setting foot on the mould.

15

There was no cook in the kitchen
  That got not a gown of gray ;
And a' was blithe and gladsome ;
  But Lady Maisry was wae.

16

There was not a groom in the stable
  That got not a coat of green ;
And a' was blithe and gladsome ;—
  Lady Maisry, she was wi' wean.

'garl,' gravel (?)

17

When mass was sung, and bells were rung,
  And all men bound for bed,
Lord Ingram and Lady Maisry
  In one bed they were laid.

18

When they were laid upon their bed,
  It was baith soft and warm,
He laid his hand over her side :
  Says he, ' You are with bairn.'

19

' I told you once, so did I twice,
  When ye came as my wooer,
That Childe Vyet, your one brother,
  One night lay in my bower.

20

' I told you twice, so did I thrice,
  Ere ye came me to wed,
That Childe Vyet, your one brother,
  One night lay in my bed.'

21

' Then father your bairn on me, Maisry,
  And on no other man ;
And I'll gie him to his dowry
  Full fifty ploughs o' land.'

22

' I will not father my bairn on you,
  Nor yet on no wrong man,
Though ye gave him to his dowry
  Five thousand ploughs o' land.'

23

From the curtain leap'd out Childe Vyet,
  Shed by his yellow hair,
And he gave Lord Ingram to the death
  A deep wound and a sair.

24

Then up did start Lord Ingram,
  Shed by his coal-black hair,
And gave Childe Vyet to the death
  A deep wound and a sair.

25

There was pity enough for those two lords,
  When they were lying dead;
There was more for young Lady Maisry,
  In that chamber when she went mad.

LIX

The Baron of Brackley.

1

DOWN Dee-side came Inverey whistling and play-
    ing;
He's lighted at Brackley yates at the day dawing.

2

Says, ' Baron o' Brackley, O are ye within ?
There's sharp swords at the yate will gar your
    blood spin.'

3

The lady rase up, to the window she went;
She heard her kye lowing o'er hill and o'er bent.

'kye,' cows.

4

' O rise up, ye baron, and turn back your kye ;
For the lads o' Drumwharran are driving them
    bye.'

5

' How can I rise, lady, or turn them again ?
Whare'er I have ae man, I wat they hae ten.'

6

' Then rise up, my lasses, tak' rocks in your hand,
And turn back the kye ;—I hae you at command.

7

' Gin I had a husband, as I hae nane,
He wadna lye in his bed, see his kye ta'en.'

8

Then up got the baron, and cried for his graith ;
Says, ' Lady, I'll gang, tho' to leave you I'm laith.

9

' Come, kiss me, then, Peggy, and gie me my
    speir ;
I aye was for peace, tho' I never fear'd weir.

10

' Come, kiss me, then, Peggy, nor thınk I'm to
    blame ;
I weel may gae out, but I'll never win in !'

11

When Brackley was busked, and rade o'er the
    closs,
A gallanter baron ne'er lap to a horse.

<hr/>

    ' rock,' rod that holds the tow on a spinning-wheel.
    ' graith,' armour.   ' weir,' war.   ' closs,' close.

12

When Brackley was mounted, and rade o'er the
    green,
He was as bauld a baron as ever was seen.

13

Tho' there cam' wi' Inverey thirty and three,
There was nane wi' bonny Brackley but his
    brother and he.

14

Twa gallanter Gordons did never sword draw;
But against four and thirty, wae's me, what is
    twa?

15

Wi' swords and wi' daggers they did him sur-
    round;
And they've pierced bonny Brackley wi' many a
    wound.

16

Frae the head o' the Dee to the banks o' the Spey,
The Gordons may mourn him, and ban Inverey.

17

'O came ye by Brackley yates, was ye in there?
Or saw ye his Peggy dear riving her hair?'

18

'O I came by Brackley yates, I was in there,
And I saw his Peggy a-making good cheer.'

19

That lady she feasted them, carried them ben;
She laugh'd wi' the men that her baron had slain.

'ban,' curse.   'ben,' within.

20

'O fye on you, lady! how could you do sae?
You open'd your yates to the fause Inverey.'

21

She ate wi' him, drank wi' him, welcom'd him in;
She welcom'd the villain that slew her baron!

22

There's grief in the kitchen, and mirth in the
    ha';
But the Baron o' Brackley is dead and awa'.

LX

Burd Ellen.

1

LORD JOHN stood in his stable door,
    Said he was boun' to ride;
Burd Ellen stood in her bower door,
    Said she'd rin by his side.

2

He's pitten on his riding boots,
    And fast awa' rade he;
Burd Ellen's cut her yellow locks
    An inch above her e'e,
She's clad hersell in a page's dress,
    And after him ran she,

3

Until they came to a wan water,
    And folk do call it Clyde;
Then he lookit o'er his left shoulder,
    To see if she wad bide.

4

The firstan step the lady stept,
  The water cam' till her knee :
' Ochon, alas !' said the lady,
  ' This water's o'er deep for me.'

5

The neistan step the lady stept,
  The water cam' till her middle ;
And sighin' said that fair lady,
  ' I've wat my gouden girdle.'

6

The thirden step the lady stept,
  The water cam' to her pap ;
And the bairn that was in her twa sides
  For cauld began to quake.

7

' Lie still, my babe ! lie still, my babe !
  Ye work your mother wae ;
Your father rides on high horseback,
  Cares little for us twae.'

8

Near the midst o' Clyde water
  There was a yeard-fast stone ;
He lightly turn'd his horse about,
  And took the lady on ;
He brought her to the other side,
  And there he set her down.

9

' O tell me this now, good Lord John,
  And a word ye winna lie,
How far is it to your lodgin',
  Whar' we this night maun be ?'

'yeard-fast,' earth-fast.

10

'See ye na yon castle, Ellen,
　That shines sae bright and hie?
There's a lady in it, Ellen,
　Will sunder you and me.'

11

'I wish nae ill to your lady,
　She ne'er comes in my thought;
But I wish that woman maist o' your love,
　That dearest has you bought!'　.

12

O four and twenty gay ladies
　Welcom'd Lord John to the ha';
But a fairer lady than ony there
　Led his horse to the stable-sta'.

13

O four and twenty gay ladies
　Went wi' Lord John to the green;
But a fairer lady than ony there
　At the manger stood alane.

14

When bells were rung, and mass was sung,
　And a' men boun' to meat,
Burd Ellen was at the bye-table
　Amang the pages set.

15

'O eat and drink, my bonny boy,
　The white bread and the beer.'
'The never a bit can I eat or drink,
　My heart's sae fu' o' fear.'

16

'O eat and drink, my bonny boy,
  The white bread and the wine.'
'O how sall I eat or drink, master,
  Wi' heart sae fu' o' pine?'

17

But out and spak' Lord John's mother,
  And a wise woman was she:
'Whar' met ye wi' that bonny boy
  That looks sae sad on thee?

18

'Sometimes his colour waxes red,
  Sometimes it waxes wan;
He's liker a woman big wi' bairn
  Than a young lord's serving-man.'

19

'O it makes me laugh, my mother dear,
  Sic words to hear frae thee;
He is a squire's ae dearest son,
  That for love has follow'd me.

20

'Rise up, rise up, my bonny boy,
  Gie my horse corn and hay.'
'O that I will, my master dear,
  As quickly as I may.'

21

She's ta'en the hay under her arm,
  The corn intill her hand,
And she's gane to the great stable
  As fast as e'er she can.

22

'O room ye round, my bonny steeds!
O room ye near the wa'!
For this pain that strikes me through my sides
Fu' soon will gar me fa'.'

23

She lean'd her back against the wa',
Strong travail cam' her on ;
And e'en amang the great horse's feet
Burd Ellen brought forth her son.

24

'O open the door, Burd Ellen!
O open and let me in ;
I want to see if my steed be fed,
And my greyhounds fit to rin.'

25

'How could I open, how shall I open,
How can I open to thee,
When lying amang your great steed's feet,
And your young son on my knee?'

26

He strack the door hard wi' his foot,
Sae has he wi' his knee ;
Iron hinges and wooden bars
Into the floor flang he.
'Be not afeard, Burd Ellen!' he says ;
'There's nane comes in but me.'

27

'An asking, an asking, sweet Lord John,
An asking I beg of thee,—
The meanest woman about your place,
To tend my young son and me.'

28

'Tak' up, tak' up my bonny young son!
  Gar wash him wi' the milk;
Tak' up, tak' up my fair lady!
  Gar row her in the silk.

29

'Be of good cheer, Burd Ellen!' he says,
  'O be of good cheer, I pray;
Your bridal and your churching both
  Shall be upon one day.'

LXI

The Lament of the Border Widow.

1

My love he built me a bonny bower,
And clad it a' wi' lily flower;
A brawer bower ye ne'er did see
Than my true love he built for me.

2

There came a man, by middle day,
He spied his sport, and went away;
And brought the King that very night,
Who brake my bower and slew my knight.

3

He slew my knight, to me sae dear;
He slew my knight, and poin'd his gear;
My servants all for life did flee,
And left me in extremetie.

'gar,' make.　　'row,' roll.　　'poin'd,' seized.

4

I sew'd his sheet, making my mane;
I watch'd the corpse, myself alane;
I watch'd his body night and day;
No living creature came thàt way.

5

I took his body on my back,
And whiles I gaed, and whiles I sat;
I digg'd a grave, and laid him in,
And happ'd him wi' the sod sae green.

6

But think na ye my heart was sair,
When I laid the moul' on his yellow hair?
O think na ye my heart was wae,
When I turn'd about, awa' to gae?

7

Nae living man I'll love again,
Since that my lovely knight is slain;
Wi' ae lock of his yellow hair
I'll chain my heart for evermair.

LXII

Willy's Lady.

I

SWEET Willy's ta'en him o'er the faem,
He's woo'd a wife and brought her hame;
He's woo'd her for her yellow hair.
But his mither wrought her mickle care,

'faem,' foam.

And mickle dolour gart her dree ;
For lighter can she never be,
But in her bower she sits wi' pain,
And Willy mourns for her in vain.

2

Now to his mither he is gane,
That vile rank witch, who lives her 'lane ;
He says, ' My lady has a cup,
O' siller wrought, wi' gouden lip ;
This gudely gift ye now sall airn,
And let her be lighter o' her young bairn.'

3

' O' her young bairn she's never be lighter,
Nor in her bower to shine the brighter ;
But she sall die and turn to clay,
And ye sall wed anither may.'
'Anither may I'll marry nane,
Anither may I'll ne'er bring hame.'
But, sighing, said his bonny young wife,
' Alas, I'm weary o' my life !'

4

He did him to his mither again,
That vile rank witch, who lives her 'lane ;
And says, ' My lady has a girdle,
It's a' pure goud around the middle,
And set wi' fifty pearls and ten,
And fifty diamonds round the hem ;
This gudely gift ye now sall airn,
And let her be lighter o' her young bairn.'

'gart her dree,' caused her to suffer.   'her 'lane,' alone.
      'airn,' earn.   'may,' maid.

5

' O' her young bairn she's never be lighter,
Nor in her bower to shine the brighter ;
But she sall die and go to clay,
And you sall wed anither may.'
'Anither may I'll marry nane,
Anither may I'll ne'er bring hame.'
But, sighing, said his bonny young wife,
'Alas, I'm weary o' my life ! '

6

He did him to his mither again,
That vile rank witch, who lives her 'lane ;
He says, ' My lady has a steed,
The like o' him no in the lands o' Leed ;
At ilka tett o' that horse's mane
There's a gowden chess and bell ringin' :
The steed and bells ye now sall airn,
Let her be lighter o' her young bairn.'

7

' She's never o' her bairn be lighter,
Nor in her bower to shine the brighter ;
Die she must, and go to clay,
And you sall wed anither may.'
'Anither may I'll marry nane,
Anither may I'll never bring hame.'
But moaning said his bonny young wife,
'Alas, I'm weary o' my life ! '

8

Then out it spak', the Billy Blind,
He spak' aye in a gude time ;

' Leed,' Liddesdale (?)   ' tett,' tassel.   ' chess ' (qu. ' jess ') ?
' Billy Blind,' a sort of Brownie, Lar, or House-Spirit.

Y

'Ye'll do ye to the market-place,
And there ye'll buy a loaf o' wace. ·
Ye'll shape it bairn and bairnly like,
And in it twa glassen een ye'll pit.

9

'And do ye to your mither then,
And bid her come to the christenin',
For dear's the boy he's been to you ;
Then notice weel what she sall do ;
And do you stand a little away,
And listen weel what she will say.'

10

He did him to the market-place,
And there he bought a loaf o' wace ;
He shaped it bairn and bairnly like,
And in it twa glassen een he pat.
He did him to his mither then,
And bade her to his boy's christenin';
And then he stood a little away,
And noticed weel what she would say.

11

'O wha has loosed the nine witch-knots
That were amang that lady's locks ?
And wha's ta'en out the kaims o' care
That were into that lady's hair ?
And wha has kill'd the master kid *
That ran aneath that lady's bed ?
And wha has untied her left-foot shee,
And letten that lady lighter be ?'

'wace,' wax.   'een,' eyes.   'pit,' put.   'pat,' put.
          'kaims,' combs.   'shee,' shoe.
   * One of the Witch's familiars, we may imagine, taking the
shape of a pet kid.

12

O Willy has loosed the nine witch-knots
That lay amang his lady's locks ;
Willy's ta'en out the kaims o' care
Were set into his lady's hair ;
And Willy's kill'd the master kid
That ran aneath his lady's bed ;
And Willy's untied her left-foot shee,
And letten his lady lighter be ;
And now he has gotten a bonny son,
And mickle grace be him upon.

LXIII

Hughie Graham.

1

OUR lords are to the mountains gane,
  A-hunting o' the fallow deer,
And they hae grippet Hughie Graham,
  For stealing o' the Bishop's mare.

2

And they hae tied him hand and foot,
  And led him up thro' Carlisle town ;
The lads and lasses met him there,
  Cried, 'Hughie Graham, thou art a loun.'

3

' O loose my right hand free,' he says,
  ' And put my braid sword in the same,
He's no in Carlisle town this day,
  Daur tell the tale to Hughie Graham.'

4

Up then bespake the brave Whitefoord,
　As he sat by the Bishop's knee,
'Five hundred white stots I'll gie you,
　If ye'll let Hughie Graham gae free.'

5

'O haud your tongue,' the Bishop says,
　'And wi' your pleading let me be ;
For tho' ten Grahams were in his coat,
　Hughie Graham this day shall dee.'

6

Up then bespake the fair Whitefoord,
　As she sat by the Bishop's knee,
'Five hundred white pence I'll gie you,
　If ye'll gie Hughie Graham to me.'

7

'O haud your tongue now, lady fair,
　And wi' your pleading let it be ;
Altho' ten Grahams were in his coat,
　It's for my honour he maun dee.'

8

They've ta'en him to the gallows knowe,
　He looked to the gallows tree,
Yet never colour left his cheek,
　Nor ever did he blin' his e'e.

9

At length he looked round about,
　To see whatever he could spy,
And there he saw his auld father,
　And he was weeping bitterly.

'stots,' oxen.　　　'knowe,' little hill.

10

'O haud your tongue, my father dear,
    And wi' your weeping let it be ;
The weeping's sairer on my heart,
    Than a' that they can do to me.

11

'And ye may gie my brother John
    My sword that's bent in the middle clear,
And let him come at twelve o'clock,
    And see me pay the Bishop's mare.

12

'And ye may gie my brother James
    My sword that's bent in the middle brown,
And bid him come at four o'clock,
    And see his brother Hugh cut down.

13

'And ye may tell my kith and kin
    I never did disgrace their blood ;
And when they meet the Bishop's cloak,
    To mak' it shorter by the hood.'

LXIV

Lord Thomas and Fair Annet.

1

LORD THOMAS and fair Annet
    Sat all day on a hill ;
When night was come, and the sun was set,
    They had not talk'd their fill.

2

Lord Thomas said a word in haste,
  Fair Annet took it ill :
' I winna wed a tocherless maid
  Against my parents' will.'

3

O Annet's gane off intill her bower ;
  Lord Thomas rode swiftly doun ;
And now he has come to his mither's ha'
  By the lee'light o' the moon.

4

' O sleep ye, wake ye, mither?' he says,
  ' O are ye therewithin ?'
' I sleep right aft, I wake right aft ;
  What want ye wi' me, son ?

5

' Where hae ye been this night, Thomas ?
  Where hae ye tarried sae lang ?'
' O I hae been courtin' fair Annet,
  But I think she used me wrang.

6

' Now rede me, rede me, mither,' he says,
  ' A gude rede gie to me :
O sall I tak' the nut-brown girl,
  And let fair Annet be ?'

7

' It's an ye wed the nut-brown girl,
  I'll heap the gold wi' my hand ;
But an ye wed her, fair Annet,
  I'll straike it wi' a wand.

'tocherless,' without a fortune.   'lee light,' calm light.
'rede me,' advise me.   'straike it wi' a wand,' give bare
measure, as if in measuring a gallon of oats you were to stroke off
the top grains with a stick.

8

'The nut-brown girl has houses and lands,
    Fair Annet has nane,' she said ;
'And I charge you, for my benison,
    The nut-brown girl to wed.'

9

'But alas, alas !' Lord Thomas he says,
    'O fair is Annet's face !'
'What matter for that, Lord Thomas my son ?
    She has nae ither grace.'

10

'Alas, alas !' Lord Thomas he says,
    'But fair is Annet's hand !'
'What matter for that, Lord Thomas my son ?
    She hasna ae rood o' land.'

11

'Sheep will die in cots, mither,
    And owsen die in byre;
And what's the land or gold to me,
    If I lose my heart's desire ?'

12

Then he has till his sister gane :
    'Now, sister, rede ye me ;
O sall I marry the nut-brown girl,
    And set fair Annet free ?'

13

'I'se rede ye tak' fair Annet, Thomas,
    She'll bring neither dool nor shame ;
But the crabbit brown girl wad gar ye cry,
    O what is this we brought hame !'

'dool,' grief.   'gar,' make.

14

'No, I will tak' my mither's counsel,
　And marry me out o' hand;
And I will tak' the nut-brown girl,
　With her houses and her land.'

15

His sister has found a bonnie boy,
　Wad fain win hose and shoon;
One that will rin to fair Annet's bower,
　By the lee light o' the moon.

16

The boy he is come to Annet's bower,
　And tirled at the pin,
And wha sae ready as Annet hersel'
　To open and let him in.

17

'Ye are bidden come to Lord Thomas's weddin',
　At twal o' the clock at noon;
Ye are bidden come to Lord Thomas's weddin',
　And ye cannot come ower soon.

18

'Ye mauna put on the black, the black,
　Nor yet the dowie brown,
But the silken blue, and your kerch sae white,
　And your bonnie locks hangin' down.'

19

'It's I will come to Lord Thomas's weddin',
　At twal o' the clock at noon;
It's I will come to Lord Thomas's weddin'—
　I thought it would be my own.

'dowie,' mournful.　　'kerch,' kerchief.

20

' My maids, come to my dressing-room,
   And dress to me my hair ;
Whare'er ye laid a plait before
   See ye lay ten times mair.

21

' Lay out my smock o' needlework
   Wrought on the holland fine ;
Lay out my skirts, and silken suits,
   And choose the best o' nine.'

22

At each tate o' Annet's horse's mane
   There hung a silver bell ;
When there came a tift o' the southern wind,
   They all began tò knell.

23

She pass'd through the crowd in Mary's kirk,
   She sat upon the dais;
The light that came frae the fair Annet
   Enlighten'd a' that place.

24

She sat close by the nut-brown bride ;
   And her e'en they shone so clear,
That Lord Thomas he forgot the bride,
   Since ever his love drew near.

25

' O wha is this, my father dear,
   That blinks in Lord Thomas's e'e ?'
' O this is Lord Thomas's first true love,
   Before he loved thee.'

'tate,' tassel.   'dais,' platform.

26

Lord Thomas held a rose in his hand,
    And he gave it kisses three,
He reached it past the nut-brown bride,
    Laid it on Annet's knee.

27

The bride she drew a long bodkin
    Out o' her gay head-gear,
And struck fair Annet to the heart,
    That word she never spak' mair.

28

'O Christ thee save !' Lord Thomas he said,
    ' Methinks thou look'st wondrous wan ;
Thou used'st to look with as fresh a colour
    As ever the sun shone on.'

29

He saw fair Annet wax pale and faint,
    And wondered what might be ;
But when he saw her dear heart's blood
    A' wood-wroth waxed he.

30

He drew his dagger frae his side,
    His dagger sae sharp and meet,
And drave it into the nut-brown bride,
    That fell dead at his feet.

31

Now stay for me, dear Annet,' he said,
    'O stay, my dear !' he cried ;
Then struck the dagger intill his heart,
    And fell dead by her side.

'wood-wroth,' mad-angry.

LXV

Lizie Lindsay.

1

'WILL ye go to the Hielands, Lizie Lindsay
    Will ye go to the Hielands wi' me?
Will ye go to the Hielands, Lizie Lindsay,
    And dine on fresh curds and green whey?'

2

Then out spak' Lizie's mother,
    A good old lady was she:
'Gin ye say sic a word to my daughter,
    I'll gar ye be hanged hie!'

3

'Keep weel your daughter for me, madam;
    Keep weel your daughter for me.
I care as little for your daughter
    As ye can care for me!'

4

Then out spak' Lizie's ain maiden,
    A bonnie young lassie was she;
'Now gin I were heir to a kingdom,
    Awa' wi' young Donald I'd be.'

5

'O say you sae to me, Nelly?
    And does my Nelly say sae?
Maun I leave my father and mither,
    Awa' wi' young Donald to gae?'

6

And Lizie's ta'en till her her stockings,
   And Lizie's ta'en till her her shoon,
And kilted up her green claithing,
   And awa' wi' young Donald she's gane.

7

The road it was lang and weary ;
   The braes they were ill to climb ;
Bonnie Lizie was weary wi' travelling,
   A fit further couldna she win.

8

' O are we near hame, dear Donald ?
   O are we near hame, I pray ? '
' We're no near hame, bonnie Lizie,
   Nor yet the half o' the way.'

9

Sair, O sair was she sighing,
   And the saut tear blin'd her e'e :
' Gin this be the pleasures o' loving,
   They never will do wi' me ! '

10

' Now haud your tongue, bonnie Lizie ;
   Ye never shall rue for me ;
Gie me but your love for my love,
   It is a' that your tocher will be.

11

' O haud your tongue, bonnie Lizie,
   Although that the gait seem lang ;
And you's hae the wale o' good living
   When to Kincaussie we gang.

'fit,' foot.   'gait,' road.   'wale,' choice, best.

12

' My father he is an auld shepherd,
    My mother she is an auld dey ;
And we'll sleep on a bed o' green rashes,
    And dine on fresh curds and green whey.'

13

They cam' to a homely poor cottage ;
    The auld woman 'gan to say :
' O ye're welcome hame, Sir Donald,
    Ye've been sae lang away.'

14

' Ye mustna call me Sir Donald,
    But call me young Donald your son ;
For I hae a bonnie young lady
    Behind me, that's coming in.

15

' Come in, come in, bonnie Lizie,
    Come in, come in,' said he ;
' Although that our cottage be little,
    I hope we'll the better agree.

16

' O make us a supper, dear mither,
    And make it o' curds and green whey ;
And make us a bed o' green rashes,
    And cover it o'er wi' fresh hay.'

17

She's made them a bed o' green rashes,
    And cover'd it o'er wi' fresh hay.
Bonny Lizie was weary wi' travelling,
    And lay till 'twas lang o' the day.

' dey,' dairywoman.

18

'The sun looks in o'er the hill-head,
   The laverock is liltin' gay;
Get up, get up, bonnie Lizie,
   Ye've lain till it's lang o' the day.

19

'Ye might hae been out at the shealin',
   Instead o' sae lang to lie;
And up and helping my mither
   To milk her gaits and her kye.'

20

Then sadly spak' Lizie Lindsay,
   She spak' it wi' mony a sigh:
'The ladies o' Edinbro' city
   They milk neither gaits nor kye.'

21

'Rise up, rise up, bonnie Lizie,
   Rise up and mak' yoursel' fine;
For we maun be at Kincaussie,
   Before that the clock strikes nine.'

22

But when they cam' to Kincaussie,
   The porter doth loudly say,
'O ye're welcome hame, Sir Donald;
   Ye've been sae lang away!'

23

It's down then cam' his auld mither,
   Wi' all the keys in her hand;
Saying, 'Take you these, bonnie Lizie,
 .   For all is at your command.'

'laverock,' lark.   'shealin',' shed.   'gaits and kye,' goats
                        and cows.

LXVI

Sweet William's Ghost.

1

THERE came a ghost to Marjorie's door,
  Wi' many a grievous groan,
And aye he tirled at the pin,
  But answer made she none.

2

' O say, is that my father?
  Or is't my brother John?
Or is it my true love Willy,
  From Scotland new come home?'

3

''Tis not thy father, Marjorie,
  Nor yet thy brother John ;
But 'tis thy true love Willy,
  From Scotland new come home.

4

' O Marjorie sweet! O Marjorie dear!
  For faith and charitie,
Will ye gie me back my faith and troth
  That I gave once to thee?'

5

' Thy faith and troth thou gavest to me,
  And again thou'lt never win,
Until thou come within my bower
  And kiss me cheek and chin.'

6

'My lips they are sae bitter,' he says,
'My breath it is sae strang,
If ye get ae kiss from me to-night,
Your days will not be lang.

7

'The cocks are crawing, Marjorie—
The cocks are crawing again ;
The dead wi' the quick they mustna stay,
And I must needs begone.'   ·

8

She follow'd him high, she follow'd him low,
Till she came to yon churchyard green ;
And there the deep grave opened up,
And young William he lay down.

9

'What three things are these, sweet William,
That stand beside your head ?'
'O it's three maidens, Marjorie,
That once I promised to wed.'

10

'What three things are these, sweet William,
That stand close at your side ?'
'O it's three babes,' he says, ' Marjorie,
That these three maidens had.'

11

'What three things are these, sweet William,
That lie close at your feet ?'
'O it's three hell-hounds, Marjorie,
That's waiting my soul to keep.'

12

And she took up her white, white hand,
  And struck him on the breast ;
Saying, ' Have here again thy faith and troth,
  And I wish your soul good rest.'

LXVII

Lady Elspat.

1

' Brent's your brow, my Lady Elspat ;
  Gouden yellow is your hair !
O' a' the maids o' fair Scotland,
  There's no anither half sae fair.'

2

' O keep your vows, sweet William,' she says,
  ' The vows which ye ha' made to me ;
And at the back o' my mither's castell,
  This night I'll surely meet wi' thee.'

3

But wae be to her brother's page,
  That heard the words thir twa did say ;
He's tauld them to her lady mither,
  Wha wrought sweet William mickle wae.

4

For she's ta'en him, sweet William,
  And she's gar'd bind him wi' his bow-string,
Till the red bluid o' his fair bodie
  Frae ilka nail o' his hand did spring.

' brent,' straight.

Z

5

She kept him in a tower o' strength,
　　Till the Lord-justice came to town ;
Out has she ta'en him, sweet William,
　　Brought him before the Lord-justice boun'.

6

'And what is the crime, now, lady,' he says,
　　'That has by this young man been dane?'
'O he has broken my bonny castell,
　　That was weel biggit wi' lime and stane.

7

'And he has broken my bonny coffers,
　　That was weel bandit wi' aiken ban';
And he has stown my rich jewels ;
　　I wot he has stown them every ane.'

8

Then out it spak her Lady Elspat,
　　As she sat by Lord-justice's knee ;
'Now ye hae tauld your tale, mither,
　　I pray, Lord-justice, ye'll now hear me.

9

'He hasna broken her bonny castell,
　　That was weel biggit wi' lime and stane ;
Nor has he stown her rich jewels,
　　For I wat she has them every ane.

10

'But though he was my first true love,
　　And though I had sworn to be his bride,
Because he hadna a great estate,
　　She would this way our loves divide.'

'aiken,' oaken.

11

Syne out and spak the Lord-justice,
  I wat the tear was in his e'e ;
' I see nae faut in this young man ;
  Sae loose his bands, and set him free.

12

' And tak your love, now, Lady Elspat,
  And my best blessin' you baith upon ;
For gin he be your first true love,
  He is my eldest sister's son.

13

' There stands a steed in my stable,
  Cost me baith gold and white monie ;
Ye's get as mickle o' my free land
  As he'll ride about in a summer's day.'

LXVIII

Willie and May Margaret, or the Water of Clyde.

1

WILLIE stands in his stable,
  A-clapping of his steed ;
And over his white fingers
  His nose began to bleed.

2

' Gie corn to my horse, mither ;
  Gie meat unto my man ;
For I maun gang to Margaret's bower,
  Before the night comes on.'

z 2

3

'O stay at hame, my son Willie !
  The wind blaws cold and stour ;
The night will be baith mirk and late,
  Before ye reach her bower.'

4

'O tho' the night were ever sae dark,
  O the wind blew never sae cauld,
I will be in May Margaret's bower
  Before twa hours be tauld.'

5

'O bide this night wi' me, Willie,
  O bide this night wi' me !
The bestan fowl in a' the roost
  At your supper, my son, shall be.

6

'A' your fowls, and a' your roosts,
  I value not a pin ;
I only care for May Margaret,
  And ere night to her bower I'll win.'

7

'O an ye gang to May Margaret
  Sae sair against my will,
In the deepest pot o' Clyde's water
  My malison ye's feel ! '

8

He mounted on his coal-black steed,
  And fast he rade awa' ;
But ere he came to Clyde's water
  Fu' loud the wind did blaw.

'stour,' strong.   'mirk,' dark.   'malison,' curse.

9

As he rade over yon hie hie hill,
  And doun yon dowie den,
There was a roar in Clyde's water
  Wad fear'd a hundred men.

10

But Willie has swam through Clyde's water,
  Though it was wide and deep;
And he came to May Margaret's door
  When a' were fast asleep.

11

O he's gane round and round about,
  And tirled at the pin,
But doors were steek'd and windows barr'd,
  And nane to let him in.

12

'O open the door to me, Margaret!
  O open and let me in!
For my boots are fu' o' Clyde's water,
  I'm shivering to the chin.'

13

'I daurna open the door to you,
  I daurna let you in;
For my mither she is fast asleep
  And I maun mak' nae din.'

14

'O gin ye winna open the door,
  Nor be sae kind to me,
Now tell me o' some out-chamber,
  Where I this night may be.'

'dowie den,' doleful hollow.   'steek'd,' fastened.

15

'Ye canna win in this night, Willie,
  Nor here ye canna be ;
For I've nae chambers out nor in,
  Nae chamber but barely three.

16

'The tane is fu' to the roof wi' corn,
  The tither is fu' wi' hay ;
The third is fu' o' merry young men,
  They winna remove till day.'

17

'O fare ye weel, then, May Margaret,
  Sin' better it mauna be.
I have won my mither's malison
  Coming this night to thee.'

18

He's mounted on his coal-black steed,
  O but his heart was wae !
But e'er he came to Clyde's water,
  'Twas halfway up the brae.

19

When down he rade to the river-flood,
  'Twas fast flowing ower the brim ;
The rushing that was in Clyde's water
  Took Willie's rod frae him.

20

He leaned him ower his saddle-bow
  To catch his rod again ;
The rushing that was in Clyde's water
  Took Willie's hat frae him.

21

He leaned him ower his saddle-bow
  To catch his hat by force ;
The rushing that was in Clyde's water
  Took Willie frae his horse.

22

' O I canna turn to my horse's head ;
  I canna strive to sowm ;
I've gotten my mither's malison,
  And it's here that I maun drown ! '

23

The very hour this young man sank
  Into the pot sae deep,
Up waken'd his love, May Margaret,
  Out of her heavy sleep.

24

' Come hither, come hither, my minnie dear,
  Come hither, read my dream ;
I dream'd my love Willie was at our gates,
  And nane would let him in.'

25

' Lie still, lie still, dear Margaret,
  Lie still and tak' your rest ;
Your lover Willie was at the gates,
  'Tis but two quarters past.'

26

Nimbly, nimbly rase she up,
  And quickly put she on ;
While ever against her window
  The louder blew the win'.

'sowm,' swim.   'pot,' deep pool.   'minnie,' mother.

27

Out she ran into the night,
　And down the dowie den ;
The strength that was in Clyde water
　Wad drown five hundred men.

28

She stepped in to her ancle,
　She stepped free and bold ;
Ohone, alas !' said that lady,
　'This water is wondrous cold.'

29

The second step that she waded,
　She waded to the knee ;
Says she, ' I'd fain wade farther in,
　If I my love could sec.'

30

The neistan step that she waded,
　She waded to the chin ;
'Twas a whirlin' pot o' Clyde's water
　She got sweet Willie in.

31

' O ye've had a cruel mither, Willie !
　And I have had anither ;
But we shall sleep in Clyde's water
　Like sister and like brither.'

32

When the water o' Clyde left roaring
　And the sun shone warm and fair,
They found these twa in each ither's arms,
　Like lovers true as they were.

LXIX

The Duke of Gordon's Daughter.

1

THE Duke of Gordon's three daughters,
   Elizabeth, Marg'ret and Jean,
They left bonny Castle Gordon
   And lived in Aberdeen.

2

They had not lived in Aberdeen
   A month but only two,
Captain Ogilvie courted Lady Jean,
   And she loved him fond and true.

3

Word came to the Duke of Gordon,
   In the chamber where he lay,
Lady Jean was in love with a captain,
   And from him she would not stay.

4

' Go saddle to me the black horse,
   My servant on the grey,
I must mount and gallop to Aberdeen
   And bring Lady Jean away.'

5

They were not a mile outside the town,
   A mile but barely ane,
When he met his daughters walking,
   And look'd hard for Lady Jean.

6

Then up came Lady Elizabeth fine,
  And Lady Margaret fair ;
But Lady Jean was the flower o' the three,
  And he could not see her there.

7

'O where is your sister, maidens?
  O where is your sister now?
Come, tell me where is your sister
  That she is not walking with you?'

8

'O pardon, pardon, father !
  O give us no fault, we pray !
Lady Jean is Captain Ogilvie's wife,
  And with him she will gae.'

9

Fast he spurr'd and gallop'd,
  Till he came to Aberdeen ;
And he saw brave Captain Ogilvie
  Training his men on the green.

10

'Woe be to you, Captain Ogilvie !
  And an ill death shalt thou dee.
For wiling away my daughter,
  High hangèd thou shalt be.'

11

The duke has wrote a broad letter,
  Sent to the king's own hand,
For to hang brave Captain Ogilvie,
  If ever he hanged a man.

12

'I will not hang Captain Ogilvie,
    Whatever the duke may say ;
But I'll cause him to put the gold lace off,
    For a common soldier's array.'

13

Now word came to Captain Ogilvie,
    In the chamber where he lay,
To cast off the gold lace and scarlet,
    And put on a soldier's array.

14

'If this be for bonny Jean Gordon,
    This penance I can take wi' ;
If this be for dear Jeanie Gordon,
    All this and more I'll dree.'

15

Lady Jean had not been married
    A year but only three,
Till she had a babe on every arm,
    And another upon her knee.

16

'O but I'm weary wandering !
    O but my fortune's bad !
It sets not a Duke's own daughter
    To follow a soldier lad.

17

'O but I'm weary wandering !
    O but I think it lang !
It sets not a Duke's own daughter
    To follow a simple man.'

'dree,' endure.

18

'Now hold thy tongue, bonny Jeanie !
    O hold thy tongue, my lamb !
I once was a noble captain—
    For your sake a simple man.'

19

And when they came to the Highland hills,
    Cold was the frost and snow ;
Lady Jean's shoes were torn to bits,
    And no farther could she go.

20

'O were I in the glens o' Foudlen,
    Where hunting I have been,
I would go to fair Castle Gordon,
    Without either stockings or sheen !

21

When they came to fair Castle Gordon,
    And crossing over the green,
The porter gave out with a loud loud shout,
    'Yonder's our Lady Jean !'

22

'O welcome bonny Jean Gordon,
    You are dearly welcome to me !
O welcome, dear Jeanie Gordon,
    But away with your Ogilvie !'

23

Over-seas went the Captain,
    As a soldier under command ;
But a messenger soon followed after,
    Bade him home to heir his land.

'sheen,' shoes.

24

'Your uncle is dead and buried ;
  He has left all his land to thee.'
'Sail home, sail home ! ' says brave Ogilvie,
  ' For now my dear Jeanie I'll see.'

25

He came to fair Castle Gordon,
  Outside the gate stood he ;
The porter gave out with a loud loud shout,
  ' O here's Captain Ogilvie ! '

26

'You are welcome, sweet Captain Ogilvie !
  Your fortune's advanced I hear ;
No guest could come to this castle
  More welcome than you, or more dear.'

27

'The last time I came to your castle,
  You kept me outside your door ;
I am come for my wife and children,
  And I ask you for nothing more.'

28

Down the stair she came laughing,
  And the tears upon her face ;
With two little children, one on each side,
  Another in her embrace.

29

'O welcome, my bonnie Jeanie,
  And dearly welcome to me !
Now come away home with our children,
  Parted never to be ! '

LXX

Fair Margaret's Misfortunes.

1

' I AM no love for you, Margaret,
   You are no love for me.
Before to-morrow at eight of the clock,
   A rich wedding you shall see.'

2

Fair Margaret sat in her bower-window
   Combing her yellow hair ;
There she espied sweet William and his bride,
   As they were a-riding near.

3

Down she laid her ivory comb,
   And up she bound her hair ;
She went away out of her bower,
   But never returnèd there.

4

When day was gone and night was come,
   And all men fast asleep,
There came the spirit of fair Marg'ret,
   And stood at William's feet.

5

' Are you awake, sweet William ?' she said,
   ' Or, William, are you asleep ?
God give you joy of your gay bride-bed,
   And me of my winding-sheet.'

6

When day was come, and night was gone,
　And all men waked from sleep,
Sweet William to his lady said,
　'Alas, I have cause to weep.

7

'I dreamt a dream, my dear ladye,—
　Such dreams are never good,—
· I dreamt my bower was full of red swine,
　And the walls ran down with blood.'

8

He called up his merrymen all,
　By one, by two, and by three ;
Saying, 'I'll away to fair Margaret's bower,
　By the leave of my ladye.'

9

And when he came to fair Margaret's bower,
　He knocked at the ring ;
And who so ready as her seven brethren,
　To let sweet William in.

10

He turned down the covering-sheet,
　To see the face of the dead.
'Methinks she looks all pale and wan ;
　She hath lost her cherry red.

11

'I would do more for thee, Margaret,
　Than would any of thy kin :
And I will kiss thy pale cold lips,
　Though a smile I cannot win.'

12

With that bespake the seven brethren,
  Making most piteous moan,
'You may go and kiss your jolly brown bride,
  And let our sister alone!'

13

'If I do kiss my jolly brown bride,
  I do but what is right ;
I ne'er made a vow to yonder poor corpse,
  By day, nor yet by night.

14

'Deal on, deal on, ye merrymen all,
  Deal on your cake and your wine ;
Whatever is dealt at her funeral to-day,
  Shall be dealt to-morrow at mine.'

15

Fair Margaret died as it might be to-day,
  Sweet William he died the morrow,
Fair Margaret died for pure true love,
  Sweet William he died for sorrow.

16

Margaret was buried in the lower chancel,
  And William in the higher ;
Out of her breast there sprang a rose-tree,
  And out of his a briar.

17

They grew till they grew unto the church-top,
  And then they could grow no higher ;
And there they tied a true-lover's knot,
  Which made all people admire.

18

At last the clerk of the parish came,
As the truth doth well appear,
. And by misfortune he cut them down,
Or else they had now been here.

LXXI

Lord Ronald.

1

' O WHERE hae ye been, Lord Ronald, my son ?
O where hae ye been, my handsome young man ? '
' I hae been to the wood ; mother, make my bed
soon,
For I'm weary wi' hunting, and fain would lie
down.'

2

' Where gat ye your dinner, Lord Ronald, my son ?
Where gat ye your dinner, my handsome young
man ? '
' I dined wi' my love ; mother, make my bed soon,
For I'm weary wi' hunting, and fain would lie
down.'

3

' What gat ye to dinner, Lord Ronald, my son ?
What gat ye to dinner, my handsome young man ?
' I gat eels boil'd in broo ; mother, make my bed
soon,
For I'm weary wi' hunting, and fain would lie
down.'

A A

4

'And where are your bloodhounds, Lord Ronald,
    my son ?
And where are your bloodhounds, my handsome
    young man ?'
' O they swell'd and they died; mother, make my
    bed soon,
For I'm weary wi' hunting, and fain would lie
    down.'

5

' O I fear ye are poison'd, Lord Ronald, my son !
O I fear ye are poison'd, my handsome young
    man !'
' O yes, I am poison'd! mother, make my bed soon,
For I'm sick at the heart, and I fain would lie
    down.'

LXXII

Young John and his True Sweetheart.

I

A FAIR maid sat at her bower-door,
    Wringing her lily hands ;
And by it came a sprightly youth
    Fast tripping o'er the strands.

2

' Where gang ye, young John,' she says,
    ' Sae early in the day?
It gars me think, by your fast trip,
    Your journey's far away.'

' gars,' makes.

3

He turn'd about wi' an angry look,
 And said, 'What's that to thee?
I'm gaen' to see a lovely may
 That fairer far than ye.'

4

'Now hae you played me this, fause love,
 In simmer, mid the flow'rs?
I sall repay ye back again
 In winter, 'mid the show'rs.

5

'But again, dear love, and again, dear love,
 Will ye not turn again?
For as ye look to ither women
 Sall I to ither men.'

6

'O make your choice o' whom you please,
 For I my choice will have;
I've chosen a fairer may than thee,
 I never will deceive.'

7

She's kilted up her claithing fine,
 And after him gaed she;
But aye he said, 'Turn back, turn back,
 Nae further gang wi' me!'

8

'But again, dear love, and again, dear love,
 Will ye never love me again?
Alas for loving you sae weel,
 And you nae me again!'

9

The firstan town that they cam' till,
  He bought her brooch and ring ;
But aye he bade her turn again,
  And nae farther gang wi' him.

10

' But again, dear love, and again, dear love,
  Will ye never love me again ?
Alas ! for loving you sae weel,
  And you na me again ! '

11

The second town that they cam' till,
  His heart it grew mair fain ;
And he was as deep in love wi' her
  As she wi' him again.

12

The neistan town that they cam' till,
  He bought her wedding-gown ;
And made her lady o' ha's and bowers,
  In bonny Berwick town.

LXXIII

Helen of Kirkconnell.

I

I WISH I were where Helen lies ;
 Night and day on me she cries ;
O that I were where Helen lies,
  On fair Kirkconnell lea !

' neistan,' next.

2

Curst be the heart that thought the thought,
And curst the hand that fired the shot,
When in my arms burd Helen dropt,
    And died to succour me !

3

O think na ye my heart was sair
When my love dropt, and spak' nae mair !
There did she swoon wi' meikle care,
    On fair Kirkconnell lea.

4

And I went down the water side,
None but my foe to be my guide,
None but my foe to be my guide,
    On fair Kirkconnell lea.

5

I cross'd the stream, my sword did draw,
I hack'd him into pieces sma',
I hack'd him into pieces sma',
    For her sake that died for me.

6

O Helen fair, beyond compare !
I'll mak' a garland o' your hair,
Shall bind my heart for evermair,
    Until the day I dee !

7

O that I were where Helen lies !
Night and day on me she cries ;
Out of my bed she bids me rise,
    Says, 'Haste, and come to me !'

'burd' (bird), damsel, young lady.

8

O Helen fair!   O Helen chaste!
Were I with thee I would be blest,
Where thou liest low and tak'st thy rest,
   On fair Kirkconnell lea.

9

I wish my grave were growing green,
A winding-sheet drawn o'er my e'en,
And I in Helen's arms lying,
   On fair Kirkconnell lea.

10

I wish I were where Helen lies!
Night and day on me she cries,
And I am weary of the skies,
   For her sake that died for me.

LXXIV

Glasgerion.

1

GLASGERION was a harper gude,
   He harpit to the King ;
Glasgerion was the best harper
   That ever harp'd on string.

2

He'd harp a fish from the river,
   Or water out o' a stane ;
He harpit the heart frae a maiden's breast,
   To love but him alane.

3

He's ta'en his harp intil his hand ;
  He harpit and he sang ;
And aye he harpit to the King,
  Wha never thought it lang.

4

' I'll gie you a robe, Glasgerion,
  A robe of the royal pa',
Gin ye will harp i' the winter's night
  Afore my nobles a'. '

5

The King but and his nobles a'
  Sat birling at the wine ;
And he wad hae nane but his ae daughter
  To wait on them at dine.

6

Glasgerion's ta'en his harp in hand,
  Till he's harpit them a' asleep ;
A' except the young Princess,
  Whom love did waking keep.

7

And first he has harpit a grave tune,
  And syne he has harpit a gay ;
And mony's the sigh and the loving word
  That pass'd atween them twae.

8

' Come to my bower, Glasgerion,
  When all men are at rest ;
As I am a lady true of word
  Thou shalt be a welcome guest.'

'pa',' pall, rich cloth.   ' birling,' drinking festively.

9

Home then came Glasgerion ;
  A glad man, lord ! was he :
' And come thou hither, Jack, my boy,
  Come hither unto me.'

10

' For the King's daughter,' Glasgerion said,
  Hath granted me my boon :
And at her bower-door I must be,
  By the setting of the moon.'

11

' Lie down in your bed, dear master,
  And sleep as sound as you may ;
I'll keep gude watch, and I'll waken you
  Afore it be time to gae.'

12

But up he rose, that lither lad,
  His master's clothes did on ;
A collar he cast upon his neck,
  He seem'd a gentleman.

13

And when he came to the lady's bower
  He tirlit at the pin :
The lady she was true of her word,
  She rose and let him in.

14

He did not kiss that lady's mouth,
  Nor when he came nor yode ;
And sore that lady did mistrust
  He was but of churl's blood.

'lither,' lazy, dissolute, deceitful (slippery ?).   'tirlit at the
pin,' lightly rattled the latch.   'yode,' went.

15

Home then came that lither lad,
  Did off baith cloak and shoon,
And cast the collar from off his neck :
  He was but a churl's son.

16

'Won up, won up, good master !
  For I fear it is day-dawn,
And there's nae a cock in a' the land
  But has wappit its wings and crawn.'

17

Then quickly rose Glasgerion,
  Did on his hosen and shoon,
And cast a collar about his neck ;
  For he was a lord's own son.

18

And when he came to the lady's bower,
  He tirlit at the pin :
The lady was more than true of her word,
  She rose and let him in.

19

'O whether now have you left with me
  Your bracelet or your glove ?
Or are you returnèd back again
  To know more of my love ?'

20

Glasgerion swore a full great oath,
  By oak and ash and thorn,
'I was never before in your chamber, lady,
  Sith the day that I was born.'

'wappit,' flapped.   'crawn,' crow'd.

21

' O then it was your lither foot page ;
    He hath beguilèd me :'
Then she pull'd forth a little sharp knife
    That hang down by her knee.

22

O'er her white feet the red blood ran
    Or ever a hand could stay ;
And dead she lieth on her bower-floor,
    At the dawning o' the day.

23

Home then he runs, Glasgerion,
    And woe, good lord ! was he :
Says, ' Come thou hither, Jack my boy,
    Come hither unto me.'

24

' If I had taken a life to-night,
    Jack, I would tell it to thee ;
But if I have taken no life to-night,
    Jack, thou hast taken three.'

25

And he pullèd out his bright brown sword,
    And drièd it on his sleeve,
And there smote off that lither lad's head,
    Who did his lady grieve.

26

He set the sword's point to his breast,
    The pummil to a stone :
Through the falseness of that lither lad,
    These three lives were all gone.

LXXV

The Gardener.

I

THE gard'ner stands in his bower door,
　Wi' a primrose in his hand, ·
And by there cam' a maiden,
　As jimp as a willow wand.

2

' O lady can ye fancy me,
　For to be my bride?
Ye'se get a' the flowers in my garden,
　To be to you a weed.

3

' The lily white sall be your smock;
　It becomes your bodie best;
Your head sall be buskt wi' gilly-flower,
　Wi' the primrose in your breast.

4

' Your goun sall be the sweet-william;
　Your coat the camovine;
Your apron o' the sallads neat,
　That taste baith sweet and fine.

5

' Your hose sall be the brade kail-blade,
　That is baith brade and lang;
Narrow, narrow, at the cute,
　And brade, brade at the brawn.

'jimp,' slender.　　'weed,' dress.　　' camovine,' camomile.
　　　'cute,' ancle.　　'brawn,' calf.

6

' Your gloves sall be the marigold,
　All glittering to your hand,
Weel spread owre wi' the blue blaewort,
　That grows amang corn-land.'

7

' O fare ye weil, young man,' she says,
　' Fareweil, and I bid adieu ;
If you can fancy me,' she says,
　' I cannot fancy you.

8

' Sin ye ve provided a weed for me
　Among the simmer flowers,
It's I'se provide anither for you,
　Amang the winter-showers :

9

' The new fawn snaw to be your smock ;
　It becomes your bodie best ;
Your head sall be wrapt wi' the eastern wind,
　And the cauld rain on your breast.'

LXXVI

Tamlane.

I

O, I forbid ye, maidens a',
　Who are sae sweet and fair,
To come or gae by Carterhaugh,
　For young Tamlane is there.

2

Fair Janet sat within her bower,
　Sewing her silken seam,
And wished to be in Carterhaugh,
　Amang the leaves sae green.

3

She let the seam fa' to her foot.
   The needle to her tae,
And she's awa' to Carterhaugh,
   As quickly as she may.

4

She hadna' pu'd a wild-flower,
   A flower but barely three,
When up he started, young Tamlane,
   Says ' Lady, let a-be !

5

' What gars ye pu' the flowers, Janet ?
   What gars ye break the tree ?
Or why come ye to Carterhaugh,
   Without the leave o' me ? '

6

' O I will pu' the flowers,' she says,
   ' And I will break the tree,
And I will come to Carterhaugh,
   And ask nae leave o' thee.'

7

But when she came to her father's ha',
   She looked sae wan and pale
They thought the lady had gotten a fright
   Or with sickness sair did ail.

8

She dinna comb her yellow hair
   Or mak' mickle o' her head ;
And ilka thing that lady took
   Was like to bring her deid.

' tae,' toe.   ' mak' mickle,' make much of.   ' deid,' death.

9

It's four-and-twenty ladies
  Were playing at the ba' ;
Janet, that wightest wont to be,
  Was faintest o' them a'.

10

Out and spak an auld grey knight,
  Lay o'er the castle wa',—
'Ever alas for thee, Janet !
  And we'll be blamèd a'.'

11

'Now haud your tongue!' fair Janet she says,
  'Or an ill deid may you dee !
Father my bairn on whom I will,
  It bringeth nae blame to thee.

12

'O gin my Love were an earthly knight,
  As he is an elfin gay,
I wadna gie my ain true Love
  For ony lord that we hae !'

13

She prink'd hersell and preen'd hersell
  By the ae light o' the moon,
And she's awa to Carterhaugh,
  To speak wi' young Tamlane.

14

No sooner had she pu'd a leaf,
  A leaf but only twae,
When up he started, young Tamlane,
  Says, 'Lady, thou pu's nae mae !'

'wightest,' nimblest.   'dee,' die.   'prink'd hersell and preen'd
   hersell,' deck'd herself and pinn'd herself.   'ae,' only.

15

' O tell me truth, Tamlane!' she says,
　'A word ye mauna lee ;
Were ever ye in a holy chapel,
　Or sain'd in Christentee ?'

16

' The truth I'll tell to thee, Janet,
　A word I winna lee ;
I am a knight's and a lady's son,
　And was sain'd as well as thee.

17

' But once it fell upon a day,
　As hunting I did ride,
As I rade east and o'er yon hill,
　Strange chance did me betide.

18

' There blew a drowsy, drowsy wind,
　Dead sleep upon me fell,
The Queen of Fairies she was there
　And took me to hersell.

19

'And never would I tire, Janet,
　In fairy-land to dwell ;
But aye at every seven years
　They pay the teind to hell ;
And though the Queen mak's much o' me,
　I fear 'twill be mysell.

20

' To-morrow night it's Hallowe'en,
　Our fairy court will ride,

'lee,' lie.　　'sain'd,' sanctified, baptized.　　'Hallowe'en,'
　　　　eve of Allhallows.　　'teind,' tithe.

Through England and through Scotland baith,
   And through the world sae wide ;
And if that ye wad borrow me,
   At Miles Cross ye maun bide.

21

' Ye'll gae into the Miles Moss
   Atween twelve hours and one ;
Tak' holy water in your hand,
   And cast a compass roun'.'

22

' But how shall I ken thee, Tamlane,
   Or how shall I thee knaw,
Amang sae mony unearthly knights,
   The like I never saw ?'

23

' The first court that comes along
   Ye'll let them a' pass by ;
The second court that comes along
   Salute them reverently.

24

' The third court that comes along
   Is clad in robes o' green,
And it's the head court o' them a',
   And in it rides the Queen ;

25

' And I upon a milk-white steed
   Wi' a bright star in my crown ;
Because I am a christen'd knight
   They gave me that renown.

borrow,' ransom   'cast a compass,' draw a circle.

26

' My right hand will be gloved, Janet,
  My left hand will be bare ; .
And when ye see these tokens
  Ye'll ken that I am there.

27

' Ye'll seize upon me at a spring,
  And to the ground I'll fa',
And then ye'll hear a ruefu' cry
  That Tamlane he's awa.

28

' They'll turn me cauld in your arms, Janet,
  As ice on a frozen lake ;
But haud me fast, let me not pass,
  Gin ye would be my maik.

29

' They'll turn me in your arms, Janet,
  An adder and an aske ;
They'll turn me in your arms, Janet,
  A bayle that burns fast ;

30

They'll shape me in your arms, Janet,
  A dove, but and a swan ;
And at last they'll shape me in your arms
  A mother-naked man :
Cast your green mantle over me,
  And sae sall I be wan.'

'maik,' mate.   'aske,' a kind of lizard.   'bayle,'
        a large fire.   'wan,' won.

B B

31

The very next night unto Miles Moss
    Fair Janet she is gone,
And she stands beside the Miles Cross
    Atween twelve hours and one.

32

There's holy water in her hand,
    She casts a compass round ;
And soon she saw a fairy band
    Come riding o'er the mound.

33

And first gaed by the black, black steed,
    And then gaed by the brown ;
But fast she gript the milk-white steed .
    And pu'd the rider down.

34

She pu'd him frae the milk-white steed,
    And loot the bridle fa' ;
And up there rase an eldritch cry,
    ' He's won amang us a' ! '

35

They turned him in fair Janet's arms
    Like ice on frozen lake ;
They turn'd him into a burning fire,
    An adder, and a snake.

36

They shaped him in her arms at last
    A mother-naked man ;
She cuist her mantle over him,
    And sae her true-love wan.

       ' eldritch,' elvish.   ' cuist,' cast.

37

Up then and spak' the Queen o' Fairies,
  Out o' a bush o' broom,
' She that has borrow'd young Tamlane,
  Has gotten a stately groom ! '

38

Up then and spak' the Queen o' Fairies,
  Out o' a bush o' rye,
' She's ta'en awa the bonniest knight
  In a' my companie !

39

' But had I kenn'd, Tamlane,' she says,
  ' A lady wad borrow'd thee,
I wad ta'en out thy twa grey e'en,
  Put in twa e'en o' tree.

40

' Had I but kenn'd, Tamlane,' she says,
  ' Before we cam' frae hame,
I wad ta'en out your heart o' flesh,
  Put in a heart of stane.

41

' Had I but had the wit yestreen
  That I have coft this day,
I'd paid my teind seven times to hell
  Ere you'd been won away ! '

'tree,' wood.   'coft,' bought.   'teind,' tithe.

NOTES.

I. THOMAS THE RHYMER.—Thomas Learmont, of Erceldowne (a
village on the river Leader, two miles above its junction with
the Tweed), was a Scottish gentleman who lived in the thir-
teenth century;[1] and to him, commonly called 'Thomas the
Rhymer,' and sometimes 'True Thomas,' many poems and
'prophecies' in circulation among the common people were
attributed. The ruins of an ancient tower are still pointed out
as his; and therein it seems, sometime in the last century,
one Murray, a quack-doctor of the humbler sort, attempted
for a while to revive the business of Wizard.[2] A rhymer no
doubt was Thomas in his day, but nothing that now survives
is really traceable to his hand. He was carried off into Fairy-
Land, said the storytellers, and came back with gift of pro-
phecy; and on this peg various ballads and 'prophecies' were
hung. There is a defective MS. of perhaps the fourteenth
century in the Cathedral Library of Lincoln containing parts
of a poem on Thomas of Erceldowne, and parts of the same
poem exist in two other defective MSS., one in the University
Library, Cambridge, and one in the British Museum.[3] It is
an old form of the story how Thomas met the Queen of
Elfland, and has much beauty; but the ballad given in *Border
Minstrelsy*, as mainly from oral tradition, is more simple
and suitable to our purpose. With Sir Walter's 'altered'
second and 'modern' third parts, in continuation of the same,
we have no business. He has placed the three parts together
in the volume of 'Imitations.'

II. THE TWA CORBIES.—Scott's *Border Minstrelsy*; from Mr. C. K.
Sharpe, 'as written down, from tradition, by a lady.' It
much resembles 'The Three Ravens,' given by Ritson in
Ancient Songs, from *Melismata*, London, 1611; a ballad,
says Ritson, 'much older, not only than the date of the book,
but than most of the other pieces contained in it.'

III. HYND HORN.—('Hynd,' courteous, gentle.) Cromek's *Select
Scottish Songs*: Kinloch: Buchan: Motherwell. A popular
ballad-abridgment of an ancient metrical romance which is
preserved in Harleian MS. 2253, British Museum, written
apparently (thinks Ritson) in the reign of Edward II., and

---

[1] Deed or charter by Thomas's son, dated in 1299; in Advocates'
Library, Edinburgh; given by Scott in *Border Minstrelsy*.
[2] Scott.
[3] Laing, *Select Remains of Ancient Popular Poetry of Scotland*,
as quoted by Prof. Child.

POEM

which itself is a translation and abridgment of a French original. This romance, 'The Geste of King Horn,' is given in Ritson's *Ancient English Metrical Romances*, ii. 91.

IV. THE BANKS O' YARROW.—Of this ballad, said to be popular in Ettrick Forest, there are many various versions; it is supposed to be founded on fact, but, in searching for the fact, one finds only loose and contradictory traditions—nothing at all worth attending to.

The river Yarrow, much famed in song, runs through a wide vale in Selkirkshire between lofty green hills, and joins the Tweed above the town of Selkirk.

'*The Tennies*' is a farm below the Yarrow Kirk.

V. EARL MAR'S DAUGHTER.—From Buchan, with some verbal alterations. The version, like most of Buchan's, is by him presented in the form given by the reciter; but that form is very evidently vulgarised. For example, take such a line as this:—

'Your lovely face did me enchant,'

or the last stanza in his copy (omitted by us on the demerits):

'When that Earl Mar he came to know
  Where his dochter did stay,
He signed a bond o' unity,
  And visits now they pay.'

Our version, keeping unchanged every incident and turn of thought, is, in form, *essentially* much more a true old ballad than Buchan's.

VI. BROWN ADAM.—*Border Minstrelsy*. 'There is a copy of this ballad in Mrs. Brown's collection. The editor has seen one printed on a single sheet. The epithet, "Smith" implies, probably, the sirname, not the profession, of the hero, who seems to be an outlaw. There is, however, in Mrs. Brown's copy a verse of little merit here omitted, alluding to the implements of that occupation.'—*Scott*.

VII. EDOM O' GORDON.—Printed by Foulis, Glasgow, 1755, as taken down by Sir. D. Dalrymple 'from the recitation of a lady;' in Percy's *Reliques*, 'interpolated and corrupted,' says Ritson. Ritson gave a copy, from a collection in the Cotton Library, in his *Ancient Songs*; a version called 'Loudoun Castle' is given in *The Ballads and Songs of Ayrshire* (First Series).

This ballad refers, but with the inexactness usual in ballads, to an event of 1571, when Adam Gordon, Deputy-Lieutenant of the North of Scotland for Queen Mary, sent Captain Carr or Ker with a party of men to seize Towie, a mansion of the Forbes family. Forbes was not at home, and his lady refused to open the gates, taunting Carr from her walls, who at last set the house on fire and burned all the inmates, thirty-seven in number. Some versions name Captain Carr as guilty of the cruel deed; but others Adam or Edom of Gordon, who sent him; and the latter name has settled into this ballad. Other names of places and persons mentioned differ in the different versions.

POEM

VIII. YOUNG WATERS.—Given by Percy 'from a copy printed not long since at Glasgow, in one sheet 8vo. The world was in-debted for its publication to the Lady Jean Hume, sister to the Earl of Hume' [very vague !]. Buchan has a much longer, but a weak and vulgar version. The ballad has been supposed to allude to the fate of the Earl of Murray, murdered by the Earl of Huntley, 1592, under prompting (as people said) of the jealous king. There is, at most, a resemblance in the *motive.*

IX. THE WIFE OF USHER'S WELL.—*Border Minstrelsy.* Two verses, 'Lie still,' &c., and 'O it's they've ta'en up,' &c., are from Mr. R. Chambers's version, recovered from recitation—one 'Our mother has nae mair,' has been added to complete the sense, and 'fish be in the flood,' &c., put instead of 'fishes in the flood'—Scott's, which he notes as obscure and probably corrupted by reciters. Mr. Aytoun has 'freshes in the flood'; Mr. Lockhart suggested 'fashes,' i. e. troubles. This ballad is by some thought to be a fragment of a longer one, 'The Clerk's Twa Sons o' Owsenford'; but the part is much better than the whole (an acknowledged *composite*) as given by Mr Chambers. 'Martinmas,' feast of St. Martin, November 11, the customary time to kill winter beef and pork, and a season of rustic jollity.
'Mantle.'—A peasant woman's mantle lasted many years, and was a kind of homely-sacred object to the children of a family.

X. THE DEATH OF PARCY REED.—First published in the *Local Historian's Table-Book*, by Mr. Robert White, from the chanting of an old woman. Percival or Parcy Reed, proprietor of Troughend, in Redesdale, Northumberland, having brought to justice certain moss-trooping relatives or allies of the Croziers, was by these Croziers set upon and murdered, with connivance of the Halls of Girsonsfield, a farm near Troughend. The ballad (which, with some awkwardness, is a simple and effec-tive narrative of the realistic kind) is said to keep close to facts; date and authorities not given.

XI. WALY, WALY.—First published in Allan Ramsay's *Tea Table Miscellany*, in 1724, and marked 'Z,' as an Old Song. Some have dated it about the middle of the sixteenth century. Part of it (by Mr. Chambers all of it) has been pieced into a later ballad on the Marchioness of Douglass, married 1670 and deserted by her husband.

XII. THE LAIRD O' DRUM.—Kinloch: Buchan: Percy, Society, vol. xvii. Professor Aytoun gives a version from collation, which we have taken the liberty to follow, except a line or two. Alexander Irvine of Drum (one of Charles I.'s Scottish ad-herents) married, in 1643, Mary, daughter of the Marquis of Huntly; but for his second wife chose Margaret Coutts, a girl of humble rank, thus offending his family,—but not the public, for whom this ballad was made. The love of an untitled youth for a noble maiden is a usual source of interest in German novels, and so is a courtship between persons of very unequal rank in our ballad literature. Many of the current Irish ballads turn upon this; for example, 'The Bonny Labouring Boy,' 'Willy Reilly,' 'Willy of Lough-Erne Shore.'

XIII. ANNAN WATER.—*Minstrelsy of the Scottish Border*, 'from tradition.' It is said that a bridge was built over the Annan after the drowning which the ballad narrates.

XIV. THE HUNTING OF THE CHEVIOT.—This ballad (of Henry VIII.'s time?) is here presented in modern spelling. Hearne printed it in the preface to his *Gulielmus Neubrigensis*, from an MS. in the Ashmolean collection at Oxford. It has no ascertained historical basis whatever; some of the incidents and verses are borrowed from the ballads on 'The Battle of Otterbourne,' relating to an encounter between Percy and Douglas in the year 1388. The better known but inferior ballad of 'Chevy Chace,' is a modernised version of this, done probably in the time of James I.

XV. BESSIE BELL AND MARY GRAY.—Recovered by Mr. Sharpe, says Mr. Chambers. Given in Lyle's *Ancient Ballads and Songs* (1827), as collated 'from the singing of two aged persons.' Bessie Bell and Mary Gray, daughters of two country gentlemen near Perth were intimate friends. Bessie being on a visit to Mary at her father's house of Lynedoch when the plague of 1666 broke out, the two girls, to avoid contagion, went to live in a bower, or summer-house of some kind, in a retired and picturesque place called the Burn-braes, about a mile west of Lynedoch House. But the plague found and slew them, and their bodies were buried at Dornoch Haugh, a secluded spot by the river Almond. (Pennant's Tour.) Allan Ramsay wrote a song with the same title, and using the first verse of this ballad.

XVI. SIR PATRICK SPENS.—Percy: Scott: Jamieson: Buchan: Motherwell. A ballad, the subject of much discussion, into which for once we may dip a little, as a specimen of such debates and what they come to. It is 'very old, but evidently retouched,' say some; refers to an ineffectual expedition, Sir Walter Scott guesses, that *may have been* sent for Margaret, called the Maid of Norway (daughter of Eric King of Norway and Margaret daughter of Alexander III. of Scotland), after the death of her grandfather Alexander in 1285, which made her Queen of Scotland: but she remained in Norway, and in a short time died there. Mr. Finlay thinks it more likely to have to do with James the Third's marriage with Margaret daughter of the King of Denmark. 'No memorial of the subject of the ballad exists in history,' says Ritson. Mr. Motherwell has no doubt whatever, that 'the ballad is founded on authentic history,' and sings the fate of certain Scottish nobles who accompanied Margaret, daughter of Alexander III., to her nuptials with Eric, King of Norway, and were drowned on their homeward voyage, *teste* Fordun's History of Scotland. Mr. Robert Chambers in his collection of Scottish Ballads published 1829 says 'the occasion of the ballad is now known to have been' &c., (as Motherwell says)—and 'thinks it extremely probable that Sir Patrick Spens lived near the little

POEM

port of Aberdour,' &c. But in 1859 (*Essay on the Romantic Scottish Ballads*) Mr. Chambers 'feels assured that *Sir Patrick* is a modern ballad, and suspects or more than suspects that the author is Lady Wardlaw.' Percy's version ('from two manuscript copies transmitted from Scotland') says not a word of Norway, or of any king's daughter: Scott's (made up from two MS. copies, collated with several verses recited by a friend) has—

> 'The King's daughter of Noroway,
> 'Tis thou maun bring her hame.'

Professor Aytoun alters these two lines into—

> 'The King's daughter to Noroway,
> It's thou maun tak' her hame'—

which Mr. Chambers calls 'unjustifiable' conduct. Buchan's version (taken down from the recitation of a blind wandering minstrel in the North of Scotland, who learned it in his youth from a very old person) has—

> 'To Noroway wi' our King's daughter,
> A chosen queen she's now.'

There is no old MS. of the ballad. All the 'foundation' which really seems attainable is this, that in old times there was much intercourse between Scotland and Norway, and between the royal courts of the two countries, and that some shipwreck, not altogether unlike this, may probably have happened. In fine, let not our readers trouble themselves about the connection of this, or any other of these ballads, with 'authentic history,' and they will be gainers in comfort, and no losers otherwise. At Dunfermline, on the north side of the Firth of Forth, was a palace of the Scottish Kings. Aberdour is a little port, about five miles distant. There is an extremely fine tract of hard white sand (says Mr. Chambers) to the east of Aberdour.

XVII. KING JOHN AND THE ABBOT.—From Percy's *Reliques*: there marked with '*‚*', the sign of 'considerable liberties' taken by the editor. 'The common popular ballad (says he) of *King John and the Abbot* seems to have been abridged and modernised about the time of James I. from one much older, entitled *King John and the Bishop of Canterbury.* The Editor's folio MS. contains a copy of this last, but in too corrupt a state to be reprinted; it, however, afforded many lines worth reviving, which will be found inserted in the ensuing stanzas.'

XVIII. THE DOUGLAS TRAGEDY.—*Border Minstrelsy.* Motherwell gives an imperfect version. Scott says this ballad 'is one of the few to which popular tradition has ascribed complete locality. The farm of Blackhouse, in Selkirkshire, is said to have been the scene.' He does not attempt to give a date. There are very similar Swedish and Danish ballads.

XIX. KEMPION.—*Border Minstrelsy* 'chiefly from Mrs. Brown's MS., with corrections from a recited fragment.' The ballad of 'Kemp Owain' ('Champion Owen' perhaps) given by Buchan and by Motherwell, tells the same story, with differences of

POEM

. detail. 'The Laidly Worm of Spindlestonheugh,' often printed in ballad-books, is a partly modern version of the same. The subject is a favourite one in popular fiction.

XX. JOHNNIE OF BRAIDISLEE.—'Johnny of Breadislee,' in *Border Minstrelsy*: 'Johnie of Braidisbank,' in Motherwell's *Minstrelsy*: 'Johnny Cock' (two versions) in Fry's *Pieces of Ancient Poetry*, Bristol, 1814: 'Johnie of Cocklesmuir' (North of Scotland version) in Kinloch's *Ancient Scottish Ballads*: also in Buchan's *Scottish Traditional versions of Ancient Ballads*, Percy Society, vol. xvii. These are various versions of one story. We have compared and selected, but added nothing. Scott, whose version was first published, says 'the hero of this ballad appears to have been an outlaw and deerstealer—probably one of the broken men residing upon the Border. There are several different copies, in one of which the principal personage is called "Johnie of Cockie-law." The stanzas of greatest merit have been selected from each copy.' This is what we also have endeavoured to do, with the advantage of additional copies to select from.

XXI. THE BIRTH OF ROBIN HOOD.—Jamieson, from the recitation of Mrs. Brown, 'without the alteration of a single word.' It is not one of *the* 'Robin Hood Ballads,' as printed in the *Garlands*, and collected by Ritson. Buchan gives a queer version,—

'What aileth my love Clementina?' &c. &c.

XXII. FAIR ANNIE.—Herd: Scott: Jamieson: Motherwell: Chambers. The story of 'Fair Annie,' of which we have in print several different Scottish versions, is found in old French, in Swedish, in Danish, in Dutch, in German.

XXIII. CHILDE MAURICE.—Of this ballad, before it appeared in Percy's *Reliques*, two editions are known to have been printed in Scotland under the title of 'Gil Morice.' An advertisement to the second edition (Glasgow, 1755) states that 'its preservation was owing to a lady who favoured the printers with a copy, as it was carefully collected from the mouths of old women and nurses,' and 'any reader who can render them more complete' is requested to make public his information. On this, four other stanzas were forthcoming, which Percy inserted when he published the ballad in his *Reliques*, though, 'perhaps, after all, only an ingenious interpolation:' they began thus:

'His hair was like the threeds of gold
Drawne frae Minerva's loome' (!).

But besides this particular piece of ingenuity, and other very evident though unacknowledged patches, this Ballad, according to Scott (see Motherwell's *Minstrelsy*, p. 259), had undergone '*a total revisal*, about the period when the tragedy of 'Douglas' [founded thereon] was in the zenith of its popularity:' that is, before Percy took it in hand. The Bishop had found in that mysterious Folio MS., in whose existence Ritson was so slow to believe, 'a very old imperfect copy of the same ballad;' but greatly prefers the modern version:

POEM

'the colouring is much improved and heightened, and many additional strokes are thrown in.'

In 1806, Jamieson printed from the Folio MS. the ballad of 'Childe Maurice.' A few lines, perhaps half a dozen, are wanting, but the story is complete. There seems to be little or no doubt that the name 'Gil Morice' itself is a modern corruption. A version was recited to Mr. Motherwell, about the year 1825, by an old woman who gave the name of 'Chield Morice,' and said she recollected when the new set of the ballad under the title of 'Gil Morice' began to supersede the old form. Mr. Motherwell also got a version of the ballad, in 1825, from the recitation of Widow McCormack, of Paisley, under the title of 'Child Norice.' This version, which is brief, and has several good points, he considers as the true original of all the others, and that 'Child Norice' (i.e. Nurseling) is the right form of the name. This, however, remains unproven, and if we go by internal evidence, the version in the Folio MS. is certainly the oldest we have. In it the slayer of 'Child Maurice' is named John Steward.

For our version we have collated (adding nothing) the Folio version and the sets of Motherwell's two old women; disregarding the thoroughly corrupt version of the *Reliques.*

XXIV. BROWN ROBYN'S CONFESSION.—This curious ballad-version of a Catholic miracle is from Buchan, i. 110, who does not say where he found it.

XXV. THE YOUNG GOSHAWK.—Mainly from Motherwell. Scott's 'selected' version ('The Gray Goss-Hawk') is much sophisticated. Buchan has a version entitled, 'The Scottish Squire.'

XXVI. ALISON GROSS.—Jamieson, 'from the recitation of Mrs. Brown.'

XXVII. OF 'JOHNNY ARMSTRONG,' the best version is in *Wit Restor'd* (1658); another, with additional stanzas, is in *A Collection of Old Ballads* (London, 1723); another, being a Scottish version, and very different from these, in Ramsay's *Evergreen* (1724). This Ballad no doubt gives one a true notion, as far as it goes, of the times of Border freebooting; but while making use of a real name and event, it has not the least claim to historic accuracy. King James V. of Scotland (he who 'made the rush-bush keep the cow'), being on an expedition through Ettrick and elsewhere against the Borderers, perhaps in 1529, was boldly accosted by the famous freebooter John Armstrong, at the head of some thirty or forty horsemen, who asked pardon and offered his services; but the king had them all seized and 'hanged upon growing trees' at Carlenrig, ten miles from Hawick. 'The bodies were buried in a deserted churchyard, where their graves are still shown.' [Pitscottie's *History*, p. 145. Scott's *Border Minstrelsy*, i. 402.]

XXVIII. KATHARINE JANFARIE.—Scott's *Border Minstrelsy*: Motherwell ('Catharine Johnstone): Maidment's *North Countrie Garland*: Buchan's *Gleanings.* In Scott's version the English bridegroom is named 'Lord Lochinvar;' and Scott

POEM

founded his lyric of *Lochinvar* on this ballad, but gave that name to the unsuccessful suitor.

Young Child Dying, translated by Jamieson in *Illustrations of Northern Antiquities*, is an old Danish ballad on the same story.

XXIX. ROBIN HOOD RESCUING THE WIDOW'S THREE SONS.—In Ritson's *Robin Hood*, from *Robin Hood's Garland* (earliest edition known, 1670); probably 'one of the oldest' ballads of Robin Hood, thinks Ritson.

XXX. FAIR ANNIE OF LOCHROYAN.—Herd: a fragment in Johnson's *Museum*: Scott's *Border Minstrelsy*, 'selected' from five versions: Jamieson, from MS. transmitted from Aberdeen by Professor Robert Scott: Buchan ('Love Gregory').

Lochroyan or Loch Ryan, a bay on the south-west coast of Scotland, holding the seaport of Stranraer.

XXXI. A LYKEWAKE DIRGE.—This *Lyke-Wake* [i. e. Dead-Watch] *Dirge* is of the North of England, and is said to have been sung, in Yorkshire, over corpses, down to about 1624 (see Brand's 'Pop. Antiq.' 1841, ii. 155). Scott, publishing it in his *Border Minstrelsy*, noted 'The late Mr. Ritson found an illustration of this dirge in a MS. of the Cotton Library, containing an account of Cleveland, in Yorkshire, in the reign of Queen Elizabeth. . . . . "When any dieth, certaine women sing a song to the dead bodie, recyting the jorney that the partye deceased must goe; and they are of beliefe (such is their fondnesse) that, once in their lives, it is good to give a pair of new shoes to a poor man, forasmuch as, after this life, they are to pass barefoote through a great launde, full of thornies and furzen, except by the meryte of the almes aforesaid they have redeemed the forfeyte; for at the edge of the launde, an oulde man shall meet them with the same shoes that were given by the partye when he was lyving; and, after he hath shodde them, dismisseth them to go through thick and thin, without scratch or scalle."—*Julius*, F. vi. 459.'

'The *Bridge of Dread*, lying in our road when we pass from this world, is described,' says Sir Walter, 'in the legend of *Sir Owain*, No. xl. in the MS. collection of Romances, W. xli. Advocates' Library, Edinburgh.' The Orientals have a similar fancy, of a narrow bridge over an abyss.

In the *Border Minstrelsy*, it is noted that *sleet* seems to be corrupted from *selt*, i. e. salt, which it was customary to lay in a platter on the breast of the corpse. In Brand we have *fleet*, but the whole version there seems inferior. The sixth and seventh verses of the dirge (if no more) are lost.

XXXII. ETIN THE FORESTER.—A fragment of it is given by Kinloch ('Hynde Etin'); by Buchan a complete version ('Young Akin'), and, by the same (through Motherwell), a modernised copy. There is a similar Swedish ballad. 'Etin' seems to mean, or be a name for, a Giant, and in some forms of the story the hero is obscurely spoken of as a supernatural or preternatural being. This character, however, was not kept up by the reciters, and at last slipped away from the ballad, which is consistent and com-

POEM

plete as a purely human story; Etin being taken (if not as a mere name) as designating a man living a wild sylvan life.

XXXIII. THE LOWLANDS O' HOLLAND.—A fragment of it in Herd (1769): a version in Johnson's *Musical Museum.* 'This ballad, the Editor is informed, was composed about the beginning of last century by a young widow in Galloway, whose husband was drowned on a voyage to Holland. The third verse in the *Museum* is spurious nonsense, and Johnson has omitted the last stanza altogether.'—Mr. Stenhouse, Notes to *Musical Museum* (1853), iv. 115. It is probably an old strain readapted.

XXXIV. THE TWA SISTERS O' BINNORIE.—A short burlesque version, 'The Miller and the King's Daughter,' in *Wit Restor'd* (1658): a manufactured version in Pinkerton's *Tragic Ballads*: another manufactured version in *Border Minstrelsy*, 'compiled,' says Scott, 'from a copy in Mrs. Brown's MSS.,' intermixed with a beautiful fragment, of fourteen verses, transmitted to the Editor by J. C. Walker, Esq., the ingenious historian of the Irish Bards,' who had it from Miss Brook, who had it from an old woman. Jamieson gives a version, *verbatim* from the recitation of Mrs. Brown, but with no less than ten interpolated stanzas of his own.

In Mrs. Brown's copy the burden ran:

> 'Edinborough, Edinborough—
> Stirling for aye ;⁓
> Bonny St. Johnston stands upon Tay :'

in the Irish fragment thus :

> 'Hey ho, my Nanny, O ;
> While the swans swim bonny, O.'

Both Scott and Jamieson adopted the 'Binnorie' burden, without saying distinctly where it came from. On the pronunciation of this word the doctors differ ; 'it may be necessary, *euphoniæ gratiâ*,' says Jamieson, 'to caution the English reader that the burden is pronounced Binnôrie.' 'Pronounced Binnôrie,' says Mr. Lockhart curtly, in a note in *Border Minstrelsy*, and is backed by Professor Aytoun. There are Scandinavian ballads with a similar story.

XXXV. GLENLOGIE.—Smith's *Scottish Minstrel*; a book in which, according to Motherwell, 'great liberties' are taken with the songs. Mr. Sharpe, in his *Ballad Book*, gives another version, which is preferred by Mr. Chambers and by Professor Aytoun.

XXXVI. THE CHILDREN IN THE WOOD.—Perhaps the best ballad in the *pedestrian* style. Reprinted by Percy 'from two ancient copies, one of them in blackletter, in the Pepys Collection.' The ballad was entered on the Stationers' books in 1595. A play by Robert Yarrington, published 1601, has a very similar plot ; the scene laid in Padua.

XXXVII. YOUNG BEICHAN.—Jamieson: Kinloch: Percy Society, vol. xvii ; &c. This very popular ballad, of which there are numerous versions (including the modern one of *Lord Bateman*), seems founded on an adventure of Gilbert Becket, father

POEM

of the famous archbishop; see Robert of Gloucester's *Life and Martyrdom of Thomas Beket* (Percy Society, vol. xix.). The fair foreigner on reaching London could speak no intelligible word but her lover's name, and constantly asking for 'Gilbert! Gilbert,' she at last found him out.

Our version is mostly from Jamieson, omitting his acknowledged interpolations. He gives a second and inferior ballad, 'Young Bekie,' on the same subject. Kinloch has a version which seems to have been recast by some vulgar modern hand, but it gives the story clearly, and has supplied us with some verses. We have added none.

XXXVIII. CLERK SAUNDERS.—*Border Minstrelsy*,—'From Mr. Herd's MSS., with several corrections from a shorter and more imperfect copy in the same volume, and one or two conjectural emendations in the arrangement of the stanzas.' Other versions in Jamieson (with additions by him): Kinloch: Buchan. *Clerk* Saunders was so-called, probably, for his learning; one version describes him as 'well-learned at the school.' 'Crystal wand' needs explanation or emendation.[1] Some think the verses from 'The clinking bell' to the end to be separate and distinct from those which precede them, and that Scott adapted and combined the two into one story. But, though several other ballads have a very similar conclusion, we find no proof that 'Clerk Saunders' is not as well entitled to it as any of the rest, and it would certainly take very strong proof to induce us to break in pieces so complete and impressive a poem. Jamieson's version, 'transmitted by Mrs. Arrott, of Aberbrothick,' has the ghost:

'She was lookin' o'er her castle high,
To see what she might fa';
And there she saw a grieved ghost
Comin' wauking o'er the wa',' &c.

and Margaret follows it to the grave.

XXXIX. THE BAILIFF'S DAUGHTER OF ISLINGTON.—Percy's *Reliques*, 'from an ancient blackletter copy in the Pepys collection, with some improvements communicated by a lady as she had heard the same recited in her youth.'

XL. A LYTELL GESTE OF ROBYN HOOD. See *Preface*.

XLI. BONNIE GEORGE CAMPBELL.—*The Scottish Minstrel* (1820-24), vol. v., words and music. For rhyme's sake we have altered the sixth line of each stanza. They ran thus:—

I. 'And gallant rade he;'
II. 'And booted rade he;'
III. 'And booted rade he;'

XLII. LORD THOMAS AND FAIR ELLINOR.—In *Collection of Old Ballads*, London, 1723, vol. i. In Percy's *Reliques*, 'given

---

[1] 'The clinking bell,' &c. It was formerly the custom at funerals to ring a handbell before the corpse as they carried it along, so that those who heard it might offer a prayer for the soul of the deceased.

POEM

(with corrections) from an ancient copy in blackletter, in the Pepys collection.' In Ritson's *Ancient Songs*, ii. 89. We have for once (in this and in No. LXIV.) given two ballad versions of the same story,—for example's sake, and because each has merit and a standing of its own.

XLIII. 'HUGH OF LINCOLN.'—Herd: Percy: Jamieson: Motherwell: and several other versions. Percy's MS. copy 'sent from Scotland,' begins—

> 'The rain rins down through Mirry-land toune,
>   Sae dois it doune the Pa:'

and the bishop learnedly argues that Milan and the Po must be meant, 'although the Adige, not the Po, runs through Milan.' Other versions give other corrupt forms, 'merry Linkim,' and 'Maitland town;' Jamieson's copy 'from Mrs. Brown's recitation' has the right reading, 'merry Lincoln.' In 1255, *teste* Matthew Paris (but a so-so witness), the Jews of Lincoln stole a little Christian boy named Hugh, tortured and crucified him, and flung his body into a pit, where his mother found it. The occupant of the house confessed the crime, and that the Jews every year thus killed a Christian child. He was hanged, as also were eighteen of the richest Jews in Lincoln. The child's body was buried with honours in Lincoln Cathedral (where they still pretend to show his tomb). Chaucer's *Prioress's Tale* is on the same subject. Horrible tales against the poor rich Jews were abundant in the Middle Ages.

XLIV. BARBARA ALLEN.—Ramsay's *Tea-Table Miscellany*. Percy gives the same, 'with a few conjectural emendations,' and also another version, 'with some corrections, from an old blackletter copy.' Pepys in his *Diary*, Jan. 2, 1665-6, names 'the little song of Barbary Allen.'

XLV. MAY COLVIN.—Herd: Buchan: Motherwell: Sharpe's *Ballad Book*, &c. A story found in various forms, not only in English, but also in Swedish and in German ballad-literature. The country people on the coast of Carrick, in Ayrshire, point out 'Fause Sir John's Loup,' and an equally authentic claim in this matter is made for a locality in the North of Scotland.

XLVI. 'EDWARD, EDWARD.'—First printed in Percy's *Reliques*, 'transmitted to the editor by Sir David Dalrymple, Bart., late Lord Hailes;' written, some say, (but where is proof?) by Lady Wardlaw,—who *was*, in all probability, authoress of the overpraised 'Hardyknute.'

XLVII. THE OUTLAW MURRAY.—*Border Minstrelsy*. Compiled by Scott from various sources; no ascertained historical foundation.

XLVIII. THE CRUEL BROTHER.—Herd: Jamieson 'from recitation of Mrs. Arnott:' Gilbert's *Ancient Christmas Carols*, &c. There are Danish, Swedish, and German ballads more or less like to this.

POEM

XLIX. LITTLE MUSGRAVE, &c.—In *Wit Restor'd* (1658): 'The Old Ballad of Little Musgrave and Lady Barnard'; in Percy (altered by him): a Scottish version in Jamieson: another in vol. xvii. of the Percy Society. The ballad is quoted in Beaumont and Fletcher's burlesque play of *Knight of the Burning Pestle* (produced 1611), thus:

> 'And some they whistled and some they sung,
> *Hey, down, down!*
> And some did loudly say,
> Ever as the Lord Barnet's horn blew,
> Away, Musgrave, away.'—*Act* v. *Scene* 3.

L. KINMONT WILLIE.—*Border Minstrelsy.* In 1596, Salkeld, deputy of Lord Scroope, English Warden of the West Marches, and Robert Scott, for the Laird of Buccleuch, Keeper of Liddesdale, met on the border line for conference, and under the usual truce, which lasted till next day at sunset. William Armstrong, of Kinmont, a notorious freebooter, returning from this conference, was seized and lodged in Carlisle castle. The Laird of Buccleuch, after treating in vain for his release, raised two hundred horse, and on the 13th of April surprised the castle and carried off the prisoner, on hearing of which, Queen Elizabeth 'stormed not a little.' Scott gives a long account of this in the *Border Minstrelsy.* 'This ballad,' he says, 'is preserved by tradition on the West Borders, but much mangled by reciters, so that some conjectural emendations have been absolutely necessary to render it intelligible.'

LI. FINE FLOWERS IN THE VALLEY.—Given in Johnson's *Musical Museum*: also by Motherwell, as 'The Cruel Mother,' with the burden

> ' *Three, three, and three by three ;*
> *Three, three, and thirty-three.*

and by Kinloch, with the burden

> ' *All alone, and alonie ;*
> *Doun by the greenwud sae bonnie.*'

Our version is Johnson's (to a word or two), adding the last verse from Kinloch. The burden, singing of flowers and leaves, at once deepens and softens the tragedy.

LII. ROBIN HOOD'S DEATH AND BURIAL.—Printed in *Robin Hood's Garland* (York), and given by Ritson, 'from a collation of two different copies, containing numerous variations.'

LIII. YOUNG REDIN.—A ballad found in various versions and under various names: 'Earl Richard,' 'Young Hunting,' 'Lord William,' 'Young Redin.' A fragment of it in Herd: a 'selected' version in *Border Minstrelsy*: a version in Buchan: one, 'from recitation of Miss E. Beattie,' in Kinloch: another, 'from recitation,' in Motherwell: a factitious version, in pseudo-antique spelling, in *Scarce Ancient Ballads*, Alexander Laing, Aberdeen, 1822.

LIV. THE FRAY O' SUPORT.—*Border Minstrelsy.* This odd and forcible outburst 'is usually chanted in a sort of wild recitative.

POEM

except the burden, which swells into a long and varied howl, not unlike a view-hollo. . . . An Englishwoman, residing in Suport [Cumberland], near the foot of the Kers-hope, having been plundered in the night by a band of the Scottish moss-troopers, is supposed to convoke her servants and friends for the pursuit, or *Hot Trod.* . . . The present text is collected from four copies, which differed widely from each other.'—*Scott.*

LV. THE SHIP O' THE FIEND.—In *Border Minstrelsy* as 'The Dæmon Lover' (a name which we have ventured to alter, being evidently not old), 'taken down from recitation by Mr. William Laidlaw.' In Buchan, 'James Herries': In Motherwell, a fragment.

LVI. LAMKIN.—A very popular ballad; found in Herd as ' Lammikin:' in Jamieson as ' Lanekin:' in Finlay in two versions: in Motherwell as 'Lambert Linkin:' also in *A New Book of Old Ballads* as 'Bold Rankin:' and in the *Drawing-Room Scrap Book,* 1837, as 'Long Lonkin.' All these we have collated (as usual, adding nothing to the traditionary matter), and with these a copy taken down from the mouth of an Irish nurse in the family of a relative of the editor. The murderer is called by various names, 'Lamkin,' 'Lammikin,' 'Lankin,' 'Linkin,' 'Belinkin,' 'Balcanqual,' 'Lambert Linkin,' 'Lammerlinkin,' 'Rankin.' One version begins:

> ' Belinkin was as gude a mason
> As ever pickt a stane;
> He built up Prime Castle
> But payment gat nane.'

LVII. THE FROLICKSOME DUKE.—From Percy's *Reliques.* The plot of this ballad is immeasurably old. It appears in a story of the *Arabian Nights,* a play of Shakespeare, and many other forms.

LVIII. CHILDE VYET.—Maidment's *North Countrie Garland*: Buchan: in Jamieson a fragment of a similar story ('Lord Wa'yates and Auld Ingram').

LIX. THE BARON OF BRACKLEY.—Jamieson. Buchan has another version in his *Gleanings.* Between John Gordon of Brackley, in Aberdeenshire, and Farquharson, of Inverey, was a fray in September, 1666, wherein the former was killed.

LX. BURD ELLEN.—Given by Percy from his 'MS. collection' (touching it up a little) as 'Child Waters': by Jamieson as 'Burd Ellen:' by Buchan in another version under the same name: by Kinloch as 'Lady Margaret.' Mr. R. Chambers gives a composite version, with some lines from a MS. supplied by Mr. Kinloch.

LXI. LAMENT OF THE BORDER WIDOW.—*Border Minstrelsy.* 'This fragment, obtained from recitation in the Forest of Ettrick, is said to relate to the execution of Cockburne of Henderland, a Border freebooter, hanged over the gate of his own tower by James V. in the course of that memorable expedition in 1529,

C C

POEM

which was fatal to Johnie Armstrong, Adam Scott of Tushie-law, and many other marauders.'—*Scott.*

LXII. WILLIE'S LADYE is given by Scott, and the same story by Jamieson under the title of *Sweet Willy.* Jamieson gives also a modernised version; and Lewis in his *Tales of Wonder* dished up a ballad upon it in his own taste. Professor Aytoun has given it mainly from Jamieson with a few touches. *Billy Blind* seems to be a comic name, taken from the game of Blindman's Buff, for a familiar and good-natured house-spirit, a sort of *Brownie* or *Lar.* Scott never met the name else-where than in Mrs. Brown's ballads. It seems that in Scot-land the blinded person in the aforesaid game is also called the *Bogle* (i. e. goblin); and hence, by a metathesis, the domestic Bogle may have come to be called 'The Billy Blind.'

LXIII. HUGHIE GRAHAM.—From *The Scots Musical Museum,* sent by Burns 'from oral tradition in Ayrshire.' Burns certainly dressed up the ballad, and wrote some of the present stanzas. Allan Cunningham again retouched the Burns' version for his *Songs of Scotland.* Scott's version in the *Border Minstrelsy,* was 'long current in Selkirkshire,' but it also is more or less improved by the editor. A corrupt copy of the ballad is found in *Wit and Mirth,* &c. (London, 1714).

Our version is precisely that of Burns, changing or restoring 'Stirling' into Carlisle, in accordance with all the other copies, and omitting one verse, in which Hughie Graham sends a message to his wife accusing her of misconduct with the Bishop, a verse that in point of art is no gain to the ballad. It makes a statement which, if referred to at all, ought to be woven into the whole narrative.

Mr. Stenhouse [*Scots Musical Museum,* new edit. 1853, iv. 297] says, that 'according to tradition' the Bishop of Carlisle about 1560, did so wrong a border chief, who in revenge made a raid into Cumberland. But all this is, as usual, vague and intangible. The ballad is a spirited little picture from the rude times on the Border, and we should only weary ourselves in vain by trying to make more of it.

LXIV. LORD THOMAS AND FAIR ANNET.—Given by Percy, 'with some corrections from a MS. copy transmitted from Scotland.' He says, it 'seems to be composed out of' two English ballads, 'Lord Thomas and Fair Ellinor' and 'Fair Margaret and Sweet William.' There is a similar Swedish ballad.

LXV. LIZIE LINDSAY.—Jamieson: Buchan: Whitelaw (from recita-tion of a lady at Glasgow). We have collated, but not added. Verse 19 one suspects to be partly Jamieson's; but it is useful to the situation, and its prettiness, though of a modern cast, ap-pears harmless enough. There is a well-known song founded on this ballad.

LXVI. SWEET WILLIAM'S GHOST.—First given in Ramsay's *Tea Table Miscellany,* imperfectly, and with at least two spurious stanzas: also by Kinloch, as 'Sweet William and May Mar-garet:' and by Motherwell as 'William and Marjorie,' a

POEM

better version, from recitation. We have added nothing in presenting a complete and consistent ballad, distinct from 'Clerk Saunders.' Some of the versions seem little else than variations of the latter part of 'Clerk Saunders.' There are corresponding ballads in Danish and Swedish, and similar stories are found in the ballad literature of many other lands.

'Sweet William's Ghost' is very dreamlike and awful. The need of getting back the faith and troth once plighted is one of the strange laws of the ghostly kingdom.

LXVII. LADY ELSPAT.—Jamieson; from Mrs. Brown's recitation. Here given with two or three merely verbal alterations.

LXVIII. WILLIE AND MAY MARGARET.—Jamieson (imperfect copy), 'from the recitation of Mrs. Brown.' Buchan, 'The Drowned Lovers.'

LXIX. THE DUKE OF GORDON'S DAUGHTER.—The version here given is founded, with numerous verbal alterations, on a copy (without date or place) bound up with other ballads in a volume in the British Museum. I have lost the exact reference to this volume, which I examined among other such, several years ago.

LXX. FAIR MARGARET'S MISFORTUNES.—Percy (from a modern printed copy, picked up on a stall): Herd: Ritson. Verse 5 is quoted in Beaumont and Fletcher's *Knight of the Burning Pestle*, act ii. 8, in this form:—

'When it was grown to dark midnight,
    And all were fast asleep,
In came Margaret's grimly ghost,
    And stood at William's feet.'

We retain the popular ending of 'the rose and the briar,' which, slightly varied, is common to many ballads, though it comes in here not very harmoniously. Probably it was used, in this and other instances, to carry off somewhat lightly a too tragical story. The full title of the stall copy, as given by Percy, is *Fair Margaret's Misfortunes; or Sweet William's frightful Dreams on his Wedding Night, with the sudden Death and Burial of those noble Lovers.* But he has entitled the ballad, 'Fair Margaret and Sweet William.'

LXXI. LORD RONALD.—*Border Minstrelsy* ('Lord Randal'). 'The hero is more generally termed *Lord Ronald* (Scott admits), but I willingly follow the authority of an Ettrick Forest copy for calling him *Randal*; because, though the circumstances are so very different, I think it not impossible that the ballad may originally have regarded the death of Thomas Randolph or Randal, Earl of Murray, &c. &c.,' mere antiquarian moonshine.

Kinloch gives a version wherein 'Lord Donald' is poisoned by a dish of *toads*, served up as fish. Getting 'frogs for fish,' i. e. foul play, is a phrase used in the ballad of 'Katharine

Janfarie,' p. 110. Buchan's version 'Willie Doo,' is in the form of a nursery song. Sweden and Germany have similar ballads.

LXXII. YOUNG JOHN.—From Buchan's *Ancient Ballads and Songs of the North of Scotland.*

LXXIII. HELEN OF KIRCONNELL.—*Border Minstrelsy*—from tradition. There given with a worthless 'First Part' of six verses—('My captive spirit's at thy feet!' &c.) Other versions are given by Herd, Ritson, Jamieson, and others. Wordsworth has a ballad (*Ellen Irwin*), of little merit, on the same story.

Adam Fleming, says tradition, loved Helen Irving, or Bell, (for this surname is uncertain, as well as the date of the occurrence,) daughter of the Laird of Kirconnell, in Dumfriesshire. The lovers being together one day by the river Kirtle, a rival suitor suddenly appeared on the opposite bank and pointed his gun; Helen threw herself before her sweetheart, received the bullet, and died in his arms. Then Adam Fleming fought with his guilty rival and slew him.

LXXIV. GLASGERION.—In Percy's *Reliques*, 'from the editor's folio MS.' Jamieson gives a Scottish version ('Glenkindie'), mainly 'from the recitation of an old woman.' Chaucer, in his *House of Fame* (iii. 118), names 'Glaskyrion' as a renowned British harper.

LXXV. THE GARDENER.—Kinloch: Buchan.

LXXVI. TAMLANE.—A fragment of this ballad is given by Herd ('Kertonha'): a version in Johnson's *Museum* ('Tom Linn'). In *Border Minstrelsy*, Scott gives a much longer version 'prepared from a collation of the printed copies, with a very accurate one in Glenriddel's MSS., and with several recitals from tradition. Some verses are omitted in this edition, being ascertained to belong to a separate ballad.' Besides collating and omitting, Scott was 'enabled to add several verses of beauty and interest to this edition of Tamlane, in consequence of a copy obtained from a gentleman residing near Langholm, which is said to be very ancient, though the language is somewhat of a modern cast.' The stanzas alluded to in this evasive manner are undoubtedly modern, and we have therefore omitted them, with several others equally spurious. Yet one of these was quoted the other day in a periodical of high rank, in a paper on the fairy mythology, as from 'the old ballad of Tamlane,' which we mention to show again how very loose are the prevailing notions with regard to 'Old Ballads,' even among literary men. This was the stanza quoted:—

'Their oaten pipes blew wondrous shrill,
  The hemlock small blew clear;
And louder notes from hemlock large,
  And bog-reed, struck the ear;
But solemn sounds, or sober thoughts,
  The Fairies cannot bear.'

Then follows : —

> ' They sing, inspired with love and joy,
>   Like skylarks in the air :
>   Of solid sense, or thought that's grave,
>   You'll find no traces there.'

Pretty enough in its own way, but certainly not the ' true thing.' A fragment, ' Tom Linn,' is given in *A New Book of Old Ballads*, Edinburgh, 1844. The hero is elsewhere named ' Tom a lin,' and ' Thomlin.' ' The Tale of the Young Tamlene' is mentioned in *The Complaynt of Scotland* (1548).

Carterhaugh is a plain about a mile from Selkirk, and the peasants are said to point out the localities where the incidents of the ballad took place.

- corruption viii
- over editing — vs eloquence ... × ×
  ... apology
- editing procedures
  xxvi xxviii
- what a mouthful wd have done xxix
- Scottish ... ×××

INDEX OF FIRST LINES.

PRINTED BY
SPOTTISWOODE AND CO., NEW-STREET SQUARE
LONDON

GOLDEN TREASURY SERIES.

With Vignette Titles by Sir NOEL PATON,
T. WOOLNER, W. HOLMAN HUNT, J. E. MILLAIS,
ARTHUR HUGHES, &c. Engraved on Steel by JEENS.

Bound in extra cloth. 4s. 6d. each.

The Golden Treasury of the best Songs and Lyrical Poems in the English Language. Selected and arranged, with Notes, by Professor FRANCIS TURNER PALGRAVE.

The Children's Garland from the Best Poets. Selected and arranged by COVENTRY PATMORE.

The Book of Praise. From the best English Hymn Writers. Selected and arranged by the EARL of SELBORNE (Sir ROUNDELL PALMER).

The Fairy Book: The best Popular Fairy Stories. Selected and rendered anew by the Author of 'John Halifax, Gentleman.'

The Ballad Book. A Selection of the Choicest British Ballads. Edited by WILLIAM ALLINGHAM.

The Jest Book. The Choicest Anecdotes and Sayings. Selected and arranged by MARK LEMON.

Bacon's Essays and Colours of Good and Evil. With Notes and Glossarial Index by W. ALDIS WRIGHT, M.A.

The Pilgrim's Progress from this World to that which is to Come. By JOHN BUNYAN.
₄ Large Paper Edition. 7s. 6d.

The Sunday Book of Poetry for the Young. Selected and arranged by C. F. ALEXANDER.

A Book of Golden Deeds of all Times and all Countries. Gathered and narrated anew by the Author of 'The Heir of Redclyffe.'

The Adventures of Robinson Crusoe. Edited, from the Original Editions, by J. W. CLARK, M.A.

The Republic of Plato. Translated into English, with Notes, by J. LL. DAVIES, M.A., and D. J. VAUGHAN, M.A.

The Song Book. Words and Tunes from the best Poets and Musicians. Selected and arranged by JOHN HULLAH.

La Lyre Française. Selected and arranged, with Notes, by G. MASSON.

Tom Brown's Schooldays. By AN OLD BOY.

A Book of Worthies. Gathered from the Old Histories and written anew by the Author of 'The Heir of Redclyffe.'

Guesses at Truth. By TWO BROTHERS.

The Cavalier and his Lady. Selections from the Works of the first Duke and Duchess of Newcastle. With an Introductory Essay by EDWARD JENKINS, Author of 'Ginx's Baby' &c.

Scottish Song. A Selection of the Choicest Lyrics of Scotland. Compiled and arranged, with brief Notes, by MARY CARLYLE AITKIN.

Deutsche Lyrik. The Golden Treasury of the best German Lyrical Poems. Selected and arranged, with Notes and Literary Introduction, by Dr. BUCHHEIM.

Chrysomela. A Selection from the Lyrical Poems of ROBERT HERRICK. Arranged, with Notes, by Prof. F. T. PALGRAVE

Poems of Places—England and Wales. Edited by H. W. LONGFELLOW. 2 vols.

Selected Poems of Matthew Arnold.

The Story of the Christians and Moors in Spain. By CHARLOTTE M. YONGE.

Lamb's Tales from Shakespeare. Edited, with Preface, by the Rev. A. AINGER, M.A.

Shakespeare's Songs and Sonnets. Edited, with Notes, by Professor F. T. PALGRAVE.

Poems of Wordsworth. Chosen and Edited by MATTHEW ARNOLD. *⁎* Large Paper Edition. 9s.

Poems of Shelley. Edited by STOPFORD A. BROOKE. *⁎* Large Paper Edition. 12s. 6d.

The Essays of Joseph Addison. Chosen and Edited by JOHN RICHARD GREEN.

Poetry of Byron. Chosen and arranged by MATTHEW ARNOLD. *⁎* Large Paper Edition. 9s.

Sir Thomas Browne's Religio Medici; Letter to a Friend, &c. Edited by W. A. GREENHILL, M.D.

The Speeches and Table-Talk of the Prophet Mohammad. Chosen and Translated by STANLEY LANE-POOLE.

Selections from the Writings of Walter Savage Landor. Arranged and Edited by SIDNEY COLVIN.

Selections from Cowper's Poems. With an Introduction by Mrs. OLIPHANT.

Letters of William Cowper. Edited, with Introduction, by Rev. W. BENHAM, B.D., F.S.A.

The Poetical Works of John Keats. Edited by Professor FRANCIS TURNER PALGRAVE. *⁎* Large Paper Edition. 9s

Lyrical Poems of Alfred Lord Tennyson. Selected and Annotated by Professor FRANCIS TURNER PALGRAVE. *⁎* Large Paper Edition. 8vo. 9s.

In Memoriam. By ALFRED LORD TENNYSON, Poet-Laureate. *⁎* Large Paper Edition. 8vo. 9s.

The Trial and Death of Socrates. Being the Euthyphron, Apology, Crito, and Phaedo of Plato. Translated into English by F. J. CHURCH.

MACMILLAN & CO., LONDON.